Nevil Shute Norway was born in London in 1899.

He was educated at Shrewsbury, then at Balliol College, Oxford, where he studied engineering. He went to De Havilland Aircraft as an aeronautical engineer, then joined Vickers in 1924 to work on the airship R100 in competition with the British Air Ministry to develop the R101. Shute's first novel, *Marazan*, was published while he was working on the airship. It was then that he shortened his writing name to protect his engineering career.

After the crash of the R101, airship design was written off as a lost cause and the Vickers team disbanded. Shute decided to set up his own company, Airspeed Ltd, in 1931. While doing this, he wrote *Lonely Road*, which was published in 1931. He was bought out of the company in 1939 by the other directors following a dispute.

He served in both world wars, and as a commander in the Royal Navy Volunteer Reserve in the Second World War, working on secret projects.

Shute flew his own aircraft to Australia in 1948–49 to do research for his novel *On the Beach*, published in 1957. He settled there permanently in 1950 living in Langwarrin, in Victoria, Australia.

His knowledge of engineering and the aircraft industry was often woven into his novels.

He died in 1960.

NEVIL**SHUTE**
Round the Bend

HOUSE OF
STRATUS

This edition published in 2000 by House of Stratus, an imprint of House of Stratus Ltd, Thirsk Industrial Park, York Road, Thirsk, North Yorkshire, YO7 3BX, UK.

www.houseofstratus.com

Typeset by House of Stratus, printed and bound by Short Run Press Ltd., Exeter

A catalogue record for this book is available from the British Library and the Library of Congress.

ISBN 1-84232-289-3

Cover design: Marc Burville-Riley
Cover image: Telegraph Colour Library

In my Father's house are many mansions; if it were not so I would have told you. I go to prepare a place for you.

ST JOHN. 14.2.

ACKNOWLEDGEMENT

Thanks are due to Mrs Flecker for permission to reprint lines from *The Collected Poems of James Elroy Flecker*, *The Golden Journey to Samarkand*, and *Hassan*; also to Dr John Masefield, O M, and The Society of Authors for similar permission in respect of quotations from his works.

CHAPTER ONE

Some men of noble stock were made, some glory in the
  murder blade,
Some praise a Science or an Art, but I like
  honourable Trade!

JAMES ELROY FLECKER

I CAME INTO aviation the hard way. I was never in the RAF,
and my parents hadn't got fifteen hundred pounds to spend
on pilot training for me at a flying school. My father was,
and is, a crane driver at Southampton docks, and I am one
of seven children, five boys and two girls. I went to the
council school like all the other kids in our street, and then
when I left school dad got me a job in a garage out on the
Portsmouth Road. That was in 1929.

I stayed there for about three years and got to know a bit
about cars. Then, early in the summer, Sir Alan Cobham
came to Southampton with his flying circus, NATIONAL
AVIATION DAY, he called it. He operated in a big way,
because he had about fifteen aeroplanes, Avros and Moths
and a glider and an Autogiro, and a Lincock for stunting
displays, and a big old Handley Page airliner for mass
joyriding, and a new thing called an Airspeed Ferry. My, that
was a grand turnout to watch.

I knew from the first day that to be with that circus was
the job for me. He was at Hamble for three days, and I
was out at the field each day from early in the morning till

dark. The chaps fuelling and cleaning down the aircraft let me help them, coiling down a hose or fetching an oil drum for them to stand on; when there was nothing else that wanted doing I went round the enclosures picking up the waste paper that the crowd had left behind and taking it away to burn in a corner of the field. It was fun just doing that, because of the aeroplanes.

I got the sack from the garage on the second day.

On the evening of their last day, I went to the foreman of the ground crew and asked him for a job. He said I was too young, and they were full up anyway. He said that he was sorry.

I went home all down in the dumps that night. I must say, Dad and Mum were good. They didn't lay in to me for getting the sack from the garage, although they might well have done. I'd told them airily that I was going to get a job with the circus, and when I went home I suppose they saw by my face I hadn't got it. They were ever so nice; Ma opened a small tin of salmon for tea to make a bit of a treat for me. The show was going on to Portsmouth, twenty miles away, and when I told them I was going over there next day, all Dad said was, "That's right. Keep trying."

I went to Portsmouth on an early bus and I was out at the airport long before the first machines flew in, helping the ground crew to put up the first enclosures round the edges of the aerodrome. The foreman scratched his head when he saw me, but they were always shorthanded so they didn't turn me off. He must have said something to Sir Alan, though, because while I was holding a post straight for another chap to hammer into the ground, Sir Alan himself came up behind me.

"Who are you?" he asked. "I thought we'd left you behind at Hamble."

"My name's Tom Cutter," I said.

"Well, what are you doing here, Tom?"

"Helping to get this post in, sir," I said. I was a bit shy at being talked to by a knight.

"Haven't you got a job?"

"Got the sack day before yesterday," I said. It sounded bad, but I didn't know what else to say.

"Is that because you spent so much time out here with us?"

"I suppose so," I said reluctantly.

He snorted. "Well, don't be such a young fool. Go back and ask to be taken on again. There's no work for you here. What was the job?"

"I was in a garage, sir. I can't go back. They took on another boy."

"Well, we can't take you on here. We're full up. I've got hundreds of boys writing to me for jobs every day, hundreds and hundreds. I've got no jobs to give."

"Mr Dixon told me that there wasn't any job," I said. "I just thought that if I came over while I'm doing nothing, I could help, picking up the paper and that."

He stared at me so long in silence that I felt quite awkward. I know now what a good answer that was. "I'm blowed if I know," he said at last, and turned away. I couldn't make head or tail of that.

I went on all that morning helping put up the enclosures, and when dinner-time came round the foreman said I'd better go and get my dinner in the mess tent with the rest of the men. It was good of him, because being out of work I hadn't got any money to chuck around. I went and helped park the cars in the car park when they started to come in for the afternoon show, and then I watched the show again. They had stunt displays, and wing walking, and a parachute descent, and a pretty girl flying a glider. They had a public address loudspeaker system rigged up, and the announcer stood up once and said that Sir Alan Cobham had offered to let any pilot of the last war try his hand at flying again. A

3

pilot dressed up as an old tramp came out of the crowd and did a bit of clowning with the announcer, and tripped over his umbrella and fell flat, and got into an Avro back to front and took it off the ground facing the tail, holding his hat on, waving his umbrella, and shouting blue murder, and went into the best bit of crazy flying ever seen in England, bellowing all the time to be told how to land it as he went crabbing down the enclosures three feet up, and the announcer bellowing back to him. My, that was fun! They finished up with a Gretna Green elopement of a couple in a terrible old Model T Ford, with father chasing after them all over the aerodrome in a Moth and bombing them with little paper bags of flour and rolls of toilet paper. I'd seen it all before, but I could have watched that show forever. I'd go and see it again, even now.

I went and helped unpark the cars and get them away after the show. Sir Alan had been flying the Handley Page himself most of the afternoon, joy-riding, taking up twenty-five passengers at a time. He handed over to another pilot at about five o'clock and came through the car park to his caravan for his tea. He was always in a hurry, but never in too much of a hurry to notice the humblest detail of his big concern, and he checked when he saw me.

"You still here?" he asked.

"I been helping park the cars and that," I said.

"Oh. Get any tips?"

"Three and six," I said.

"Fair enough. Want to earn five bob?" I grinned and nodded.

"I'll give you five bob if you'd like to do the girl in Gretna Green this evening. Think you can do it?"

"Oh, aye," I said. "I can do that all right. Thank you, Sir."

I was young, of course, and I'd got a fresh, pink and white face in those days, so I could make up as a girl quite well. All I had to do was to dress up in the most terrible women's clothes and drive about on the aerodrome in the old Ford, trying to get out of the way of the Moth. The Ford was driven by a boy about my own age, Connie Shaklin. Connie was short for Constantine; he was a cheerful, yellow-skinned young chap with straight black hair who put me in the way of things. He was dressed up as a young farmer in a sort of smock and we did the turn together; we never turned that Ford over, but we came bloody near it sometimes. It was good fun; we wheeled and skidded the thing all over the aerodrome, shrieking and hugging and kissing while the Moth dived on us and bombed us. The show ended, of course, with my skirt getting pulled off and me running off the field in a pair of red flannel knickers, covered in flour and with streamers of toilet paper all over me, while the crowd laughed fit to burst.

I got the five bob and Sir Alan himself said I'd done very well. That was the first money that I ever made in aviation.

I made eight and six that day in all, and when I got home I'd got four and twopence left, clear profit, after paying for my bus fares and my tea. I showed it to Dad and Mum and told them I was going over to the show again.

Next day they let me do the Gretna Green girl in both performances, and gave me ten bob for the two. For the rest of the day I picked up paper and carried things about for the ground engineers; there was always something to work at. Then I helped in the car park again and got some more tips, and when I went back home that night Dad said I was getting my nose in.

The show moved on to Winchester and I followed it there, but after that it was going to Newbury and that was too far for me to go over every day. I asked the foreman about a job again then, and he said he'd speak to Sir Alan for me. Next day was a Saturday and Dad was off in the afternoon, so I got him to come over in case they said I was too young again. Sir Alan saw Dad for a minute and said I was a smart boy, but if I came I'd have to be laid off in the winter. Dad said he thought it was best for me to do what I was keen on, and we'd take our chance about the winter. When we got on to the bus that night to go back home I'd got my job in the air circus, four quid a week, which was more than I'd been getting in the garage.

Thinking back over my life, I know of two or three times when I've been just perfectly, radiantly happy. That was one of them.

I went all over England, Scotland, and Wales with the show that summer, from Falmouth to Inverness, from Kings Lynn to Swansea. I did labouring work and Gretna Green, and helped with the aeroplanes whenever I got a chance. That was mostly when some passenger had been sick on the floor. From that I got to washing off the dirty oil with a bucket of paraffin and cleaning down generally, and by the time the season ended I'd picked up quite a bit of knowledge about those particular aeroplanes, just by keeping my ears open and working on them whenever I got the chance.

I got laid off when the show packed up for the winter, but Mr Dixon said that I could come along next year if I wanted, and if I turned up or wrote in the first week of April there'd be a job for me. Sir Alan himself came round on the last evening and shook hands with us all and thanked us, and when he came to me he asked what I was going to do.

I said, "I'll get a job of some sort for the winter and come back again next year, if that's all right."

"Mr Dixon tells me that you want to be a ground engineer," he said.

"That's right, sir," I replied. "I was going to go to evening classes in the winter."

"Fine," he said. "If you do that, bring along some kind of a report with you next spring. If it's a good one, I'll see you get a bit more to do with the aeroplanes."

I went back home, and I got a job with a coal merchant, going round with the driver of one of those chariot coal carts drawn by a horse, delivering coal at the houses. It was all right as a job because it didn't tire your mind, and I got off sharp at five every evening with plenty of time to clean up and have tea and go out to my classes at the Southampton Polytechnic.

I did mathematics and mechanics and engineering workshop that winter, and it kept me pretty busy. On top of that I read two technical books about aeroplanes that I got out of the library, and understood about a quarter of them. When the spring came round I got a good report, and I took it along with me in April when I went to Littlehampton to join up with the circus again. I showed it to Mr Dixon and he showed it to Sir Alan, and he sent for me and asked me if I'd like to be an apprentice with the ground engineers. That meant I'd be working on the aeroplanes all the time. My, I was pleased, and so were Dad and Mum when I wrote home. I liked humping the coal all right, but it wasn't half as much fun as working on an aeroplane.

Being an apprentice didn't mean that I did anything very difficult upon the aeroplanes. I still had the job of cleaning out the cabins and washing off the oil from fuselages and wings, but there were also sparking plugs to be cleaned and filters to be checked, and as time went on I got to working with the ground engineers more and more. I still did the Gretna Green girl with Connie twice each day although I had begun to shave, and this brings me to Connie.

When I joined the show the first year, it never struck me that there was anything unusual about Connie. After all, the whole show was a bit unusual from start to finish, and Connie was a part of it; the fact that he looked strange was just another one among a mass of new, strange things. He looked a bit foreign. He was about my age, but taller and rather thin. He had straight black hair and a yellowish tinge to his skin; in spite of that he had firm, well cut features. He was a good-looking, striking chap. He was a darned good friend to me, right from the first.

Once one of the pilots, irritated over something that Connie had or hadn't done, said, "Where's that bloody Chink?" It was a surprise to me at the time, but when he said that I thought of the Chinese laundry at the corner of our street at home, and I could see what he meant. Connie was much taller than either of the two men in the laundry and he'd got a leaner look about his face, but he did look a bit Chinese, when you came to think of it. Still, that didn't mean a thing to me; Connie was just like any other boy except that he knew a good bit more than most of my other friends.

He was an apprentice like me, but he'd started a bit higher on the ladder; he'd been to a good school. Sir Alan had had some trouble at Penang on his first pioneering flight out to Australia, and Connie's father had helped him, I think; that's how Connie came to be an apprentice in the air circus. Connie and I became very close friends, perhaps because our backgrounds were so different. Our Gretna Green turn brought us very close together in more senses than one; we were always thinking up new gags for it, most of which Sir Alan stopped us doing after the first time because he said they were too rude.

Again, that second summer we went all over the British Isles, staying a day in each place and giving two shows each day. There was never a whole day off; in an air circus like that you take your weekends in the winter. We were improvising all the time to keep the aircraft in the air; we had plenty of tools and good materials to work with, but all the work had to be done out in the open field. It was a grand training for an engineer, because in each emergency you had to work out quick what was the best way to tackle it with the facilities at your disposal. I've changed an engine many a time in the lee of a haystack, by lashing up a sheer-legs of scaffold poles over the nose of the machine and borrowing the farmer's tractor to pull the wire rope, like a crane.

It's not quite true to say that we had no time off, however. We often stayed at the same place over the weekend. We had the afternoon and evening shows on Sunday as usual, but there was never very much to do on Sunday morning. Connie sometimes used to go to church, but Connie was unusual; I can't remember that anybody else did.

I knew more about church than most boys in our street, because until my voice broke I was a choirboy at St John's. I never talked about it on the circus because it sounds a bit sissy to say you've been a choirboy, but I was. I wouldn't have been, but for Mum. She said that if I'd got a good voice it was my duty to use it, and she made me go. I never got anything for it but the outing to the Isle of Wight each summer, and when my voice broke I got out of it. If I'd been working in Southampton Mum would have made me join up as a tenor when my voice steadied down, but the air circus got me out of that, of course. It wasn't worth doing just for the winter months.

The thing that interested me in Connie's church-going was that he just went to any old church there was. He went to the nearest, whether it was Anglican or Methodist or Presbyterian or Roman Catholic. He went to a synagogue one time, at Wolverhampton. If it was raining or if we'd had too much beer on Saturday night he wouldn't go at all, but if it was a nice fine morning and nothing particular to do, he'd ask somebody where the nearest church was and go to it.

I asked him once if it was all right, just going into any church like that. He grinned and said, "Blowed if I know. I've never been chucked out."

"I'd be scared of doing the wrong thing," I remarked. "However do you know what to do in a synagogue?"

"Just sit at the back and watch what other people do," he said. "If they start doing anything comic, like going up to the altar or anything like that, I just sit still and watch."

"Don't they mind you doing that?"

"I don't think so. A Roman Catholic priest came up one time as I was going out and asked me who I was. I told him I was just looking, like in a shop. He didn't mind a bit."

He collected churches, like another boy might collect cigarette cards or matchbox covers. The gem of his collection was at Woking, where he found a mosque to go to. He had a bit of a job getting to that one because the big day at a mosque is on a Friday, but he was a very good apprentice and a hard worker, so the foreman let him go.

Once, I remember, I asked Connie what he really was, Church of England, or Presbyterian, or what. "Blowed if I know," he said. "I was born in Penang and my father was a Buddhist. But he died four years ago, and then we came to England. I was Church of England at school."

I stared at him. "Where's Penang?"

"Just by Malaya," he told me. "But we don't live there now. Mother brought us to England when my father died. She was born in Irkutsk, so she's Greek Orthodox."

Connie knew an awful lot more than me, of course, and I didn't want to go on looking stupid, so I let Irkutsk go. The Greek part stayed in my mind, and I remember months afterwards looking at a map of Greece in the Public Library, trying to find Irkutsk where Connie's mother had been born. But all that came later; at the time I only asked him, "Is your mum in England now?"

He shook his head. "She's in California, at a place called San Diego, with my sister. Mother got married again."

It was quite outside my range, of course: California was somewhere abroad where they made Syrup of Figs. "Oh ..." I said vaguely.

I was young, of course, and I was loaded down with new experiences. Until I joined the circus I'd never been more than five miles from my own street in Southampton, and I'd got an awful lot to learn. I must have seemed slow at times, because it wasn't till that second season was half over that I realised what being an apprentice meant. It meant that I'd got a regular job, that I wasn't going to be laid off in the winter, like I had before. Connie and I were going to spend the winter at Littlehampton working on the aeroplanes, overhauling them for their certificates of airworthiness so they'd be all ready for the spring.

The circus ran for four years and that was the end; the last season wasn't so good as the first three had been, and it looked as if the public were getting a bit tired of it. Sir Alan packed it up, and went on with his development work on refuelling aeroplanes in flight. He was very good with us apprentices. He went to a great deal of trouble to find us jobs in other places in the aircraft industry. He got me a fine apprenticeship with Airservice Ltd at Morden aerodrome, just south of London, overhauling and repairing aeroplanes in a big way in a grand, modern shop. I owe a great deal to Sir Alan over that.

I had to say goodbye to Connie then. Like me, he wanted to go on and take his ground engineer's tickets, but neither of us could do that till we were twenty-one years old. He was going out to California to his mother; he told me that there were aircraft factories out there in San Diego and he wanted to get into one of those. I was very sorry to part from Connie, because we'd been together for three and a half years and had a lot of fun; although he knew such a lot more than I did, he was never stuck up about it. Being with him in those early years was very good for me. We said we'd keep in touch by writing, and of course we never did.

I went to Airservice in the autumn of 1935, and I stayed with them for ten years. It was a good firm to work for, and

I got on well. I got my A and C certificates for the maintenance of engines and airframes as soon as I was old enough, in 1936, and I got the B and D certificates for complete overhauls in 1938; by that time I was earning over ten pounds a week, including overtime. I didn't spend it on girls, and I didn't spend much of it on beer. I spent it mostly on flying. The firm had a scheme that gave cheap flying instruction to its staff, and I took my first private pilot's "A" licence in 1937. By the middle of the war, when pilots were short and regulations lax, I was test flying the Tiger Moths we had rebuilt after a crash as a regular thing. I used to finish the inspection in the shop and then just take it out and fly it. It saved such a lot of time and bother looking for a test pilot.

I stayed a civilian all the war, working at my normal job of repairing crashed aircraft. I was put in charge of a repair section in 1940 and got to foreman's rank. In 1943 the firm had to strengthen the repair side of their branch in Egypt, and they asked me if I'd go out there for a bit. I was twenty-eight years old, and up till then I'd never been out of England. Of course I said I'd go.

It was on account of that I married Beryl Cousins.

I've not said much about girls up till now because, to tell the truth, I never had a lot to do with them till then. I was so stuck into my job and so keen on aeroplanes and flying that girls passed me by, or I passed them by, whichever way you look at it. Till I got my B and D tickets I was working at classes three or four evenings every week; then when I'd got them, and might have had time to look around a bit and have a bit of fun, the war came. That meant that I was working overtime every night till eight o'clock and sometimes later than that, which sort of limits the time that a chap has to look around and pick himself a girl. Maybe when it's like that he's apt to pick the first that comes along.

I lodged in a suburban road at Morden and Beryl lived two doors up the road from me, and worked in the stores at Airservice Ltd. She was a sort of clerk there, working on the inwards and the outwards files. She was a slight, pale girl with ash-blonde hair. We used to walk to work together in the mornings. We got to having lunch together and tea if she was working late, all in the works canteen, and Saturdays I'd take her to the pictures, or we'd go dancing at a Palais. After six months of that we came to the conclusion that we were in love, and we'd get married when the work let up a bit. We didn't realise we both loved something better than each other. I was in love with aeroplanes, and she was in love with love.

I heard about this job one morning, and when they said they wanted me to go out to Egypt they said it would be for two years and I'd have to go in about three weeks' time. I met Beryl at our usual table for lunch with other people all round us in the works canteen, so I said to her, "Eat up quick. I've got something to tell you, but not here."

We walked out on the grass up the aerodrome hedge when we'd finished; it was September, and a lovely sunny day. I told her all about it as we walked along by the scrap dump of wrecked airframes and engines, and she said, "Oh Tom! Have you really got to go?"

I hadn't got to, but I wasn't going to miss that chance. "They put it to me pretty firm," I said. "You don't get much choice, these days."

She turned to me, and her eyes were full of tears. "I thought we were going to get married about Christmas. That's what we said."

I was a bloody fool, of course, but one does these things. I couldn't bear to see her cry. I took both her hands in mine. "I know," I said. "What say if we get married now, before I go?"

She said softly, "Oh Tom! Do you want us to be married?"

13

I wasn't really sure I did, but I was twenty-eight and I'd never got that far with any girl before. I said, "Do I want to!" and took her in my arms and kissed her.

After a bit we got to thinking about ways and means. There wasn't time for doing it the regular way with banns called in church and all that. We should have to do it with a special licence, and I found out pretty soon that Beryl knew all about those. Girls study things of that sort more than men. I wouldn't be able to set her up in a house in the time we'd got, and she didn't want to leave her job at Airservice because if she did, and didn't have a baby, she'd only have got directed into something else since it was wartime. So we fixed that we'd get married as soon as we could and she'd go on working just the same, and living with her people.

We went and saw her dad and mum that evening and told them all about it. They were pleased all right, because I was making good money and I think they felt that I was likely to get on. Next day was Friday, and I asked for the day off and took Beryl down to Southampton and introduced her to my folks, and ten days after that we got married at a registrar's office.

We got a week at Southsea for our honeymoon; it was a fine September that year so that although there wasn't much to do we could sit on the front and look at the ships going in and out of Portsmouth harbour, and the Bostons and the Spitfires going out on strikes. I think Beryl was happy, and if I was thinking of the work more than a man ought to do upon his honeymoon, well, it was wartime and the flying schools were waiting for the Tiger Moths I mended, to train pilots. Beryl understood – at least, I think she did.

Looking back upon it now, it must have been a poor sort of a honeymoon. It was wartime in England, and everything was short. There was complete darkness at night, of course, there on the coast, and the cafés and the dance halls and the picture houses were full of men and girls in uniform; a civilian didn't get much priority. You couldn't get down to the beach to bathe except in one little place because of the anti-invasion barbed wire and tank obstacles and land mines, and there weren't any motor coach tours or steamer trips or concert parties on the beach, or anything like that. This was all normal to us because that's the way things were in England then, and we didn't grieve over what we couldn't have, but when I think about the sort of honeymoon I could have given her if it had been in peacetime, I feel a bit sore. It might have made a difference.

It was better for me than for Beryl. I had Egypt ahead of me. I was going out to an important job in a warm, spacious country, into all the glamour of a successful war in North Africa. There would be luxury in Cairo, and sunshine on the desert, and the Pyramids, and the Nile, and travel to our various outstations in Africa and Persia and Iraq. For me, this week in Southsea was the last of the drab misery of war in England. Ahead of Beryl was a long, indefinite vista of it, cold and monotonous in the same job, and lonely with me away. We neither of us thought about it like that – or, if I thought of it, I didn't talk about it. But that's the way it was.

We didn't look ahead. I can't remember that we ever discussed where we were going to live after the war, or anything like that. It didn't seem to be much good, with things as they were. The war had been going on for four years; for four years we had been directed where to work and we were getting out of the way of thinking about our future for ourselves. This job in Egypt was to be for two years, and after that I should come back to wartime England, so we thought, and it would be the same except that every thing would be scarcer and more difficult than ever. We never looked ahead to think about the peace, that I remember.

I was flown to Egypt by BOAC. It wasn't possible for Beryl to come and see me off because the time and place of departure were secret. The best that she could do was to come down with me to Morden Underground station late one afternoon as I carried my suitcase down from the digs. We walked silent together down the suburban streets; on that last walk we didn't seem to have anything left to say to each other. Maybe she was only realising then what the separation was going to mean. She hadn't got a lot of imagination.

By the entrance to the station we stopped and looked at each other. It was raining a bit, and the red buses starting and stopping at the halt just by us made a great clatter with their diesels. I put down my suitcase and took her hands. "Well, girl," I said, "this is it."

She was pretty down in the mouth. "Write to me a lot, Tom," she said. "I'll be ever so lost without you."

"Cheer up," I said. "I'll write as soon as ever I get there, but don't get worried if you don't hear for a while. If they're sending letters round the Cape it might take anything up to six weeks."

"I won't be able to sleep till I hear."

I grinned. "Bet you do. Tuck a bolster in beside you and make believe I'm there, and you'll sleep all right."

She smiled, though she was very near to tears. "Now stop it ..."

I took her in my arms. It didn't matter that there were people all around at the bus stop; you saw this every hour of every day, with people going off on draft. "It's only for two years, girl," I said softly. "It'll soon be gone."

"It sounds like as if it was forever," she said miserably.

There was no sense in prolonging the agony; it was only making things more difficult for her, and we'd said all that there was to say. We kissed, and kissed again, and then I said, "I'll have to go now, girl. Look after yourself."

She released me. "You look after *yourself.* Cheer-oh, Tom." She was crying now in earnest.

I squeezed her hand clumsily. "Cheer up, girl. It's not for so long." And with that I turned and picked the suitcase up and left her, and went and got my ticket. I looked back over the turnstile and she was there waving goodbye to me with tears running down her face, and I waved back to her, and then I had to turn round and go down to the train.

I went in a Liberator, squashed in with about twenty others in the rear fuselage. We took off at about ten o'clock that night from an aerodrome somewhere in the south; we didn't know what aerodrome it was, nor where we were going to. We flew on for about eight hours, and then in the dawn we landed. We couldn't see anything out of the aeroplane, and when we got out on to the tarmac we found that we were in a sandy sort of place with palm trees and white houses. They told us it was Tripoli.

We weren't allowed outside the aerodrome; they gave us breakfast in a tent while the Liberator was refuelled, and we took off again for Cairo. We landed at Almaza in the middle of the day and it was good and hot; I had English clothes on, and I envied the chaps working on the aircraft in just a pair of shorts and no shirt. I got passed through the various formalities, and then I went and reported to the manager of Airservice Ltd on the aerodrome.

That two years was a fine experience for me. I was in charge of airframe repairs and general maintenance. I lived in a small hotel about a mile from the airport, and I had my office at the back of the hangar. We operated a large number of aircraft all over the Near East and North-East Africa, and I was responsible for keeping them in the air, all except engine overhauls, which were the business of another chap. If a Rapide ran off the runway and bent its undercarriage at Luxor or at Lydda, the responsibility for getting it into the air again was mine. If it was a simple and straightforward repair I would send one of my ground engineers to it by air or truck, but if it was a difficult or complicated job I would go myself and see the work put in hand the way I wanted it. We had an old Hornet two-seater that I used to go in if the journey was anything less than five hundred miles, but there was always a difficulty about finding a pilot who could spare the time, and after a while the firm agreed that I should fly myself about in this thing. It wasn't worth much if I crashed it, and I didn't want any flying pay or insurance.

On these repair jobs, flying myself or being flown by a pilot, I travelled very widely in the last two years of the war. I went to Beirut and Baghdad and Aleppo and Nicosia, and down south as far as Khartoum and Addis Ababa. I got to know about Syrian and Iraqi and Egyptian aircraft hands, what they could do and what they couldn't, what days they had to take off for their religion or their festivals, and why. I tried to learn about all that. It's no good going round and saying that those boys are just a lot of monkeys, that they aren't reliable and you can't use them. You can use them all right if you take the trouble to learn about them, and if you do that you'll find the work is liable to come out a good deal cheaper, because their wages are much less.

I got some experience of negotiating with officials, too. That was a type of job I'd never done before. Whenever parts for a repair had to be taken into Syria or Lebanon or Iraq there were Customs duties to be paid or talked out of; in the usual way I'd get to Aleppo or some place like that and find that the repair parts I'd sent up had got stuck in a bonded warehouse, the Government were asking for a hundred and fifty pounds before they would release them, and the ground engineer had got angry and had insulted the Minister for Air. There was nobody to straighten all that out but me, and I got into the way of taking it easy, going to drink a cup of coffee with the Minister, saying what a happy little town it was and how my wife would like it if we came to live there, and sending over a big bouquet of flowers for the Minister's wife. I'd usually get the parts next day without any trouble at all, and nothing to pay. The most I ever had to do was to fix up a joyride for the Minister's children when the aircraft was flying again.

I used to write to Beryl regularly once a week wherever I was, telling her as much about what I'd been doing as I thought would pass the censor. She used to write to me, but not so often. It was once a week at first, but then it got a bit irregular and sometimes I wouldn't hear anything for three weeks, and then two letters would come together, written within a couple of days of each other. She never seemed to have much to say, but that was natural because life in England was all just the same. Often most of a letter was about some film she'd seen.

There was one of those long gaps in her letters, nearly a month, about October 1944, when I'd been out in Egypt just a year. Airmail was coming through all right. I got a bit angry, because I'd written regularly myself and I didn't see why she couldn't find time to write to me, so I sent her a sharp one. Nothing happened for a bit, and then about ten days later I got a letter from her dad.

It read:

DEAR TOM,

We've been having trouble here, I'm sorry to say, and Beryl wants me to write and tell you before she writes herself, and her Ma and I think that's best too. It's been very dull for her since you went away, and she went up to the West End some time ago and got in with some Polish officers, very nice and well behaved, she says. She took to going about with one of them, a Captain Wysock, and the long and the short of it is, Tom, she's going to have a baby in January.

I know this will be a great blow to you, and I can't tell you how sorry we all are. Captain Wysock has been down to see us and we had a long talk. He was heartbroken about you, but we talked it all out and we thought that it would be best if there was a divorce and he was to marry Beryl; they are very much in love and that is what they want. Beryl will be writing to you in a day or so, but we thought I had better write and tell you first.

Captain Wysock comes of a very high-born family. His father is a Count and has big estates near a place called Jabinka and a town house in Warsaw. He has been very generous to Beryl, and we feel that as things have turned out a divorce would be the fairest thing all round, and I hope you will think so too.

Beryl wants me to say she sends you her love, and we all send our sympathy in what must be a shock to you. But I am sure that it will all be for the best.

Your affectionate father-in-law,

ALBERT COUSINS.

I was at Damascus when this letter came to Cairo, and I didn't get it till I got back to Egypt a few days later. By that time the letter from Beryl had just come in, so I got them both together. That one read:

DARLING TOM,

I saw Dad's letter before he sent it off and I have waited a bit before I wrote so as you should get his first. I don't know what you must be thinking, Tom, and believe me I wouldn't have had things happen like this for the world. It's such a mix up. But I'm sure the best way to get it straight now is for you to divorce me. I couldn't come back and live with you again not after what has happened, not even if you wanted me which I suppose you don't, not now. Feodor and I are very much in love

20

and we want to get married, so if you divorce me that will be best and you'll be free to look for someone else. I'm so terribly sorry it's turned out like this. I never thought a thing like this would ever happen to me.

I wish you could meet Feodor, Tom – he's such a dear. His family is terribly rich with a big castle in the country and everything; I do hope they'll approve of me. He hasn't seen them since the war began, but he knows they're all right. After the war, when we're married, we're going there to live. He's given me the most lovely engagement ring, diamonds and emeralds, but first of all we've got to get the divorce.

Don't be miserable about all this, Tom. I know it's all for the best.

Your loving,

BERYL.

I was up to the eyes in work at that time. I read these letters through with my mind half occupied with the problems of getting enough aircraft serviceable to maintain our scheduled services, and they were just another thing to me. It was like when you're counting on an aircraft being finished for the morning flight to Khartoum, and an engineer comes up at six o'clock in the evening and tells you he needs a right-hand contact breaker and they've only got left-hand ones in the store and they've been telephoning all round and there aren't any right-hand ones in Cairo. Beryl and her boy friend, in my mind, took their turn in the queue with all my other worries, and must wait for attention till I got the decks cleared a bit. At the same time, I was sick and angry when I got these letters, because there'd been a lot of this sort of thing going on in England. Somebody once told me that ten per cent of the wives of men serving overseas had been unfaithful to them. Now I was in with that ten per cent.

21

In the brief moments that I had to think about my own affairs that day I wondered how in hell she expected me to set about a divorce in a foreign country like Egypt, in the middle of all my work, in war time. And then I wondered if they were all mad to go believing such a transparent, cock and bull story as this Polish soldier had told them, about his father being a Count, and huge estates, and all that. It was a crazy, miserable business that they'd written out to plague me with; the only thing to do was to put it out of my mind and get on with the work.

I had to go to Luxor next day, where a young fool of a pilot had run one of our Ansons into the tail of a Dakota of Transport Command. I had to clear up the accumulation of paper work on my desk before going off again in the morning; I worked on late that night. It was after ten o'clock when I had time for my own affairs and I was dead tired, but I had to write to Beryl because I should be away for another two or three days. I got the letters out and read them through, and I was bitterly angry once again that they should plague me so.

I pulled a sheet of paper to me, and I wrote:

DARLING GIRL,
I got your letter and your Dad's together when I got back here after being away for a few days. I won't say what I think because you probably know that, but I'll say this. I think you must be bloody well daft, all the lot of you.

First of all, I'll bet you a hundred quid to a sausage that this Polish officer's father isn't a Count and that he hasn't got any estates and that the ring he gave you is either stolen or phoney. For God's sake snap out of it and act like a grown up woman, and tell your Dad to do that too. You've been sucked in and fallen for the oldest story in the world, my girl. That's what's happened to you.

Now about this divorce you want. I don't know how in hell you expect me to get you a divorce from here even if I wanted to, and I've not made up my mind about that yet. What do you think this is – the Court of Chancery, with lawyers going round in wigs and gowns and that? I'll tell you what it is. It's a bloody hot, dirty, dusty aerodrome, no fans and blinding sun, and grit all over my desk. I've come five hundred miles from one just like it today, and I'm going off to another like it tomorrow. There's no English lawyers here and no English law. If it's a divorce you're thinking of, you'll have to wait till I get back to England in a year from now, and then I'll see if I'm prepared to give it you. Some of you girls seem to think you can get a divorce just by putting a penny in the slot.

You think this over a bit more, and then write and tell me how you're going on. If I was in England now we'd soon find out if this Polish officer is a Count or not, and you'd find out what the end of a strap feels like, my girl. I'm not at all sure that you'd find out what a divorce feels like. You can't just pick up being married and put it down, like that. You think it over a bit more.

Ever your loving husband,

TOM.

Considering this letter, it seems to me that I said everything that was in my mind, except that I still loved her. I didn't think to tell her about that. Perhaps I thought she knew.

Nothing much happened then. She didn't write again, and nor did I. I was very sore about this Polish officer, and till that was all cleaned up I hadn't got much to say to her. If I'd been in England I'd have cleaned it up fast enough. I did sit down once or twice to write, but I never finished a letter. I could never think of anything to say that wouldn't be pleading with her for our marriage, and I was damned if I'd do that.

I had an arrangement to send her money through the bank, deducted from my salary when it was paid in, and this went on as usual; she still took my fifteen pounds a month in spite of her Polish Count with his large estates. I was content to leave the matter so. I was far too busy in those Cairo years of war to bother about any other girl. I used to wonder sometimes if I was married or not, and how it was all going on, and then I'd put it out of my mind. Time enough to start and sort out that one when I got home. I think I felt that so long as she went on taking my money there was nothing that couldn't be ironed out when finally we got together.

The end of the German war came, and the end of the Japanese war, but there was still a vast amount of transport needed in the Near East, and I had to serve my full time out. It wasn't till the middle of November 1945 that I finally got a date for my air passage home, and then I wrote to her quite shortly and told her I was coming and I'd come and see her at her dad's house as soon as I landed in England, probably on the Tuesday of the following week.

I landed in England on the day I'd said, and went up to London on the airline bus. It was pretty late in the afternoon when we got in to Town, and I decided to stay in London that night rather than go down to Morden there and then; I didn't want to have to stay in the same house if this Polish officer was living with her or anything like that. I took my bag to a hotel I knew about just off the Euston Road, that wasn't too expensive, and I got a room there.

I went out and walked about the streets after my tea, down Tottenham Court Road to Cambridge Circus and to Piccadilly. The V-bombs had made a good bit of blitz damage since I was there, but London seemed much the same as ever. I was the one who was different. When I left England I hadn't been too sure of myself; I was good enough on the bench or in the hangar, but it always seemed to me that other people knew much more about the world and business than I did. Coming back after my two years in the East, I felt self-confident. I knew that I could hold my job alongside anyone, and teach them a thing or two besides. When I worked in England I was just Tom Cutter in Airservice Ltd. When I left Cairo I'd been Mr Cutter to everybody for a long time, from the managing director down.

I was looking forward to meeting Beryl again, and I wasn't much worried about this Pole. I reckoned I could sort out that one without too much trouble. She couldn't be married to him, and now that the war was over he'd be going back to his own country. The baby might be a problem, but I don't think I really held that much against her. I was still fond of Beryl and quite prepared to make the best of things and fall in love with her again. There wasn't any other girl.

I went down by Underground after breakfast next morning and got out at Morden station and walked up through the streets to her home. It was a fine morning for the end of November, with a pale, wintry sort of sun. I was still in light clothes and a raincoat only, and I remember walking quick, because it was chilly. I went in at the little front garden gate and knocked on the front door, and her young brother came and opened it.

"Morning, Fred," I said. "Remember me?"

He hesitated, and I looked at him more closely; it was almost as if he had been crying. And then he said, "Oh – yes. How are you, Tom?"

"I'm fine," I said. "Beryl in?"

"Wait a mo'," he said. "I'll go and tell Mum." And with that he turned and fairly scuttled off into the kitchen at the back of the house.

I waited at the door. It was bound to be a bit awkward for them, but I didn't care; I hadn't made the awkwardness. I could hear a lot of whispering going on in the kitchen and then her mother came out to me, wiping her hands nervously upon her apron. And when I saw her face I knew that she'd been crying, too, and for the first time I felt fear of what was coming.

"Morning, Tom," she said hesitantly. "You didn't get our letter?"

I shook my head. "No."

She opened the door of the sitting-room. "Come in here." She led the way in. "I wish Father was here to tell you, but he's just stepped out."

"What is it?" I asked her. I think I knew by that time what it was.

"It's Beryl," she said. The tears began to trickle down her cheeks. "She did it with the oven, with the gas, some time in the middle of the night when we was all asleep."

She was weeping unrestrainedly now. "Her dad told her it'ld be all right," she sobbed. "We all told her. But she was terribly afraid of meeting you."

CHAPTER TWO

> – And I was but a dog, and a mad one to despise
>   The gold of her hair, and the grey of her eyes.

> JOHN MASEFIELD

THERE WASN'T ANY Count, of course, and there weren't any estates at Jabinka or anywhere else. Captain Wysock had disappeared one day, and her dad had gone up to London to the Polish Embassy after a time to ask about him. He found that he had been drafted out to Italy. He had been a waiter at a hotel in Warsaw before the war, and he'd got a wife and family out there. They never heard any more of him. The ring was genuine enough, and was worth about sixty quid. I often wonder where that came from.

He beat it soon after the baby was born, in February or March. Her dad wanted to write and tell me, but Beryl wouldn't let him. I think she was too proud to want to come crawling back to me as soon as he'd left her flat. She told her people straight to let her affairs alone; she'd sort them out in time the way she wanted to. So they shut up, and probably that was the best thing.

They told me that they thought that in a general sort of way she'd been looking forward to me coming home, although she didn't tell them much. When my letter came, however, saying that I'd be home in a week, they said she seemed to go all to pieces. First she wanted to go away and not meet me, and then there wasn't anywhere convenient for her to go to, and then she said she'd have to meet me some time so she'd better get it over. They said she didn't know what to do. She wasn't sleeping much, they thought. She'd come down to breakfast one day and say she'd made up her mind to go away, and then by dinner-time, they said, she seemed to have forgotten about that and was wondering if the butcher would put by a sheep's heart for them, because she said I was always partial to heart for dinner if it was on the menu at the canteen.

They said that she was much calmer on the last day, sort of quiet-like, and they went to bed quite happy about her. They never heard anything in the night. The baby slept in her room, of course, and at about six in the morning they heard it crying, which was normal, but as she didn't get up and attend to it her ma got up after a bit and went in, and she wasn't in her room, and she hadn't been to bed. Her ma called her dad and went downstairs, and when they opened the door the kitchen was full of gas. Her dad held his breath and dashed in and turned it off at the oven, and opened the back door and got out into the garden, and then they had to wait a quarter of an hour before they could get in to her. Her dad went down the road to the call box and telephoned the police.

She had put a cushion in the oven and put her head on that, and lain down to die. She had a copy of *The Picturegoer* in her hand, open at an article about Anna Neagle and Michael Wilding, the great lovers.

There was no letter, or anything like that.

Her father was inclined to be apologetic to me. "I dunno if we should have written to tell you, after he went off," he said. "At the time it seemed the best thing to let time go by a bit, like. We knew you'd be home before so long, and we thought things'ld settle down ..."

To comfort him I said, "I couldn't have done much, if I'd known." And while I said it, of course, I knew that I was lying. I could have done one thing. I could have written and told her that I loved her.

They had the inquest the day after I arrived, and I went to that with her dad and mum. Her dad had to give evidence about our marriage and this Captain Wysock, and the baby, and me coming home, and how he found her. The coroner asked me if I'd written to her lately, and I said no, and told him about the first letter when I said I wasn't going to divorce her till she'd thought it over a bit longer. The doctor gave formal evidence about the cause of death, and then the coroner summed it all up.

"We have here one of those unfortunate cases for which the war is largely responsible," he said. "The evidence is perfectly clear. The deceased woman was unfaithful to her husband during his absence overseas, and gave birth to a child born out of wedlock. She was deserted by her lover, himself a married man, so that in any event no divorce and marriage with her lover would have been possible. Her husband seems to have behaved with commendable restraint and wrote nothing to her which would have led her to take her life, and her family appear to have treated her with sympathy and understanding. The deceased appears to have been the victim of her own conscience, and as the time for the return of her husband drew near she became mentally upset. I find that the deceased committed suicide while the balance of her mind was temporarily deranged."

He turned to us with fishlike, stupid eyes blinking behind his spectacles. "I must express my sympathy with the husband and the parents of the deceased woman." With her dad and mum I said, "Thank you, sir," mechanically, and as I did so indignation rose in me that such a fool should be a coroner. Because I killed her, slowly, like a chap might do with small doses of arsenic over a period of years. I started killing her when I married her without giving her a home.

A bit was said about the baby, and a woman, a police court missionary or somebody like that, came up and talked about it to her dad and mum. They wanted to keep it and bring it up as a grandchild, which of course it was, and that seemed the best thing to do. Then the inquest was over, and we went back for the funeral which happened in the afternoon.

I left her parents at the cemetery when it was all over; they wanted me to go back home with them for tea, but I said I had to get down to Southampton that night. I hadn't, but I had got to be alone. I went back to my cheap hotel near Euston station, and went up into the bare, white bedroom, and sat down on the bed. I must have sat there for two hours or more, just staring at the wall ahead of me.

You can only do a thing for the first time once, and that goes for falling in love. You may do it over and over again afterwards, but it's never the same. When you chuck away what's given to you that first time, it's chucked away for good. I started chucking it away when I married Beryl and went off to Egypt, leaving her alone.

You can be very, very cruel just by acting with restraint, and everyone will say what a good chap you are.

You can kill somebody just by doing nothing, and be complimented at the inquest.

You can be absolutely right all through. And what you'll get for it is a memory of happiness that might have been, if you had acted a bit kinder.

I might have dozed a bit that night – I don't know. I know that I heard every hour strike from a church clock outside my room.

I had to go and report to the Company next day, and that, of course, was at Morden, just by her house. I had to go down again to the same Underground station, and there were the same red buses rattling the same diesel engines at the bus stop by the entrance where we had said goodbye. She had said, "I'll be terribly lost without you." She had been.

I stood staring at the place by the Metroland poster where I had stood holding her in my arms, stood there in a daze. I had told her that it was only for two years. She had said miserably, "It sounds like as if it was forever." It had been.

It was there that she had stood waving me goodbye.

I turned away, and walked up the main road through the shopping part before turning off up Aerodrome Lane to the works. And now I was scared stiff that I'd meet her dad or mum out doing the shopping, or some of her family. I don't know why it was, but I was afraid to meet them, and I knew as I walked up to the works that I could never work in that place again. I'd never have the courage to walk round those streets as we had walked together, or go to the picture house that we had used, or lunch in the works canteen where we had lunched.

The managing director, Mr Norman Evans, he was very nice to me. I think he must have heard about my trouble, because when I said that I'd been back two days and I'd had personal things to see to first, he said quickly, "I know, Cutter. Things get a bit tangled up when one's away for a long time. I'm very sorry indeed." And then he went on to talk about the work, so that I didn't have to answer.

The business was all upset, of course, because it had been expanded greatly in the war years with war orders, and now those had come to an end and it was having to contract again. It's easy enough to expand an aviation business, but it's bloody difficult to get it back to what it was before. Mr Evans couldn't have been nicer. "I want to tell you how much I appreciate the job you did in Egypt," he said. "We've got to make a lot of changes now. What I want you to do is to take over the whole of our repair and servicing side in the British Isles – here, and at Bristol and at Belfast."

It was a first-class job, of course, as good as any I could hope to get. I was only thirty-one years old. "The main office would be here, sir, I suppose?" I asked. "I'd do most of the work from here, and travel to Bristol and Belfast?"

"That's right," he said. "I thought you might take over Mr Holden's old office. I'll have that room next to it divided into two, and you can have your secretary in there unless you want her in the room with you." Then he went on to talk about the salary, which was good, and as we talked I knew that it would never work. Unless I came to work each day by helicopter I'd have to use the same streets and the same Underground and the same passages and roads about the works that I had walked with Beryl.

I said presently, "I've got a month's leave due to me, sir. Can I take that now?"

"That's right," he said. He glanced at the calendar. "Oh well, that takes us up to Christmas. Suppose we say you'll start immediately after that."

I thanked him, and agreed, and then he took me for a walk around the works and we talked about the layout of the place, and what parts we would shut down or use as stores, and how the rest of it should be reorganised. I had only half my mind on the job. At every corner there was some new place I had forgotten about where I had walked and talked with Beryl in the lunch hour. When finally Mr Evans asked me to stay and lunch in the canteen I couldn't take it any longer, and I said that if he'd excuse me I'd get off down to my home in Southampton that afternoon.

As I walked down to the Underground, looking furtively around in case there were some of the Cousins family about, I knew it was impossible. I couldn't go back there to work. I'd have been off my rocker in a fortnight.

I got my bag and paid my bill at the hotel, and went to Waterloo and caught a train down to Southampton. I got there in the late afternoon, and took a bus to the gas works, and walked home from there. Our street, between the gas works and the docks, hadn't suffered much in the blitz; old Mrs Tickle's house had gone, and Mrs Tickle with it, but that was the only damage actually in our street, and that had been done before I went to Egypt.

I was surprised at how small it all looked now. I knew it was dirty, because you can't keep houses clean between the gas works and the docks, but I had not realised till then how small the houses were, how small and mean the shops. As I got near our house I could see that an upstairs window was broken and shut up with windowlite tacked over the frame; they had written to tell me about that, done by a flying bomb that fell into Montgomery Street in July 1944. I thought that while I was home I'd build up the frame and get a bit of glass and do that for them, even if it was the landlord's job.

I went in at the street door that opened straight into the living room and there was Ma laying the table for tea; it was getting on for five o'clock when Dad would be knocking off at the docks. I put my suitcase down. "I'm back, Ma," I said quietly.

She said, "Oh Tom! You're looking so brown!" And when she'd kissed me she said, "We know about poor Beryl, Tom. We're all ever so sorry."

"How did you get to know?" I asked.

"Mrs Cousins wrote and told us," she replied. "There was a bit about it in the paper, too. It's been a sad home-coming for you, boy."

"That's right," I said heavily. "Nothing to be done about it now, though, and the least said the better." She took the hint and she must have dropped a word to Dad, because they never bothered me with questions.

We had plenty of other things to talk about, though, specially when Dad came home. I'd written to them regularly while I was away, and they'd got young Ted's school atlas and marked on it all the places that I'd been to, and it made a sort of spider's web all over the Near East. I had some photographs that I'd collected from time to time, and after we'd done the washing up I got these out and showed them and told them all about it, and my sister Joyce came in with her husband, Joe Morton, who kept the greengrocer's shop in Allenby Street just round the corner, and he brought a couple of bottles of beer in, and I sat talking and telling them about it all till nearly ten o'clock.

When they had gone and Dad and I were sitting with a final cigarette before the fire, and Ted and Ma had gone up to bed, Dad said to me, "What comes next, boy?"

"I don't know." I told him about the job I had been offered that morning, and I told him something about my great unwillingness to go back to Morden. He asked, "What's the pay like?"

"Nine hundred a year," I told him.

He opened his eyes. "That's twice what I get. Three times what I ever got before the war. You're getting on in the world, boy."

"I know," I said. "It's a good job and I'd be a bloody fool to turn it down. But it's no good working in a place that's going to send you round the bend."

"You're looking tired," he said. "You'll feel different when you've had a bit of a rest. How long leave have you got?"

"They're giving me a month," I told him. "Till after Christmas. I haven't had a day off since I went out to Egypt."

He said in wonder, "I never had more'n a week's holiday in all my life. Are they paying you?"

"My Cairo pay goes on till the end of December," I said.

"Do you spend it all?"

I shook my head. "I've got a good bit saved up." I hesitated. "I was saving up for furniture."

Ted was the only one of the family still living at home; he was just eighteen and due to go off for his military service pretty soon. He worked for a firm of contractors and Dad had had him taught to drive, so he was all set to be a truck driver. We had three bedrooms in that house; when I was a boy it had been Dad and Mum upstairs in one room and the girls in the other, and for us boys there was a room downstairs built out behind the scullery in the garden. It was a good big room, and it had need to be because four of us had slept together there when I was a boy, in two beds. Ted had got the girls' room upstairs, and Dad and Mum had titivated up the big old room for me, colourwashed it and all when they heard I was coming home; they'd gone to a lot of trouble over it, working at it over the weekend. I slept there that night, comforted a bit by memories of childhood, and although I stayed awake some time, I did sleep.

I went out early next day and got a chisel and a brass-backed saw, and started on that window. I worked on it all that day and the next and got it finished and glazed for them, with a coat of white lead paint. I did a lot of odd jobs round the house in the next few days, and got an electric water heater and installed it over the sink in the scullery for Ma. While I worked at these things, I was making up my mind what I was going to do. By the end of the first day, I think I knew what it was to be.

I took a bus one day and went out to the airport at Eastleigh. There's a firm there, Kennington's, who do quite a big business in overhauling and servicing aircraft; I had thought once or twice of putting in for a job with them. Now I went to the sales side, to a young chap called Warren that I knew slightly, and asked if he knew where I could get a Fox-Moth.

The Fox-Moth is a de Havilland type, obsolete now; it was produced about 1933. It has a little cabin for the passengers and an open cockpit for the pilot, and an engine of a hundred and thirty horsepower. Mine cruised at about ninety miles an hour. It would carry the pilot and two passengers comfortably, or four passengers if they were very little ones, and there was a good long runway to take off on with the overload. The type hasn't been in production for a long time and there weren't many of them left, but Warren said he thought he knew of one in Leicester, dismantled and unused for years, and wanting a lot of work done on it. We got on the telephone from his office, and found that it was there all right, and about to be put out on the scrap heap.

I went to Leicester next day and bought it with a second-hand engine for a hundred and twenty pounds, and arranged for it to be sent down to Eastleigh on a truck. That's how I started in the air transport business.

I was headed for the Persian Gulf. I'd been to Abadan and Basra and Kuwait and as far down as Bahrein for a night, and I'd seen conditions there. I had an idea that a chap with a little aeroplane for charter, that could land on any decent bit of desert, might do all right for himself. There's no way to get about that country except by plane or car, and travelling by car on those sand tracks is no fun at all. There was nobody doing charter work in that part that I knew of. I had a hunch that if I went there with a Fox-Moth I might make a living. Anyway, it would be something different; if I lost my money I'd always got my trade to fall back on.

Kenningtons were very helpful. I made a deal with them to pay for overheads and for any labour that I used, and when the Fox-Moth came they put it in a corner of a hangar and let me get on with the work myself, with a boy to help me; they knew I hadn't got much money. The plane wasn't in too bad condition. I got it all stripped down and had the Air Registration Board inspector to agree what wanted doing, and by Christmas time I'd got the airframe finished all except the final spraying. I was working on it by half-past seven every morning, and I never left till eight o'clock at night; I hadn't got much time to spare, because with every day my money was running out.

I wrote to Mr Evans at Morden about the middle of December, turning in my job. I told him that it was for personal reasons, that I didn't want to come back there, and that I was going to do something totally different for a change. He wrote me a very nice letter telling me to let them know if ever I wanted to come back into the repair business, and with that I felt I had something behind me to fall back on.

I finished the engine and got it through a test run on the bench about the end of the first week in January, and got it installed in the aircraft a couple of days after that. I made a test flight on January 12th, and there was nothing then to do but the final spray-painting and lettering, and make the arrangements for my journey to the Gulf.

Ma was good to me while I was working out at Eastleigh on the Fox-Moth. I used to go out there on a bicycle to save money, six miles each way, and sometimes I wouldn't be home till nearly ten o'clock at night. Whatever time I came home there would be something hot for me in the oven, and a kettle boiling ready for my tea, and a bit of cheese or cake to eat after. Once while I was eating my supper, Ma said,

"How long will you be away for this time, Tom?"

I grinned at her. "Three months," I said. "I'll be broke by that time, and home looking for a job."

She was knitting, and she went on for a minute. "I don't think so," she said quietly. "I don't think you'll go broke."

"Lots of people do go broke," I said, "and doing less daft things than this I'm playing at."

"I don't think you will," she repeated.

I grinned at her again. "Well, I've never starved in the winter yet."

"No, and I don't think you will."

She knitted on in silence for a time. "This place Bahrein where you're going to," she said. "What sort of place is it? How will you be living?"

"It's a fair-sized town," I said. "An Arab town, of course. There are some white people living there – the RAF, and the chaps in the Government. And then, inland there are sort of special towns like Awali run by the Bahrein Petroleum Company, where a lot of British and Canadian engineers live with their families."

"Will you live there?"

I shook my head. "I think there's an Arab hotel in the town. I'll probably be there, at first at any rate."

"Will there be any white girls there?" she asked.

I knew what she was getting at, of course. "Not one," I said. "There might be some WAAFs with the Air Force, but I wouldn't get a look in there."

"Try and find someone, Tom," she said quietly. "I know you don't feel like it now, and maybe that's right. But I would like to see you settled comfortable in a nice home, with a nice girl and some children. Don't give all of your life to your work."

"Blowed if I know where I'll find the nice home, but it won't be in Bahrein," I said. "Nor the nice girl, either. But I'll bear it in mind, Ma."

"That's right," she said. "Just keep it in your mind. I do want to see you settled and comfortable, like your Dad and I have been."

Ma never wanted anything better than she'd got. She knew it was a lousy little house, of course, but it was home and near Dad's work, and there she had lived all her married life, and had her children, and watched them grow up and get out into the world. She never wanted anything better; she had a happiness quite independent of the quality of her house. It's convenient for Dad's work and she's accustomed to it. She'll never move.

I finished off the Fox-Moth a few days after that, and she really didn't look so bad, with a new aluminium spray all over her and green registration letters, and a broad green line running backwards down the fuselage from the prop. I had had the cabin seats reupholstered, too, and replaced the scratched perspex in the windows, so that by the time I'd done with her she looked almost new.

Dad and Mum came out to see her when she was finished, one Sunday, and I took them up for a joyride over Southampton. Then I was ready to start.

It was a bad time of year to fly from England, and the Fox-Moth was a very little aeroplane, with no blind flying instruments, or radio, or anything like that. On the day I wanted to start, Monday the 21st, there was a dense fog and it would have been crazy to leave the ground even if the airport officers had let me, which they wouldn't. Next day was better. Ma came out with me to Eastleigh to see me off. I got the aircraft out and ran the engine to warm her up, and got my stuff through Customs, and went and made my flight plan at the Control. Then I was ready to get in and go.

"This is it, Mum," I said. "I'll be back in a year or so."

She kissed me. "Goodbye, Tom," she said. "Look after yourself, and don't go killing yourself or anything of that."

"I won't do that, Mum," I said smiling. One always thinks, of course, those things can't happen to me.

"Don't forget what I was telling you, about finding a nice girl."

"I won't. Goodbye, Mum."

"Goodbye, son."

I swung the little propeller, and the engine fired, and I went round and got into the cockpit, clumsy in my leather coat. Then I waved to Mum and taxied forward, and the Control gave me a green light and I moved to the end of the runway and took off from England.

I'm not going to say much about that trip out to Bahrein; there was nothing to make it interesting but my own inexperience and the inadequacy of the aircraft for so long a journey. I could fly the thing all right, but my total flying experience was only about five hundred hours and I didn't know a lot about navigation, when I started. I knew a bit more by the time I reached the Persian Gulf.

I had to land a good many times for fuel on the way. The extreme range of the Fox-Moth was only about three hundred and fifty miles; later on I fitted an extra tank. I went by way of Dinard, and across France to Cannes, landing at Tours and Lyon. From there I went to Pisa and Rome and Brindisi and Araxos and Athens, and from there to Rhodes and Cyprus. I rested a day there and did a quick run round the engine, and went on by way of Damascus to a place called H3 in the middle of the desert; then to Baghdad, Basra, Kuweit, and so to Bahrein. It took me eight days of trundling along at ninety miles an hour, and I was tired when I got there.

I landed one evening on the big RAF and civil aerodrome on Muharraq Island. There was a hangar there, and the place is an RAF station, but there were no service aircraft stationed there at that time. Several used to come through every week, and at that time the BOAC flying-boats called there, as well as several foreign lines.

It was a lovely, summery evening as I taxied to the hangar after landing, just like a warm day in June in England. It had been very cold over most of the route, until I got south of Baghdad, and then it had begun to warm up. A couple of RAF flying officers strolled out to the machine as I switched off in front of the hangar, and I got out of the cockpit to talk to them.

"Come far?" one asked.

"Eastleigh," I said.

They raised eyebrows and grinned. "How long did it take you?"

"I left England last Tuesday," I said. "Eight days."

"Going on to India?"

"No," I said. "I was thinking of staying here a bit, and see if I can pick up a bit of charter work."

We talked about it for a time, and then I left them and went up to the Control Tower to report. When I got back to the machine the officers had got some airmen and we pushed the Fox-Moth into the hangar and got my stuff out of the cabin. As we did so one of the young officers that I later came to know as Mr Allen said, "Pity you weren't here yesterday."

"Why's that?" I asked.

"Party of three engineers going down to Muscat. They're consulting on a new water supply or something. They came in by BOAC from England. If you'd been here you might have got a job."

"What happened to them?" I asked.

"Went on down to Sharjah in a chartered dhow. They left this morning."

"How far is it to Sharjah?"

"About four hundred miles. I wouldn't like to do that in a dhow. It'll take them three or four days."

"How far on is it to Muscat?"

"About two hundred and fifty miles. They were going to charter a truck to take them from Sharjah to Muscat."

I said, "Is there any fuel at Muscat?"

Allen nodded. "We keep a small party there. There's a strip there, and there's hundred-octane fuel."

This was too rich and rare a fuel for my common little engine, but I could mix it with motorcar petrol. I said, "Can I get a telegram to Sharjah offering this Fox for charter to them?"

"I should think so. They'll probably send it from the Control Tower if you ask them nicely, over the R/T. They're always talking to Sharjah. It's more reliable than the land telegraph line. That's always falling down."

I got the name of the leader of the party from him, and the rest house where they would stay in Sharjah, and went back to the Control Tower. The Control officer knew all about this party, and advised me to wire them care of the Political Agent. I sent off a message detailing the accommodation and range of my Fox-Moth and offering it for charter for eight pounds an hour from Bahrein.

I had a bit of luck then, because one of the wireless operators, Dick Reed, spoke up and asked me where I was going to stay. He lived in a house in Muharraq town just outside the aerodrome with all the other operators; they ran it as a chummery, and they had a spare room, normally occupied by a chap who was on leave. They offered this to me and I moved in there that night and messed with the radio crowd.

At the aerodrome, they made me a member of the sergeants' mess, which meant that I could go in there at any time for lunch, or for tea if I was working late. That was a great help, in those early months.

I spent next day working on the aircraft to get it overhauled and fit for work after the flight out from England, and in typing out circular letters, five copies at a time, to send out to the eighteen or twenty possible employers of a charter aircraft in the Persian Gulf. I got a job next day, to take two engineers from Awali up to Kuweit for a conference, leaving early in the morning and coming back at night. They paid my eight pounds an hour without blinking, and the job went off all right, so by the end of the day I was fifty-six pounds in pocket and everyone seemed satisfied, specially me. My eight pounds an hour worked out at about two bob a mile, but we had travelled six hundred miles in seven hours flying time.

Next, a reply to my Sharjah wire came in, ordering me down to Sharjah at once. Three days in an Arab dhow had made my eight pounds an hour seem cheap to the water engineers, even though I couldn't carry the party in one load but had to ferry them everywhere in two trips. I took them down to Muscat and stayed with them for a week. In all I was away from Bahrein for ten days, and I got back at the end of the job with thirty-eight hours of flying done for them, and a cheque for three hundred and four pounds in my pocket.

That's the way it went on all the time. The Persian Gulf is full of industry – new oilfields being laid out, wells being sunk, pipelines being laid, new docks and harbours being built all over the place. There are no roads outside the towns and no railways, and no coasting steamers and few motorboats. The country is full of engineers to whom time is money, and there are always people wanting to get about in a hurry. The country is mostly sand desert, good for landing a small aeroplane when you have learned the different look of hard and soft sand from the air, and I was right up to the neck in work from the day I got there. Most of the oil companies had their own aircraft, but there was plenty of work left over for me.

I have been asked sometimes what led me to the Persian Gulf, what instinct told me that I could build up a business there. It's really perfectly simple. If you go to the hottest and most uncomfortable place on the map you'll find there's not a lot of competition; in my experience most British pilots would rather go bankrupt than get prickly heat. If you can find, as I did, a place where there's a lot of business for a modest charter operator, that's also hot and uncomfortable – well, it's money for jam. Only, of course, you can't afford to pay the wages of a European staff.

To start with, I had no staff at all. For the first two months I did everything myself, serviced the aircraft, washed it down, did the correspondence on my typewriter in the evening, kept the accounts, sent out the bills, and – easiest of all – flew the thing. Presently it got a bit too much, and I got in help for the washing down. I got an Arab boy about fifteen years old called Tarik and paid him twenty rupees a month, about thirty bob, at which he was highly delighted. I taught him to wash and clean the aircraft while I worked upon the engine, and when he wasn't doing that he was running errands for me to the souk – the market. He wasn't fully employed in those early days, of course, but it was useful to have somebody to help with the refuelling.

It was three months before anyone woke up to the fact that I wasn't licensed to carry passengers for hire or reward. I only had a private pilot's licence. An ARB inspector turned up from Egypt one day, travelling around to see what was going on in civil aviation in the Persian Gulf, and told me that I was breaking the law every time I went up. I knew that, of course, but I hoped that nobody else did.

He was quite nice about it. I told him that next day I had to take Mr Cassidy and Mr Hogaarts of the Arabian-Sumatran Petroleum Company from Abu Ali to Kuwait, and if I didn't turn up they'd be stuck at Abu Ali, and after some hesitation he agreed that I should make this one trip. While we were talking the telephone went, and it was Johnson of the Bahrein Petroleum Company wanting to book me for the following Thursday to take a couple of his chaps down to Dubai. I knew Johnson well, and I never believe in hiding things up, so I told him I was with a bloke who said I couldn't carry passengers for hire because I'd only got an "A" licence.

"For Christ's sake," he said. "Let me have a talk to him." I handed over the receiver, and he talked to the inspector, saying that they couldn't do without me and all that sort of thing. The upshot of it was that it was agreed that I should do that one trip also, and by next morning the inspector had thought it over and said that he would recommend that I should be granted a provisional "B" licence.

The point of this argument was that I could get a "B" licence without much difficulty on the basis of the experience I had, but I could only go through the examinations for it in England, and I was in the Persian Gulf. I couldn't have got it when I left England; I wasn't good enough. I knew that I could keep them talking for some months and in the meantime I could go on operating, and after that I might well find myself in England.

By that time, it was dawning on me that I should have to make a quick trip back to England before long to buy another aeroplane. There was far more work than I could cope with. I was flying four or five hours practically every day, and maintaining the aircraft and doing the correspondence for the rest of the time. At that I was only tackling the fringe of the job. It wasn't only taking engineers about the country, though I could have used a six-passenger machine on that to supplement the Fox-Moth. There was machinery to be taken out to places in the desert, drilling machinery to be fetched in for reconditioning, spare parts for trucks and bulldozers – all sorts of things, some of them requiring really large aircraft. Nobody was doing more than scratch the surface of the work that was offering, and over and above the lot of it there were things like the transport of pilgrims to Jiddah and transport of food to relieve the perennial famines in the Hadramaut.

If I didn't nip in and get myself established, someone else would come along and do it over my head.

On Bahrein aerodrome the local RAF and civil air staff began to get quite interested in me. It was obvious at the end of the three months that, licence or not, I was on to a good thing and I was doing pretty well. British NCOs with the RAF used to come along and watch me working with young Tarik, and suggest that they were due to be demobilised in a few months and what about a job? I never engaged one of them. I knew from my own experience the wages that you have to pay British engineers in the East, and I knew that if once I started on that sort of wage bill I'd be bust in no time. Moreover, I didn't need them. I had all the ground engineer's licences myself. Young Tarik, brown though he might be, was keen and quite intelligent, and I reckoned that with two or three more like him I could service several aircraft myself.

It was about that time that Gujar Singh turned up.

Gujar Singh was a young Sikh, who worked as a cashier in the Bank of Asia. He might have been twenty-six or twenty-eight years old at that time, and he was the fiercest thing I had ever seen. Being a good Sikh he never cut his hair, and he had a great black beard that stuck out forward from his chin in a manner that would have frightened any gunman trying to hold up the bank into a fit. When I got to know him better, and travelled with him, I found that he slept every night with a bandage round his head to make this beard grow fiercely outwards from his face. He wore European clothes and was usually dressed in a neat, light grey tropical suit, but he always wore a turban. Beneath this turban there was long black hair that reached down to his waist, coiled round his head out of sight and fastened with a comb. He wore a plain iron bangle on his wrist, and beneath his jacket he wore a ceremonial dagger belted round his waist. He didn't smoke or drink, because of his religion.

Gujar Singh was always pleasant when I met him in the bank; he was a smiling, soft-spoken, friendly young man in spite of his fierce appearance. He was reserved and discreet; he was evidently interested in me and in my business, but he never asked questions. Once he did ask me what the weather had been like the day before, when I had been down to Yas Island or somewhere, and afterwards the remark stuck in my mind, because it had been a thundery sort of day and something in the words he used were well informed for a bank clerk. He seemed to speak my language.

My whole life at that time centred round my work. If I had had more time I think I should have been very lonely. I lived with the four radio operators but I wasn't one of them, and I was never one for lying on the charpoy reading or sleeping, as they did in their spare time. The memory of Beryl was never very far from my mind; whenever I had leisure I was moody and depressed, so that it's a good thing in a way that I had little leisure. I must have been bad company in the chummery. Perhaps it was this moodiness and loneliness that made me interested in the Sikh cashier at the bank, and when next I went there I asked him where he learned to speak such very good English.

He smiled. "I was educated in Lahore," he said. "I went to Lahore College. But apart from that, my father was a captain in the Army. We often spoke English at home."

"I wish I could speak Arabic as well as you speak English," I said. "It'ld make things a lot easier. Were you in the Indian Army in the war?"

He smiled again. "I was in the Royal Indian Air Force. I did about three hundred hours on Hurricanes."

I struck up quite a friendship with Gujar after that. He told me all about his squadron and what they had done in the Burmese war against Japan; he showed me his pilot's logbook one day and I found that he'd done about four hundred and fifty hours in all, with only one minor crash upon a Tiger Moth in the early days of his training. He was deeply interested in my venture, not only because it had to do with flying, but because it was apparent from the bank account that it was very profitable.

He came down to the aerodrome several times in the evenings after that, and I found that he was quite willing to take his coat off and give me a hand with the maintenance. Once a man has had to do with aeroplanes it gets into the blood, whether he is Western or Asiatic, and Gujar Singh used to potter about with me from time to time cleaning the filters and draining the sumps and checking the tyre pressures of the Fox-Moth. Presently, one evening in the hangar, he asked me to remember him if ever I wanted another pilot.

The thought had been in my mind for a week or two. I had been at Bahrein about four months when that happened, and clearly if I got another aeroplane I'd have to have another pilot. This gentle, ferocious-looking Sikh was certainly a possibility. I said, "What about the bank, Gujar? You want to think a bit before giving up a steady job like that. I may go bust at any time."

He smiled. "It may be a breach of confidence, but of necessity I know the balance of your account, what it was when you came here and what it is now. I am prepared to take the chance."

I liked Gujar. He was modest and careful. It did not seem to me that he was likely to crash an aircraft. I knew nothing of him as a navigator, or how steady he would be in an emergency. But in these things one has to trust one's judgment, and my whole instinct now was to give this a trial.

"Tell me," I said. "Are you married? I don't want to pry into your affairs, but I'd like to know that."

"I am married," he said. "My wife is a Sikh also. I have three children. I live at the north-west side of the souk."

I knew that part. It was in a part of the town where only Asiatics live, a part where there are no made roads, just alleys between the houses. Probably he lived in one room, or at the most in two.

"How much money would you want?" I asked.

"I will tell you," he said. "At the bank I am paid two hundred and fifty rupees a month, and I can increase that by ten rupees a month for every year of service." He smiled. "Our needs are less than yours, and we are quite comfortable on that. I would come to fly for you for the same money as I am getting at the bank, but if you should take on another pilot under me I should expect promotion."

That was fair enough, of course. I always have to translate rupees into English money in my mind, because most of the aircraft costs and contracts are in terms of sterling. Two hundred and fifty rupees a month, which he was getting in the bank, was about two hundred and twenty pounds a year, less than the wage of a farm labourer in England. On that he was quite happy with a wife and three children. If I were to get an English pilot out from England to fill this job I should have to pay at least a thousand a year, more than four times the wage that Gujar Singh wanted. The balance would pay for a good many minor crashes if my judgment proved to be wrong. But I didn't think it was.

"Look, Gujar," I said. "We'd both better think this over for a bit. Until I've got another aeroplane I don't want another pilot. It'll be three months or so before the thing becomes acute. But I'll certainly bear it in mind."

"That is all I want," he said. "Just keep it in your mind. I would rather work for you than continue to work in the bank. What sort of aeroplane do you think that you will buy?"

"There's a new thing just out called a Basing Airtruck," I said. "That's what we want out here. High wing, two of these engines, and a great big cabin for a ton of freight. I've got the specification in my room, if you'd like to come in and see it."

I had a good many talks with Gujar after that, and I confirmed the good opinion I had formed of him. His knowledge of aircraft wasn't very deep, but then it didn't have to be. He hadn't got a licence of any sort, of course, but I had little doubt that he could get a "B" licence in the lowest category, making it legal for him to carry passengers in the Fox-Moth.

That spring the Air Ministry sent an RAF Tiger Moth to Bahrein, an old instructional type that was used for *ab initio* training in the war. They were evidently getting worried that morale would suffer if flying officers were stationed there indefinitely with nothing to fly, and a large RAF aerodrome with no aeroplanes at all looks rather odd to foreigners. The Tiger Moth is a small open two-seater with dual control, and for a time this thing was in the air all day, mostly inverted. When the rush for it subsided a bit, I asked the CO if one of the officers might give Gujar a run round in it and check up on his flying for me. It wasn't strictly according to King's Regulations, of course, but I have always found the RAF to be quite helpful, and Allen and Gujar went off and did circuits and bumps in this thing for an hour one evening while I watched the landings from the shade of the hangar. When they came in, Allen told me he was all right. Gujar was as pleased as a dog with two tails.

That evening I told him he could give his notice in to the bank and start as soon as he liked.

I had his licence to negotiate then I had been given a provisional "B" licence for myself which had to be renewed each month, and was only given on the understanding that I went to England very soon to take it properly. I started in to battle then for another provisional licence for Gujar Singh so that he could carry on in the Fox-Moth while I was in England. Officialdom came back at once and asked who was going to maintain the Fox-Moth and sign it out while I was in England, and I threw back the ball that Flight Sergeant Harrison had "A" and "C" ground engineer's licences and would do it in the evenings. Officialdom replied that Flight Sergeant Harrison was licensed for Dakotas, it was true, but not for a Fox-Moth, and I replied that surely to God if he could sign for a Dakota he could sign for a pipsqueak thing like a Fox-Moth. So it went on.

Presently it came out that Gujar Singh was an Indian subject, and we found that he could get a "B" licence with the greatest of ease in Karachi. There was a York of RAF Transport Command going through to Mauripur the week that he joined me, and the CO very kindly gave him a passage in that. He was back three days later in a Dakota of Orient Airways that was going through to Baghdad, and he had a brand new "B" licence, valid for six months. I wished I was an Indian.

The way was clear then for me to go to England. I sent Gujar off in the Fox-Moth for a couple of charter trips and he came back all right from those; I turned over the books to him and told him to do the best he could with the business while I was away, and transferred most of the cash in the account to London. When I'd left sufficient for him to carry on with safely in my absence, I found that I'd got two thousand two hundred pounds to transfer – not bad for six months work with one little aeroplane. But I'd had to work for it.

I left Bahrein six months and two days after I landed there. I got a cheap ride as far as Rome on a Norwegian Skymaster that had taken a load of Italian emigrants to Australia and was on its way back to pick up another lot. There was nothing going to England from Rome except regular services which would have charged me the full fare, so I took a second class ticket by rail. It took me longer to get from Rome to London than it had to get from Bahrein to Rome, and when finally I got out of the train at Victoria station I was thankful that, if all went well, I should be going out by air in a week or two.

I got on the Underground and went to the same hotel near Euston that I always stayed at because it was cheap. I had written to Basing Aircraft from Bahrein on my cheap notepaper, and they had sent me out details of the Airtruck. I rang up their sales manager, a Mr Harry Ford, first thing next morning and said that I was coming down to see them right away. He told me a train and said he'd send a car to meet me. I drove from Basingstoke station to the works behind a chauffeur like a lord, the first time I'd ever been to an aircraft works like that. It felt very odd.

Harry Ford was quite a decent chap, but I could see he didn't quite know what to make of me. He'd been in aviation a long time; I knew of him, though I had never met him. I think he knew a little about me. He gave me a cigarette, and then he said:

"We got your letters, Mr Cutter. What did you think of the stuff about the Airtruck we sent you?"

"Looks all right, for what I'm doing," I said. "I'd like to have a look at one in the shop."

"We'll go out in a moment," he replied. "There are just one or two things I'd like to clear up first. What's the name of your Company?"

"I haven't got a Company," I said. "There's nobody in this but me."

He was a little taken aback, I think. "You mean, you're trading as an individual?"

"That's right."

"You're doing charter work?"

"That's right," I said. "I've got a Fox-Moth, but I want something a bit bigger now."

"Just one Fox-Moth?" He was smiling, but in quite a nice sort of way.

"Just one Fox-Moth," I said firmly. "Maybe you'd think more of me if I'd got fifty thousand pounds of other people's money, and a dozen disposals Haltons, and a staff of three hundred, and a Company, and a thumping loss. As it is, I've got just one Fox-Moth and a thumping profit. Show you my accounts if you like."

"Have you got them here?"

I pulled the envelope from my pocket, and unfolded the various papers: the accounts certified by the Iraqi accountant in Bahrein up to three days before I left, together with the complete schedule of the jobs I'd done, the hours flown on each, and the payments received to balance with the income side of the accounts. "I'm showing you these," I said, "because I want to buy an Airtruck if it's the aeroplane I think it is, and I've not got enough money to pay for it."

"Fine," he said. "I wish some of my other clients came to the point so quickly."

He ran his eye over my papers, and I saw his eyebrows rise once or twice. He did not take more than a couple of minutes over it; it was clear that he was very well accustomed to this sort of thing. "On the face of it, that's a very good showing, Mr Cutter," he said. "I don't suppose many Fox-Moth operators can show profits like that."

"I don't suppose many Fox-Moth operators work as hard as I've worked," I said.

"You do all the maintenance yourself, as well as the piloting and the business?"

"That's right."

"I see." He thought for a minute. "I take it that if you bought an Airtruck you would want credit."

I nodded. "I'd want a hire-purchase agreement, over a year."

"Could you find anyone to guarantee your payments?"

"No," I said firmly. "I've got no rich friends. I've got the record there of what I do, and that shows I can keep up the payments. If we can't do business for an Airtruck upon those terms I'll have to go elsewhere, and buy a cheaper aeroplane."

"I see." He took up the papers. "We'll go outside and you can have a look at an Airtruck, and talk to our test pilots, Mr

Cutter. They'll be interested to hear about your operations in the Persian Gulf. While we're doing that, would you mind if our secretary has a look at these figures of yours?"

"Not a bit," I said, "so long as they're kept confidential. I wouldn't want any other operator to see them."

He left me for a time and took my papers out of the room with him; when he came back we went out to see the Airtruck. He took me through the works; there were a lot of Airtrucks there on an assembly line, and there were two or three new ones in the flight hangar, unsold. They could give delivery at once. If I'd been able to pay cash I'd have got one at a discount off list price, I'm sure.

I spent a couple of hours going over the machine from nose to tail, and had a short flight in one with a test pilot. When I had finished, I knew that that was the machine I wanted for the Gulf. It had a big, wide cabin with low loading, high wing which would keep the cabin cool upon the ground in the tropical sun, and full blind flying instruments. With the addition of a small VHF radio set it made an aeroplane that would take a ton of load anywhere, and very cheaply. I knew that I could make money with that out in the Gulf, and I knew that I could learn to fly it without much difficulty. I was very pleased, although I did my best not to show it.

We went back to the office to talk turkey. Harry Ford got the secretary to come along to his office, a lean Scotsman called Taverner. He had been through my figures and gave the papers back to me, and then we talked about a hire purchase deal.

"How much could you pay in the way of a deposit, Mr Cutter?" the secretary asked.

"A thousand pounds," I said.

"That's only twenty per cent of the cost of the aircraft. From the profits you show, you should be able to do better than that."

"I've got to keep some liquid capital in the business," I said. "The cost of flying out the Airtruck to Bahrein is one thing. I don't think I can do more than that."

"Mm. I think that leaves too much for your business to carry. Ye can't pay off four thousand pounds in a year."

"Why not? You see what I can make with just a Fox-Moth."

"Aye," Mr Taverner said. "Ye've done very well, but you won't go on like that. You're paying no insurance, for a start. Maybe that's wise with just the Fox-Moth, and in any case, you've got away with it. But if we give you credit terms upon this Airtruck, you'll have to insure it with a policy that we approve. That's a bit off your profits."

He paused. "But the big difference is going to be, that from now on you've got to employ pilots and ground engineers. Up till now you've been doing everything yourself, and you've made close on two thousand five hundred pounds profit in six months. But you've taken no pay yourself. I'll guess that you've been working like a horse, and you've been making money at the rate of five thousand a year, and maybe you're worth it. But it's going to be different from now on."

He turned to Ford. "What will he have to pay a pilot, working from Bahrein?"

"A thousand to twelve hundred."

"And a ground engineer?"

"About eight hundred."

The secretary turned to me. "Ye've got to have staff now, Mr Cutter, with two aeroplanes, and that's going to alter the whole picture. Put in the wages of yourself at fifteen hundred and a pilot at twelve hundred, and a ground engineer at eight hundred, and there's three thousand five hundred pounds added to your overhead expenses right away. I'm not saying that there'll be no profit left, but I doubt, I doubt very much, if you can pay off four thousand pounds on an Airtruck within a year on the work you'll do with it. It does not seem possible to me, or in two years either." He paused. "Ye'll not get the utilisation with the larger aeroplane that you get with your Fox-Moth."

"I agree," said Ford. "All operators find the same thing. When you're operating just one aeroplane, a charter service can look very promising. Directly you have to start in and employ a staff, the whole thing alters and the costs go leaping up. I've seen it happen over and over again."

There was a pause.

"That may be," I said. "This thing of mine is different."

They smiled. "In what way?" Ford asked.

"If other operators go on the way you say, they must all be bloody well daft," I said. "I can't afford to go paying pilots twelve hundred a year. I've got a pilot flying the Fox-Moth for me now while I'm away, a darned good pilot, running the business side as well. Do you know what I'm paying him?"

"What?"

"Two hundred and fifty rupees a month," I said. "That's two hundred and twenty pounds a year."

They stared at me. "With flying pay?"

I laughed shortly. "No. Two hundred and twenty pounds a year, flat," I paused. "I've got a boy of sixteen cleaning down the aircraft. He'll work up and be a ground engineer one day. Do you know what he gets? Thirty bob a month." I snorted. "I'm not surprised that charter operators go broke right and left if they pay the wages that you say."

They sat staring at me. Then Ford said, "Are these natives?"

"That's right," I said. "The pilot's a Sikh. The boy's an Arab."

"Oh. Would you propose that this native pilot should fly the Airtruck?"

"I don't see why not."

"We'd have to think about that one, if you're going to want credit terms on the sale. We should have an interest in the machine."

"Think all you like," I said, "so long as you do it quick. This Sikh I've got is an ex-officer of the Royal Indian Air Force, and he's done over three hundred hours on Hurricanes without an accident, much of it operational flying. If your Airtruck's so bloody difficult to fly that he's not safe on it, I don't know that we can go any further."

Ford laughed. "You know I don't mean that. Anybody could fly an Airtruck. The proposal to employ a native pilot is a bit of a novelty, you know."

I shrugged my shoulders. "You've got to go on the record. If he's got a record of safe flying and if he's got a 'B' licence, that's good enough for me."

"I suppose so. If the business grows, would you propose to employ more than one?"

"I'll answer that in six months' time," I said. "If Gujar Singh is the success I think he will be, he'll be the chief pilot, under me. In that case, any other pilots I take on may very well be Sikhs. I don't see that there'd be any place in a setup like that for British pilots at a thousand a year."

Taverner asked, "What about the ground staff? Would you use Asiatic ground engineers for your maintenance?"

"I don't know," I said frankly. "That's much more difficult than the pilots. I'm fully licensed as a ground engineer myself, 'A', 'B', 'C', and 'D'. I can use Asiatic labour for a time, under my supervision. Then we'll have to see. But I think by the time I need them Asiatics will turn up. I had some working under me in Egypt during the war. They were all right."

Harry Ford laughed. "You're planning an air service staffed entirely by Wogs!"

I was a bit angry at that. "I call them Asiatics," I replied. "If you want to sell an Airtruck you can quit calling my staff Wogs."

"No offence meant, Mr Cutter," he said. "One uses these slang phrases ... I take it that the point you're making is that by the use of native staff you can reduce your overheads to the point when you can bear the hire-purchase cost of eighty per cent of an Airtruck spread over a year."

I nodded. "That's right. I can pay off the aircraft in a year, and still make money." I thought for a moment. "I don't want you to think that a native staff is solely a question of money," I said slowly. "If I extend my operations, it will be in the direction of India, not towards Europe. Europe's crowded out with charter operators already, all going broke together. There's more scope for charter work as you go east. If I develop eastwards, then by using Asiatic pilots and ground engineers exclusively, I shall be using the people of the countries that I want to do business with. That's bound to make things easier."

Taverner chipped in then, and we went over my prospective overheads in the light of the payments I would have to make for Asiatic staff, and the sum naturally came out a good bit better. They left me then to go off and have a talk about it by themselves, and when they came back they said, fifteen hundred down and the machine was mine. I stuck my heels in and refused to pay a penny more than twelve hundred, and when I left the works that evening the machine was mine for delivery in about ten days, subject to the completion of all the formalities.

I went to Southampton that night, and got home at about nine o'clock. There was no telephone at home, of course; I'd sent a telegram from the works to say that I was coming, but it was nearly six o'clock when I telephoned it and after delivery hours, so Ma hadn't got it. I walked in at the street door and put my bag down. Ma was in the scullery, and when she heard the door go she called out, "That you, Alf?" She thought it was Dad.

I said, "It's me, Ma – Tom!" She came rushing out and put her arms round me and kissed me, and ticked me off for not letting them know which day I was coming. And then she said, "My, Tom, you do look brown. How long have you got at home?"

"Only a week or two," I said. "I'm getting a bigger aeroplane, and flying out again as soon as it's ready."

"Not bust yet?" she asked.

"Not quite," I said. "Where's Dad?"

"He stepped out to the 'Lion' for his game of darts," she said. "He should be back now, any minute."

"Mind if I go down there and fetch him, Ma?"

She nodded. "He'll like you to meet his friends, Bert Topp and Harry Burke, and Chandler. Don't be more'n a quarter of an hour, Tom. I'll start getting supper now."

I went down to the pub, and there was Dad playing darts with Harry Burke. I said, "How do, Dad," and he said, "How do, Tom," and I told him I'd been home, and he told the barman to give me a pint, and went on with his game. The barman said, "Been out in the sun?" and I said, "Persian Gulf," and he said, "Uh-huh," and I sat and watched Dad going for the double at the finish of the game. It was just as if I'd never been away at all, as if Bahrein and Gujar Singh, and Sharjah, and Yas Island were places and people I'd read about in a book.

I walked home with Dad when he'd finished the game, and told him something about what I'd been doing on the way. Back home when we sat down to the light supper that they had before going to bed, Ma asked me, "What's it like out where you're working, Tom? What does it all look like?" She paused. "Is it all palm trees and dates and that?"

"Not in the country," I said. "Nothing grows outside the towns, because of the water. There's no water at all. The land is desert – great flat stretches of sandy sort of earth, with maybe rocky hills or mountains here and there. All yellow and dried up under the sun. You get groves of date palms and greenery outside Bahrein and outside most towns, where they irrigate with water from wells."

Dad said, "Sounds a bad sort of country."

"I rather like it, Dad," I said. "It gets hold of you, after a bit. It's good for people – you don't get any of the pansy boys out there. It can be lovely when you're flying, too. Some places and in some lights, the desert goes a sort of rosy pink, all over, and then if you're flying up a coast the sea can be a brilliant emerald green, or else a brilliant blue, with a strip of white surf all along the edge like a girl's slip showing."

"Ever had a forced landing in it and got stranded?" Dad asked.

I shook my head. "Not yet, and I don't want one. I had to put down once because of a sand storm, and sit it out in the cabin for five or six hours; then it got better and I took off and went on. I always take a petrol can of water in the aircraft."

Ma said, "My ..."

They wanted to know if I'd got anyone to help me, and I told them about Gujar Singh and Tarik. It was difficult, of course, to make them understand, however hard I was trying, however much they wanted to. Dad said,

"Like niggers, I suppose they'd be?"

I shook my head. "No, not like niggers. Gujar Singh's an Indian."

"Lascars are Indians, I think," Dad said. He only knew the types he'd seen about the docks, of course.

"That's right," I said. "But this is a different sort of Indian. A better sort than lascars, more of an Army officer type." I went on to describe what Gujar looked like, but I don't know that a description of him really helped me in describing what I had come to feel: that our minds ran on similar tracks.

Ma said, "They'd be heathens, I suppose?"

The question worried me a bit, because I wanted her to like them. I wanted her to understand. "I don't know," I said slowly. "Both of them believe in God – just one God, not a lot of Gods. I suppose you'd call them heathens. They don't believe in Jesus Christ as God – the Moslems think He was a prophet, just like Moses. But I must say, they seem to say their prayers very regular, which is more'n we do."

Ma was trying her best. "They don't go to church, I suppose?" she asked. "Just have heathen temples, like?"

"They've got their own places where they go to pray," I said. "Friday is the big day, like our Sunday, when they all go to the mosque. Most businesses shut up shop on Friday, and the offices and the banks shut on Friday, too. We don't work on Fridays, but we work on Sundays. They're very particular about Fridays, and then, of course, they're always at their prayers. I told young Tarik after the first day, I said, You do your praying in the lunch hour and after we knock off, lad – not in the time I pay you for. A chap in the radio set-up put me wise to that one. They'll swing it on you if you let them. But then, on your side, you've got to be reasonable and fix the hours of work so they can get their praying in."

"Do you mean they go off to the mosque on a working day?" Dad asked.

I shook my head. "They can do it on any quiet little bit of ground, it seems. A Moslem has to say his prayers five times a day. What young Tarik does, he goes out on a little bit of flat ground just beside the hangar and he faces west, about in the direction of Mecca. That's their holy city, where they go for pilgrimages. He takes off his shoes and stands up straight, and puts both hands up to his ears, and prays. Then he stands with his arms folded in front of him and prays. Then he bends forwards with both hands on his knees, and prays. Then he goes down on hands on knees and puts his head on the ground, and prays. Then he sits down for a bit and thinks about it all, and then he starts in and goes through it all again. He goes on like that for about ten minutes, like doing physical jerks. Only you can't laugh about it, Dad, when you see them at it. They take it all so serious, just like us in church. It means a lot to them."

"Five times a day they go through all that?"

"That's right," I said. "Young Tarik's hours are sort of fluid, 'cause there's only just him there at present. He's supposed to start at seven in the morning, and I must say he's usually there on time. He works till nine, and then gets a break for a cup of tea or a bit to eat, and prayers. Starts again at nine-thirty and works till twelve, and gets an hour then for his dinner and prayers. Works from one to four-thirty, and knocks off for prayers. That makes an eight-hour day. If he works over, then I give him a bit more at the end of the month."

Ma said, "Seems like they're not heathens at all, if they say their prayers that much."

"They're not Christians, Ma," I said. "But honestly, I don't think you could call them heathens, either. They believe in God all right."

Dad asked about the aeroplanes, and I told him about the Airtruck, and got out a picture of it from my case to show him. He asked how much it cost, and I told him, and then I told him about the money that I'd made, and that was all going back into the business. Dad and Ma were so pleased, it was just fine; they thought far more of my little success, and took more pleasure in it, than ever I did. It was worth that six months of heat and work and sweat and fright, to see the pleasure they got out of it.

They asked what I was going to do and how long I could stay, and I told them that I'd have to go for a week to Air

Service Training Ltd at Hamble and get a radio operator's licence; that was only six miles out of Southampton, so I could live at home and go out on the bus each day.

Young Ted had gone off to do his military service so Dad and Ma were all alone at home. Ma asked where I'd like to sleep, upstairs or down, and I said down in the big room where we'd all slept together as kids. I lay there for a while that night thinking of all sorts of things, of the Airtruck, of my radio licence, of Bahrein and the Persian Gulf country, of the last time I came to sleep there in the misery of Beryl's death. If Beryl had lived, my life would have been a very different one, I knew. She wouldn't have fitted in at Bahrein, and she'd have hated it. But then, I'd never have got out there if she'd lived.

I got up with Dad and Ma next morning and had breakfast at seven with Dad before he went off to the docks. I hung around then and helped Ma with the washing up, because there was no point in getting out to Hamble before ten. As we were drying the dishes Ma said, "Ted brought ever such a nice girl home last weekend, Tom. Lily Clarke, her name is. Her folks live at Fareham. Father's a petty officer in the Navy."

"Starting young," I said.

"Mm. Met her at a dance. I don't know if there's anything in it."

"Better wait till he gets through his service and in a proper job," I said. "Besides, he's only just nineteen."

"Your pa was only twenty when we got married, Tom. I had Elsie when I was nineteen."

I grinned at her. "Ought to be ashamed of yourself, Ma, and Dad too."

"Well, I don't know. It worked out all right with us. I often wish you'd married young, Tom, but you were always so stuck into your books."

"I know," I said quietly. "I got around to it too late."

"There's always another chance. You didn't meet anybody out there?"

I shook my head, smiling a little. "It's not that sort of a place, Ma. You get more snowstorms in the Persian Gulf than unmarried white girls."

She sighed. "I wish you didn't have to work in a place like that. Will you ever come back and work in England, Tom?"

"I expect I will some day," I replied. "The trouble is, I rather like it in the East. I'd like to go further if I get a chance, into India and Burma, and on past those."

"Well anyway," she said, "it's not as if you had to be out there for ever. Being in the air business, you do seem to be able to get home now and then."

She kept on trying, Ma did. I went out that day and fixed up my course at Air Service Training, and got them to start me off next day on account of the urgency. Two nights later I came back to tea about six, and there was a girl in to tea with Ma, Doris Waters, daughter of old Waters the plumber. She was a pretty kid and quite intelligent, about twenty-two or twenty-three years old; she taught in a school. If I'd been different to what I was, things might have been different, too. But I wasn't, and they weren't. I was sorry for Ma.

With all the examinations for the radio operator's licence and the "B" licence, and the renewal of my ground engineer's licences, I was busy in a maze of paper work for the next three weeks. I had to go three times to London, and then in the middle of it all the August Bank Holiday came and everything stopped dead for about four days. I finally got away from England in the Airtruck on August the 22nd having been in England nearly a month. Dad and Mum came out to see the machine, as they had done before with the Fox-Moth. But this was a bigger and a better aircraft altogether. I had about three hundredweight of spares and tools with me, and quite a bit of luggage, and it made a little heap in one corner of the big cabin that you'd hardly notice.

The Airtruck was faster than the Fox-Moth, and better equipped, and so much easier to fly. Having two engines I took the sea crossing from Cannes to Rome direct, and then over the top of the Appenines through cloud to Brindisi instead of going round the coast. Short cuts like that made a lot of difference to the time, and with the greater range of the Airtruck I didn't have to land so often for fuel. I got to Bahrein in five days from England, and as I turned downwind on the circuit I saw the Fox-Moth standing in front of the hangar, and Gujar Singh and Tarik standing by it looking up at the Airtruck and waving to me. They hadn't broken the Fox, which took a load off my mind. As I came in to the runway on the final and put her down, I felt like it was coming home again. The wide, bare, sandy field under the blazing sun, the blue sea beside, the shimmer from the tarmac, the white houses with their wind-towers – these were the things that pleased me; this was where I wanted to be.

Gujar and Tarik came up to the machine as I switched off in front of the hangar, and they opened the door, and came in to greet me as I sat quiet in the cockpit for a few minutes, tired after a long day of flying from Damascus via Baghdad and Basra, writing up the journey logbook on my knee. They were very much impressed with the Airtruck. "There will be a great deal of work to be done with this," said Gujar, "once the oil companies get to know that it is here."

I found that evening that he had done quite well in my absence with the Fox-Moth. He had had a job to do most days, and the bank account, which was two hundred pounds when I went away, was now over seven hundred. There were a good few bills outstanding because I hadn't left him power to draw cheques, but so far as I could see he had made a profit of over three hundred pounds in the month or so that I had been away. I was very pleased with that, and I told him so. It meant that I could go away on jobs myself without the feeling that everything was going to collapse.

I got Evans of the Arabia–Sumatran Petroleum Company to come down and have a look at the new machine next day, with one or two from the other companies. The response was good, and by the end of a week the Airtruck was going hard every day. Spare parts for motor transport was one of our big, constant loads. The oil companies have a great number of trucks in various parts of the Arabian deserts in connection with the oil wells and pipelines and docks. These trucks give continuous trouble; however ruggedly they may be built a country that has no roads and a lot of sand is hard on things mechanical. We could fly in spare back axles, wheels complete with tyres, drums of oil, or engine parts to stranded trucks, and it's extraordinary how many stranded trucks there are. Apart from that, we took surveying parties and all their gear about the place continuously, and cases of tinned foods – all sorts of stuff. From time to time we took quite big loads of people, employees going in and out of some inaccessible place; I had no seats for the Airtruck and took them sitting or squatting on the floor. Presently, of course, the inevitable official popped up and told me that was illegal because they all ought to have a safety belt.

After a time I decided I should have to have another aeroplane. Gujar Singh was used to flying the Airtruck by that time, though I did most of the work on it myself and let him fly the Fox-Moth. Now things were piling up on us. There was still far more work than we could tackle, and the Fox-Moth was due for its annual overhaul for the Certificate of Airworthiness. I had engaged an Iraqi ground engineer with "A" and "C" licences called Selim, but I didn't trust him much and anyway he wasn't licensed for complete overhauls; I should have to do that myself. I wanted another Airtruck, and that meant another pilot.

I was up to date with my payments on the first Airtruck, and had about two thousand pounds profit again in hand. I wrote to Harry Ford and told him how I stood and sent him the accounts, and said, what about another Airtruck on the Never-Never? I think they must have had a lot of trouble selling them, because he wrote back at once and said, come and get it. It wasn't very suitable for ordinary charter operators, perhaps, but it fitted my work like a glove.

I had a talk with Gujar Singh about another pilot then. He didn't himself know of another Sikh pilot. In ten days' time, however, we had to take a load to Karachi, a trip which I proposed to do myself in the Airtruck. He suggested that he should come with me; he knew Karachi very well, of course. We went together and stayed for a couple of days. At the end of that time we found quite a good pilot called Arjan Singh, with another big black beard and another iron bangle just like Gujar; he had been instructing on Harvards at Bangalore in the war and had done a bit of time on Dominies. I took him on and put up Gujar's salary to three hundred rupees, and we all went back to Bahrein together. I started Arjan on the Fox-Moth and turned over the Airtruck to Gujar, and went back to England in a chartered Halton that had taken a ship's propeller shaft out to Singapore and was on its way back with a load of silk goods.

I was only home about four days that time, because the second Airtruck was all ready and waiting for me on Basingstoke Aerodrome. In fact there were eleven of them standing in a row, unsold; I kicked myself that I'd got to have credit and so had to pay full price. However, it was better to have it so than to get outside money in; I wanted to keep the show in my own hands. I still wasn't a company, and I didn't see any reason why I should become one, for the time being. There's no income tax in Bahrein.

I stayed three of the four days with Dad and Ma as usual, and took them up for a joyride in the Airtruck. Then I was off again back to Bahrein. I was getting to know the route by that time, and I was a much better pilot than when I went out first with the Fox-Moth.

When I got back to Bahrein I started in to put the business on a proper basis. With the two Airtrucks flying all day long and the Fox in for overhaul for its Certificate of Airworthiness, I had to take on a good bit more staff. I got another ground engineer, an Egyptian who'd been with me at Almaza, and two more Arab boys under Tarik, who was shaping quite well; these boys worked as loaders when we wanted labour. Sometimes we parachuted loads down instead of landing if the ground was bad, especially to stranded trucks, and these boys went along then in the aircraft to put the stuff out of the doorframe; for those jobs we flew without the door.

I had to start an office going, too. I found a young Bengali clerk called Dunu who could work a typewriter and keep books; he came from Calcutta and was working in a shipping office in the town. I managed to lease a disused hutment from the RAF on a strictly temporary basis, and I set the office up in that.

From that time onward my own work began to change. I had to spend more time on the ground, because I was the only ground engineer in the show who was licensed for aircraft overhauls; I couldn't be away all day piloting while a machine was in for its annual overhaul, and with three machines coming up for annual overhaul in turn it was clear that I should have to spend a lot more time in the hangar. Having to do that, I was able to attend more to the bookkeeping and costs, and it was about that time I set to work to get the prices down. It had been all very well to charge a high figure for my transport in the early days, but I knew that if I went on doing that the oil companies would start to kick, and either get their own aircraft or else, much worse, encourage someone else to start up at Bahrein in competition with me. Within a month of my return with the second Airtruck I cut my own prices by twenty-five per cent, and let them all know what I'd done, and why I'd done it.

I still did all of what one might describe as the pioneering flying. Whenever we had to make a landing at a place we hadn't used before, I used to take the machine myself if possible, sometimes with Gujar or Arjan with me in the machine so that they could see it and get the gen. That was the position some months after I got back to Bahrein, at the end of November, when Evans of the Arabia–Sumatran rang me up and asked if I could quote for taking a load of fifteen hundred pounds of scientific instruments and one passenger from Bahrein to Diento, in Sumatra, where they had another refinery.

Diento is in the south of Sumatra, about four hundred miles south of Singapore, not very far from Batavia in Java. It was by far the longest haul that had come my way, and I regarded it as something of a compliment and as a sign of confidence in me that they had asked me to quote. It meant a flight of about five thousand miles all through the East, across India and Burma, through Siam and down Malaya, into Sumatra and past Palembang to this place Diento. I knew I could do it in an Airtruck and I was determined to go myself, of course, for an important job like that. I had a lot of difficulty with the quotation, though.

The trouble was in finding a return load. If I charged him for the double journey the figure came out so high that it frightened me; I wanted to do the job very badly, but I wasn't going to do it and lose money. In the end I took my figures to him and put the cards on the table. I told him he would have to guarantee payment for the return journey to Bahrein, and I suggested he should put his Sumatran organisation to work to find me a return load either from their own requirements or else from Batavia; in that case we would set off anything that we could get for the return load against his invoice, with appropriate mileage adjustments if the return load was to a destination off my direct return route. We thrashed out an agreement on these lines. He told me that he would send a copy out to their office in Batavia and I should probably receive instructions in Diento to go on there for whatever freight load they could get together for me.

I started almost immediately, in the new Airtruck. I'm not going to say much about that first hurried journey through the East; this isn't a travel book. It took me a week to get to Diento, flying seven or eight hours every day and servicing the aircraft in what was left of the day. We got good weather all through India and Burma, but we struck a lot of monsoon rain in what they call the Inter-Tropical Front as we went through Malaya; it got to be fair weather again by the time we reached Diento.

I never saw anything of all these countries, hardly, on that trip. I was working all the time when the machine was on the ground, and it was dark each night by the time we could drive in from the aerodrome to a hotel. I got just tantalising glimpses of brown men and pretty Chinese girls in flowered pyjamas, enough to make me realise what I was missing.

Diento was a huge refinery town of over twenty thousand employees, many of them Dutch. It had a good airstrip, and I put down there about midday after flying in from Palembang. The strip wasn't much different from any other aerodrome in any part of the world, but the grass was a bit darker in colour. The cars and trucks and roads were all the same. It's a funny thing about the tropics, I have found. You go expecting everything to be quite different, and there's so much that's the same.

My passenger was a young Dutch-American scientist; he knew all about Diento, because he'd been there before. They sent a truck down for the laboratory gear, and his boss came down to meet him in a car. We waited to see the stuff unloaded and safely in the truck, and then I went up with them in the car to the refinery offices. That was a big place. It stretched for miles out into the bush and along the bank of a river, rows and rows of storage tanks, and pipes and cylindrical towers and all sorts of things. Full-sized ocean-going tankers came into Diento to take the oil away to ports all over the world.

As I expected, in the office they had instructions to send me to Batavia, about a hundred and fifty miles further on; they thought there was a small return load waiting for me there, but they didn't know what it was. I would have gone back to the aerodrome and got off there and then, but the Dutchmen wouldn't hear of it. They insisted that I stay the night and have a party with them and relax, and after all that flying I was quite glad to. They had a club by the riverside and they gave me a fine bedroom in that. There was a swimming pool and pretty girls out of the offices in it, and a concert and a dance after dinner, all by the riverside with sampans going past, and lights over the water, and flying foxes wheeling overhead in the velvety darkness, and a huge tropical full moon. I drank more Bols than I wanted to, but they were so kind and so pleased to see a strange face, one couldn't refuse. I got rather tight, but so did everyone. A good party.

They sent me down to the aerodrome next morning in a car. I made a check over the machine, cleaned filters, drained sumps, swept out the cabin, and refuelled. Finally I took off at about ten-thirty for the short flight down to Batavia across the Sunda straits, and found the aerodrome, and came on to the circuit behind a Constellation of the KLM. The Dutch pilots were all speaking English on the radio to their own control tower, which seemed odd to me. It certainly made everything very easy, because I couldn't speak a word of Dutch.

I landed and taxied to the parking position, and locked up the machine and went to the Control and Customs for the necessary clearances. It all took a long time because Java was in an uproar with a full-scale war going on against the Indonesian republicans, and there were military officers in all the offices wanting to see every sort of document. The KLM people had been warned to expect me and were very helpful, and got me through the various offices as quickly as anyone could, and laid on transport for me, and took me into town to the Nederland Hotel.

The hotel was crowded out with military, and the best that they could do for me was a dormitory room with three other beds in it, and other chaps' gear lying round all over the place. I was used to that sort of thing; we'd had it at several other places on the way. I dumped my stuff on an empty bed and saw the room boy, and went down to the dining room for lunch. I had been warned by the KLM chap that most offices took a siesta in that hot place after the midday meal; a suitable time to get to the Arabia–Sumatran office would be between three and four. I took the tip, and went up after lunch for an hour on the charpoy myself.

There was another chap in the room now, lying stretched out on the bed under his mosquito net, naked but for a short pair of trunks. I couldn't see him very clearly through the net. I said conventionally, "I hope none of this stuff's in your way."

He turned and looked at me, and then he sat up and lifted the side of the net to see me better. I stood there gaping at him for a moment in surprise.

It was Connie Shaklin.

CHAPTER THREE

We travel not for trafficking alone:
By hotter winds our fiery hearts are fanned:
For lust of knowing what should not be known
We make the Golden Journey to Samarkand.

JAMES ELROY FLECKER

IT WAS THIRTEEN years since I had seen Connie and a lot had happened in that time, but I knew him at once. I said, "Connie Shaklin! You remember me – on Cobham's Circus? Tom Cutter."

He pushed back the net, got out, and shook me by the hand. He was leaner than I remembered him, especially in the face. In some ways he looked more Chinese than ever, but alongside a Chinese you could see he wasn't one. He was too tall, too aquiline. His Russian mother was responsible for that. He was a striking-looking man; he reminded me of something, but for a time I couldn't think of what it was.

He said, "Tom! What are you doing now? Last time I heard was years ago. You were still at Airservice then."

I offered him a cigarette, but he said he didn't smoke. I lit one and sat down on the charpoy. "I left them last year," I said. "I'm on my own now."

"Still in aircraft?"

"Yes. I'm operating in the Persian Gulf. I came down here on a charter job."

I was terribly glad to see Connie again. He was a part of my youth, part of the fine time you have before you have to take responsibilities. Presently, as you go through your life, you undertake so many duties that you haven't time for making new, close friendships any more; you've got too much to do. For the remainder of your life you have to make do with the friends you gathered in in your short youth, and for me, Connie was about the only one I ever had. I started getting serious pretty early in my life, I suppose.

I told him all about my charter service in the Gulf as I stripped my few clothes off and stretched out on the bed. In return he told me what he had been doing. From Cobham's Circus he had gone to California; he had got a job with the Lockheed Company in their service and repair department, and he had stayed with them for six years or so. Then the war had come, in 1939. He was a British subject, of course, and England was at war; he felt it was his duty to serve, although he had queer ideas about fighting, and so he went north over the border to Edmonton and joined the Royal Canadian Air Force as an engine fitter.

"Were you in aircrew?" I asked.

He shook his head. "I think that it is wrong to kill," he said simply. "I told them that, when I volunteered for the RCAF I told them also that if one could not kill in time of war, one ought to work very hard. I had the American ground engineer's certificates, of course, for Lockheed and Pratt and Whitney stuff, and they were glad to have me for a fitter on the ground."

He had spent the whole of the war in Canada working at various aerodromes in connection with the Empire training scheme and, later, on some cold-weather research projects at Trenton. He had sat for the Canadian ground engineer's licences at the end of the war and had got the lot without difficulty, and at the beginning of 1946 he had gone out to

Bangkok and had worked for a time as a ground engineer with Siamese Airways.

I opened my eyes at that. Siamese Airways is the national airline of Siam and, I thought, staffed exclusively by Asiatics. "What on earth made you go there?" I asked.

"Karma," he said, smiling. I didn't understand him, but his old magic was upon me once again and I didn't interrupt; he knew so much more than I did. "I went back home to San Diego for a few months and worked at the Flying Club, but I couldn't settle there. I didn't really like America, and I wanted to know more, much more, about the Lord Gautama and the Four Noble Truths. I wanted to hear people talk about the Buddhist faith who really *knew* something – not the sort of people you find in Los Angeles. And presently I found I had to go to Bangkok to find out about all that. There was no alternative except the bughouse."

I grinned. This was the same old Connie, different to anybody else that I had ever met. He had been good for me when I was a callow and an ignorant youth; he was good for me now. I said, "Were you able to get into Siamese Airways?" And then I said, perhaps a little thoughtlessly, "I thought they were all Asiatics."

He smiled. "Well, what do you call me?"

"You're British," I said, wondering.

"I was born in Penang," he replied. "My father was a full Chinese. My mother was a Russian who got out in 1917, at the time of the Revolution. I speak Cantonese, and a little Mandarin. I spell my name in two parts now that I'm out here, Shak Lin, like my father did. I'm an Asiatic."

"Not a proper one," I said loyally.

He grinned. "Proper enough to get a job with Siamese Airways. I think they were very glad to get me; I got to Bangkok just as they were starting up. They bought a lot of disposals Dakotas and had them converted in Hong Kong. I was with them up till about four months ago."

"What are you doing now?" I asked.

He said, "I'm with Dwight Schafter."

"Who's Dwight Schafter?"

"Don't you know about him?"

I shook my head. "No."

"He's a gun-runner," said Connie. "He flies arms in to the Indonesian Republicans, or he did. The Dutch have got him now, here in Batavia."

"You're working for him?"

"Yes."

"Well, I'm muggered," I said in wonder.

As we lay there on our beds in the hot afternoon he told me about Dwight Schafter. Dwight was an American, a soldier of fortune by profession. Wherever there is trouble in the world the Dwights of all nations foregather. There are not very many of them, thirty or forty perhaps, and they are all supremely competent men because the others have been killed.

Dwight had spent some years in Central and South America, and he had flown for Franco in the Spanish Civil War. He had been flying for the Chinese against the Japanese in 1938 and 1939, and he had come into the United States Army Air Force via Major Chennault's Flying Tigers. He delivered two or three disposals B25s from America to the warring Israelites in Palestine just after the war, but by the middle of 1946 he was back in the East, flying loads of sub-machine-guns from the Philippines to Indonesia for the benefit of brown men fighting the Dutch.

At that time there was considerable sympathy in South East Asia for the Indonesians in their struggle against the Dutch. In Indo-China the Viet-Minh forces were engaged in a similar rebellion against French rule. In Siam there was sympathy with the Asiatics in both cases, though it would probably be quite wrong to suggest that the Siamese Government connived at gun-running. It would probably be quite right to say that when strange freight aircraft turned up at Don Muang aerodrome outside Bangkok with thin stories of journeys to improbable places, the Siamese Government saw no reason to initiate officious and unnecessary investigations.

Dwight Schafter was a small, quick, dark-haired man from Indiana. He turned up at Don Muang one day flying a brand new Cornell Carrier. The Carrier was a great big American freight aeroplane in the same class as the British Plymouth Tramp; it was powered by two Pratt and Whitney engines of about seventeen hundred horsepower each, and it was very completely equipped. It cost about two hundred and fifty thousand dollars in the States; quite an aeroplane.

Dwight Schafter said that he was starting an air service with it from Saigon in Indo-China to Manila in the Philippines. He did not explain what he intended to carry between these cities in this expensive freight aircraft, and no one bothered to ask him. He was known at Don Muang. He had a Dakota which turned up from time to time for servicing by Siamese Airways, and he had always paid his bills with cash on the nail, usually small cubical gold ingots, of which he seemed to have an inexhaustible supply.

He wanted the Carrier serviced with a routine engine check. He said that there were no licensed ground engineers in Saigon, which at that time may or may not have been true; conditions in Indo-China were certainly very disturbed. In any case, he brought the aircraft into Don Muang to be checked over, and Connie Shaklin was put on the job with two Chinese ground engineers to help him. There was about two days' work to be done.

When Connie told me this, I had not, at that time, seen him at work. I can now say that he was the most thorough and careful engineer that I have ever met. He was quick enough in doing a job, but he would never take the slightest thing on chance; in consequence he added to his work far more than another man would have thought necessary.

Dwight Schafter was clearly very much impressed, because on the evening of the second day, when they were in the cockpit together at the conclusion of an engine test run, he said: "Say, Shak Lin, why don't you leave this outfit, 'n come and work for me? I'll need somebody like you to help me run this baby." He caressed the bakelite control wheel of the Carrier.

Connie stared out over the wide brown stretches of the airfield, glowing golden in the evening light, to the dim blue line of the hills up the north. "Where are you based?" he asked. "Where would the job be?"

"I run from the Philippines to Saigon," said Schafter carefully. "But the job's not there. I've got a private strip way out in the country, where we do the maintenance. It's very quiet there, of course – no Europeans nearer than a hundred miles. But that won't worry you, because you speak Chinese."

"I speak Canton," said Connie. "Does that go at your strip?"

He nodded. "The people that you'd come in contact with understand Canton. Not the peasants, but you wouldn't have to worry about those." He paused. "It's very isolated, but the job will probably be over in six months. Give you eight hundred American dollars a month, and transportation back here to Bangkok."

Eight hundred dollars a month is at the rate of £2,500 a year, a high wage for a ground engineer even in the East. In all his later life, I never knew Connie to take the least interest in money. He always earned a good salary because he was first-class at his job, but he lived on the Asiatic standard. I know that he had no money at the time of his death; I think he gave it all away. While he worked for me he preferred to be paid in cash each month. I don't think he had a bank account at all.

It certainly wasn't for money, then, that he left Siamese Airways and went to work for Dwight Schafter. I know now that he had been in close touch with the ecclesiastics of

Buddhism while he was working in Bangkok, and he spoke once of his horoscope. My own belief is that he felt the need to go out into the wilderness for a few months, to get away from the crowd for a time to meditate on what he had learned of Buddhism. That is a possible explanation, and it certainly fits in with the life that Dwight Schafter offered him, a time of long periods of inactivity while Dwight was away flying, with only Asiatics for his company, upon the abandoned airstrip at Damrey Phong.

He had no illusions about the job. "I maintain aircraft," he said, there in the beautifully finished cockpit of the Carrier, with the long rows of black-faced instruments in front of him below the windscreen. "I take no part in wars. I would not fly with you to any foreign country to deliver any load."

"You don't have to do that," said Schafter, looking at him curiously. "I don't want you for an aircrew. I've got a C47 and I've got this baby, and I guess there's plenty for you to do keeping those two in the air. I want somebody that I can trust to stay back at the strip and keep the maintenance of the one ship going while I'm away with the other. I think I can trust you. What do you say?"

He said, yes. He left Siamese Airways a week later. Dwight Schafter reappeared at Don Muang in a Dakota with a brown man called Monsieur Seriot as his copilot, and Connie got into it with his small luggage, contained in an old parachute pack and a tool chest. The Dakota cleared for Prachaub in Siam and flew towards the sea and down the coast of Cambodia into Indo-China. Two hours later they landed on the strip at Damrey Phong.

Damrey Phong lies on the river Kos about fifteen miles from the coast. It is about a hundred miles from the Siamese border, and about a hundred and eighty miles as the crow flies from Saigon. It is a small Asiatic village of palm thatch houses, the homes of a purely rural community. Superimposed on this was the civilisation of the airstrip, built for strategic purposes during the war. There were two houses built of wood in European style, and a store building; there had been a hangar, but the roof had fallen in with neglect and the remains of the wooden building were rapidly disintegrating. There was a wharf to which small coasting motor vessels could come up the river, and here there was a petrol store with a good stock of fuel and oil in drums. The Cornell Carrier was parked beside the strip.

The place was in territory held by the Viet-Minh forces in rebellion against the French, and the pattern of the operations was soon explained to Connie. The loads carried up till that time had been exclusively trench mortars, sub-machine-guns, and small arms. They came from somewhere in the Philippines, he thought the island of Negros. The Dakota would fly there across the China Sea once every two or three days, a flight of twelve or thirteen hundred miles. It would return to Damrey Phong loaded with these arms, all of which were ex-American Army weapons, mostly in poor condition owing to neglect since the war. Consignments of ammunition arrived in the same way from time to time.

About half of these weapons and ammunition were sold to the Viet-Minh forces, but the supply was greater than they could pay for or recondition. The loads not required remained in the Dakota while it was refuelled, and it then took off again for some destination in Indonesia. This flight was made direct, but the empty Dakota frequently returned to the home airstrip via Bangkok to pick up any stores or spare parts that might be required.

Connie gathered that it was a very profitable trade.

Whoever financed it, indeed, found it so profitable that he was able to plough back profits into the business. Wherever the arms came from, there was larger stuff than sub-machine-guns going for scrap price. There were anti-tank guns, bazookas, and seventy-five-millimetre field guns, and ammunition for them, too, neglected and rusty maybe, but still capable of being put to use. These guns were worth their weight in silver to the Indonesians, and since the gold and silver mines of Bencoolen and Madoen were both in rebel hands, there was little difficulty in paying for them in negotiable currency. The Cornell Carrier was just the aircraft for the job.

"Six journeys, and this baby will be paid for," said Dwight Schafter. "After that, it's all clear profit." When Connie got to Damrey Phong the Carrier had already made two trips, and was loaded and fuelled, ready to start on a third.

Connie settled down at this out-of-the-way tropical village quite happily. He had two indifferent engineers under him, one a Burmese lad, and one a Chinese from Hong Kong. They messed together in one of the European-style houses where these two engineers lived with two girls of the village serving as their wives, simple and attractive girls who did the cooking and housework for them, and who volunteered at once to bring along a selection of their friends for Connie to choose from. There was genuine kindness and good feeling behind the offer as well as the desire to ease the housework caused by a third man, but he refused and chose an older woman as his servant. He had not come to Damrey Phong for a domestic life.

Dwight Schafter and his copilot, Seriot, lived in the other house upon the strip, each with a local girl. These girls had an easy time, because their lords were hardly ever there. There was no other aircrew; Schafter and his brown copilot flew every trip together, alternately in the Dakota and the Carrier. They were superb as a crew. They flew practically every day, long, difficult journeys with no meteorological reports except what they could glean by listening to the scheduled radio weather forecasts from Singapore, Hong Kong, Manila, and Bangkok; they were very cunning at that. There were no ground aids to guide them on their way in the dark night; they always flew the last stages by night. Alone they had to make their landfall on dark, inaccurately mapped coasts, alone they had to find the secret airstrips where a few flickering flares of paraffin laid on the grass served as the sole help to them for putting down these large, heavily loaded aircraft. Over all was the continual danger of detection, and a quick burst of tracer into them from some defending fighter, unseen and unsuspected, that would end it all. They must have been men of iron, for they came and went over and over again, and showed no sign of any mental stress. It was a job to them like any other job, except that it was an exceptionally good one.

In the thirteen weeks that Connie was with them at Damrey Phong the Carrier made eleven or twelve trips to Indonesia, loaded with two field guns every time. They kept no records or logbooks, and Connie could not recollect exactly how many journeys each machine had made. Between the Carrier journeys the Dakota flew in field-gun ammunition and small arms, about the same number of trips. It took the Indonesians about that time to recondition the first guns. They got them into action against the Dutch Army after about two months, and raised a hornet's nest for Dwight Schafter.

The Dutch were no fools, and they knew fairly well where all these arms were coming from. The trouble was that at that time they controlled only small areas of Java and Sumatra round about the larger towns, and it was fairly easy for a resolute pilot coming in by night to land upon an Indonesian airstrip to discharge his load. The Dutch Air Force pilots were ready and valiant in flying on night fighter patrols, but sheer bravery cannot replace the technical equipment necessary for a successful interception, and at that time they hadn't got it. A number of Dutch Mustangs were lost on these night fighter patrols; the pilots, if they survived, were executed immediately by the Republicans, who fought their war according to an Eastern code. For a time the loss of aircraft and pilots was more serious to the Dutch than the continued landing of small arms, and the night patrols became infrequent.

When artillery appeared in rebel hands, the defence was galvanised again. Coincident with the increased activity, a few airborne radar equipments came to hand in Batavia, and these were fitted hurriedly in the B25s. For the first time the Dutch Air Force had a reasonable chance of intercepting Dwight Schafter on his night flights, and this, of course, was quite unknown to him. They saw him on the radar screen as he was going away one night, the first night they had used it operationally, but on that occasion they were unable to get within fifteen miles of him. They now knew his route, however, and they kept machines from Palembang continuously in the air from then on during the hours of darkness. On the fifth night he came again in the Dakota, and they got him.

It was his habit to fly from Damrey Phong southwards and parallel with the east coast of Malaya and about a hundred miles off-shore, checking his course by wireless bearings from the broadcasting stations of Bangkok and Singapore. He flew on on his course to Jogjokarta, the rebel headquarters in Java, passing somewhat to the east of the island of Banka, and it was here that the Dutch fighter first made contact with him. The pilot was under orders not to shoot the intruder down into the sea as it was necessary to get evidence, and so he held the Dakota in his radar and followed about three miles behind for an hour and a quarter till Dwight Schafter crossed the north coast of Java a hundred miles or so to the east of Batavia, making his usual landfall at a distinctive turn of the coast north of Tjerebon. There the Mitchell closed up on him, and shot him down upon the foothills of Mount Tjareme.

Schafter and Seriot were quite prepared for such a thing to happen; it was one of the occupational hazards of their way of life. The first thing that they knew was a long burst of tracer fire into the port wing. The engine stopped with a rending jerk that shook the machine through; it may have fallen out. Fire broke out immediately from the pierced petrol tanks.

They had their drill for this contingency all worked out. Both flew in parachute harness. Escape was by the door at the aft end of the cabin, and the cabin was always loaded, with an avenue down the middle to provide a clear run. Seriot was flying the aircraft at the time and Schafter was at the navigator's table. Schafter plucked him by the arm and nodded, and then turned and ran aft to snap on his parachute and jettison the door. The brown man at the wheel counted ten slowly, trimming the aircraft as he counted; then he left his seat and ran down the fuselage after his captain, snapped on his parachute, and followed Schafter into the black void below. The Dakota went on for a few seconds burning fiercely, then it fell over in a spiral dive and went down in a shapeless mass of flame. The ammunition started going off before it hit the ground, and for a time made an interesting display upon the forest slopes.

Seriot reached the ground uninjured, landing in some paddy-fields on the edge of the forest. Schafter had bad luck; he fell on the tree-tops, which checked him, and his parachute collapsed. He was perhaps fifty feet from the ground. The top branches broke beneath his weight after a moment and he fell through the branches to the forest floor, clutching at every branch as he fell. Finally he dropped helplessly from a height of about twenty feet and fell across a root. He broke his thigh in two places.

That was the end of it for him. That part of Java is fairly well populated and villagers found him before dawn; then the Dutch, moving quickly in trucks, threw a cordon round the district and picked him up without much difficulty. Seriot put on native clothes supplied by the villagers and attempted to get through to Jogjokarta, but the Dutch were too clever and he was arrested a day later.

Schafter was now in hospital in Batavia; when he was well enough to appear in court he would be tried and sentenced. Seriot was in jail in Batavia, awaiting trial, but as he was an employee he would not be tried before his captain.

News of this disaster came to Connie Shaklin at Damrey Phong within twelve hours, by way of broadcast news from Singapore and from Bangkok. He had the Carrier at Damrey, and he was working on it when the news came in. He had a short talk with his two engineers. Clearly the party was over, and all that there was left for them to do was to wind it up and disperse. The only real problem was, what should become of the Cornell Carrier, an aeroplane which only a short time before had cost nearly seventy thousand pounds, and was presumably worth about that figure still.

In Dwight Schafter's absence, Connie was responsible at Damrey, and he took his responsibilities seriously. He paid the month's wages out of money that had been left with him by Schafter, and went to Bangkok, travelling by fishing vessel up the coast. It took him about four days. In Bangkok he went to the Dutch Embassy and explained the position, well aware that they could not proceed against him upon Siamese territory. He said that there were stocks of fuel, tools, and spares for the Dakota at their base in Indo-China and he wanted instructions from Dwight Schafter as to the disposal of these assets, which were the property of this American citizen. He did not tell them anything about the Carrier.

His request added one more headache to the many headaches that Dwight Schafter had given the Dutch. It was impossible for them to be too high-handed with the donors of Marshall Aid, and the United States consul had already intervened to ensure that this criminal awaiting trial should be imprisoned with all the amenities proper to an American citizen. The question of his assets upon foreign territory was quite outside the jurisdiction of the Dutch. In Java they cogitated over it for twenty-four hours and then decided not to irritate the State Department any further. They instructed their Ambassador to give Shaklin a visa for a visit to Batavia to interview his boss in hospital, and promised that he would be allowed a safe conduct to depart out of Dutch territory at will. To make assurance doubly sure, Connie Shaklin went to the American Embassy in Bangkok and told them all about it before flying down to Batavia.

He arrived at the Nederland Hotel the day before I did. When I found him lying on his bed after lunch, he was thinking over his interview in hospital that morning.

By the time he had told me all this it was three o'clock, and time for me to go to the Arabia–Sumatran office to find out about my return load for the Airtruck. They knew all about me. They had found a load of radio apparatus that had to get back to Holland in quick time for a rebuild; I was to take this back as far as Bahrein and arrangements would be made to get it on to Holland from there. It would be ready for loading into the Airtruck next morning.

I went back to the Nederland Hotel. Connie was in the room still, lying on his bed. I had been thinking as I walked back through the palm-lined streets by the canal. "Look, Connie," I said. "I've got a proposition to put to you. Let's go downstairs and have a drink, out in the cool." The sun was going down, and it was getting cooler out in the open than it was in the bedroom.

"Okay," he said. "I've got one for you."

He put his shirt and trousers on, and came downstairs with me to the open piazza in front of the hotel, with all the little tables under sunshades. He wore a pair of khaki drill trousers and a white shirt open at the neck, and sandals. As we turned the corner of the stair I saw his face in profile, lean, Eastern, and ascetic, and I knew what he reminded me of. He looked like a priest.

He wouldn't touch anything alcoholic, so I ordered fresh lime squash for us both. "Look, Connie," I said, "this is what I had in mind. My show at Bahrein is growing, and the ground side's getting a bit out of hand. I've been looking after that myself so far, with two Asiatics A-and-Cs to help me. God knows how it's all going on up there now. Probably not so good. Would you like to come and work for me as chief engineer? I need somebody like you."

"I'm still working for Dwight Schafter," he said. "I've got his Carrier to look after."

"He can't go on employing you for long," I said. "From what you tell me he'll get a prison sentence as soon as he comes out of hospital."

He nodded. "Yes, he will go to prison, probably for years. But that doesn't mean that he won't want to employ me. He's made enough money to employ a dozen people while he serves his sentence, and still be a wealthy man when he comes out. The Dutch can't touch his money. That's not here." He paused. "If he wants me to stay on and serve his interests while he is in prison, I will do so. I would like to come and work for you in Bahrein, Tom. I could help you with your Asiatic engineers and labour. But until Dwight Schafter comes out of prison I will stay with him."

I took a drink of my lime squash and lit a cigarette. It was no good saying that Dwight Schafter was a mercenary soldier of fortune, about to be sentenced very rightly on a criminal offence, that he had been gun-running for the money there was in it, that he richly deserved all he got. That was the Western way of looking at things, but they seem different to Asiatic eyes. Connie probably liked and respected the man, probably regarded him as one who risked his life and liberty to help millions of Asiatics in their struggle for freedom. When liberty was lost, Connie would not abandon Dwight Schafter.

I sat there smoking for a time in silence, looking out over the canal to the white buildings on the other side.

"What's going to happen to the Carrier, Connie?" I asked at last.

"I said I had a proposition for you," he replied. "Shall I make it now?"

I glanced at him and nodded.

"I think you should take over that Carrier and fly it to Bahrein and operate it there," he said.

Frankly, that thought had never entered my head, although I suppose it might have done. The Carrier was a real aeroplane compared with the small stuff I was operating. I measured my resources in hundreds of pounds at that time, but the Carrier cost more than sixty thousand. It was so far beyond my capabilities that I had never bothered even to consider the economics of operating a thing like that. But now that Connie mentioned it, I knew at once that in the Persian Gulf that aeroplane would pay. It could carry a big truck. It could carry five tons of machinery. It could carry a fair-sized boat, or about ninety pilgrims at a time over Arabia to Jiddah for their pilgrimage to Mecca. It was a logical extension of the business I was doing.

"I couldn't pay for it," I said. "I've not got the money. And what makes you think that Schafter would want to part with it?"

"What else can he do? If he leaves it on the field at Damrey Phong some warlord will turn up before long and take it, and probably crash it. If he has it flown down here, the Dutch will take it from him. If he has it flown back to America, his own Government may take it from him to appease the Dutch. There are not many things that he can do with that aeroplane, if he wants ever to see his money again. But one of the first things he must do is to find somebody to fly it away out of this area to some other part of the world altogether, and preferably into the British Empire, where the laws of property are clearly framed and easy to understand. I think if you could use it, he would charter it to you, provided you would take it to Bahrein and operate it there."

He paused. "If you did that, I would ask Schafter if I might go with it, and work for you. I think he would agree to that, because that aeroplane is by far the greatest of the responsibilities that I now have for him. I think that he would want me to stay with it."

We talked this over for half an hour, and the more I thought of it the more I liked the idea. I wanted Connie to come and take over the maintenance of my little fleet, and he wouldn't come unless I took the Carrier too. Well, I was willing enough provided that I didn't have to pay for this large aeroplane; anybody would have been. And the way he put it, my fairy godmother was going to give it to me free.

He got up presently and hailed a rickshaw, and went off in it to the hospital to see Dwight Schafter again before the nurses packed him up for the night. I sat on in front of the hotel in the cool of the evening, smoking and resting, with the fatigue oozing out of me. I was tired. It was very, very good to have found Connie again. It was like seeing a bit of light at the end of a tunnel.

He came back presently, and found me sitting in the same place. He dropped down into the same chair beside me. "I told Dwight about you and your business at Bahrein," he said. "I said that you would take the Carrier on charter if it was available, and I would go with it to maintain it. He will think it over during the night. He wants you to go and see him early in the morning, before you leave."

I nodded. "You'll come along?"

He shook his head. "It will be better if you talk your business with him alone. I am a technical man. I am not interested in money matters."

"Okay," I said. "One little thing, though. Did you tell him I could fly it?"

"You can fly it," he replied.

"It's ten times heavier than anything I've ever flown before, ten times," I said. "I don't want there to be any misunderstanding about that. What happens if I crash it?"

"You can talk about that with Schafter," he replied. "But I know this, that you will fly it, and you will not crash it."

I glanced at him, but he was quite serious. He spoke almost as if it was a prophecy. "Oh, you know that, do you?" I replied. "More than I do. I'm used to flying things that I land with my arse down on the ground, not twenty feet up in the air. Still, I don't mind having a stab at it if nobody else minds."

"You will have no difficulty," he said. "It is just like any other aeroplane. They are easier to fly as they get bigger, provided you are not afraid of them. And you will not be afraid."

I grinned. "It's a long time since I've been afraid of an aeroplane."

I went to see Dwight Schafter early next morning. He was in a good ward in a normal hospital; the ward sister was a Dutchwoman, the nurses Javanese girls. The only thing that marked him as a prisoner was a sentry on the door of the ward, a Dutch soldier in American battledress, armed with a rifle. He let me pass to see his prisoner without any question, which relieved me; I had thought that I might have to get all sorts of permits.

I sat down by Schafter's bed and told him who I was, and he came to the point at once. "Shak Lin said you were here," he said. "He told me about you. Said you wanted to charter my Carrier."

"I can use it," I said. "But I can't pay much for it. If I'm to take it to my operating base – that's Bahrein, in the Persian Gulf – it's going to cost me six hundred pounds in fuel and oil and landing fees to get it there, as a start. That's got to be recovered out of profits before I can pay you anything at all for the hire."

"Bolony," he said. "Fuel will cost you nothing. There's over twelve tons of hundred-octane fuel in the store at Damrey Phong right now. You can fill her up before you start and take five tons with you in the cabin. That'll get you there. If you don't take it, someone else will. There's oil there, too. The rest is chicken feed."

"Maybe it's chicken feed to you," I said. "It's not to me. I've got to fly another pilot out to Bangkok to take over the machine I'm flying now. I suppose his fare is chicken feed, too."

"That Carrier's worth five thousand bucks a month in charter fees," he said.

"You'd better find someone who can pay that much, then," I replied. "I can't. I'm operating in a small way. You'd better offer it to Pan American."

"All right, wise guy," he said. "What's your angle on it?"

We started in then, and in a quarter of an hour we had thrashed out what I still think was equitable in the circumstances. I was to take the machine to Bahrein with any fuel and spares from Damrey that I could carry in it, with Connie Shaklin as my engineer. I was to hold it insured as soon as it reached Bahrein; insurance from Damrey was hardly practical. I was to charter it at the rate of a dollar a month for three months or three hundred hours flying time after reaching Bahrein, whichever was the least. In that three months Schafter's attorney in Indianapolis would make contact with me at Bahrein and I would deal with him if I wanted to buy it, or charter it further, or surrender it to him. The machine was not to be flown into Dutch or US territory.

"Jesus," he said. "I wish some guy had given me a deal like this when I was young. I wouldn't have needed to go flying guns."

"It's fair enough," I said.

"Maybe. But you're a darned lucky guy all the same."

I left the hospital, and went to the Arabia–Sumatran office, and borrowed a typist, and had copies of our draft charter agreement made, and took them back to the hospital for him to sign. We talked for some time about the flying qualities of the machine; he already knew from Connie that I had no large aeroplane experience. He was more phlegmatic about that than I had thought he would he; from something he said I knew that Connie had given me a good character. "I bring her in about a hundred knots," he said. "Hundred and ten if it's full load or very rough. Take it easy, and you'll find her quite all right. You'll have Shak Lin with you as flight engineer?"

"That's right," I said. "He'll be with me."

He turned and glanced at me from the bed. "Say," he said. "You've known that guy a long time, haven't you?"

"We started off together as boys in the same air circus," I said. "I haven't seen him since those days."

"Oh … Well, he's a good engineer. And he's one you can really trust. You see the way he's come down here to find out what I wanted done. But – say, he's a queer sort of a guy in other ways, isn't he?"

"I don't know," I said. "I only met him yesterday. What sort of ways?"

"He's got some mighty strange ideas for an engineer," said Schafter. "It's a thing you ought to know about, since you're taking him on. About religion, and all that."

I nodded slowly. Connie always had been one for going to odd churches, and he had the look of a priest. It was a pity. "Does it affect his work?" I asked.

"I'll say it does. It makes his work a whole lot better."

I glanced at this American gun-runner in enquiry. It wasn't quite the answer that I had expected.

"I've been away a lot of the time," he said. "I don't know all of what's been going on at Damrey Phong. He's got a statue of a Buddha set up in a little sort of a pagoda just by where we park the aircraft. One of these painted clay Buddhas, you know, like you see in the villages. He has a sort of a prayer meeting there each day before they start work on the machines, and after they knock off."

I blinked at him.

"That's right. He runs a sort of Buddhist prayer meeting, all in Chinese or Siamese or something. He's got both the other engineers coming to it, and the local labour, and the girls – they come along, too. See them all kneeling down in front of this Buddha with flowers in their hands, saying their prayers, every morning. Then up they get, and straight off to start work on the machines. And the same thing, as soon as they knock off. Down they go on their knees before that painted image, and pray for about ten minutes. Then off they go."

"Is that usual with ground staff in this part of the world?" I asked.

"I'll say it's not. I've never seen it done before."

"Did Shak Lin start it, then?"

"I think he did. I think he must have done."

"Did you ask him why he did it?"

"I never had much time," he said. "I've always been flying. I did say something once, and all he said was something like, men worked better if they prayed." He grinned. "Just like a preacher back in Indiana. But I will say this, those boys at Damrey Phong did a good job for me. Most Asiatic engineers, you know – you just can't trust a thing they do. They mean all right, but they're not responsible. Well, these boys weren't like that. They'd look you right in the eye and tell you when they'd done a job on the aircraft that wasn't quite so hot. Like using copper wire for locking instead of steel because they were out of steel wire, or putting gasket cement on an old washer to make it tight because there weren't any new ones. Things like that. They'd just come and tell you. Like as if they were as good as you, and weren't afraid of being bawled out." He paused. "I never knew Asiatic engineers like that before," he said. "It's always been the other way." He glanced at me. "Pack of lying, crawling rats, mostly. *You* know."

I knew it only too well. "I don't know the East," I said. "I worked in Egypt in the war, but this is my first time out here. I've never met an Asiatic engineer I'd like to trust. Except Shaklin, of course, and he's really British."

"I'll be interested to hear how you made out with him one day," said Schafter. "Maybe there's something in this religion business after all. I wouldn't know." He hesitated. "My copilot – he's an Asiatic, he used to go to these prayer meetings in front of the Buddha, regular. See him kneeling there with all the others, with a gladiola blossom in his hands. Funny, to see a pilot doing that ..."

I smiled. "You didn't go yourself?"

"I did once," he said unexpectedly. "The morning we were taking off in the C47 for this last trip here." He hesitated. "I guess I was kind of worried, or I wouldn't have done a thing like that. I reckoned that the artillery must be in action by that time and the Dutchmen, they'd be hopping mad, 'n we might meet more opposition than we'd had till then. And when I came out of the John that morning there was nobody around, no girls or anyone, and there they all were praying at the Buddha. So I didn't want to be snooty, see? I went and picked a flower and knelt down with them, too. I couldn't understand what Shak Lin and the rest were saying, and I got to thinking about the white wooden church at home with all the cars parked outside, and the minister preaching, and the sun coming in through the stained glass, back home in Shelbyville where I was raised, in Indiana." He paused. "I guess it does you good to have a quiet time to think, like that, before you take off on a dicey trip."

I would have liked to have stayed and talked to him longer, but my load would be arriving at the airport, and I had to get off that day. I said goodbye to him, and left the hospital, and went back to the hotel and paid the bill and picked up Connie and drove out to Kermajoran. Two hours later we were in the air in the Airtruck, on our way north to Palembang.

We stayed there for the night. I sent a cable to Gujar Singh in Bahrein telling him to drop everything and come by airline to Bangkok at once to meet us there, and told him to cable me care of the Flying Control at Don Muang to say when he would arrive. Next day we made an early start and got to Songkhla in the south of Siam after landing to refuel at Singapore and at Kuantan. We landed at Bangkok about midday next day.

I saw very little of Connie in the two days that we waited at Bangkok for Gujar Singh. I had a room at the Trocadero Hotel, but he wouldn't stay there with me. He said that he had Asiatic friends who wanted to put him up, and I found later that he was staying in a Buddhist monastery just by the Wat Cheng pagoda. He came along to the hotel each morning and evening to find out the form and when I wanted him; then he would go off and I wouldn't see him again. I got a guide to take me round some of the pagodas, the loveliest sort of churches that I ever saw in all my life. I sent a lot of picture postcards of them to Dad and Mum, back home in Southampton, between the gasworks and the docks. I wanted to make them understand, if possible.

While I was waiting in Bangkok I made a few enquiries about the formalities of flying in and out of Indo-China from Siam. At that time there was no very settled government in Saigon, and the French, who were in power by virtue of their army, probably had no idea that Dwight Schafter's Cornell Carrier was in the country at all. It seemed somewhat superfluous in those circumstances to seek for a permission to take it out of Indo-China, but if I did not do that, could I bring it into Siam without getting it taken from me by the Siamese?

I mentioned this worry to Connie when he came to see me on the morning of the second day. He went, I think, to the Siamese Airways manager at Don Muang, and together they went to some department of the Government about it. Dwight Schafter's prestige amongst the Asiatics was high, and the Siamese would put no obstacle in Connie's way as the agent of Dwight Schafter in the disposal of his assets. By the time Gujar Singh arrived, Connie was able to assure us that we had leave to fly in and out of Don Muang with no questions asked. For the sake of the record, when we left for Indo-China in the Airtruck we cleared for Hua Hin, a Siamese seaside resort about a hundred miles to the south.

I unloaded my cargo of radio apparatus for Holland from the Airtruck before taking off and left it in the bonded store at Don Muang; if anything should happen to the Airtruck in Indo-China, I didn't want to lose the cargo. I took off from Don Muang early one morning with Connie and Gujar squatting on their bags behind me in the empty cabin. Three hours later I was coming in to land upon the strip at Damrey Phong.

That strip was very beautiful. There was a mountain about two thousand feet high just to the north of it which made things a bit awkward on the circuit, but this mountain was covered in flowering trees, the Flame of the Forest, and these trees were all in bloom, so that the side of the mountain was covered with orange-red splashes on the jungle green. The little atap village was just by the strip, and there were flowers everywhere, bougainvillaea and hibiscus and frangipani all over the houses and the little streets. Beyond the village was the river, and a flat plain with hills again in the blue distance beyond. It was a quiet, happy, beautiful little place. Nothing had ever happened there before the airstrip came, and now that Dwight Schafter had passed on, probably nothing would ever happen there again.

The Cornell Carrier was parked just off the middle of the strip by the two European houses. I put the Airtruck down and taxied to park her by the Carrier; as I did so men and women came streaming from the village. I swung the Airtruck quickly into the parking position and stopped the propellers in case the natives came crowding round, but they formed a sort of circle round the aircraft at a safe distance, waiting for us to get out.

I turned in my seat, and said to Connie, "It's a pretty little place."

He smiled. "I am glad to see the Carrier still here. I was worried that some warlord might have gone off with it."

We got out of the machine, and he introduced us to his two mechanics, U Myin, the Burmese lad, and Chai Tai Foong, the Chinese from Hong Kong. U Myin spoke no English and seemed a bit dumb generally, but Tai Foong could make himself understood in English and seemed brighter all round.

We went at once to have a look at the Carrier. The people parted to let us through; they were mostly men and children, some of the men very old. Such young women as were there were, I think, the mistresses or housekeepers of the engineers. Relations were evidently very good with these people. They paid little attention to me or to Gujar, but when Connie spoke to any of them, or even when he turned his head, they touched the right hand to the forehead and bowed to him.

The Carrier was in very good order. She was only four or five months old, of course, and she had only done about three hundred hours flying – nothing in the life of a machine like that. In the cabin, or hold, where the load was carried, she had had rough usage, but externally the paint was hardly scratched, and in the pilot's cockpit everything looked new. She had been very carefully maintained by Connie and his boys; in the cockpit everything was spotlessly clean, the windscreens newly polished, the safety belts folded neatly across each seat as if for an inspection. I was amazed that fortune should have brought so fine an aeroplane into my hands. The only thing now was – could I fly her?

She was only half full of fuel, which suited me for a first solo. We had a meal of rice and little side dishes of curried fish and chillies, served by the girls in the house of the two engineers, and then Connie and I went out to the Carrier to try my luck. We spent about an hour on the machine together, mostly in the cockpit, till I knew all the controls by heart. Then, with Connie by my side in the copilot's seat, I started up the engines, ran her warm and ran them up to power for the engine check. Then I throttled back to idling and eased the brakes, and taxied out on to the strip.

A queer thought came to me then as I taxied down to the far end, in that lovely place. I leaned over to Connie by my side in the wide cockpit. "We've come a long way since we used to drive that Ford in Gretna Green, in Cobham's Circus," I said. I had not sat beside him since, that I could recollect.

He smiled. "Those were good days."

I turned the machine at the end and the strip lay stretched out before us; there was little or no wind. I was in no hurry. I sat there for a few minutes doing the final cockpit check and getting comfortable; then when I was ready to go I raised my head and had a good look round. About half the people, including Gujar Singh and the two engineers, were standing watching under the shade of the wing of the Airtruck, but the rest were kneeling in front of the Buddha on his throne under a little palm thatch roof. It was all very bright and colourful upon that aerodrome.

I said to Connie, "What are they doing there? Praying?"

"Yes," he said.

"For me, that I'm not going to make a muck of this?"

He laughed. "For us both. Probably more for me than for you."

"Well," I said, "it's nice to know somebody cares." And with that I pushed the throttles open and we took off down the strip.

As Connie had said, she handled just like any other aeroplane, except that she had better manners than most. I climbed her slowly straight out over the sea to about five thousand feet, then turned and came back over Damrey Phong. I played about with her up there for twenty minutes till I had the feel of her with engines on or throttled, flaps up or down, and then I brought her down and did a circuit and made a long approach. The landing went all right; the undercarriage was so good it didn't seem to matter how you put her down. I took her off again; in all I did four landings on her without incident. When I taxied in beside the Airtruck I was very pleased with myself. I could fly that thing. Fuelling at Damrey Phong was quite a business. The petrol was in forty-gallon drums in a store down by the river, and these drums had to be rolled up by hand to the machine, a distance of about half a mile. We needed about six hundred gallons to put into the Carrier, and about twenty-five more drums to load into the cabin to be taken with us on the flight. There was a small portable motor pump to lift the fuel from the drums twenty feet up into the wing tanks, but even with this help the work was severe and lengthy. Damrey Phong, though healthy, is a humid place, and we were all sweating in torrents before long.

We could not get it done that evening. As the sun went down I told Connie to knock off the men; we would finish in the morning. I had an idea that he would want some daylight for his worshipping before the Buddha, and we couldn't go on working after dark, anyway. I walked across to the house that had been occupied by Dwight Schafter and his copilot Seriot, which was where I was to sleep, and threw off my wet shirt and trousers, and stood under the kerosene-tin shower, and put on dry clothes.

When I came out, it was evening. There was still a golden sunlight on the big hill by the strip, but overhead the sky was getting blue, and the light was going. I had guessed correctly about Connie. He was standing in front and to one side of the Buddha, and all the people were kneeling in front of it, with flowers in their hands, as Dwight Schafter had said.

I strolled up closer to see what was going on. I could not understand what he was saying, but it was clear that he was leading them in prayer. One phrase of four words was continually repeated, as in a litany. Connie would say a sentence or two, facing the statue, and the rest of them would then repeat this phrase with him, very reverently.

It was with something of a shock that I saw Gujar Singh kneeling there amongst them, his turban on his head, a flower in his hands beneath his great black beard. I was the only one who was not praying, the only one from the West in Damrey Phong.

Perhaps, like Dwight Schafter, I didn't want to be snooty. Perhaps it was that I couldn't bear to be left out. It couldn't do any harm, in any case. I went forward and went down upon my knees in the last row; I couldn't understand what it was all about, but that didn't seem to matter. There was an Asiatic by me, a coolie who had been rolling barrels all the afternoon; he had a sheaf of gladiola blossoms in his hand. Quietly he parted them, and gave me two to hold.

Beryl had put her head in the gas oven because I had been proud, and righteous in the eyes of other people, and unkind. That had set my life upon the course that in the end had brought me to this place, far from Southampton docks and my own people, worshipping with natives in an Eastern village. Beryl had died because I was proud and unkind. How many other people should I kill like that before I died too?

Presently I realised that Connie was speaking in English. He had not altered his posture or his tone, but he was saying, "It is written in the Dhammapada, 'You yourself must make the effort. Buddhas only show the way. Cut down the love of self as one cuts the lotus in the autumn. Give yourself to following the Path of Peace.' " And then he repeated, and the others with him, the phrase that I had noticed before, Om Mani Padme Hum.

I stayed there on my knees with them till it was nearly dark.

CHAPTER FOUR

O spiritual pilgrim rise: the night has grown her single horn:
The voices of the souls unborn are half a-dream with
Paradise.

JAMES ELROY FLECKER

WE GOT THE loading finished next morning and got the fuel drums lashed down in the cabin. I had no intention of flying the Carrier by night till I was more used to her, and so we made the first day's stage to Bangkok only. We had to stop there anyway, to load the cargo that I had left there back into the Airtruck.

On Connie's advice I engaged Chai Tai Foong to come with us to join the staff at Bahrein; he was a good lad who spoke a little English, and he knew the Carrier. The other one, U Myin, I had no place for, but I offered him a passage in the Carrier to Rangoon, where we should land after Bangkok. I didn't quite know how Gujar would get on in foreign countries and I meant to stay with him as far as Calcutta, where he would be on his own ground. After that I would leave him and go ahead, because the Carrier was much faster than the Airtruck and had a much greater range.

We had a meal at midday, and got off for Bangkok after lunch. It was affecting in a way, because the people of the village were so deeply grieved to see Connie go. He had his service at the Buddha in the morning before starting work and most of the village turned up for it, women as well as men; there must have been over two hundred people there on the strip. It only lasted about ten minutes. The people hung about the strip all day. They paid no attention to the rest of us, but their eyes followed Connie everywhere. A curious thing was that three monks turned up in yellow robes, with shaven heads and bare feet. They made the same obeisance to him that the villagers made, touching their fingers to the forehead and bowing low. This seemed odd to me, but I was sorting out the maps with Gujar at the time and didn't take much notice of what they were doing. The trouble was that we had only one set of maps for the two aircraft, which made things a bit tricky. We couldn't fly in company, because the Airtruck cruised at a hundred miles an hour and the Carrier at a hundred and fifty. At the cruising speed of the Airtruck the Carrier would have been just about falling out of the air.

There was quite a good assortment of spares for the Carrier in Dwight Schafter's house, and several valuable bits of ground equipment – towing bars, hydraulic jacks, and all that sort of thing. In all there was over a ton of stuff. We put this in the Airtruck for the flight to Bangkok as the Carrier was loaded to the limit, meaning to transfer it at Don Muang when the Carrier had used up some of her fuel load. In this way we managed to take with us everything of importance that Dwight Schafter had at Damrey Phong except about four tons of petrol; that we had to leave in the store for the benefit of whoever came along.

We taxied down to the end of the strip together and took off in turn, Gujar Singh first in the Airtruck with the two engineers; I followed in the Carrier with Connie by my side. I turned after taking off and followed Gujar round upon a left-hand circuit before getting upon course, and having raised the flaps and throttled back the boost and set the revs I glanced out of the window at the strip on my left side. The whole village seemed to be standing by the Buddha looking up at us; they were not waving. They were just standing there motionless and sad, watching us as we flew away.

We flew past Gujar Singh and waved at him, and went on on a compass course that would bring us to the Menam river between Bangkok and the sea. I had given our one map to Gujar, having made a few extracts from it on a sheet of paper. The Carrier had an automatic pilot, and at our sector height and on our course I put this in and sat for ten minutes watching that it was working all right. Then Connie and I left our seats and went to the wireless, and found Bangkok broadcasting station, and took a series of bearings on it to check our course. In the course of an hour the bearings gradually crept round from 319 degrees to 357 degrees magnetic, which should have brought us to the river, and when we got to that point and stood up to look out of the windscreen, there was the river. It was as easy as that. We landed at Don Muang about an hour ahead of Gujar Singh. The Siamese Control officers knew the Carrier well; they were most tactful, and asked no questions.

We transferred the loads next morning and took off about midday for Rangoon, flying by the Three Pagodas Pass and the line of the Burma-Siam railway made in the war with the labour of Asiatics and prisoners of war at a vast cost in human life. Again we got to Rangoon an hour or so before Gujar, plodding along behind us at a hundred miles an hour. I was able to raise some more maps at Mingadon airport; we stayed the night in the hostel there and said goodbye to U Myin and went on at dawn next day. That day we landed to refuel the Airtruck at Chittagong after flying up the coast of Arakan, and took off in the early afternoon for Calcutta.

At Calcutta I left Gujar to follow on behind at the best speed he could make, and went ahead with Connie in the Carrier. We made one long hop to Karachi in the day, flying right over India at about ten thousand feet, stayed there the night, and left next morning for Bahrein direct. We got there in the early afternoon and circled the familiar airport in our new large aircraft. There was the other Airtruck parked outside, and Arjan Singh with the ground staff standing looking up at this strange freight aircraft that was coming in to land. They didn't know it was a new addition to the fleet.

In the next few weeks I had a lot of work. I reorganised the ground staff and put Connie in charge of all maintenance. I wanted to get Gujar Singh on to flying the Carrier as soon as possible, but I was resolved that he should do a hundred hours on it with me as copilot before taking it on alone. With two of us off nearly every day in the Carrier, because there was a lot of business for it from the start, it was urgently necessary for us to get another pilot. By that time I was getting letters in almost every mail from British pilots wanting a job, but I was getting on all right with Asiatics at a quarter the salary and probably harder working. I got an Iraqi called Hosein who had been an officer in the Iraqi Air Force; he could fly twin-engined stuff and so Gujar put him on the Airtruck right away. I now had four aircraft all going hard, and so I found I had to get another boy clerk and more labourers. It was getting to be quite a business.

There was work for the Carrier, more work than we could handle, from the first day. For the first time we had an aircraft in the Persian Gulf that was really designed to carry heavy commercial loads; we could take a motor pump out four hundred miles into the desert, or a concrete-mixer, or a truck. We could fetch a crashed aircraft from Sharjah or Kuweit and take it to Egypt in a few hours for repair, and we did that more than once, returning with loads of cases of machinery or engineering stores. There was all manner of work for a big freight aircraft, we discovered, in the Persian Gulf, and it showed no sign whatsoever of getting any less.

In Batavia, Dwight Schafter came up for trial by the Dutch, and got three years' imprisonment; his copilot Seriot got twelve months. I wrote to Schafter about that time saying that the Carrier was safe and earning its keep, and I should be willing to negotiate with his attorney to buy it at my own price by instalments over a period. So far as I could see, the thing would have paid its cost in about two years; if I could spread the instalment payments over that time I should get it without having to put down any capital at all. Dwight Schafter, I felt, wouldn't need the money till he'd done his sentence; it might well be that he would agree to such a scheme.

In the hangar, Connie got the organisation into order in a very short time. I had increased the staff by the Chinese, Chai Tai Foong, that we had brought from Damrey Phong and by another Iraqi, so that I now had Connie, four licensed engineers, and five engineering labourers, the latter all Arabs from Bahrein. I had suggested to Connie that I should get him into the radio operators' chummery with me, but he wouldn't have it. "I am an Asiatic," he said. "It would lead to difficulties."

"I don't see why it should. You're only technically an Asiatic, after all."

He smiled. "Perhaps. But I should prefer to live in the souk. I must learn Arabic now, and anyway, I shall feel freer there."

He had a great ability to learn languages, I was to discover; three months seemed to be quite enough for him to become fluent in any Eastern language. "All right," I said. "I don't want to press you to live on the station. Where are you staying now?"

"Gujar Singh has found me a room near his place," he said. "A room in the house of an Arab merchant who sells silks. I shall be all right there."

"It's a good long way from the hangar," I said. "What will you do – walk it?"

He grinned. "Do what Gujar Singh does – get a bicycle." My chief pilot came to work each day on an old rusty lady's bicycle, his black beard flowing fiercely in the breeze.

All this expansion made a considerable stir on Bahrein aerodrome. Practically every month I had to go to the RAF and ask if I could lease another building. Although in theory I was making money hand over fist, there was never any of it in evidence; it all went back into aeroplanes and tools and spares – into various capital accounts. I should have been hard put to it to find the money to erect the simplest wooden hut, but fortunately there were plenty of empty buildings belonging to the RAF that had been put up in the war and had been empty ever since. The accountant officer was very helpful; whenever I wanted a new store or office he could usually produce something, although on a very short-term lease. I was lucky in the officers I had to deal with, perhaps; certainly without the help and encouragement of the RAF I'd never have been able to build up the business in those early years.

I had no time, of course, for any social intercourse, nor could I have kept my end up in such matters. I got my education at the fitter's bench, not at a university. The Persian Gulf states are advised by a British Resident, Sir William Faulkner, who lives at the Residency in Bahrein with Secretaries and whatnot from the Foreign Office; I saw these people sometimes as they came and went in aircraft at the aerodrome, but I never spoke to any of them for years. I never did any work for them because my business was freight alone. I've never put a passenger seat into an aeroplane unless its weight was charged for, or employed a stewardess, and I hope I never shall. I went into that business to make money, not to lose it, and my sort of aircraft weren't the sort to carry diplomats about the place.

I went on living at the radio operators' chummery and in the sergeants' mess.

I got to know some of the young officers quite well, however. When they went on leave I could often give them a free ride to India or to Egypt if they didn't mind sitting on their luggage with the load in an unheated and unsoundproofed cabin, and I was always glad to help them in this way, as they helped me. A lot of them had nothing much to do, and they were keen on aeroplanes. I did far more flying at Bahrein in those post-war years than ever the RAF did, and these boys used to come down to the hangar sometimes and just sit around and watch. Some of them got to know as much of what was going on in my crowd as I did myself, or a bit more.

Flight Lieutenant Allen came into my office once for something or other – I forget what it was. As he turned to go he grinned and said, "How's old Harpic getting on?"

"Who do you call Harpic?" I enquired. It was a new one to me.

"Sorry," he said. "Mr Shaklin. Your chief engineer."

"Doing all right," I replied. "Why do you call him that?"

"He's clean round the bend."

"He's a bloody good engineer," I said. "He's brisking up the other boys. I'm getting the maintenance properly done now that I've given up trying to run everything myself."

"He talks religion to them all the time."

"Well, what of it?" I said. "Do some of you young muggers good if you thought about your immortal souls a bit."

"You can't maintain aircraft with the Koran in one hand and a spanner in the other. Or can you?"

"Course you can," I said. "He's doing it. Who told you, anyway?" Because I knew that anything of that sort that was going on in my hangar went on in Arabic. I was starting to understand a bit of Arabic myself by that time, but I was pretty sure that Flight Lieutenant Allen didn't know a word.

"The barman in the mess was telling us. It's getting talked about all over the town. They say that if you want religion you can go and listen to the Imam in the mosque or you can go and listen to old Harpic in the hangar."

I grinned. "Do you a bit of good to go to either." He went away, and I sat on at the bare table that I used as a desk, listening to the typewriter in the next room, slightly uneasy. Connie was getting talked about, it seemed. I should know more of what was going on.

I knew it happened mostly in the afternoon, in the last hour of work before they knocked off for the afternoon prayer. I went down to the hangar that afternoon and got into the cockpit of the Fox-Moth with a pencil and a notebook; I had intended for some time to fit a blind flying panel in the instrument board and I wanted to scheme it out. But that wasn't really the reason that I went.

Standing beside the Fox was the first Airtruck, and Connie was doing a top overhaul on the port engine. He had a working platform rigged up by the engine of a couple of planks on trestles, and he was up on this thing with a ground engineer and one of the Arab boys. Most of the rest of the staff seemed to have arranged their work to get within earshot; they were all doing something, but they were listening at the same time. Up on his platform working on the engine Connie was talking to them.

He was speaking partly in English and partly in Arabic, which he could already speak much better than I could. "We are a peculiar people," he was saying, "we who care for aeroplanes. For common men it is enough to pray five times in each day, as the Imam dictates and as is ordained in the Koran. But we are different, we engineers. We are called to a higher task than common men, and Allah will require much more from us than that." He paused, and said to the man working with him, "Got a five-sixteenth box there? Thanks. Now hold it, just like that."

They worked on for a time in silence. "You have heard from the Imam of the journey that the Prophet of God made, when he was roused from sleep by the angel Gabriel who mounted him upon the horse with eagle's wings, Al Borak. You know how he passed by the Three Temptations and traversed the Seven Heavens till he came to the House of Adoration and the Presence of God. God then gave to the Prophet the main doctrines of the Faith, and ordained that prayers should be said by the faithful each day." He paused, and slipped the nuts collected in his hand into an old cigarette tin. "Now, draw her off gently. Wait a minute – the gasket's sticking on this side." They disengaged the cylinder head, and passed it down carefully from hand to hand to the ground.

Connie straightened up. "How many times were prayers to be said each day?"

There was a momentary silence. Then two or three said at once, "Fifty times." And someone added, " – Teacher." I noted that for thinking over later on. This thing was going deeper than I knew about.

"That is correct," said Connie. "Fifty times. I see you all don't know this story, or you have forgotten it, and yet of all men you should know it. Do you not know that when the Prophet descended from the Presence he met Moses?" One or two of the men nodded. "Moses asked how many times God had required the people to pray, and Mahomet said, fifty times. And Moses told him that it was impracticable, that he had tried it with the Children of Israel and he had never succeeded in getting anybody to pray fifty times a day. He said that the Prophet should go back to God and humbly beg that this number of prayers each day should be reduced. Mahomet did so, and on coming from the Presence he met Moses again, and told

110

him that the number was reduced to forty prayers a day. 'That is still too much,' said Moses. 'The people will not pray so many times. You must go back and ask Him to reduce it further.' " He paused. "Let's have that No.2 cranked cylinder head spanner."

Presently he went on, "Urged by Moses, it is written that the Prophet went back and back to God until the number of prayers was reduced to five each day. And still Moses said, 'Do you think you can exact five prayers a day from your people? By Allah, I have been through this with the Children of Israel, and it cannot be done. Go back and ask Him to reduce it yet again.' But the Prophet said, 'No, I will not go back. I have asked His indulgence already until I am ashamed. My people are not Israelites, and they shall worship Him five times a day.' That is the reason why every Believer has to say his prayers to God five times each day."

He spoke again to the other engineer about the cranked spanners, and then decided to loosen a part of the induction manifold to get at the nuts. He went on, "That is the story that you know and have been taught as true Believers, only some of you seem to have forgotten it. But you will see that five prayers is the minimum; the number was brought down to be within the power of the unlettered, common man – a camel driver, or a shepherd. But we are not like that, we engineers. We are men of understanding and of education, on whom is laid responsibility that men may travel in these aeroplanes as safely as if they were sitting by the well in the cool of the evening. We are not men like camel drivers or shepherds, and God will demand much more from us than from them. From men like us, the full tally of fifty prayers a day will be demanded. Five of them must be made in public or in private, according to the way you know, but this is the bare minimum for all men. From men like you another forty-five prayers are demanded. I will tell you about them."

111

They detached a part of the induction manifold and passed it down to the ground, and started to slack off the nuts of the next cylinder head. "Forty-five prayers a day may seem a lot to you," he said in Arabic. "They did to Moses. Yet forty-five more prayers a day was the commandment of God, and God is All-Seeing, and All-Knowing, and All-Merciful; He would not command that you should do more than you can perform. Men who work as you do upon aeroplanes can pray to God forty-five times a day quite easily, and I will tell you how."

He straightened up upon the trestle and looked down on them, spanner in hand. He was wearing a soiled khaki shirt and khaki shorts; he wore old oil-stained shoes with socks rolled round about his ankles. Beads of sweat were making little glistening streaks upon his face in the heat of the hangar, and the shirt clung to his back in dark, wet patches. His hands and forearms were stained and streaked with oil from the engine, mixed with sweat.

"I inspect some of the work you do upon these engines and these aeroplanes," he said. "God, the All-Seeing and All-Knowing, He inspects it all. You come to me and say, 'I have replaced this manifold and the job is finished.' I come to look at it to see if there is any fault, and I see everything in place. I look at the nuts, and I see the locking wires correctly turned the right way to prevent the nuts unscrewing, and that is all that I *can* see. I cannot see if the nuts are screwed only finger-tight; I cannot see if you have put a lever on the spanner and strained them up so tight that the bolts are just about to fail in tension. These things are hidden from me, but nothing is hidden from the All-Seeing Eye of God."

He paused. "God, the All-Knowing, knows if you have done well or ill," he said quietly. "If you ask Him humbly in prayer to tell you, He will tell you if you have done well or ill; in that way you will have a chance to do the job again, and try to do it better. Or you can come to me and say, Help me to do this work, because I cannot do it right. God is All-Merciful, and He will not hold bad work against you if He sees you striving to do right. So I say this to you."

He paused again. "With every piece of work you do, with every nut you tighten down, with every filter that you clean or every tappet that you set, pause at each stage and turn to Mecca, and fold your hands, and humbly ask the All-Seeing God to put into your heart the knowledge whether the work that you have done has been good or ill. Then you are to stand for half a minute with your eyes cast down, thinking of God and of the job, and God will put into your heart the knowledge of good or ill. So if the work is good you may proceed in peace, and if it is ill you may do it over again, or come to me and I will help you to do well before God."

He turned back to the engine. "If you do this," he said, "you will soon find that you are praying to God forty-five times a day or more, as He directed the Prophet in the first instance. Moses and Mahomet were quite right to get the tally reduced, because the people of that day were nomads and camel drivers. But you are educated men doing the most skilled work in all the world, and so much closer to God. God will require more of you than of common men; you are worth more than many camel drivers, because men look to you to see how good work should be done. And now I tell you, good work can be done only with the help and power of the All-Knowing God."

It was only then that I noticed what young Tarik was doing. He had got out a penny exercise book, bought in the souk or stolen from a school, and he was writing busily in it with a pencil, using the workbench as a desk. He was obviously having difficulty in keeping up and I would have given a good deal for a look at the book; I didn't know that Tarik could write. But equally obviously, he was doing his best to write down everything that Connie said. I wondered when I saw him how long he had been doing it.

It was five o'clock presently, and time for the men to knock off. Those who were Moslems, which meant most of the men working in the hangar, went out to the little patch of ground beside the hangar and turned to Mecca and commenced their afternoon *Rakats*. I had noticed a couple of days before that they had fallen into the habit of doing this together in a little crowd or congregation, and I was surprised to see some of the Arab servants from the RAF camp join them. One of these I thought I recognised as the barman in the officers' mess, though I had only seen him once or twice and I couldn't be sure.

Connie did not join them in their devotional postures. He went with them and knelt in prayer a little way apart from them, facing to Mecca as they did, but kneeling all the time. I guessed that this was because he was not a Moslem, and for the first time I wondered what he was.

I must say, I was rather impressed. In aircraft work of the somewhat pioneering sort that I was doing you have to be adaptable. When a new situation arises without precedent, you have to go to first principles and make the precedent yourself, and this religious turn that my maintenance crew were taking was just one of those things. I had chosen to staff my enterprise entirely with Asiatics. Having done that with my eyes open, I could not expect to run the non-essential parts of my business wholly in the European way; there must be tolerance on my part, and I must adapt my way of doing things to suit their ways of life. You can run a workshop in the Western style with time clocks and job cards and rate-fixers and premium bonus schemes, but to make a success of that you've got to have some people from the West to work in it, and I myself was the only one in the party. Or, you can run it in the Eastern way, and that's not necessarily a bad, or inefficient, or a slovenly way. Connie had introduced into my shop a form of discipline that was quite new to me, but the proof of the pudding, after all, was in the eating, and I was coming to the conclusion that the results were pretty good. The aeroplanes were being well maintained.

Dwight Schafter had commented on that when I had met him in the hospital in Batavia; he had said that Asiatic engineers who worked with Connie became confident and responsible people. My own experience was tending in the same direction and I began to watch the work that went on very closely. I must say I was very pleased indeed, so pleased that I mentioned it to Gujar Singh one day to get his views.

Gujar and I had flown the Carrier to a place called El Hazil in the Arabian desert about halfway between Kuweit and Egypt, with a load of machinery for the pipeline. El Hazil at that time was little more than a sand airstrip, three wooden huts, and half a dozen tents, with a Bedouin encampment in the middle distance. It was nearly dark when the unloading was finished and there was some stuff to go back to Bahrein that was coming in to the strip in the morning, so we stayed there for the night, sleeping on camp beds in the cabin of the aircraft, as we often did.

We had supper with the engineers in their mess hut, and strolled over to the aircraft presently, smoking in the cool of the night. It was very quiet in the desert; the dark blue sky was sown with millions of bright stars. I said to Gujar, "How do you think things are going in the hangar now?"

He said, "I think very well."

I nodded. "I think so, too." We walked on for a few paces. "I think Shak Lin is very good with them," I said at last. I had fallen into the habit of using his Asiatic name when speaking to an Asiatic. "I'm just a little worried about all this religion. I suppose that's quite all right?"

He smiled. "I do not think you have anything to worry about. I think it is a very good thing."

I hesitated. "One of the RAF officers – Flight Lieutenant Allen – was saying the other day that he's getting talked about, in the souk. Do you think that's true?"

He said, "There is talk in the souk about him."

"Not going to make any trouble, is it?" I had in mind vague stories of religious riots and that sort of thing.

"I don't think so," he said. "You know that he is great friends with the Imam?"

"I didn't know that."

"Oh yes," he told me. "They have long talks together, very frequently."

That was something, anyway; if the Imam knew what was going on in the hangar it was unlikely that there would be trouble with the orthodox Moslems. "What is he, Gujar?" I asked. "Is he a Moslem?"

He smiled. "He is not a Moslem. When I met him first I thought he was a Buddhist, at Damrey Phong. Now I don't know what he is."

I glanced at him. "I saw you praying with him there before the Buddha. I thought you were a Sikh."

He laughed. "I saw you, too, Mr Cutter. I thought you were a Christian."

"Oh, well …" And then I stopped, a bit embarrassed. I was about to say that that was different, and then it seemed to me to be a bit silly to say that. I didn't know what to say. It was infinitely quiet and blue and peaceful in the desert night.

"Perhaps," said my chief pilot presently, "he is just an ordinary man like you and I, who has the power to make men see the advantage of turning to God. As you have power to make men see the advantage of sending new tracks for a bulldozer by air."

It seemed a funny sort of way to look at things. "Maybe," I said vaguely. "The part that concerns me, of course, is the maintenance, and I'm bound to say I think that's going a lot better since he came."

"I think it will do so," Gujar said. We strolled on together for a while in silence. Presently he said, "People get into

116

such bad habits when they start to learn the techniques of the West."

"Bad habits?" I said.

He struggled to express himself in English. "I am not trying to be rude. You English and Americans have your own way of life, which is different to ours. I know you have your own codes of behaviour which are based upon the Christian religion, and very good they are. But you are not religious people, as we understand it in the Asiatic countries. Few of you pray to God in public or in private even once a week." He paused. "But God, and prayer to God, is necessary to us.

"When one of our boys starts to learn an English or American technique like the maintenance of aircraft," he said, "he learns from men who are materialistic in their way of life. He learns that science is the ruling force in the world, that every effect has a certain cause. Only when men are old and wise can they begin to see the Power of God even behind these things of science, and our young men are neither old nor wise. They see that railways run and ships steam and aeroplanes fly without the help of God. So they abandon God and turn to science, and then, because religion is necessary to us, they are bewildered."

He smiled. "I know what English pilots say about Asiatic ground engineers," he said. "I myself prefer to fly an aircraft serviced by a British engineer. With God taken from their way of life, our engineers become slovenly and irresponsible; they need a British or an American foreman who can check their work all the time if the aircraft are to be safe to fly. I think that Shak Lin understands this very well. He is showing your men that God is with them in the hangar, and making them turn to God for help in doing their work well. He is giving back to them the thing that has been taken from their lives. I think that you may find that in a year's time your ground engineers are as good or better than any English engineer." He laughed. "If that happens, you will have a maintenance staff that is unique in Asia, in more ways than one."

We went to bed soon after that. I let him go first, because in the cabin of the Carrier there was no privacy, and he had a lot to do with combing his long black hair, bandaging up his beard, and saying his prayers, that did not seem to be any concern of mine. I stood outside leaning against the tail of the aircraft, thinking about what he had said. I was starting to get an uneasy feeling that there was more in this business than operating the aircraft and cutting the costs and charging enough to show a decent profit. There were things going on that I didn't really understand, and though they seemed to be beneficial, I found them worrying.

They did not become less worrying as time went on. The three months nominal hire of the Carrier came to an end and left me, of course, with a very substantial profit on its operation, for it was flying several hours every day. I had engaged in a protracted three-cornered negotiation to buy it in instalments, conducted by means of letters and cables to Dwight Schafter in prison in Batavia and to his attorney in Indianapolis. It wasn't an easy deal because they wanted dollars for it, and I could only pay in blocked sterling; however, they weren't in any position to sell it in America while it was his property, which gave me some advantage. We finally settled on a price of twenty-four thousand pounds for it, to be paid in equal instalments of a thousand pounds a month. At that it was a cheap aeroplane, and I was very well pleased.

In the hangar, after a month or two, there was a tendency for casual Arabs to drift in and sit about around the machines, especially in the afternoon when Connie was in the habit of talking to the men in the last hour of the day. Apparently these people came from Muharraq and even across the causeway from Bahrein for the sole purpose of listening to what was going on in the hangar and saying their prayers with the party afterwards. The aerodrome was an RAF station and there was a guard on the road, but so many Arabs were employed about the camp that there was never any difficulty about getting in. There was the obvious danger that tools would be stolen, and apart from that the people were a nuisance to the work.

I had a talk with Connie about it in the office one day. "We'll have to keep them out," I said. "I don't want to be unreasonable, but we can't have all these bodies round the aircraft."

He nodded. "I quite agree. I'll get a notice put up on a board, in Arabic. Then we'll string a cord across the mouth of the hangar, and have one of the labourers on guard. But I'm afraid they'll probably come all the same. You won't mind if they come and sit outside the hangar, behind the rope?"

"I don't mind what they do so long as they don't come into the hangar," I said. "What do they come for?"

"The engineers have been talking about the prayers we have after work," he said. "The people come to join in those."

"They walk all the way from Bahrein to say their prayers outside our hangar?"

"Yes," he said. "It's a bit of a novelty for them, you see."

"Well, it's all right with me," I told him, "so long as we keep them out of the hangar. I don't want the tools stolen."

He said, "Oh, they wouldn't do that."

"Says you."

"They wouldn't. All they want to do is to come here and pray. They wouldn't steal things from a mosque. I should be very much surprised if we lost anything."

"You mean, they come to our hangar as a mosque?"

"In a way."

"Well, I dunno," I said, a little at a loss. "Anyway, let's keep them out."

"I'll see to that." He got up to go, and then he said, "My mother died last week."

He had never mentioned his family to me at all; he was a queer, solitary man. "I say, I'm sorry about that," I said. "I'm very sorry indeed, Connie. Was that in San Diego?"

He nodded. "These things have to happen," he said quietly. "She had been ill for several months. My sister had been looking after her."

"I'm very sorry," I repeated. And then I said, "You've got just the one sister, haven't you?"

He nodded. "She lived with my mother."

"Not married?"

"No."

One has to try and help one's staff when they are in trouble, and I had known Connie since I was a boy. "What's she going to do?" I asked. "Does she work there?"

He nodded. "She's got quite a good job. She's a secretary with an American export firm – Collins and Sequoia Inc. She speaks and writes Chinese, you see."

"Shorthand typist?"

He nodded.

"Too bad you've got to live on opposite sides of the world," I said. "If she'd like to join you here, I'll give her a try-out in the office for a couple of months. No hard words if she doesn't suit, though, and the job comes to an end after two months." I had never had a shorthand typist, and though the Babu clerk was good up to a point, the correspondence was always on top of us. A semi-Asiatic girl might be the answer.

He said, "That's good of you, Tom. I don't know that she'd fit in here, but I'll certainly write and put it to her."

I nodded. "Do that, Connie. I'd like to help if I can. And I'm damn sorry about your mother. I really am."

The rope across the mouth of the hangar and the notice in Arabic did the trick all right. Most afternoons people used to collect outside the hangar at about four o'clock; they would squat down on their heels in the shade beside the rope and look at what was going on inside, and listen to what they could. On some afternoons there were as many as twenty of them, mostly elderly men. They were quite orderly and never made any trouble. For Moslems there is extra virtue in prayer as a congregation, and these chaps used to sit around until the engineers knocked off, and then they would all go together to the bit of vacant land beside the hangar and do their *Rakats* in a group, Connie kneeling a little way apart. The Chinese, Chai Tai Foong, took to coming to the prayer meeting after a bit; he was not a Moslem and he knelt apart behind Connie.

I used to keep an eye on what went on in the hangar in the afternoons because it all seemed a bit difficult to me; however much work I had on my desk on the days when I wasn't flying, I usually took a stroll down to the hangar about that time. I did this one afternoon about a month after the rope went up and found a big new Hudson saloon parked just by the rope and four very well-dressed Arabs squatting by the rope a little apart from the crowd, looking at what was going on inside. One of these men was very old. I knew him and one of the others by sight; it was the Sheikh Abd el Kadir and his Wazir, Hussein.

There is a great big barren island by Bahrein which is the Sheikhdom of Khulal. It's practically all desert, with a few tiny hamlets scattered round the coasts where fishermen and pearl divers live. The place is about a hundred miles long and fifty or sixty across, but it is quite waterless and uninhabited in the middle. I suppose there may be six or seven thousand Arabs in the whole Sheikhdom, about three thousand of whom live on the east coast in the one place that can be called a town, the capital, Baraka. There is an airstrip there marked out upon the desert with small cairns of stones painted white, and in Baraka, Sheikh Abd el Kadir had his palace, about a hundred miles as the crow flies from Bahrein.

Khulal produces a little dried fish, a few pearls of poor quality, a negligible quantity of dates, and a vast amount of crude oil. The Arabia–Sumatran Company have a field of oil wells near the south-west corner of the island and a refinery at a place on the west side called Habban; there is a pier here to which the tankers come, and a town of modern, standardised houses where about a thousand Europeans live. They pay a royalty to the Sheikh for every barrel of his oil they take away, and I had heard various opinions of his income from this source. Some said he had an income of a million pounds a year, but others said that it was nothing like so much as that, not more than three hundred thousand. Whatever his financial position was, the old man had sufficient for his daily needs, considering that he paid no taxes whatsoever. He lived quite modestly in a small palace just outside Baraka, white and rococo, and surrounded by a grove of date palms. I had flown a new Packard to him in the Carrier a month or two before, and had met the Prime Minister, Hussein. Now there they all were, sitting gravely before the rope that kept them out of the hangar, trying to hear what was going on inside.

I didn't quite know what to do, but I walked up to them and smiled at Hussein, who got up from the ground to meet me. The others looked up and rose too, even the old Sheikh. I said, "This is a great honour, Mr Hussein. The rope wasn't meant to keep *you* out."

He smiled, and bowed, and then, speaking in Arabic, he introduced me to the Sheikh, who bowed to me. I said in my halting Arabic, "So many people come to hear what Shak Lin says to the engineers that we have had to put up this rope, or the men could not work. But if you want to hear more, will you not come inside?"

The old man replied, but he was very old and he mumbled so that with my poor knowledge of Arabic I couldn't understand him. I said, "Forgive me, I speak Arabic so badly," which was one phrase that I knew by heart.

Hussein said in English, "The Sheikh wishes very greatly to hear the Teacher, but he is rather deaf. It is very kind of you." I lifted the rope for them, and the four men moved majestically across the floor of the hangar, their long white skirts swishing with every step.

I could not take any part in their devotions or in their relations with Shak Lin. He was doing something with one of the engineers on the bench – checking the gap of a contact breaker, I think. I crossed to him and said, "Connie, this is the Sheikh of Khulal and his party. I've told them they can come into the hangar any time. Is that all right with you?"

He looked up. "I can deal with them."

"All right, then. I'll leave them with you." I took him forward with me and introduced him to the old Sheikh in my halting Arabic, and they bowed to each other, and then I said that I had a great deal of work waiting for me in my office, and went away. I felt at the time that it was cowardice, but it was a situation that I really couldn't cope with at all. When I looked out after the men had knocked off, there was the Sheikh and his party outside the hangar with the rest of them, going through the *Rakats*, but a little to one side of the crowd. Later they got into the Hudson and drove off.

They didn't come to the aerodrome again, that I know of, but Connie used to go to them, usually on Friday, which is the Moslem day of prayer. He made these visits to Baraka at irregular intervals, sometimes once a month and sometimes at less frequent intervals than that. Baraka, although only a hundred miles away, is pretty inaccessible; there is no post or telegraph service, and no regular boat service or land transport. I always knew when he was going there because he came and booked the Fox-Moth and got one of the pilots to fly him over; he never learned to pilot a machine himself. I used to charge him the full rate for these trips, less ten per cent.

We went on steadily for some months after that, building up the business. I got a Proctor, a single-engined four-seat aircraft, cheap in Egypt as a replacement for the Fox-Moth, which was really much too slow and too short in range for the work we put it to in the Persian Gulf. We kept the Fox-Moth in commission for short trips about Bahrein, and the two Air-trucks were working steadily, but the bulk of the turnover, of course, was done by the Carrier. I charged sixty pounds an hour for the Carrier, which came to about a penny for every pound weight carried a hundred miles, and at that the machine was working practically to capacity all over the Persian Gulf and far beyond. In those months I took on another Sikh pilot, a chap called Kahan Singh.

I still did the longest trips upon the Carrier myself, though Gujar normally now flew it as chief pilot, with one of the others with him as copilot. We got a big job for the Carrier one day, to fly to Burma. The Arabia–Sumatran Oil Company had interests in the oilfields at Yenanyaung in central Burma and had a load of machinery to send there from Bahrein; the return load was to be a number of the European staff coming home on leave. These men were to ride home as far as Bahrein in the Carrier, and would go on to England or to Holland by the normal airlines.

I took the Carrier upon this trip myself, with Arjan Singh; I wanted to see how Arjan carried on before approving him as the chief pilot of the Carrier in Gujar's absence. I used this as a training flight, in fact, and sat in the copilot's seat all the way, making Arjan act as captain of the aircraft as well as doing all the navigation and the radio. I only helped him when it was physically impossible for him to be doing two jobs at the same time. I made him do all the formalities upon the ground – the manifests, the Customs clearances, the immigration formalities, the flight plans – everything.

He got on all right, of course; he had, in fact, a good many more hours flying experience than I had myself, and on more types. But one likes to be certain, and he didn't know the route beyond Calcutta.

While cruising across Baluchistan and India upon this journey, in the long hours of sitting relatively idle in the copilot's seat while Arjan Singh did all the work, I had leisure to consider my business as a whole. The various oil companies in the Persian Gulf were growing accustomed to the use of a large freight aircraft in their daily work, and I was offering the service to them at an economic rate. It would not have paid them, individually, to keep such a large machine as a Carrier for their private use, but amongst the lot of them there was more than enough work for one such aeroplane. Much more. It was this aspect of the matter that was worrying me a bit. On this journey to Burma I was taking the Carrier away from the Gulf for a week; in that week the heavy air transport business would be at a standstill. Having accustomed them to the advantages of heavy air transport I could not expect them to tolerate that for long. I might have to get another large aeroplane, or there would be competition cropping up.

Moreover, this journey to Yenanyaung was only to be the first of many. The Arabia–Sumatran people had made that fairly clear to me. They had these interests in Burma, and they had their big establishment at Diento in Sumatra, which I had visited in the Airtruck. In addition, they were starting to develop an oilfield on the East Alligator River, about a hundred and fifty miles to the east of Darwin, in North Australia. These four oil centres formed a chain stretching from the Persian Gulf to Australia. Before the days of air transport each of these centres would have been equipped with the necessary scientific staff and laboratory and field scientific equipment for it to function entirely as a separate entity. With air transport, it was now becoming possible for the Arabia–Sumatran Company to transfer scientists and their equipment quickly and readily from one oilfield to another, and this they were doing in an increasing degree. There were obvious economic advantages to them in doing so, and they were quite prepared to use my organisation for the transport job. It meant, however, that if one large aeroplane was to be cruising most of its time between Australia and the Persian Gulf, I should have to have another for the day-to-day business at Bahrein.

To buy another Cornell Carrier would be out of the question; I should never get an allocation of the dollars. It would have to be a British aeroplane, and the Plymouth Tramp was the obvious British counterpart. The Tramp was about the same size as the Carrier and had certain advantages in easy loading; I knew that I could use a Tramp very profitably if I could add one to my fleet. The trouble was the purely mechanical business of paying for it, always a bugbear.

A new Tramp cost about fifty-five thousand pounds, and of course I hadn't got a hope of raising such a sum. It was too much to expect that I should find another gun-runner operator of a Tramp on his way to prison, and though I could try for a second-hand Tramp I very much doubted if there were any on the market. I wasn't sure what sort of a reception I should get from the Plymouth Aircraft Company if I went along as an individual, Tom Cutter, with very little money to put down upon the table, and asked for an expensive aeroplane upon hire-purchase terms without any guarantees or backing whatsoever. The Plymouth Aircraft Company were a very large and powerful concern, full of the most important work, with no need to scratch for orders or to provide finance for small operators wanting to use their products. I had a notion that I should be shown the door pretty quick if I went to their sales department with the only sort of proposition I could offer.

All these matters occupied my mind as I sat idly in the copilot's seat from Bahrein to Rangoon. We left about midday one day and made Karachi in one hop, making a night landing there at about seven o'clock. We slept at the airport and flew on early next day across India to Calcutta, and on the morning of the third day we flew to Rangoon down the coast of Arakan and crossing the Arakan Yoma south of the island of Ramree. We landed at Mingadon airport about midday.

That day was a Saturday and there was trouble at Rangoon because all the Government's civil servants were on strike. This included the Customs officers, and Mingadon airport was in confusion. The police were very active and there were two other charter aircraft full of freight parked under a police guard when we got there, delayed until the Customs officers resumed work and could clear them. Passenger aircraft were allowed to function normally; it was the freight that they were interested in. The Control officer explained the position to me quite politely; I must park my aircraft under guard alongside the other two. They hoped to make arrangements to clear them all on Monday.

When travelling in the East one has to keep one's temper and take things as they come. I parked the aircraft where they said and locked it up, and rang up the Arabia–Sumatran office in Rangoon, twelve miles away. They said that one of their staff would come straight out to the aerodrome, and asked if we wanted hotel accommodation in Rangoon. I said I'd rather stay out at the aerodrome; I never like sleeping very far from the aircraft in a foreign country.

The representative of the oil company in Rangoon, a Scotsman called Macrae, turned up three-quarters of an hour later in a Chevrolet and found Arjan Singh and me at lunch in the airport restaurant. He was a pleasant young chap. He apologised to us for the delay and promised to report on the demurrage to the Bahrein office, because this affected the charter fee. He said that he had ascertained from the Customs that all aircraft would be cleared on Monday morning. In the meantime he would be delighted to show us Rangoon. He quite understood that we preferred to sleep at the aerodrome near the aircraft, but would we dine at his home that night if he sent a car for us? And then tomorrow, Sunday, he would take us to the Shwe Dagon pagoda and show us that.

It really was very good of him. I told him that we had some work to do on the machine that afternoon, but we would be delighted to dine with him that evening. He went away then, and we fetched our small luggage from the aircraft and took it to the aerodrome rest house. Then we refuelled the Carrier and looked for a small oil leak on the starboard engine and put that right. I used the last of the locking wire in the tool kit on that job. While Arjan was polishing the windscreens, putting away the maps, and making all tidy in the cockpit, I strolled over to the hangar that housed the aircraft of the Burmese National Airways to see if they could let me have a hank of locking wire from their stores.

One of the first men that I saw in the hangar was U Myin, the Burmese boy who had been with Dwight Schafter and Connie at Damrey Phong. He was working on the port engine of a Dove. He recognised me at once, and he was very pleased to see me. He seemed more upstanding and competent to look at than I had remembered him, but he had very little more English at his command than he had had then. He understood technical words, of course, and when he understood I wanted locking wire he left his job and took me up to the office of the chief engineer, Moung Bah Too.

Moung Bah Too was a friendly and smiling young Burmese who spoke perfect English. He listened to what U Myin had to say to him in Burmese, and then said to him in English, "Of course." He turned to me. "I think we have eighteen gauge and twenty-two gauge wire. Eighteen gauge? All right." To U Myin he said, "Go to the storekeeper and ask him for about a pound of eighteen gauge galvanised iron wire, and bring it back here."

The boy went off, and Bah Too offered me a cigarette. "It's really very kind of you," I said. "It's not fair to come in and want supplies like this. I hope that I'll be able to do something for you in the Persian Gulf one day."

He smiled, and we talked about our operations and compared notes for a few minutes. Presently I said, "How's U Myin getting on?"

"Oh, he is very good," his chief said. "A very good engineer. He is reliable; you can trust that work is well done if he says it is all right."

"I'm glad to hear that," I said. "I'd have taken him on myself when Dwight Schafter packed up, but for the fact that he couldn't speak much English. At that time I was running the ground engineers myself, so all the people I took on had to know English fairly well."

He nodded. "I think he was very well trained when he was with Schafter," he said. "You have a chief engineer, have you not – a Chinese called Shak Lin?"

"Yes," I said. "He was with Schafter, too. He's not exactly a Chinese, though. He's a British subject born in Penang, of a Chinese father and a Russian mother. He went to school in England."

"Is that so!" There was keen interest now upon the wide, intelligent brown face before me. "I had often wondered who he was."

"You've heard of him, then?"

"Oh yes, I have heard of him many times. U Myin talks to me and to the other engineers about him constantly, in the workshop, about his methods of teaching and inspection. In Bangkok, too, they talk of him a great deal, with Siamese Airways. I have two or three engineers from Bangkok working for me now."

I had not thought that Connie would be so well known, yet it was reasonable enough, because he was a man to be remembered, and the aviation world was small.

"He is religious, is he not?" There was no mistaking the interest that Moung Bah Too was showing.

"Yes," I said. "He's very religious."

"Tell me, what religion does he teach? Is he a Buddhist, do you know?"

It was the same question that I had asked myself several times before. "I don't know what he is," I said. "I don't think he's a Buddhist because he talks about God. You don't do that, do you?" He shook his head. "He's certainly not a Moslem, although he talks a lot about God to the Moslems in the hangar at Bahrein. I shouldn't say he's much of a Christian. I'm afraid I can't tell you what he is."

"I have heard it said," Bah Too observed, "that he has the power to make men of any religion bring that religion to their daily work upon the aircraft, and the results are very good."

"I think that's fair enough," I said slowly. "I should think that's the best definition that you'd get of what he does."

"It is very, very interesting," he said earnestly. "I am not religious myself. When U Myin and two other men came one day to this office and asked if they might set up that Buddha that you see in the hangar – " I had not noticed it, " – I did not know what to say. In England, in the de Havilland Technical School where I served for five years, you do not put a Cross up in the hangar, and I run this hangar in the way that I was taught." My heart warmed to this little brown man, whose problems had been so very similar to my own. He laughed. "I did not know what to do," he said. "In the end I told them that they might put it up, but no time was to be spent in prayer in working hours."

It might have been myself, telling somebody about my own difficulties in Bahrein. "What have the results been like?" I asked. "Does it help the work?"

"It is very good," he said seriously. "It is a very good thing. They pray before and after each shift, for five minutes or less than that. They say a few verses from the Payehtgyee, our litany of praise, and then they say a prayer that Shak Lin taught U Myin in Damrey Phong, about the aircraft, that Right Thinking is indicated in Right Work, and Right Work in Right Thinking, because both are one. By his teaching, Right Meditation, which leads to Nirvana, is only attained by the exercise of Right Work. No man cumbered with error in the Work can reach the state of Right Meditation, which is the approach to what you would call Heaven. I do not know if you are used to these ideas, but I can tell you this. Since U Myin introduced them to my hangar, the standard of maintenance of the aircraft has improved enormously."

I nodded. "I've had the same experience," I said. "I'm a Christian myself, of course, but most of the ground staff at Bahrein are Moslems. Shak Lin teaches them the same sort of thing in my hangar, but conforming to the Moslem code, so it's all a bit different. But as regards the results, I must say they're very good indeed. My people have got more responsible since he took over the hangar than ever they were under me."

He nodded. "It is the same here. I think this new teaching is a very good thing." He smiled. "The only complaint I have is that it is spreading. Most of our engineers now join in the prayers before the Buddha in the hangar. The transport drivers have been coming along, too. That is all right for our own transport drivers, but lately all sorts of other people have been coming to the hangar to pray with the engineers – transport drivers from the other companies, and from the petrol companies, and even taxi-drivers – they have been coming in. I cannot have all these people coming into the hangar. I do not quite know what to do about it."

"I had to put a rope up," I said. I told him what had been going on in Bahrein and we compared notes for a few minutes. Then U Myin came back with the locking wire. His chief took it and gave it to me, and I asked how much I should pay for it, and he smiled and said that he was glad to be able to help. I thanked him. During this U Myin was standing by the door, although Bah Too had indicated that he could go, but now he said laboriously,

"Mr Cutter, he stay two, three days?"

"Till Monday, anyway," I said. "I can't get Customs clearance until then, because of this strike."

He said, "English pongyi ..." but then his English broke down, and he turned to Bah Too, and began speaking in Burmese. His chief listened to him, nodding now and then, occasionally putting in a question. Presently he turned to me.

"He says that one of our monks living just outside Rangoon is an Englishman," he told me. "He is a very holy man. He has been a Buddhist monk, a pongyi we call them, for over thirty years. He is a very old man now, and he will not live for very much longer. His name is U Set Tahn. He has heard about Shak Lin. This boy wants to take you to see this monk, in order that you may tell him more about Shak Lin. Would you like to do that?"

"I don't mind a bit," I said. "I've got nothing much to do tomorrow, so far as I know."

U Myin understood English much better than he could speak it, because I saw his face light up when I said that, and I wondered what I was letting myself in for. Bah Too said, "It would probably be a great kindness if you can spare the time."

I got out a pencil and an old envelope and wrote the name down on the back of it, with Bah Too's help, U Set Tahn. "That is a Burmese name, of course," he said. "It means, Mr Rainbow." He spoke to the boy, but neither of them knew what the old man's English name had been.

I fixed up to meet U Myin at the office of the airline in Rangoon at three o'clock on the following afternoon and they gave me the address, in Montgomery Street, near the Sulei Pagoda Road.

I drove into Rangoon that evening dressed in a clean suit of whites to dine with the Macraes, with Arjan Singh with me in a neat grey suit and a red and gold embroidered turban, looking like a robber baron in full dress. They had an English couple to meet us, and we had a very Surbiton sort of a dinner party; but for Arjan and the two boys who served us we might have been thousands of miles away from the East. They were very kind and hospitable people, keeping up the English way of life meticulously, far from home. I asked them if they knew this English pongyi, U Set Tahn. Macrae had vaguely heard at some time that there was such a person, but it was news to the rest of the party that any Englishman in Rangoon was living as a Buddhist monk, and there was a marked indication that he was letting down the side by doing so. I didn't pursue the subject, beyond saying that I had promised to go and visit him the next afternoon. Nobody offered to come with me.

Arjan Singh had made a date for Sunday with a countryman of his own, a Sikh pilot of Indian National Airways that he had met during the war in the Royal Indian Air Force. I drove into Rangoon on Sunday morning, a long, interesting drive past lakes bordered by flame trees, very beautiful. The Macraes took me round the Shwe Dagon pagoda in our stockinged feet, and I marvelled. Then we went back to their house and changed our socks and had a drink, and went down to the Strand Hotel for them to have lunch with me. Then they left me, very kindly putting their car and driver at my disposal for the afternoon, and I went out to meet U Myin.

I picked him up at the airline office, and we drove out together northwards from Rangoon. He knew where the old man lived, and gave the driver the instructions in Burmese. We went out about six or seven miles, past the lakes, and came to a country district where the good class suburban bungalows standing in their gardens were merging into farm land and the palm thatch houses on posts of the poorer Burmese peasants. Here we drove down a side road and stopped the car and got out. A little-used footpath led through the scrub up on to a small hill with a few palms rising above the lower trees on top. "This way to ashram," U Myin said. "English pongyi live here."

He led the way, and I followed him up the path past a farmhouse; in this place that was wholly in the East I was queerly reminded of Cornwall, for there little farms lie close beneath small hills in just the same way. We went up the hill between the bushes and came to a small palm thatch house on top, shaded by the palm trees, all rather tumbledown and decaying. We stood by this and called up to it, because like all these houses it stood on posts and the floor was five or six feet from the ground, reached by a rough ladder. A very old man came to the door and looked down on us.

His head and face were shaven clean, and he wore only the coarse yellow robe of a monk. He listened to U Myin for a minute, and then said, "Good afternoon. It is very kind of you to come to visit me. Will you come up?"

We climbed up into the house. It had an inner and an outer room, all very poor. In the inner room there was a bed with a mosquito net, in the outer room a broken deck-chair, a wooden stool, a table with a few tattered books upon it, and little else. The old man made me take the deck-chair and he sat upon the stool; U Myin squatted on the floor beside us.

I knew enough about the East, of course, not to approach the subject of my visit directly. I had all afternoon and evening to spare, and it was for him to raise the subject of Shak Lin when he wanted to. I said that I was passing through Rangoon and had heard that he was living there, and had come to visit him to see if there was anything that I could do for him, or bring to him from other countries. I explained that my aircraft were likely to be passing through Rangoon fairly frequently.

He was a pleasant, and a matter-of-fact old man, whose manner contrasted oddly with his way of life. He told me that he had few needs, but under a little pressure he confessed that he wanted one thing, a British Admiralty Nautical Almanac. Astrology enters largely into Buddhist religious life, and he was hampered in his studies of the World to Come by the fact that his Nautical Almanac was out of date and he could not forecast the positions of the stars and planets upon any given day. I promised to get him that, and we talked of unimportant things for over an hour before he raised the subject of Shak Lin.

The old man had been a Colonel Maurice Spencer in the Royal Army Service Corps in the First World War, and had come to India after that for the prosaic job of organising a service of lorries in Bengal. Within two years he had become a Buddhist and had achieved a small circle of Indian Buddhist friends in Calcutta, where he must have been a great grief to the English official and business community. Presently his friends told him that they were going out as monks to walk through Bengal villages for a month, and they proposed that as some leave was due to him he should put on the red robe, red for Buddhist priests in India, and get a begging bowl, and come with them. It had been as simple as that.

He had come back from that walk, settled up his Western affairs, and had put on the Buddhist robe again for good. He had walked on foot across India and down into Ceylon, eating only what the pious put into his bowl as he walked through the village, silent, every morning. I asked what happened if they didn't put anything in, and he said that that had never happened. There was always more than he could eat. Each day he would walk on to the next village and sit talking with the elders under the village tree, giving what advice to them in local problems that he could, helping spiritually where he was able. One by one they would slip away to bed till he was left alone beneath the tree in the night; he was too holy a man to share their houses. When all were gone, he said, he would hunt about for somewhere to sleep himself. If there was a temple he would wrap his robe around him, and curl up and go to sleep in a corner of that, but you had to be careful of the snakes, which sought the warmth of a body on the cold stone floor. If there was no temple, he would go out into the country and find a haystack, or else go to sleep in the lee of a hedge. He had never come to any harm in many years of this life, though he had had fever often enough. He had walked across India and down into Ceylon, and all over Ceylon, and back up India and into Burma, in the course of ten or twelve years. He had come to rest there on the outskirts of Rangoon and had found this place, where the people had built the ashram, or small monastery, for him. When it needed repair or rebuilding, the villagers would make a day of it in a gang, and rebuild it for him. He had three or four small boys that he called his disciples; they came to him each morning and together they all walked out through the district for an hour or so with begging bowls held before them, eyes cast down, never looking to the left or the right, never speaking. The people brought out food and filled their bowls. They would return and eat, and for the rest of the day he would instruct the boys in reading and writing the Buddhist scriptures in the Pali script. At evening the boys went back to their homes.

I asked if he had ever been back to England, and he said, once, in 1936, but he found the world set upon the wrong course and was glad to return to his quiet ashram on the outskirts of Rangoon. I asked him what he wore in England, and he said, "Well, that's a damn-fool question. Do you think I walk down Piccadilly looking like this?" One could ask him anything.

A monk, he told me in explanation of his poverty, may possess only a few articles – the robe, the bowl, the drinking cup, the spectacles if he needs them, the sunshade, the needle, the fan with which he shields his eyes from the sight of women. As he was a friendly and a candid old man I asked about his mosquito net and his deck-chair, to which he replied that they were weaknesses of the flesh that he could not do without, which meant that he was not a very good man. There seemed to be no answer to that one.

Presently, as we sat talking easily about these things, he turned the conversation to Shak Lin. "U Myin has told me that you have a man working for you, a remarkable man," he said.

"He told me that you wanted to know about him," I replied. "He's my chief engineer. His name is Shak Lin."

"And he is remarkable?"

I hesitated. "Probably not, to you. In England, people would say that he was mad. I say that he's a fine engineer, who makes men reliable by bringing religion to their daily work. You can take it any way you like."

He nodded and sat in thought for a minute, stooping to scratch a brown and rather dirty leg with a lean, skinny hand. His legs and feet were covered in old scars. "I had heard of that," he said. "U Myin has given me some information, but several people have been talking to me about him."

"Have they?"

"Indeed they have. He made a great impression on the monks in Bangkok. An Arab merchant from Aden came here to Rangoon a month or two ago and told one of my religious friends about the teaching that was going on in Bahrein. A Parsee from Karachi told us the same story. And then came U Myin who had actually been taught by this man, and who was teaching others at the airport out at Mingadon, as one of his disciples. And now you come, who know more than anyone, perhaps."

"Well," I said. "What can I tell you, father? I'm not a very religious man myself, but I'll tell you anything I can."

He said, "Do you know where he was born?"

It was a question that I was not prepared for. "No, I don't," I said. "I think it was in Penang, but I can't say for certain. His father was Chinese and a British subject, I think. Shak Lin himself is certainly British. His mother was a Russian."

He looked up quickly. "A Russian? From what part of Russia?"

A vague memory of the idle chatter of boys in Cobham's air circus stirred my mind. "I seem to remember that she came from Irkutsk."

He got up from the stool and went to the table with the books on it. He had a tattered school atlas there, a little cheap thing such as children use in a council school. He stood there fingering it with fingers that trembled a little, a bowed old man with bare legs and feet, in this coarse, blanket-like yellow robe thrown over one shoulder, leaving the other skinny shoulder bare. He stood staring at the map of Asia for a time, and then closed the book and put it down.

He came back to me, and sat down on the stool again. "Do you know the date of his birth, and the hour?" he asked.

I shook my head. "I'm afraid not, father. I don't even know how old he is. I've always supposed he was about the same age as myself. I think he is, within a year or so."

"How old are you?" he asked.

"I'm thirty-three."

"So you were born in the year 1915?"

"That's right," I said.

He sat in silence for a long time after that. I shot a glance or two at him after a time. His head was shaking in the way that very old people do; it seemed to me that he was getting very tired. I had been with him for something like an hour and a half. I glanced at U Myin, and in his return look it seemed that he agreed with me; it was time we went away.

I broke the silence presently, after at least ten minutes. "Father," I said, "I think it's time we went home now, and left you to rest. I'll come again one day, if I may. And I'll send the Nautical Almanac as soon as I can get one out from England."

"Stay for a minute," he said. "I have things to tell you."

He sat in silence again, and I waited.

At last he said, "I know that you are not a religious man. I will put what I have to tell you in words as simple as I can make them. Men are weak, and sinful, and foolish creatures. When they are given something that is beautiful and good they can recognise it and they venerate it, but gradually they spoil it. Infinite wisdom, infinite purity, and infinite holiness cannot be passed from hand to hand by mortal men down through the ages without being spoiled. Errors and absurdities creep in and mar the perfect vision. All the religions of the world have become debased. According to the present code of this religion I may not take life, yet I may eat meat if somebody else kills it and puts the cooked meat in my bowl. You Christians have similar absurdities; you have a curious ceremony in which you eat your God. The Moslems fast, which is a stupid thing to do, and they

139

give far too much thought to the outward forms of prayer and pilgrimage."

He paused. "Every religion in the world requires to be refreshed from time to time by a new Teacher. Gautama, Mahomet, Jesus – these are some of the great Teachers of the past, who have refreshed men's minds and by their lives and their example brought men back to Truth. We are very far from the truth now, far enough here, even farther in the West. Belsen and Buchenwald exceeded any horrors of the war here in the East. But we are all in this together, wandering, far, far from the Truth."

He raised his head. "This thing is beyond the power of ordinary men to put right," he said. "We must look for the new Teacher. One day the Power that rules the Universe will send us a new Teacher, who will lead us back to Truth and help us to regain the Way. There have been four Buddhas in the history of this world, of whom Gautama was the last. One day a fifth will come to aid us, if we will attend to Him. Here in Burma we earnestly await His coming, for He is the Hope of the World."

I sat silent while he rambled on. He was putting into words things that I had resolutely kept in the background of my mind, in little cups that I hoped might pass from me.

"We know a little of the Teacher from our sacred learning, based upon the movements of the Celestial Universe," he said. "We know that He is very near to us in time. We think He is already born. We think that His birthplace is somewhere in that corner of the continent of Asia where Tibet and Russia and China meet. We think that He will be of a mixed eastern and western stock. We think that this man is the Saviour of the World."

I moistened my lips. "Do you know where He is going to teach, father?"

"That has not been revealed," he said. "The only certain fact we know is that His ministry will last for four years and twenty-three days."

He was silent again, and when I looked at him he was sitting with his eyes closed, perhaps in some kind of a trance, perhaps asleep. I glanced at U Myin and got his agreement; we got up to go. The old man never stirred. I waited for a minute, but there seemed to be no point in staying any longer or disturbing him, and after a time we climbed down the ladder and went back to the car.

CHAPTER FIVE

Oh, Threats of Hell and Hopes of Paradise!
One thing alone is certain, that Life flies:
    One thing is certain, and the rest is lies:
The flower that once has blown for ever dies.

EDWARD FITZGERALD:
Rubaiyat of Omar Khayyám

I GOT BACK to Bahrein about four days after that, after taking my load up to Yenanyaung. I landed back at our base with eighteen passengers from the Burma oilfield late one evening. I went into the office before going to the chummery and found, as I had suspected, that we had had to turn away or to postpone a number of important transport jobs for the various oil companies, due to the fact that the Carrier had been absent from the district for nine days. Clearly, I couldn't go on doing business in that way.

I had a talk about it to Connie and Gujar Singh in my office next day. Ours was a personal business, and all the decisions and responsibilities were mine, but I had got into the way of talking things over informally with my chief pilot and my chief engineer whenever difficult decisions had to be made. I had them in now, and told them how we were placed.

"We can't go on like this," I said. "We've brought this business into being by offering air transport to the oil companies, and now they're offering more business than we can cope with. I'm going to try and get another big aeroplane, and I think it'll have to be a Plymouth Tramp. We'd never get the dollars for another Carrier, even if we'd got the sterling, which we haven't."

We talked about the Tramp for a time. They both liked the idea; indeed, Gujar Singh said roundly that he'd rather have a Tramp for our business than another Carrier. Connie was in favour of a Tramp, but concerned at the diversity of spares that we would have to carry for another aircraft of another type. There was a great deal in what he said; already we were operating five aircraft of four different types, and if we got a Tramp we should have six aircraft of five types.

"I'll see if I can sell that Fox and get another Proctor," I said. "That makes it a bit better."

A Tramp it would have to be, and I told them then about my money difficulty. "There's nothing wrong with the business," I said. "But all the profits are taken for the time being by the instalments that I'm paying on the Carrier. All of our profit's going into that, till May next year. The most that I can raise in cash at present is about five thousand pounds, and that's less than ten per cent of the cost of a Tramp. I don't believe the Plymouth people would let us have a Tramp for that."

Gujar never forgot his banking experience, and he was quite useful at times like this. "You have sufficient assets for a considerable loan," he said. "I do not think the Bank here would advance much because aviation enterprises are not quite their business. But they would certify whatever was required to an industrial bank in London. You have a very good name in Bahrein."

We talked about that for a time. It meant a trip to England, but that was necessary in any case for the negotiations about the Plymouth Tramp; I did not then know what amount of capital I needed. What Gujar said was probably quite right, but the idea of going trailing round from office to office in the City of London trying to find somebody to lend me fifty thousand pounds or so at some crippling interest rate was not one that I relished. From the point of view of the business it was wrong, utterly wrong from start to finish. Inevitably it meant a big mortgage or debenture held by some stranger, Gentile or Jew, whose interests would be purely financial and possibly divergent from my own, who would have to be consulted whenever I took a chance, who would have to be argued with when things went wrong. Not a happy outlook, and it worried me a lot. I didn't see what else I could do, however.

I pointed out these disadvantages to them. "If I boob on this one it'll mean the finish of the business," I said. "I'm not taking any bouquets for what we've done up to date. We've done it all together. But there's one basic factor that's been at the bottom of our success, and that is that the man who controls the money has been working out here on the job – that's me. If the money control had been by an accountant in a London office, we'd have been bust long before this. And that's just what may happen to us, if we don't look out."

They saw that point, and we broke up the meeting with nothing decided on the financial point. I hung about at Bahrein for a week although I should have been in London looking for money. I could not bring myself to start on what I knew to be a wrong road, and I stuck around at Bahrein flying the Carrier on local day flights, trying to think of some better finance, moody and bad-tempered. I had got myself into a jam, and I couldn't see how to get out of it.

I came in from Ras Mushaab one evening in the Carrier with a three-ton truck on board with a broken differential for repair. As I passed the hangar on the circuit before landing I saw a big maroon car outside my office that looked like the Hudson that Sheikh Abd el Kadir kept in Bahrein,

144

and I wondered if the old man had taken to coming up to the hangar again to say his prayers. I landed and taxied in and stopped the motors, and Connie came forward from the hangar and met me as I got out of the cabin door.

"Wazir Hussein's waiting in the office to see you," he said.

"Hussein? What does he want?"

He hesitated. "I went over to Baraka on Friday," he said. "I go there sometimes to pray with Sheikh Abd el Kadir, and to talk to his Imam. I told them you were thinking of getting another big aircraft."

I stared at him. "Did you tell them that I hadn't got any money to pay for it?"

He nodded. "I think that Hussein may have come with a proposal."

"For Christ's sake!" I said.

He smiled. "I don't see what's wrong with that. It's local money and that's better than London money." That was true enough; if it came to a choice between having an Arab sheikh in the business or a London accountant who had never been out of England, I'd choose the sheikh. "There's just one thing," Connie said. "Watch what you say about interest, if they should offer a loan. They never take interest, you know. They're very strong against usury. It would be very easy to offend them by asking what rate of interest they want."

I left him to organise the unloading of the truck from the Carrier, and walked across to where Hussein was standing by his car outside my office, a grave, bearded figure in the Arab dress – white headcloth bound with two black cords, and a long white under-robe with a wide skirt, and a long coat of a light black linen, gold-embroidered, open down the front. He wore a plain leather belt with a gold-hilted curved dagger stuck into it, with a richly chased sheath. He bowed as I came up, and I said, "I'm so sorry to have kept you waiting, Wazir. Shak Lin says that you are waiting to see me."

He smiled, and said, "I know how hard you work." He spoke very good English. Somebody once told me that as a young man he had been at Cambridge.

We went into the office and sat down together, and I sent the boy to get coffee from the airport bar. Till it came we talked of general things, the weather, the state of the date crop, the irrigation schemes that the Sheikh had in hand around Baraka, the yield from the pearl fishing, and how the Packard was behaving. Then the coffee came and we sipped it together; when the boy had left the room, the Wazir said, "My master, the Sheikh of Khulal, was told by Shak Lin, El Amin, that you are thinking of buying another large aeroplane."

I nodded. "That is true," and I went on to tell him why I had decided that I had to have it, that there was more work than we could handle and that if we didn't do it somebody else would. Two companies both operating in the same area might split the work so badly that both would be ruined, whereas if we kept it in our hands the business should go steadily ahead. "All the profit that we make goes back into the business," I said. "I take nothing for myself beyond my living expenses."

He nodded gravely. "My master has been told that you are having to resort to usurers to find the money for this aeroplane," he said. "I have explained to him that this is common in England and that no sin is involved on either side, out he has been very much distressed."

I said, "It's very nice of him to think of us like that. You know the processes of business in the West, Mr Hussein. I've got no feeling about paying interest, provided that it's reasonable. What worries me is that if I'm not careful this business may become controlled by those who lend me money, and I think that would be a disaster."

He smiled a little, and said, "All contact with sin is a disaster." There was a little silence then, and presently he said, "I do not want to be impertinent, Mr Cutter. My master has sent me to enquire if you need money for this aeroplane, as a loan. It seems very undesirable to him that you should fall into the hands of usurers."

There was another silence while I thought about this magnificent proposal. "First of all," I said, "will you tell the Sheikh of Khulal how very deeply touched I am by his consideration. It's true that I'm in a difficulty, but I've been in difficulties before and got over them." I paused. "I'm not sure if you realise the scale of the money that is involved. The price of this aeroplane is fifty-five thousand pounds." His face did not change, but then, he was an Arab. "Spare parts and equipment will be needed for it which will cost about another five thousand – say sixty-five thousand pounds in all. That's about eight lakhs of rupees. All I have in the bank at present is about five thousand. With such an aeroplane I can earn sufficient profit to pay off its cost in three or four years, so that in four years from now I should hope to be free from debt. But if some bad luck should come to the business that we cannot foresee, I could never hope to pay back such a loan from what I can earn upon a salary. No man could do that. If your master should lend money to me in this way and bad luck comes, another war or something terrible, that we cannot foresee, I may never be able to pay him back."

He inclined his head. "I understand that point. I will explain that to my master."

I said, "This is a personal business, Wazir. I am not a company, and no person but myself has any share in it. The aeroplanes are all my personal property." I thought for a minute. "I will get the accountant to make up an account of my assets to the end of last month, and I will show that to you. I think the book figure will be able to show that the aeroplanes and goods that I own are worth about fifteen thousand pounds, to which should be added the bank credit and the balance of the money that I am owed in trade, and the money that I owe. I think the total figure of my assets will be twenty-one or twenty-two thousand pounds, which would be available towards repayment of this loan if things should go very wrong. It means that if disaster came there would be a balance of thirty-five thousand pounds or so which your master would almost certainly lose. But, as I say, I will have the accountant make a statement of my assets and give you a copy."

He inclined his head. "It is my duty to guard the interests of my master, and I shall be glad to see it. I have never known him to be harsh with a debtor who was unable to pay his debt through no fault of his own."

I sat in thought for a time. "There's one point I'd better mention," I said. "It may be that in the next year or two I shall have to form the business into a number of small companies, one in India, one in Pakistan, one in Siam, one in Burma, and so on. That may be necessary in the future, because each country reasonably demands that profits which are earned in that country shall be retained in that country and spent in the country. I do not think that this affects the matter because I shall be the only shareholder, but complications of that nature may arise as the business grows."

He nodded. "It is an interesting point, but so long as all the property is owned by you I do not think my master would complain if some of it was in Siam and could not be transferred. Repayment of the loan should be made here in Bahrein, if possible."

"Of course," I said. We went on to discuss the details. They were apparently quite prepared to lend me sixty thousand pounds without interest, to be repaid over a period of four years at the rate of £1,250 a month. I told him that I would fly over to Baraka with the statement of my assets on the following Tuesday, and he said that he would have a document ready for my signature acknowledging the loan, in Arabic and in English, side by side. Then he got up to go, and I showed him to his car. He said, "May God protect you," and got in, and drove away.

I walked over to the hangar in a daze. Connie had gone home, probably to avoid me, but Gujar Singh had just come in in one of the Airtrucks, and I told him all about it as we walked up and down on the tarmac in the evening light. He was delighted with the news, of course, and he made two comments on it that were both shrewd and illuminating.

The first thing he said was, "This puts us on very firm ground with the Arabia–Sumatran Company."

I blinked in surprise. "How does that come into it?"

He smiled. "Their refinery at Habban. It's all his oil, the refinery is on his land, and they pay him the royalty. If they started giving air transport contracts to anybody else, the old Sheikh might lose sixty thousand pounds. They wouldn't want any trouble with the Sheikh."

It was a point, of course, a sort of discouragement to competition.

The second thing he said was, "Of course, it's a religious matter."

I walked with him in silence for a minute. Then I said, "Shak Lin?"

"Yes. You say he suggested it to them."

I shook my head. The mere idea that Connie would have used his religious influence with the old Sheikh to induce him to lend me money was utterly repugnant. "That's absolutely wrong," I said. "Shak Lin could never have done that." As I spoke, I wondered why I felt so positively about it. It was inconceivable.

"I don't say that," Gujar said slowly. "I think like you, he is too good a man. But this is a religious matter, all the same."

I was silent.

"It is too near a gift for it to be otherwise," he said. "You have told them, and they must have known before, that if things should go wrong you cannot pay this back. When Sheikh Abd el Kadir dies, he cannot leave a legacy to you or to me. By Moslem law he can only leave his money to his family, or he can leave a legacy for a religious purpose – to build a new mosque, or something like that. They are very strict about such things. Legacies are governed by *hadith*, based upon the Koran. He cannot even dispose of his money as he likes within the family; his children by his concubines share the inheritance equally with his legitimate family, boys two shares and girls one share. When this old man is dead he could not possibly leave money to you, and as he is so near death now, it would be most improper for him to make you a large gift, or even an unrepayable loan."

I wrinkled my brows. "Why is he doing it, then?"

He said, "I think he must have consulted with the Imam and the Majlis, and made this loan for a religious purpose."

We were getting into deep waters. "To buy me another aeroplane?"

"No. If I may say so, I do not think he cares if you, an Englishman and a Christian, possess another aeroplane or not. But usury in the business that employs Shak Lin ... that is another matter. To him this hangar is a very holy place, and you, and I, and everyone who works here down to Tarik and the babu clerk, we are all touched with holiness. If usury threatens us, it is a pious and a godly act on his part to step in and stop it, that the shrine may remain undefiled. He could devote his money to that purpose."

We walked on in silence. "Do you really think that that's the reason behind it?" I asked at last.

"I do. I think he has consulted with the Imam and the Majlis before doing this."

"I see ..."

150

I suppose he saw that I was worried, because after a time he said, "There is no harm in it, and no reason why you should not take his loan. I know it is unusual in the West for men to give large sums for a religious purpose. Perhaps it is more common in my country than in yours."

"Perhaps it is," I said. "It all wants a bit of thinking about." I left him soon after that, but I thought about it till the small hours of the morning in the hot, brilliant night. I had told Gujar Singh the whole story except two words, which I had kept to myself. Wazir Hussein had referred to Connie as El Amin. El Amin is Arabic, and it means 'He who is worthy of trust'. Not a bad name for a chief ground engineer, of course, except for the fact that it was one of the names of the Prophet.

I got the accountant on the job next day, and the figures came out just as I had expected. I thought them over for a bit. In a negotiated sale the business was probably worth more than the book value of the assets, but if some disaster were to force a sale the aircraft might not realise the book value. In the accounts I was writing everything off over five years. I added a note about this to the accounts suggesting an additional depreciation of twenty-five per cent on the aircraft in the case of a forced sale, and then I got into the Proctor and went over to Baraka.

I circled the palace and the Wazir's house before landing, and saw a car leave for the airstrip; then I landed and parked the aircraft as the car drove up. I got out and drove to the Wazir's house. Hussein came out to meet me at the door. It was a two-storeyed house built around a court; one side of this court was a blank, windowless wall behind which lay the harem. Hussein had his son and a secretary with him. He greeted me with a grave courtesy and took me up to a room with a balcony on the first floor; there was practically no furniture in this room except two wooden long chairs, a table, and a very beautiful carpet on the floor.

We sat down and he clapped his hands, and an Arab servant came with coffee. It was delightfully cool in that top room, with a sea breeze blowing through it. We talked of casual things for a time – the weather for flying, the design of the house, the condition of the airstrip, and presently I produced my accounts and explained them to him. "I don't want to conceal anything from you," I said. "This is the true position of the business as I understand it at the moment." I paused. "Please ask anything which may occur to you. I will tell you anything I can."

He asked a little bit about my forward contracts and about my relations with the Arabia–Sumatran Company, and I told him about the long-range work which was developing for them, which had made this new large aircraft necessary. Then he laid the accounts down, and smiled. "I do not think that there is anything further," he said, smiling. "My master knows of you as an honest man. The money is at your disposal when you need it, sixty thousand pounds. Have you a bank in Bahrein?"

"I've got an account with the Bank of Asia," I said. "If you would pay it into my account there, I should be most grateful. In that case I shall transfer most of it to a London bank at once and fly to England to place the order." I paused. "I can only tell you, what I think you know already, that your help is making things very easy for me."

He said, "That is my master's wish."

He told me that the Sheikh was anxious to meet me, and presently we went downstairs and walked a hundred yards or so down the lane to the palace. This was a white house standing in a garden of flowerbeds and date palms just outside the town. It was not very large as palaces go; it was arranged in two storeys around a courtyard and might have had about ten or twelve large rooms in all. It was in a sort of Moorish style with fretted wooden sun-shutters at the windows; there was rather a beautiful little mosque immediately adjacent to it in the garden.

I had been entertained by sheikhs a good many times since I had come to the Persian Gulf, and there was very little to distinguish this lunch party from many of the others. The old man met us at the door; he spoke no English, and I had to do the best I could in Arabic; from time to time the Wazir helped me by translating when I got stuck. He had a crowd of about fifteen of his ministers and hangers-on with him, and we sat around on hard chairs in a circle in an anteroom and made polite conversation until lunch was ready. Then we went through into the dining-room or whatever they call it, where the meal was prepared upon a table-cloth in the middle of the carpet on the floor – a huge pile of rice on an enormous dish with the best part of a sheep boiled and lying on top of it, all very greasy. I knew about this, of course, and had prepared for it by eating nothing that day, and very little the evening before. One goes into training for an Arab feast.

We sat down on the floor, myself next to the Sheikh, and washed our hands in the bowls that the negro servants brought round. Then the old man tore a bit of mutton off the carcase in the middle with his hands and put it on my plate, and a servant began to hand a multitude of side dishes to me, curries and mushrooms and truffles and dates in sweet syrup and Lord knows what. I'm always very bad at eating with my fingers and I always seem to make more mess upon the carpet than the Arabs do, but I must say there's a fascination in that sort of a meal. Some of it was perfectly delicious.

Finally the old man got up, and the servants washed our hands for us, and we went back into the anteroom for coffee flavoured with cloves. It was only then that the Sheikh raised the subject that had brought me there. He said, "The

Wazir tells me that your business has been satisfactorily concluded."

"There only remains for me to express my very deep gratitude for so much help," I replied. "I say this not only for myself, but for the pilots and the engineers who work with me."

"It is good that men who bring others to the way of God should not be perplexed for money," the old man said. And I thought, Gujar Singh was right. That's what is behind it all.

Presently I took my leave of the Sheikh, and went back with Wazir Hussein to his house. The Sheikh's eldest son came with us, a young man called Fahad, and at the Wazir's house we had another cup of coffee and he produced the loan agreement. This was a document written on parchment in Arabic and in English, in vertical columns with the two languages side by side. It only had three clauses and was very simple and straightforward. Fahad, who spoke good English, explained it to me with the Wazir, and I signed it there and then, and they gave me a cheque for sixty thousand pounds. I flew back to Bahrein in the Proctor wondering when I was going to wake up.

Next day I spent an hour telephoning round to all my clients in the oil companies to tell them that I was leaving for England to bring out another large aircraft; I sent a cable to the Plymouth Aircraft Company ordering a Tramp and saying I would visit them during the following week to finalise the specification and to pay a deposit, and I sent a cable to Dad to say that I was coming home. There was a Dakota of Orient Airways going through to Almaza that day and I got a ride in that, and from Egypt I flew home by BOAC, which had a spare seat in a Constellation of the Australian service.

It was more than a year since I had been in England, and it was good to be back. It was May, and as I travelled down by rail to Southampton I thought that I had never seen a country look so green and beautiful. I had forgotten that England was lovely. I sat with my nose glued to the window in the train, just looking at the varied greens of the fields and trees and hedges, at the delicate colours of the flowering trees. It was wonderful.

I went by bus from the station to the gasworks, and carried my bag from there. It was evening, and the tall steelwork of the gas-holders and the cranked cranes of the docks were all touched with a golden light. I walked down the familiar streets, through the games of the playing children, in a dream; this was my own place, and I was home again. The places I had worked in were all very wonderful and strange, but this was my town, where I belonged.

I turned into the door of our house and went into the living room. Ma was in, as I had known she would be, and Dad wasn't; he was down at the 'Lion' playing darts. Ma came out of the scullery when she heard the door, and she said, "Tom!" And then she said, "Oh Tom, you're thinner! Whatever have you been doing with yourself?"

As I kissed her I said, "Am I, Mum?"

She said, "Of course you are! Have you been ill or something?"

I smiled. "Not a day. I'm as fit as a flea."

"Really, Tom?"

"Honest, Mum. I've not been ill at all."

She felt my shoulders. "Well, I dunno. You don't look ill, I must say, but you must be a stone lighter." She stood back and looked at me. "You're looking older, too. Have you been working overtime or night shift?"

"I've been working," I said. "I expect that's it."

"Well, now you've got to stay at home a bit and get rested up," she said. "How long are you home for now, Tom?"

"I don't know," I said. "I've come home for another aeroplane, but it may be a month or so before it's ready." In the correspondence they had said four weeks delivery.

"Well, then," she said, "you'll be able to lie in tomorrow and have a real rest."

"I've got to catch the seven-thirty-three for Plymouth tomorrow morning, Mum," I said. "I'll have to have breakfast before Dad."

"Oh Tom! You ought to get some rest. You're looking quite worn out."

"I'm all right," I said.

She told me I was sleeping in the same old room, and I took my bag through and unpacked it. None of us children were at home with the old people. Ted had been the last, but he'd gone now. He'd married his Lily as soon as he got out of the Army and he'd got a job driving a truck for a builder at Wootton; they had been living with Dad and Mum up till a week or so before, but now they'd got a council house, because she was expecting. All the kids were out in the world, and all married and settled except me.

While I was in the back room, Ma sent young Alfie Lamb from next door down to the 'Lion' to tell Dad I was home, and Dad came back ten minutes later. Ma got supper for us and we sat and talked till after eleven. I told them everything I could about the business, all except the religious part; I left that out because I didn't properly understand it myself. I didn't tell them about the loan I'd got from Sheikh Abd el Kadir, either, and they didn't know enough about business to be curious about where all the money was coming from. They thought I made it, and I didn't undeceive them.

Once Dad said, "How much money have you got now, Tom?"

"Bloody little," I said, grinning. "I've got about five thousand pounds in the bank."

Ma said, "That's a *lot* of money."

Dad said, "He's got more than that, Ma. He's having us on. Just look at him."

She said, "Tom, how much have you *really* got?"

"That's all," I said. "I've got some aeroplanes, of course."

"How much are they worth?"

"I'd only be guessing if I told you, Mum," I said seriously. "They stand me in at about fifteen thousand pounds in the books. If I went bust and got sold up, they probably wouldn't fetch that much. If I sold the business as a going concern, with goodwill, they'd probably fetch a bit more."

Dad said slowly, "So you've made twenty thousand pounds, then, have you?"

"I suppose so," I said slowly. "It doesn't feel as if I had. I mean, it just sort of happened."

"How much would twenty thousand pounds bring in if it was invested, Tom? Say in a row of houses, like it might be these?"

"Oh, I don't know, Dad. Something like seven hundred a year, I should think."

"Seven hundred a year. You could sell the business and retire and do nothing for the rest of your life, and still have close on twice as much as me each week to live on. You've not done bad for yourself, son."

Ma said quietly, "Why don't you do that, Tom, and stay at home, and get a job in England? You could buy a business with that money, and a good one, too." She meant a shop, of course.

I said, "It's not so easy to get out as that, Mum. There's a lot of other things to be considered. I mean, when you start a thing there's other people get mixed up in it, and you can't let them down. You can't pick things up and put them down just as you fancy. You've got to see things through."

"That's right," said Dad. "You've got to think about the other people in the business. But what your ma says is right,

Tom. There's no call for you to spend your whole life in the Persian Gulf."

Ma started to put the plates together. "You want to look about a bit, now that you're home," she said. "You want to find yourself a girl and settle down. That's what you want. We're none of us getting any younger."

I laughed. "Okay, Ma," I said with mock obedience. "Where shall I start looking?"

She called from the scullery, "There's two or three nice girls right in this street would do you very well. You don't have to look far. If they knew that you'd got twenty thousand pounds we wouldn't be able to get in or out of the door."

"Well, don't you go telling 'em," I said.

I was up early next morning, and took a few things in my bag, and caught the seven-thirty-three for Plymouth. It was a slow journey, and I didn't get there till after dinner. There was the hell of a fine car with a chauffeur waiting there to meet me, and I was whisked out to the works just as if I was somebody important, instead of being Tom Cutter from the sergeants' mess out in Bahrein.

It's an enormous company, of course, employing over twenty thousand hands in all the various divisions of the business. Like most big concerns, they were quite brutal about the money. Within the first five minutes I had to write a cheque for ten thousand pounds before they'd even talk to me, but when they'd got that in their hands they took me seriously, and were they good! Whenever any of them quoted a performance, or gave a price, or a date, you kind of knew that that was dead right and no bolony. What's more, they put me through the hoop about my business, to find out what kind of loads I carried or was likely to carry; they weren't going to have their aeroplane give any trouble because I was using it wrong. When they heard I carried bulldozers they pulled out a reinforced floor scheme, when they heard I aimed to carry pilgrims they pulled out a seating scheme of long, hard dural benches, very light and easily washed down. When they heard I flew normally with a crew of two they pulled out a revised crew accommodation that did away with the radio operator's position and added a hundred and ten pounds to the payload. It was an education dealing with those people.

They had machines on the production line coming through and they gave me twenty-six days delivery, from noon the next day. It was getting towards evening by that time, and they pushed me their way like as if I was a little boy. They'd got accommodation for me in their own hotel just by the works, and they gave me a mass of drawings to study that night. They arranged a demonstration flight for ten o'clock next morning for me, and they made it very clear that they expected me to confirm the order then with another twenty thousand pounds. After that I was to go away and not bother them any more – they told me the time of my train – for twenty-five and a half more days. I could come back then, with another twenty-five thousand pounds, and fly my aeroplane away exactly at noon, unless I cared to stay for lunch. The only thing they didn't make exactly and precisely clear was if I had to pay for lunch.

I'd never have got anywhere with those people if I hadn't been able to pay cash down. Their business was, quite simply, to make the best aircraft in the world – not to lend money.

I didn't have to go back to Southampton by train, as it happened. There was a Proctor there owned by my old company, Airservice Ltd, that had come over for some spares. I knew the pilot slightly and he knew me; he had been out in Cairo for a bit, and I had met him once or twice when I had taken a load there in the Carrier. He was interested to see me with the sales people, and he said that Mr Norman Evans, my old chief, would be very glad to hear I was in England, and would be sure to want to meet me. I said I'd be free for the next three weeks and gave him my

159

address; he wanted the telephone number, but of course he was unlucky. However, he was genuinely pleased to see me, and we got along so well I touched him for a lift to Eastleigh; it was a bit out of his way but he said the firm would be glad to do that for me. So I was home with Dad and Mum that evening in time for tea, instead of about midnight, as I thought I would be.

Mum wasn't expecting me so early. When I went into the house there was a girl there in the kitchen with her, Doris Waters, the schoolteacher that I'd met when I was home before, daughter of old Waters, the plumber. They'd got Ted's school atlas spread out on the table that they'd marked in ink with lines to all the places I had been to, and a lot of picture postcards that I'd sent home, and some photographs I'd brought back with me. Mum had been having a grand time, telling this girl all about me.

Ma said as I went in, "Hullo, Tom. Thought you weren't coming home till late?"

"I got a lift back to Eastleigh," I said. "Evening, Doris."

She smiled, and said, "Good evening, Tom. Your mother's been telling me about your travels. Haven't you been a long way?"

"You don't have to believe everything Ma says," I said a bit awkwardly. Doris had filled out since I was home last, got more mature; she must have been twenty-four years old or so. It was years since I'd spoken to a young woman like her. She was quiet, and graceful, and pretty; I could hardly take my eyes off her.

"He's a bad, wicked boy," said Ma. "You can believe that, anyway. Doesn't write home enough, and when he does he doesn't tell us anything. We have to wait till he comes home to hear what he's been up to, and that's only when he wants another aeroplane. When he's got all the aeroplanes he wants we shan't see or hear from him at all."

The girl said, "Oh Mrs Cutter, how terrible! He must be a great disappointment to you." She was grinning.

"Don't you ever get married, Doris," said my mother. "You'll find children more trouble than they're worth."

"One thing," I said, "is that they're always wanting their tea."

"I don't know there's anything for you," said Ma. "I didn't think you'd be home, so I only got three kippers; one for your pa, one for Doris, and one for me. I dunno what you're going to eat, Tom, unless you slip down to Albert's and see if he's got another one. There was plenty in the box this morning."

Doris said, "I'll go, Mrs Cutter."

"No," I said. "I'll go."

"Well, don't start fighting over it," said Ma. So she stayed to clear the table and put the kettle on, and Doris and I walked down to the fishmonger's together.

I knew, of course, that Ma hadn't engineered this meeting, although she was quite capable of it. Doris was in the habit of dropping in to see Mother once or twice a week; I knew that from Ma's letters. I was glad of that, because with us kids all out in the world and mostly living in other places, it must have been a bit lonely for Ma with Dad away all day, especially now that Ted and Lily had moved out and set up their own home. I tried to tell Doris something about that as we walked down the street.

"Nice of you to keep coming in so often to see Ma," I said. "She looks forward to you coming."

"I like it," she replied. "Your father and mother are such genuine people, and they're so proud of what their children are all doing. Specially you."

I walked on for a moment in silence. "Wish I wasn't so far off," I said at last. "They're neither of them getting any younger."

"I know." She hesitated. "Your mother was really worried last winter, when your father got that pneumonia."

I stared at her. "When did Dad have pneumonia?"

"Last January. Didn't you know?"

"Not a word. Are you sure?"

"Of course. It was just after Christmas, Tom. He was off work all January." She had reason to know, because the crisis had come in the school holidays, and I found out later that she had been in the house with Mother every day, and sitting up several nights.

I was worried. "Ma told me that he'd had a cold and been off work a bit," I said. "I didn't think much of it."

She nodded. "She didn't want to worry you. I mean out there, you couldn't do anything to help."

" 'Course I could," I said. "The show can get on without me for a bit, almost any time. I could have been home in thirty-six hours, if there was any trouble with Dad or Mum like that."

She said, "Flying home? It'ld cost an awful lot. Your father wasn't as bad as that."

"Not much sense in flying home just for the funeral," I said a bit shortly. "What happened? Did he go to hospital?"

"They hadn't got a bed," she said. "It was all right at home."

Mum and Dad like our house and they'd never move away from it, but it's not much of a place to nurse a serious illness in, with no running water upstairs and the only toilet out in the back yard and shared with the house next door. "Did they try and get him into a nursing home?" I asked.

"I don't think so," she said. "It comes a bit expensive, you know."

I said, "For Christ's sake!" I was worth twenty thousand pounds, all made in about three years. It wasn't real money, of course, to Dad and Mum. It wasn't very real to me.

"I wish I'd known," I said. "I'd have been home inside two days and got all that fixed up. There's plenty of money for a nursing home, or anything they need."

"I'm very glad to know that," she said seriously. "I'll remember it." We walked along in silence for a bit. I was worried, thinking what a bad son I had been. "If that happens again, Tom," she said seriously, "would you like me to send you a cable?"

I turned to her. "I wish you would. But if you do that, send it good and early, so that I can get home in good time and do something. I've got all the money in the world to help them if they're sick. Don't wait to send a cable till they're dying."

She hesitated. "It might mean bringing you home on a wild goose chase," she said. "You wouldn't thank me then."

"I would. I'd rather have it that way. I don't get home to see them enough, anyway. If you cable me like that, I wouldn't hold it against you if Dad was back at work again when I got home, or Mum out at the pictures."

"Do you really feel like that about it, Tom?"

"Of course I do. I ought to be home every six months, but I'm not. I could be, but one gets stuck into things; you get so that you can't bear to take a holiday. But for a thing like this I'd come home any time. Will you let me have that cable?"

"I'll do that," she said.

"Full rate," I said. "None of this deferred or night letter nonsense."

She laughed. "All right."

We came to the shop, and I went in and got my kipper, and they wrapped it up in a bit of newspaper for me, and we turned to stroll home. "How long are you back for this time, Tom?" she asked.

163

"Three weeks," I said. I told her about the delivery of the Tramp. "It's not worth going back to the Persian Gulf and coming out again."

"That'll be nice for your mother," she said. "She loves having you at home." We walked on in silence. "Will you fly the new aeroplane out to Bahrein alone?"

I shook my head. "I think I'll get my chief pilot back here two or three days before. We'll fly it out together."

"Gujar Singh?"

I turned to her in surprise. "Yes. You know about him?"

She smiled. "I think I know all about you that your mother knows, Tom. You mustn't mind that. She loves to talk."

"I don't mind," I said. I didn't, either. "He's a Sikh. Do you know what a Sikh looks like?"

She nodded. "I've got a book at the school with a picture of a group of Sikhs. I brought it home and showed your father and mother. They look terribly fierce. Your mother was quite frightened."

"Gujar's not fierce," I said. "He comes to work each day on a lady's old rusty bicycle. I'll introduce you to him when he comes, if you like. But he's married, so don't get any ideas into your head. Got three children, too."

She laughed, and then she said something about East being East and West being West and the twain never meeting. Poetry, I think it was. "That sounds like bolony to me," I said. "If you fly East and keep on going, past Rangoon and Bangkok and Manila and Wake Island and Hawaii, you'll find you're back in the West again, although you're still going East."

"That's only geographical," she said. "What Kipling meant was that the peoples of the East are so different to us, we'll never understand them."

"That's bolony, too," I remarked.

"You're very fond of them, aren't you?"

"I get on all right with most people," I said. "Asiatics are just the same as anybody else. I've not found them any more different to us than Spaniards, say, or Czechs."

She was quite unconvinced. "Anyway, I wouldn't want to marry Gujar Singh," she said a little stiffly. "I think mixed marriages are horrible."

"So does Gujar Singh," I replied. That put the lid on it, and we walked the last hundred yards in silence. Dad was home and Ma cooked the kippers and I told Dad a little bit about my trip and how Norman Evans wanted to see me and I'd probably go up to London one day for that. Then we all had tea, and after tea Doris Waters got up to go.

I went with her to the door. "Sorry if I was rude about Gujar," I said. "He's a friend of mine." I paused. "Like to come to the pictures tomorrow night?"

She hesitated, wondering, I suppose, if I was quite hygienic. "I'd love to," she said at last. "I don't know what's on."

"It's all one to me," I said. "I haven't seen a picture for two years."

I fixed up to call for her at her dad's house next evening after school and take her out; she knew a café where we could get fish and chips for tea. Then she went away and I went back into the house. "I'm taking Doris to the pictures tomorrow," I told Ma. "I won't be in for tea."

"Well, you might think of a worse way of spending an evening than that," said Ma. "Doris is a nice girl, Tom."

"From all I hear she's earned an evening out," I said. "What's this I hear about pneumonia?"

I spent the next day wiring up the house for power. They had electric light and a little cooker in the scullery for using when the range wasn't lit, but it had never entered their heads to have any heat upstairs in the bedrooms. When Dad had been ill they had bought an oil stove and had it upstairs in his room, which wasn't so good in a tiny room when you couldn't open a window. I got a lot of rubber-coated flex and fittings and a couple of electric stoves, and set to work to wire up all three bedrooms and the living-room with power points.

Doris and I had a grand time that night. I don't know what it was, but everything seemed to go right. The picture wasn't a particularly good one, and I've known better fish and chips, but we enjoyed ourselves. She wasn't so snooty about the East as she had been the night before; she asked a lot about it as if she really wanted to know. In turn, she told me about her school. She had never been out of England, but she had worked for a time in Leicester during the war, when the schools were evacuated from Southampton.

As we were walking home from the pictures that evening she asked, "What are you going to do, Tom? Are you going to stay out in the Persian Gulf for ever?"

It was May, and England was a very lovely place. It was a question that I had been asking myself, perhaps subconsciously. "It's where my business is," I said. "You can't run away from that."

"Is it nice out there?"

"It's all right," I said. "It's not the part of the East I'd choose to live in, if I had my pick. But there's not much to complain of, really."

"Will you ever come back to live and work in England?"

I walked on for a time in silence. "I'm King of the Castle out there," I said. "Running my own show. I'd never get to that position here in England. Not in aviation."

"Does it have to be in aviation?"

"I could run a garage," I said. "That's about the nearest thing to what I know. A garage, or a haulage contractor's business, or something like that. I'd be no good at anything else."

She nodded. "I should think you'd run a garage awfully well. Would you like that, or would it be dull after the East?"

She had put her finger on the point. "It'ld be dull," I said. "But – well, there's other things to think of, too. I'd like to

166

be in England, now that Dad and Mum are getting on. I think one could settle down all right with a big garage in a little country town, some place like Romsey or Lyndhurst or Poole. I'd like that all right."

"It would be nice for your father and mother if you ever did that," she said quietly. "Of all the children, you're the one they think the most of, you know, Tom."

"Maybe," I said. It was a fact that none of the others seemed to do much for the old folks. Ted could have put those power points in for them, but he hadn't thought of it. We walked on for a time in silence.

"Don't you ever get depressed out there?" she asked presently. "I mean, away from your own sort, with only black people to talk to?"

"They aren't black," I said patiently. She meant her question kindly enough. "They're brown, and when you've lived with them a bit you don't see them as brown people any more. You see them as just people."

She laughed. "You *are* touchy about them, Tom. But don't you ever get depressed?"

"It wasn't a riot of fun when I left England," I replied. "I was depressed when I went out there."

"You mean, about Beryl?"

"That's right," I said.

"That all happened a long time ago," she said quietly. "I don't know the rights or wrongs of that. I don't suppose anybody knows that except you. But I know this much: that there's nothing in that old story to make you spend your life out in the Persian Gulf, away from everyone you know." And then she said a very queer thing, very shrewd. "I know why you went. You went to find a sort of hermitage."

I stared at her. "Well, I dunno." I had gone there in a tenth-hand Fox-Moth because I was out of a job and wanted to make some money. Or, had I? And then I said, "Perhaps I did."

167

"I know. But it's time you came back into circulation, Tom. If you stay there alone much longer you'll go round the bend."

I smiled, and she thought I was laughing at her. She flushed a little. "I suppose you think that's silly. But people do go funny when they live isolated from their own sort, out in the Tropics."

"I don't think that's silly," I said. "What you say is right. I've got a chap working for me now that everybody says is going round the bend."

"I thought you hadn't got any white staff?"

"I haven't. He's an Asiatic."

"I meant, English people."

"I know you did. But a Chinese can be further from his home when he works in the Persian Gulf than any Englishman, and lonelier."

"Is this a Chinese that you're speaking of, who's going round the bend?"

"Half Chinese and half Russian," I said. "Born in Penang, and so a British subject just like you and me."

"What's wrong with him?" she asked. "What does he do?"

"He believes in God," I said a little wearily. "He teaches engineers who work with him to turn to God in everything they do upon the aeroplanes, and he gets people to believe that that's the sensible way to set about the job of aircraft maintenance. He's obviously going round the bend. Everybody says so." And with that my old worries and responsibilities closed down on me. A month was too long for me to be away from Bahrein. Anything might be happening in my absence.

"But surely that's not wrong?" she asked.

"I don't know if it's right or wrong," I said. "I only know it's liable to make a packet of trouble, any time."

We were just at her house, and there wasn't time to tell her any more, and I didn't want to anyway. It would have been useless to try and make her understand all that was going on out in Bahrein and further east. I turned to her. "I've enjoyed this evening," I said. "Like to do it again one day?"

She smiled. "Of course I would. I'm free most evenings, Tom. Tuesdays I bring home the essays to correct, but most of the rest are free."

"I'm expecting to have to go to London," I remarked. "There may be a letter tomorrow. I'll probably be there for a night or two. I'll drop around one evening when I get back."

She nodded. "Fine. I may be round with your mother. I have enjoyed this, Tom. It was nice of you to ask me."

I turned away. "Okay," I said. "We'll do it again."

As I had thought, there was a letter from Mr Norman Evans next morning. He said that he had heard a lot about my success out in the Persian Gulf, and he wanted to congratulate me. He went on to say that as they were operating both in Egypt and in India we ought to get together, as we'd have a lot in common to talk over. Would I like to lunch with him at the Royal Aero Club one day? He was free any day that week. Perhaps I would give him a ring and suggest a day.

I rang him from the call box at the end of our street, and went up to London a couple of days later with my bag packed for a night or two. I went to the same economical hotel in Bloomsbury, and left my bag, and took a briefcase with a few papers in it, and went out to lunch with my old boss.

He was very glad to see me. I'd never been inside a London club before, and it was all new to me. We had a drink in the bar, and I was really glad to be back with him again. One gets kind of attached to people that you work for, sometimes, and I had always hit it off with Mr Evans.

He asked how many aircraft I'd got operating, and I didn't mind a bit telling him that. I'd fixed in my own mind the day before the things I wasn't going to talk about – contract prices, and things of that sort – but except for one or two essential bits of business like that I saw no point in hiding anything up. We had a drink or two and then we had lunch. I asked him question for question, and he told me all about his staff and aircraft out in Egypt and in India, most of which I knew already, and I told him about mine.

Over the coffee he said, "What we've none of us been able to understand, here at home, is how you managed to work up such a fleet of aircraft on no capital at all, Cutter. I couldn't have done that. It looks like black magic to us. I hear you've placed an order for a Plymouth Tramp."

"You keep your ear pretty close to the ground," I said.

"Well, of course, I wish I knew what you use for money."

I smiled; there were some things I didn't mean to tell him. But I could tell him most of it. "For one thing, I've been very lucky," I replied. "For another, I probably work at a much bigger margin of profit than you do. I don't employ any Europeans at all. Not one. None of my aircraft carry upholstery or soundproofing. If anybody wants a seat he pays extra for the weight of it, at standard freight rates. Little things like that."

"Third class travel for everybody," he said thoughtfully.

"That's right."

"I've been wanting to ask you about staff," he said. "I knew, of course, that you use only Asiatic pilots and ground engineers. Are you satisfied with that?"

"Perfectly. We've had no accidents yet, and the maintenance is good. You can ask the ARB."

"It's very, very interesting. How much do you pay a pilot – say for one of your Airtrucks?"

I grinned. "I'm not telling you."

He laughed. "All right. There's quite a number of people wanting to know that."

"They may find out if they black their faces and come to Bahrein for a job," I said. "They'll have their work cut out to find out any other way."

We sat for some time upstairs with the coffee. "I still don't understand where you have found the capital," he said. "It's very wonderful, the amount that you've been able to do. You aren't a company even, are you?"

"I'm just trading as Tom Cutter. It seems to work all right." I did not want to keep anything from him that I could reasonably divulge. "I'll be quite frank with you, Mr Evans. Up till now I've been very lucky with getting easy hire-purchase terms, for the Airtrucks and the Carrier, so that I could meet the instalments out of profits. For this new Tramp, I've got in some new money, as a personal loan. Local money."

He stared at me. "Local money – in Bahrein?"

"That's right."

"And as a personal loan?"

I nodded. "It's a personal business. The aircraft are all my property – so far as they're paid up."

"I see. You must be getting to be worth quite a bit, if it's all personal."

"On paper," I said, laughing. "You wouldn't believe the struggle that it's been to pay the wages and the petrol bill sometimes."

"I would," he said. "I've had some."

Presently he said, "Look, Tom, this is just an idea that's been passing through my mind in the last month or two. I'm putting it to you without prejudice and with my fingers crossed and all that." I nodded. "You know what we do. We operate charter aircraft based here, and in Egypt, and in Delhi. We've been a bit slow over setting up an organisation in Iraq and the Persian Gulf, for a variety of reasons. Well,

171

now in a way you've stolen a march on us and you've done what we should have done ourselves, and good luck to you. As things are, no competition has developed between us, and I hope it never will. I always think of you as one of us. But, geographically, we operate each side of you. If we try to join up Delhi with Egypt we shall come into competition with you. If you try to get out and extend your operations either way, you'll come into competition with us. I've been wondering if we couldn't get together in some way."

"That's very interesting, Mr Evans," I said cautiously. "I think I'm all right as I am, but there's no harm in talking it over."

That began it, and for the next week I was up in London almost all the time. I edited an edition of my balance sheet for them and gave them that to chew over, and in return I asked for theirs. Mine was a darn sight better than theirs was, although my total business was much smaller. I met Evans again at Morden with an accountant, and then I met him again in London with his chairman, Sir Roger Sale. I told them early on that after running my own show I wasn't going to work for anyone, but that if they cared to make an offer to buy my business as a going concern I'd be interested to hear it. I told them straight that if I went on in aviation I was going on as boss of my own show, but I'd consider a proposal whereby they'd pay me hard cash for the business, and I'd get out.

I was thinking of the garage, and of Dad and Mum at home, not getting any younger.

They took a few days to think it over, and I went home. I was troubled about the whole thing, because I didn't know what I wanted to do. In three years I'd got further ahead in my own business than I had any right to expect; I couldn't suppose that I'd go on getting bigger and bigger at that rate for ever. There was nothing behind me in the way of finance; if the aeroplanes stopped operating for a month I'd be bust. I lived from hand to mouth all the time in that business; there was no cash in it. But it was my own show and I'd made it a success, and out there people depended on my efforts.

Back at home, Dad and Mum were beginning to depend on me, too, as they got older. It looked as if Airservice Ltd would make an offer, and I had a pretty good idea of what it would be. A garage in a country town was well within my reach, with a quiet, pleasant life in the south of England, close to all the places and the people that I knew. I could get married again with more chance of a success this time, and raise a flock of kids. And I knew somebody who'd marry me if I put it to her right, too.

I went around, on the morning I got back, to the garage out at Bitterne on the Portsmouth road that I had worked in as a boy, and that I had got the sack from when Cobham's circus came, seventeen years before. Mr Collier still ran it, greyer and older than when I had worked for him; he remembered me, and he had heard I was in aviation in the Persian Gulf. I asked him how one would set about buying a garage business if one wanted to, and he produced some copies of a privately issued paper called the *Garage and Motor Agent*, with a lot of businesses for sale in it. He lent me half a dozen copies and I fixed up with him to hire a little ten-year-old Ford to run around in while I was at home.

I went off in this car next day alone, and drove around, thinking. There was a business at Petersfield for sale, and another one at Arundel, and one at Fordingbridge, and one at Lymington in the New Forest, on the Solent. And there was a good big one in Bournemouth.

I got back home on the first evening and parked the car on a bombed site near our house. Doris Waters was in having tea with Mother. It was a Friday and there was no school next morning. I said to her, "Like to come for a joyride in my Rolls tomorrow?"

She smiled. "I'd love to do that. Where are you going to?"

"Fordingbridge, Lymington, and Bournemouth," I said.

"Oh, lovely, Tom. Shall I make us up some sandwiches?"

"Not a bad idea," I said. "Make us independent."

Ma asked me, "See anything you fancied today?"

"I saw two," I said. "Trouble is, I don't know if I want a business or not. Or even if I can pay for it, if I did want it. I'm just looking."

Ma said, "Well, Doris can help you look. Four eyes are better than two."

I ought to have slept well that night, but I didn't. I lay awake hour after hour in the little back bedroom we had all slept in as boys together, listening to all the church clocks in Southampton as they struck the hours, the noise of shunting engines and the clang of trucks from the goods yard, and the occasional siren from a steamer in the fairway. I couldn't sleep at all.

A man has a right to get married and have children, and I'd earned the right to have a wife, both in work and money. A man's got a right to live in his own place. A man has a right to make his life where he can look after his dad and mum a bit when they get old. I owed nothing to the East. If this deal went through I could pay back the sixty thousand that I'd borrowed from Sheikh Abd el Kadir for the Tramp. Everyone working for me at Bahrein would go on working for Airservice Ltd, just as they had for me, except that they might get a bit more money; Airservice Ltd paid higher wages than I did. I could get clean out, injuring nobody, putting nobody out of a job, and I could come back to my own place with capital to buy a garage with, and settle down. It was reasonable, and straight, and the obvious thing to do.

And I didn't want to do it.

I lay in bed tossing and turning, trying to reason out why I was such a bloody fool. It was the glamour of the East, of course. The colour, and the easy life, and the quick money. These things had got hold of me, intoxicated me, so that I couldn't break away and come back to a harder, saner, more humdrum life in England. That was the trouble with me, I told myself. Now that I'd realised it everything would be all right, and I could sleep.

That's what I told myself, but it wasn't all right at all. It was no good kidding myself like that. There wasn't any colour in Bahrein. There was an awful lot of grey dust, but no pretty girls. There wasn't an easy life out there, or if there was I hadn't had it. What I had had was hard work and bad food, prickly heat and sores that wouldn't heal because of the sweat, and nobody to talk to. If I had made money it had not been easy money, and it had done me no good whatsoever; in terms of fun or goods or holidays I'd have been better off working in England on the bench in some factory at six quid a week. It wasn't true when I tried to tell myself that the glamour of the East had got hold of me. There isn't any glamour, or if there is, it hadn't come my way.

I lay sleepless, hour after hour. Somewhere, sometime, I had read a story about a Spitfire pilot going into a dogfight with his squadron. It was near the end of his tour of ops, and he couldn't take it any longer. The story told how he fiddled with his safety harness as they dived towards the Jerries, making sure that everything was ready for him to get out quick, and slid his cockpit cover back a fraction just to make sure it was free. He knew just what he'd do. He'd carry straight on in his dive and not attempt to get a Jerry, but just go right through them. Then, while everybody else was engaged, with no eyes for anything but the Jerry in his sights or the Jerry on his tail, he'd turn his Spitfire over and bale out, and nobody would ever know he hadn't been unlucky. He did that, and got down all right, and the French Resistance boys got hold of him and hid him, and made a fuss of him as a great hero. Two days later he shot himself.

I lay awake till dawn with that damn story running through my mind. Then I slept an hour or so, and then it was time to get up and take Doris for her day in the country. She turned up about half-past nine, as pretty as a picture in a white summer frock with a little fine red and green pattern on it. She had colour in her cheeks and a sparkle in her eyes. She was carrying a basket full of lunch, with a white napkin tucked around the top of it. "Oh Tom, isn't it a heavenly day?" she said when she saw me. "I've been up since six."

I grinned; her mood was infectious, and all my gloom was rolling away at the sight of her. "What got you up so early?"

"I've been making your lunch. Tom, you can eat sardines, can't you?"

"I can eat anything," I said. "What have you got?"

"Sardine sandwiches, and brawn sandwiches, and cheese and biscuits and some little cakes I made last night. I've not got anything to drink except a thermos of coffee. Are you going to bring some beer?"

"Might as well," I said. "Shall I get some for you?"

"I don't drink it," she said. "I'll have cider."

I went out and down to the "Lion" and in at the back door, and they let me have the bottles in a bag, because it was out of hours. It was bright and sunny and fresh out in the street. I went and fetched the old Ford from the bombed site and drove it up to the door of our house, and got all the stuff and put it in the back seat. Doris came out and got into the seat beside me, and Ma stood at the door waving us goodbye, and two or three of the neighbours were peeking at us round the corner of the curtain. I let the clutch in and we moved off with a haze of blue, scorched oil rising up around us in the shabby little saloon.

Doris turned to me, "Oh Tom, this is fun!"

It certainly was a lovely summer morning when we got out on to the road. We went by Cadnam and over the open heaths of the New Forest, and we didn't go very fast because the car wouldn't go very fast; it had been nobody's darling for so many years that about twenty-five was its safe cruising speed. We couldn't talk much, either, because it kicked up a pretty fair racket. We just sat and enjoyed the colours of the country and the warm, tolerant sunshine alternating with cool shade, and we were happy.

I stopped outside Fordingbridge and showed Doris the advertisement of the garage in the paper I had with me, and then we drove in to have a look at it. It was advertised as having a two-bedroomed house, and they wanted seven thousand for it. When we got to it we found it mostly built of tin and rather dirty, and the house was nothing much. I went in and spent about half an hour with the chap looking after it; the owner had just died and previous to that he had let it run down badly. I didn't think a lot of it, but it was cheap and in a good position. We got into the car again, and went on to see the one at Bournemouth.

We stopped for lunch on the way, by a wide river, heavily preserved, full of enormous trout. There was a waterfall there, a little sort of weir; we carried our lunch along the river bank to the tumbling water, and sat down and had it there. As Doris was spreading out the white napkin for a tablecloth, we saw a kingfisher.

Doris was very positive about the garage that we'd seen at Fordingbridge. "It's all right," she said, "but it wouldn't do for you. There's not enough scope there for a man like you, Tom. It's – it's all too small."

"I'd have a bit of capital left over for building it up," I said. "It's a possibility, anyway."

She shook her head. "All right for some people, but not for a man like you."

I grinned. "Fat lot you know about me."

"I can't see you fitting in at Fordingbridge," she said obstinately. "Not after all that you've been doing. You'd be bored to tears at the end of a year."

"Give me another of those rock cakes," I said. "They're good." I knew she had made them herself. She passed them to me, smiling, and I took one and bit into it. "About Fordingbridge," I said. "You may be right, but I'm not sure you are. You think I couldn't stick it in a small town. But I've been living in one for three years."

She stared at me. "Where?"

"Bahrein," I said.

"But that's different, Tom. That's in the East."

"A small town's a small town, wherever it is," I said. "I've got no feeling against small town life. I rather like it."

She switched the subject. "It's a rotten little house, anyway," she said. "I'd hate to live in it."

I grinned at her. "I haven't asked you to."

She flushed a little, and I was sorry I'd done that. "I didn't mean it that way. It's a rotten little house, and you can't make it any better. You'd have to find another house, and that would take you away from the business."

"I know what you mean," I said gently. "You're right, too. In a place like that I think you ought to live on top of the job."

"It's a small-scale business," she said, "and it always will be. But you're not a small-scale person, Tom."

We sat and smoked a cigarette after lunch, watching the tumbling water and the birds, and presently we packed up and walked back to the car and got on the road for Bournemouth.

The Bournemouth business was a good one. It was on the west side of the town out towards Canford Cliffs, in a very good suburban district. It was clean and fairly new, on a street corner on a busy main road with a wide area behind it covered with good houses, all of which would have a car and many of them two. It had four petrol pumps with a good concrete pull in, under cover, and a very good machine shop. About ten hands were regularly employed, and there was a showroom built on to it; they held a subagency for Austins. It was a good prosperous modern business going for twenty-five thousand pounds because of the death of the owner; the price seemed a bit on the top side to me. There was no house.

I spent an hour and a half there, and had a long talk with the manager, a smart young chap who'd been in the RAF. He'd had a shot at buying it himself, but hadn't been able to raise the cash. He said there were one or two people after it as an investment. He was quite frank, and showed me everything, but I think he was a bit windy that if I came in I'd turn him out and run the show myself. He was probably about right there, because there wouldn't have been room for two of us.

We left that place at about half-past three, and drove down to the sea, and went into a café for a cup of tea and for Doris to tidy herself up in the ladies' room. She was very much taken with that garage. "It's a good business, isn't it, Tom?" she asked. "It's all so clean and nice, and in such a good neighbourhood."

"I should think it's all right," I said.

"Would you have enough money for it?"

"I think so. Yes, I think I should."

She sipped her tea. "I think you'd do awfully well there. It's big enough to give you plenty of scope."

"Yes," I said. "It's big enough for that."

"What's the matter with it? You don't sound very enthusiastic."

I sat in silence for a minute, looking out of the window at a sailing-boat tacking up and down the beach. "Well," I said at last, "it's somebody else's business."

She wrinkled her brows. "But it's for sale. If you bought it, it'ld be yours, wouldn't it?"

I nodded. "The first thing I'd have to do would be to sack that chap who showed us round, because I'd want to run it myself. The money's nothing. It's his business, really. He's worked it up." I paused. "The money's just what makes it possible for me to pinch his business off him. That's all the blasted money does."

"What a horrid way to look at it, Tom."

"It's the right way," I said quietly. "It's the truth. It's a good business, and I'll think about it. But if I go in there that chap goes out, and he knows it. His staff won't care about that much, either – he's got a good crowd there. I don't know that I want to start off on the job like that."

"I see that," she said slowly. "Couldn't you keep him on?"

"I don't know," I said. "It all wants a bit of thinking about. I couldn't keep him on as boss, which he's been up till now."

We still had one more place to see, in Lymington, and that was on our way back to Southampton. We left the café and got into the little Ford again, and drove out through Christchurch. Lymington lies about fifteen or twenty miles to the east of Bournemouth; it is a little town at the west end of the Solent, on a river near the mouth. It's a great yachting centre, with the unspoilt country of the New Forest all around. I had planned our trip to leave this till the last, because I had a hunch from the advertisement that the Anchor Garage might be what I wanted.

And it was. It was at the end of the town right down on the waterfront. It wasn't as big as it had been at one time, because in 1943 an ME 109 had come over on a tip-and-run raid and had flattened most of it with a bomb, and killed about fifteen people on the side. Half of it was still standing, and the owner had put up a couple of disposal Nissen huts for machine shop and stores. The same bomb had brought down about six houses beside the garage; the debris had been cleared away, of course, so that there was now a big open space right on the waterfront, suitable for expansion. The garage had two pumps, and a fair amount of car work, but much of the business before the war had been marine, and motorboat engines were very much in evidence in the showroom.

It was owned by an old chap called Summers, who must have been over seventy. He was a good mechanic himself, and the place was in good order considering the limitations of the premises, but he was tired and wanted to sell out and settle his affairs before he died. He told me that he was leaving everything to his married daughter, but he wanted to leave it in cash. He was quite willing to stay on and help me if I bought it till I got the hang of things. He wanted fifteen thousand pounds, and there was no house.

I spent the best part of a couple of hours there with him. He had bought one of the house sites, and he thought the others could be got without great difficulty. He expected a licence to build within twelve months, but I should have to see the council about that. The bomb had made possible a project that he had always had in mind, a slipway for motorboats in his own premises, but he would have to leave that to another man to do. He was old now, and wanted to get out.

I didn't say much, except grunt now and then, or ask a question, because I was afraid of seeming too eager. It was a lovely garage. The one bombed site he'd bought went through to the main road and had a frontage there right on a corner, so you could have the pumps and showroom up there with a good drive in. From that the ground he'd already got ran down to the original premises on the quay, and alongside that, as I say, there was vacant land for expansion along the waterfront. There was any amount of yacht work there, increasing every year as yachting grows in popularity, and yacht work is good work because it's not so cut price and people will pay for good-quality workmanship in yachting.

It was Saturday evening, and about seven o'clock by the time that I'd learned all I had to know. The old man said that several people had been to see it and were considering it, but I could see that it was rather a big proposition for the average man looking for a garage. Over and above the purchase price, a lot of money would need spending on it in the way of buildings to develop it to what it could be made into, far more than the War Damage compensation. At the same time, there wasn't much immediate return for the next year or two, till buildings could be got up, so that as an investment it wasn't so attractive as some others. I said I'd think it over for the weekend and if I wanted to go on with it I'd come over on Monday or Tuesday, and with that I got back in the car with Doris and drove off.

"It's an awfully pretty place," she shouted above the rattle of the worn little engine.

I nodded. "We'll find somewhere to stop and have a pint, and talk it over."

There is a little pub on the edge of an open heath just the other side of Beaulieu. It was a warm summer evening, and I parked the car on the grassy sward outside this place, and we went in, and got beer and cider and bread and cheese, and took them out on to the bench in front, looking out over the heath. It was very quiet there, and calm, and peaceful. "That's the place," I said. "That's what I want."

She turned to me, smiling, "Really?"

"It's marvellous," I said. "Didn't you think so?"

"I loved it," she said. "It's so pretty, with the water and the boats and everything. But there's an awful lot needs doing, Tom."

"That's what's going to make it fun," I said.

She turned to me. "Have you got enough money for it?"

"I've not got any yet," I said. "If Airservice make an offer for my business I'll hear in the next day or two. If they come through all right, there ought to be enough."

"There isn't any house," she said.

"I thought of that one," I replied. "There's a lot of building to be done. I'd like to have a big flat over one bit of the garage, for a start."

"Oh Tom! Looking out over the water, with the yachts and everything?"

I nodded. "That's what I had in mind."

She said, "A brand-new flat, that one could plan and have everything just right from the start! You do have lovely ideas."

"I don't see why not," I said. "One's got to live somewhere and that ground was all housing at one time. I think one'ld get a permit to do that all right."

I thought about it for a minute or two, drinking my beer. "Keep a boat, perhaps," I said. "I'd like to do that. A little sailing yacht that one could take away for the weekend."

She said, "It sounds just heavenly ..."

I sat there staring out over the heath. It was as she said – just heavenly, too good to be true. I was getting tired, I suppose, at the end of the day, and I hadn't slept a lot the night before. It was all within my grasp and I could grab it if I wanted to, and my other life out in Bahrein could go to hell. In time I'd probably forget all that, even if it took a year or two to do it.

I put the tankard down. "Let's get going," I said quietly. "Dad and Mum will be wondering what's happened to us."

I ought to have pulled up somewhere on the way back, in the shade under a tree in some quiet spot, and given her a kiss or two, and told her that I loved her. It would have made her day perfect if I'd done that, and mine too, perhaps. But it's no good getting into things too deep unless you're sure of yourself; I'd done that once before, with Beryl. That was how I started killing her, although I didn't see it at the time. I wasn't going to have that happen to Doris. I still had Bahrein on my mind, and so I drove straight on, and presently got home and dropped her at her father's house.

She said, "It's been a lovely day, Tom. Thank you ever so much for taking me."

I smiled. "I've enjoyed it. I'll let you know how things go on."

I went back to the house, and there was a letter for me from Gujar Singh, and another one from Connie; they wrote to me every two or three days to tell me how things were going. I opened Connie's first.

There was not much in it except news that his sister was on her way to Bahrein; she was coming in an American ship to Alexandria and from Egypt she would fly. He expected her to arrive in about a week, and said that he had fixed up accommodation for her in the house that he lived in. I wondered how a girl from San Diego would react to the conditions in the souk; it was none of my business, of course, except that I had offered to give her a trial in the office. He said that one of the ground engineers, a chap called Salim, had left and had taken a job with Sind Airways Ltd in Karachi, and he was looking for another one. I knew that Salim had worked in Karachi during the war, and I was not surprised that he had left to go back there. The rest of the letter was about the routine work going on in the hangar.

Gujar's letter was more serious. After telling me about the flights that had been made and booked ahead for the next few days, he went on:

I think it will be better when you can return. The secretary from the Residency, Mr Connop, came to the office yesterday and asked when you would come back, and when I said a fortnight he seemed angry. He did not say his business, and went away. In the bazaar men are saying that the Resident is angry with you for the loan of

money from the Sheikh of Khulal because they say that
religious influence has been used to make that old man
lend his money. There is much talk about this so that
some say that what goes on in our hangar is good and
comes from God, and others say that it is evil. I do not
think it would have entered anybody's head that it was
evil if the English people at the Residency had not been
angry, and the servants told it in the souk. And now there
is a great deal of talking going on.

Shak Lin has told you that Salim has gone back to
Karachi. I think he has gone to tell the engineers in Sind
Airways our way of doing things, but that is nothing to us,
because he is gone. Shak Lin is looking for another one.

Ma was in the room as I was reading this one. "Bad news,
Tom?" she asked.

"No," I said. "Just business." I was furious over what had
happened in Bahrein. The loan that had been offered by the
Sheikh of Khulal was not of my seeking, nor was it due to
any religious trickery on the part of Connie Shaklin. News
of it had got to the Residency as some distorted rumour, and
they had assumed that we had swindled the old Sheikh with
a confidence trick and got away with sixty thousand pounds
of his money. If they believed that, of course, it was their
duty to commence enquiries because it was their job to do
what they could to protect the Arab population from
exploitation. They had been ham-handed in the Residency
and had talked in hearing of the servants, and now God
knew what might be stirring in Bahrein. It might end in
religious riots, easily.

I didn't get much sleep that night, either. I lay and tossed
upon my bed all night, wakeful and in a weary, anxious
maze. Salim had left and gone to Sind Airways, in Karachi. I
knew Salim; he was one of the most devout of our ground
engineers. Gujar said that he had gone to teach the

engineers of Sind Airways our way of doing things. What way? The religious way? Gujar could hardly mean anything else. Was Salim, then, a missionary, spreading a new gospel amongst ground engineers? Was he starting up a cult of Shak Lin's teaching in Karachi, as U Myin had started it in Rangoon? What was ahead of us, and where was it all going to end?

If riots started in Bahrein because of Shak Lin's teaching, how far would they spread? Would the flame run from Bahrein to Karachi, to Rangoon, and on to Bangkok in Siam?

I lay unhappy and distressed all night through in our small slum house in Southampton, between the gasworks and the docks. Out in the East the situation might be getting out of control, and here was I in England, away from the job and powerless to influence events. There were eight days to go before the Tramp was ready for delivery.

I got up in the morning, tired and stale. It was Sunday, so we had breakfast late. Over the meal Dad said, "We've not heard anything about how you got on yesterday, Tom. See anything you fancied?"

I stared at him; my mind was far away in the Persian Gulf. "Anything I fancied?"

"Any garages?"

Recollection came flooding back to me, but it all seemed unreal now, and vastly unimportant. "Oh – garages. We saw one or two, but nothing very much."

He grunted. "What are you going to do – go on looking?" I had to get away and be alone, to think things over. "Yes," I said. "I think I'll go out today and look around a bit more."

Ma said, "Taking Doris again?"

I shook my head. "I'll go alone. I've got a lot of things I've got to have a think about."

She said no more, and I went out after a time and got the car from the bombed site and drove down to the central post office. I sent a very long cable to Gujar Singh from there, two sheets of it. I asked him to let me know at once by cable if I ought to return; I said I would fly back immediately if there was any need, and come back again to England a week later to fetch the Tramp. If everything was quiet and in order in Bahrein, I said, he should fly to England himself by BOAC on Friday arriving on Saturday, and I would meet him at Heathrow. We would go to Plymouth on Monday morning and take delivery of the Tramp and fly it out to Bahrein as soon as possible.

I sent this off and went back to the car. I had done the right thing, I felt, and I had done what was in my power to take control of the events that I had started, but I was most unhappily aware that I was vacillating wildly. Twenty-four hours before, I had been driving out with Doris Waters to look for a garage and an English home, perhaps with her. Now all that had gone down the wind and was almost forgotten, so that Dad had had to remind me about it at breakfast, and here I was, having just sent off a cable committing myself to go back to Bahrein.

It crossed my tired mind that I could go back for a week or two, perhaps, just to get things straightened up in order to hand over clean to Airservice Ltd.

I drove north that day, through Winchester and Whitchurch, on the road to Newbury. I drove on in a dream, not thinking much where I was going to, not really caring. I got sleepy presently for I had had two bad nights, and so I pulled into the side of the road somewhere and slept in the driver's seat a bit, nodding forward on the wheel.

I woke up half an hour later with a bad taste in my mouth, and wondered where I was, and what the hell I had come there for. There was no sense in it. I turned the car and drove back south again, and presently I found a pub and stopped, and went in for a pint and a couple of packets of biscuits as my lunch. I felt better after that.

By mid-afternoon I was running south and entering the outskirts of Winchester. I had been a choirboy once, when I was young. When you're in a bit of trouble I think your mind goes back to childhood, to the time when you had no responsibilities, when all decisions were made for you. That's a grand time, that is. I got to thinking of my time in the choir that Sunday afternoon as I drove into Winchester. I'd got nothing better to do, and I turned left down the High Street and then right, and parked by the cathedral.

It was quiet, and dim, and cool in the cathedral. I stood at the end of the nave vaguely looking round; it was restful, and a good place to think in. Presently I went into the north aisle and began to walk slowly up it, looking at all the names of famous people on the walls and on the floor I walked on, Sir Henry Wilson who was murdered, and Jane Austen. Maybe they'd had their troubles too, I thought, and like me they'd not known what to do for the best.

There was an old man in a long black cloak at the end of the aisle. He came up to me and said quietly, "The service is in the choir this afternoon, sir. May I show you a seat?" It was on the tip of my tongue to say I didn't want to go to any service, and then I thought perhaps I did, and so he took me through the carved screen and put me in a choir stall of old, carved wood, with more prayer books in front of me than you could shake a stick at.

There wasn't anything in particular about that service. Good singing, a hymn or two, an anthem, all in the familiar ritual that I had known as a boy. I was still tired, and once or twice I nearly fell asleep upon my knees. Maybe God did that for me. I know it was over and I walked out of the choir; I was rested and quite calm. I knew what I'd got to do. I'd got to go back to Bahrein and forget about the garage.

I drove back to Southampton with a mind at ease. It was bad luck on Dad and Mum and Doris, but it had to be. It was just one of those things. I parked the car upon the vacant lot and before going home I walked round to the Waters' house. The old man came to the door himself.

"Evening, Mr Waters," I said. "Doris in?"

She came to the door behind him, and he went back into the room. "Look, Doris," I said. "I've got to tell you something. Like to walk down the street a minute?"

She came out, and we walked together down the road past all the kids playing. "About that garage business," I said. "It's all off. I'm going back to Bahrein."

"Oh, Tom! Wouldn't they buy the business?"

"It's not that," I said. "It's something different. Things aren't so good out there."

"How long will you be gone for?"

"A long time," I said quietly. "When once you start a thing, you've got to see it through." I turned to her. "You mustn't count upon me coming back at all."

"I see," she said quietly. "I understand, Tom."

She didn't understand, of course, but her way was the best. "I thought I'd better let you know," I said a bit awkwardly. "I'll have to be getting back out there as soon as ever I can."

She smiled. "Then all I can do is wish you luck." She'd got plenty of guts.

I smiled with her. "Maybe I'll need it." I held out my hand, and she took it. "Goodbye, Doris. I'm sorry it's turned out like this."

"I'm sorry, too," she said. "Goodbye, Tom."

I walked back to our house, and went down to the 'Lion' with Dad and had a game of darts with him. There's no sense in agonising over what can't be helped, and it pleased Dad no end to have me in the pub with him. I only had a few days left to please them in.

Next morning there was a letter for me, from Mr Norman Evans of Airservice Ltd. He said they'd had a board meeting and he was pleased to be able to tell me that they had unanimously resolved to make an offer for my business. He went on to the details. Broadly speaking, they would take over the Tramp contract. They could pay sixty-five thousand pounds for the remainder of the assets at that date. That meant that after paying back the loan from Sheikh Abd el Kadir I'd have thirty-five thousand pounds clear profit from the sale of the business.

It was about seven thousand pounds better than I thought they'd go to. At the end of the letter, Mr Evans said he hoped that I'd be able to reconsider my decision to leave aviation. He said that if I should do so, would I get in touch with him?

I walked down to the telephone box at the corner of our street, and rang him up at Morden. As I stuck the sixpences and shillings in the slot while the children gaped at me through the glass, I felt as if I was signing my own death warrant, and perhaps I was.

He came on the line at last. "This is Cutter," I said. "Mr Evans, I've been thinking this thing over, and I'm not selling just yet. I'm in a bit of trouble out there, and I've got to get back quick. I'm sorry if I've led you up the garden."

CHAPTER SIX

To Meccah thou hast turned in prayer with aching heart and eyes that burn:
Ah, Hajji, whither wilt thou turn when thou art there, when thou art there?

JAMES ELROY FLECKER

I GOT A cable from Gujar Singh on Tuesday evening, in reply to mine. He said that there was no immediate trouble likely to arise in Bahrein, largely due to the Imam, who had visited the aerodrome and had himself conducted evening prayer outside the hangar one day; this service had been attended by about a hundred people from the town. The Liaison Officer had been up at the aerodrome that afternoon, but had taken no part in the proceedings. He said that according to the gossip in the souk the people in the Residency were still very much upset about the loan. There was no reason why he should not come to England, however, and he proposed to leave on Friday as arranged.

I met him at Heathrow airport on Saturday evening when he came in on the Constellation from Australia, and drove him down to Southampton in the little Ford. Gujar had never been in England, and this was a great thrill for him; he was amazed at the fertility of the country. "I did not know it was like this," he said. "I had read about the green grass and the fields, and seen pictures and the cinema, of course, but even so, I did not know it was like this."

191

He created quite a sensation amongst the kids in our street when he got out of the car. I had no need to apologise to him for our house because he knew quite well that I was a working man, and my father too, and anyway the house was probably a better one than the one he lived in in Bahrein. I took him in and introduced him to Dad and Mum, and fixed him up in the top bedroom, and then we all had tea together downstairs.

Dad and Mum took to Gujar, as I had thought they would. Once you got accustomed to the great black beard and the turban Gujar was all right, and before long he was telling Mum all about his kids. He didn't drink or smoke, of course, so it was no good taking him down to the 'Lion', and so we sat at home all evening, just talking.

He confirmed that there was no cause for alarm about the doings in Bahrein, largely due to the statesmanlike action of the Imam. He said that he had called at the office of the Arabia–Sumatran Company after a telephone call with Mr Johnson, and there were developments there. As I had supposed would happen, they wanted to transfer a load of scientific equipment and three technicians from Bahrein to their new oil field on the East Alligator river in the Northern Territory of Australia, and they wanted a date as soon as possible for the flight. The load totalled about three tons, so it would have to be either the Carrier or the Tramp. Gujar had discussed my absence and the Tramp delivery with them, which they already knew about, and had quoted a date about three weeks ahead, which would give me about ten days in Bahrein after I got back before leaving on this journey. Being a flight over new ground, he knew that I would want to go myself.

I took him for a joyride next day in the little Ford, finishing up at Portsmouth and taking him over the Victory, Nelson's flagship berthed for ever in her dry-dock in the middle of the dockyard. He was very much impressed with that.

Next day we went by train to Plymouth. The Tramp was standing ready for us on the aerodrome, clean and new and shining. With the sales manager we got into it and inspected it all through, and then, with one of the test pilots flying it and myself in the copilot's seat, we took it off and flew round a bit. After a landing or two we changed seats, and with Gujar standing behind us I took it off and landed it a couple of times. It handled rather better than the Carrier; everything worked and everything was right. We spent an hour on the ground then checking over the inventory, and paid the final cheque. Then the machine was mine.

We stayed that night at Plymouth in the firm's hotel, and spent a couple of hours next morning buttoning and unbuttoning every cowling with the firm's engineers, getting to know the aircraft intimately. Then we said goodbye to those efficient people, and took it off, and flew it down to Eastleigh. We landed there about dinner time, and I took a taxi and went home and fetched Dad and Mum out to the aerodrome as soon as Dad got home from work, and showed it to them.

Dad stared up at it in awe. "Bit different from the first one, Tom," he said. What impressed Ma most, I think, was the toilet in the rear fuselage. "I declare, it's nicer than what we've got at home ..." she said. I don't think the rest of the machine really registered with her; it was too big and too complicated for her to take in. "All those clocks and things in front of you," she said. "However do you get to know what they all mean?"

While I had been fetching them out, Gujar had had the Tramp refuelled; she had tankage for twelve hundred gallons, giving her a still-air range of about two thousand miles. I was taking a small load out with me, a spare engine for the Proctors and one for the Airtrucks, and a few airframe spares, and he had got all this stuff loaded in.

When we left her that night and went home with Dad and Mum we were all ready to go.

We got up at four in the morning, and Mum got up and cooked us breakfast. Then the taxi was there, and it was time to go. I went and said goodbye to Dad in bed. "Look after yourself," I said. "No more of that pneumonia," and he said, "Get on with you," and that was our parting.

I went down and kissed Mum. "Goodbye, Tom," she said. "Don't be so long away this time." She was crying a little, a thing I never saw Mum do before, but she was getting old.

"I'll try not to, Mum," I said quietly. "Cheer up. I'll be back before long." And as I said that, I couldn't help remembering Beryl, because that was what I'd said to her.

It's bad when you've got to say goodbye.

Thirty-four hours later I put the Tramp down on the runway at Bahrein, a bit different to that first journey in the Fox-Moth. As I taxied in towards the hangar all the staff came crowding out to see the new machine.

Although I was still sick at leaving Mum and home, it was good to be back.

Connie was there to meet us, of course. I left the clearing up of the pilot's duties to Gujar Singh, and walked down the length of the vast cabin and opened the rear door and got out on the hot tarmac. It was mid-afternoon, late in May, and Bahrein was warming up; the heat hit me like a blow. "Afternoon, Connie," I said. "Well, here's your baby."

He grinned. "Looks a nice job. Have any trouble on the way out?"

I shook my head. "Not a thing. Just kept going." We moved away and looked up at the engine nacelles; there were no oil leaks and everything was factory-clean. "I think she's quite all right."

I turned to him. "How have things been here?"

"Okay," he said. "Mr Johnson rang up yesterday to ask if we'd be able to do that flight to Australia. I told him I thought you were on the way, and that you'd give him a ring as soon as you got in."

I nodded. "I'll ring him this afternoon."

"Which one will you take – this or the Carrier?"

"Carrier ready?"

He nodded. "She's got about two hundred and eighty hours to go before the engine change, but that's plenty."

"I think I'll take this one," I said slowly. "I'd like to get to know her. I don't think I'll take the Carrier through the Dutch Indies till I've got to. You never know."

I strolled into the hangar with him and had a look at the maintenance that had been going on in my absence. Everything was in apple-pie order, as I had known it would be. I didn't keep him very long because I knew he would be wanting to get on to the new machine, and I had a mass of stuff waiting for me in the office.

"Okay," I said. "Better get that one inside and give her a check over. There's a sort of family bible of maintenance schedules for her, with the logbooks. Gujar knows about it. If you get started on that, I'll be out as soon as I've had a look in the office.

He hesitated. "My sister arrived the day before yesterday," he said. "Would you like to see her in the morning?"

I had forgotten about her. "Oh – yes. She'd like a job with us?"

"I think she would. There's nothing for her to do here unless she works."

"Where's she staying?" I wasn't quite sure how much of an Asiatic this girl was.

"That's all right," he said. "I've got her a room alongside mine, in the same house."

I wasn't quite sure how he lived, or where, except that it was somewhere in the souk near Gujar Singh. "That's all right for her, is it?"

"Oh yes. She won't come to any harm."

If he was satisfied, it was no concern of mine how the girl lived. "Shorthand typist?"

"Yes."

"Fine," I said. "Tell her to come up tomorrow morning, and I'll give her a try-out. Two months I said, didn't I?" He nodded. "Well, no hard words if I boot her out at the end of it."

He grinned. "I've told her that."

"All right. 'What's her name?"

"Nadezna."

I stared at him. "How much?"

"Nadezna."

"How do you spell it?"

He spelt it out for me. "Nadezna," I said. "That's a new one on me."

"It's a Russian name," he said. "It means Hope."

"Does it! I never knew anyone with a Russian name before."

He smiled. "Well, you know me. Constantine is Russian. Our mother was a Russian, so we both had Russian names. She met my father at a placed called Barkul; he was a silk merchant from Canton. She'd done something in Russia and the Tsarist police were after her. She married my father in Barkul and they went down to Shanghai, and then they emigrated and got settled down in Penang. I was born in Penang. Old Mutluq bin Aamir here, the chap whose house I live in – he's a silk merchant and he knew my father."

"Where's Barkul?" I asked.

He smiled. "Now you're asking something. It's right in the middle of Asia somewhere, but I don't know where. In Sinkiang, I think. It's somewhere about a thousand miles north-west of Shanghai."

"I've never heard of it before," I said.

"No. Nor has anybody else."

I turned away. "Well, tell your sister to come up tomorrow morning. Nadezna. I'll have to write that down."

I went into the office to the babu clerk. He had done his best while I was away, but there was a great pile of invoices and statements and ARB notices and Notams and applications for jobs and correspondence about spares and payments, over a foot high. I shuffled through this mass of stuff hoping to God this girl was going to be some good, and then I rang up Johnson of the Arabia–Sumatran.

He said, "Glad to hear you, Cutter. Gujar Singh told you about this flight we want on the 6th?"

"Oh yes," I said. "We've got all that laid on. I'll go with him myself, in the new aircraft. When are you coming down to see it, sir?"

"I want to meet you," he said. "There have been some developments; if this first trip to the East Alligator goes all right, we may want more. We might even have to have something like a regular service."

"I'd better come and see you," I said. "When shall I come?"

He thought a minute. "I'd like to see your new machine," he said. "I'll come over late tomorrow afternoon."

I settled down to plough through the pile of papers that had accumulated for me. When you run a show like mine that's what you have to do; you fly all day and come into the office tired with the strain, and start off on the real work. I'd been at it for about half an hour when a car drove up and parked outside. It was the Liaison Officer, Major Hereward. He hadn't wasted much time in coming up to see me; I suppose they'd seen the Tramp flying over on the circuit as I came in to land.

Hereward was an Indian Army officer, or had been at one time. He wasn't a bad sort, but I'd had very little to do with him. I never got invited to any of the Residency parties, of course, because only officers go to those, and I lived with the radio operators and in the sergeants' mess. I'd spoken to him once or twice upon the tarmac, and he'd always been quite friendly. I got up as he came in and gave him a chair and a cigarette.

"What I've come about," he said, "is this loan. I understand that you've been borrowing money, Cutter, from the Sheikh of Khulal."

"That's right," I said. "You may know the amount."

"Sixty thousand pounds?"

I nodded. "That's right." It struck me that he didn't care about the job he had to do.

"Well, that's a very large sum of money," he observed.

"It would be to you or me," I said. "It's a very small amount in the aircraft business. It's the cost of one aeroplane."

"That may be," he replied. "Quite frankly, Mr Cutter, we don't much care to see the sheikhs lending their money to buy aeroplanes. We should very much prefer to see them spending it upon their people, in the provision of roads, hospitals, schools, and things of that sort. There are other sources of finance for aircraft projects. But unless the sheikhs provide the schools and hospitals in their own sheikhdoms, nobody else will. It's very undesirable that they should lend their money to enterprises that are of no benefit to their people."

He had a point there, of course, but I didn't see what I could do about it. "I see what you mean," I said. "This is a local enterprise and we employ a good many local people. I should have thought local capital was rather a good thing."

"I'm afraid we don't take that view of it at all up at the Residency," he said. "In fact, you employ hardly any truly local people. Half a dozen labourers at the most. All your skilled employees come here to work for you from other parts of the East. If you were employing two or three hundred Arab labourers recruited in the district upon work that they can do, digging ditches for example, we might take a different view of this large loan. As it is, I'm afraid we consider it very undesirable, and in more ways than one."

"I'm sorry about that," I said. I sat in thought for a minute, wondering how much trouble they intended to make. "This loan wasn't my doing," I said at last. "I didn't go round asking for it. I had to get in some more money to do what the oil companies want me to do – I had to get another large aircraft. The Sheikh of Khulal heard that I was in that position and sent his Wazir to offer me this money as a loan. That's what happened."

"Where is the money now?" he asked.

I didn't like that one. "Just outside the hangar," I said evenly. "That is, unless my chaps have pushed it in."

"You mean, it's been spent upon the aeroplane that you've brought back from England?"

"That's what it was lent me for," I replied. "Fifty-five thousand pounds was the cost of that aircraft. I've got about eight thousand pounds' worth of spares on order for it."

"I see," he said. "How did the Sheikh of Khulal get to hear you needed money?"

It was no good trying to conceal anything from these people. They probably knew anyway. "My chief engineer goes over to Khulal sometimes," I said. "I think he told them I was having to expand."

"That's Shak Lin?"

For some reason his use of the Chinese version of the name annoyed me, though I did it often myself. But this was a pretty formal matter, and Connie was a British subject. "Mr Shaklin is my chief engineer," I said.

"Yes. And he goes and talks some bastard form of religion to the old man."

"I don't know anything about that," I said. "Whatever he does over there he does in his spare time, on his day off. I know, of course, that Mr Shaklin is a religious man. But I've never discussed the Sheikh of Khulal with him, or him with the Sheikh. You're not suggesting, are you, that he should have had a permit of some kind before going to see the Sheikh?"

"No ..." he said thoughtfully. "You'd better know the suggestions that *have* been made, though, Mr Cutter. It has been suggested that your man Shak Lin used his religious influence with the Sheikh of Khulal to get you a very large loan which would be free of interest under the Islamic law, whereas for a speculative business such as yours you would have had to pay large interest charges on a loan obtained from any other source."

I got up and crossed over to the window and stood looking out. I wasn't going to answer that one in a hurry; I was too angry.

"That's a nice suggestion," I said at last. "Who thought that one up?"

He said, "It seems rather an obvious deduction from the facts."

"Maybe." The trouble was that it was so very nearly true. It was the truth told with a twist. "The facts are what you say, of course. I *have* saved interest charges. The motive was completely different – the motive for taking this loan. You can believe that or not, just as you like."

"It's all very unfortunate," he said. "It lends itself to misinterpretation."

I swung round from the window; I'd had just about enough of this. "What do you want me to do?" I asked. "Give back the money?"

He smiled. "I don't suppose you can do that." I could have wiped that grin off his face with the greatest pleasure, but I didn't do it.

I crossed to the table where my briefcase was, full of the papers I had brought from England. "I could," I said. "I don't know that I'm going to. However, I'll show you something." I pulled out the letter from Mr Norman Evans and chucked it across the table to him. "That's a cash offer for this business," I said. "I've just refused it, but I could get it back again. I could pay back that sixty thousand in a month from now if I decided to. But I shan't do that just because you and the Resident have come to the conclusion that I'm a bloody crook."

He took up the letter and began reading it. "That's rather extreme language," he said mildly.

I didn't answer that, but I stood in silence staring out of the window as he read the letter. One works and struggles to build something up over the years, and then an ignorant and suspicious official, full of his own importance, comes along and tries to knock it down.

He came to the end of the letter and laid it down. "I see," he said. "You say that you have refused this offer?"

"That's right."

"Why? It seems a very good offer to me."

I crossed to the desk and sat down in my chair, and lit a cigarette. "I'll tell you why I refused it," I said slowly. "I was going to accept it first of all, and retire from the Gulf, and take my money and go back and live in England. Then I heard from my chief pilot that you people had been raising a packet of trouble out here, over this loan and over Mr Shaklin's religious doings. In England, it looked as if you'd stirred up a hornet's nest here for no reason at all. Well, when I sell a business, I sell it clean – not with a packet of unknown trouble hanging round its neck. I called the deal off and I came back here."

"Why do you think that we raised any trouble?"

"I know damn well you did. Everything was quite all right here when I went away. Then you found out about this loan, and your boys at the Residency heard you talking and spread it all over the souk. My people live down there – they know what happened. If the Imam hadn't been such a good chap you'd have had a holy war or something on your hands."

He coloured a little. "That's a considerable exaggeration," he said stiffly.

"All right," I said. "Let's leave that. Where do we go from here?"

"I beg your pardon?"

"What do you want me to do?" I asked. "I'm quite willing to co-operate with you, provided what you want is reasonable."

"Well, Mr Cutter," he said, "I shall have to go and talk it over with the Resident. Some rather large issues may arise out of this matter, concerning the whole future of commercial development in the district. If anything has to be done, I'll get in touch with you again." He paused. "In the meantime, may I take it that there will be no more borrowing money from the sheikhs?"

"You may for the next month," I said. "I've got no further expansion in mind at the moment."

"Only for a month?"

"I should have thought that was time enough for you to make your mind up what you want to do," I said. "I'm not going to accept a permanent restriction of that sort just from you, this afternoon."

That was the end of it, and I went out with him to his car. It was a bit unfortunate that sunset prayers outside the hangar were just starting up. I hadn't seen that for a month or so, and it had grown a great deal in my absence. The waste ground by the hangar had been levelled off over an area of about a hundred yards by fifty, and marked out with white stones with a semicircle in the side towards Mecca. That had been done since I went away. There were only about twenty of our people from the hangar, but there were three motorbus loads from the town, and a large number of miscellaneous Arab bodies from the RAF camp. There must have been about a hundred and fifty people there in all, all turned to Mecca and in prayer. About ninety per cent of them were Moslems, doing their *Rakats* together. The non-Moslems knelt a little way apart behind Connie, facing to Mecca like the others, but in silent prayer. Some of the men who had come up from the town in the buses I knew as merchants in the souk, and some of them were quite well dressed. A few were in European clothes.

Major Hereward stood looking at this going on in silence for a minute. His disapproval was evident, but there didn't seem to be much that I could do about it. Finally he snorted, got into his car, and drove away without a word.

It didn't look so good.

When I got to the office at half-past seven next morning, our normal time for starting work in that hot place, the girl was there waiting for me. She was in European clothes, a light cotton frock, bare legs, and white shoes. She had long black hair done up in European style upon her head, but you could see the Chinese in her as, indeed, you could with Connie. I think her Russian mother must have been a pretty woman because Nadezna had good features, and she had a sort of impish cheerfulness that may have come from the Chinese father.

"Morning," I said. "It's Miss Shaklin?"

"That's right," she said. "My brother told me to stick around here." She spoke with a slight American intonation.

"Come on in," I said. I led the way into the office and gave her a chair. "Your brother told me that you'd like a job with us."

She nodded. "That was the general idea."

"Can you take dictation at the rate I'm speaking now?"

"Why, surely, Mr Cutter. I can take quicker than that."

"I told your brother that I'd give you a try-out for a couple of months if you came here," I said. "After that, no hard feelings if we part." She nodded. "What we didn't discuss was what the wage would be. Got any ideas on that?"

She shook her head. "I just don't know what people pay out here, or what it costs to live."

"I don't pay San Diego wages."

"I know it."

I sat in silence for a minute. Then I raised my head and smiled at her. "Why did you come here, Miss Shaklin? It's a pretty dud sort of place, and rough living for you, I should think."

She smiled. "Well," she said, "it's kind of different to San Diego." She was silent for a minute. Then she said, "I suppose Connie told you about Mother dying?" I nodded, and said something or other. "Well after that there didn't seem to be much sense in brother and sister living right on opposite sides of the world, and neither of them married, nor likely to be. So as he was stuck fast here and I was sort of loose in San Diego after Mother went, I said I'd come out here for a time anyway, and keep house for him."

I wondered if she had found him living as she had expected, but there was no sense in starting a discussion of that sort with this girl. I had troubles of my own to deal with, without digging into hers. I straightened up at the desk. "Okay, Miss Shaklin," I said. "Now about the wage. I haven't an idea what a shorthand typist gets here. I don't suppose there is another one outside the bl – outside the Residency." I should have to watch the language now, with a girl in the office. "I'll tell you what I'm going to suggest. The wage of a cashier in the bank here is two hundred and fifty chips a month. That's supposed to be enough for a married man with a family, living in this town. I know that, because Gujar Singh was one before he came to me. That's on the Indian standard, but then you're a single woman. I'll give you that for a start, two hundred and fifty rupees a month, and see how it works out. If it's not enough, come and tell me about it. I don't want to put you to any real hardship, but I don't pay European wages. I'd be bust in a fortnight if I did."

She said, "That sounds fair enough, the same rate as a teller. It's good enough to make a start on, Mr Cutter. Maybe I won't be here long enough to feel the pinch."

"Right," I said. "Well, I'll just show you round and then we'll get started." I took her in and introduced her to the babu clerk and showed her our one typewriter. She said it looked as if it had come over in the Ark and spent most of the intervening time up in the snow on Mount Ararat. I said I'd get her a new one because I knew that there'd be trouble if I tried to take it from the babu or make them share it; it was a sort of badge of office to him and a sign of social elevation that he wrote letters on a typewriter. There were some new Royals in a shop down in the souk; I'd make Gujar go and buy one for me because he'd get it cheaper. Then I showed her where the ladies' room was in the airport building about a quarter of a mile away, and then we got settled down to the dictation.

I heard no more from Major Hereward, but Johnson of the Arabia–Sumatran came out to see me that afternoon. The Tramp was in the hangar, and I took him and showed him that, and we climbed all over it and opened the big nose doors to show him how a truck was driven into it. It was absolutely brand-new, of course, and everything was clean and shining and polished; he was quite impressed. Then we went over to the office and I sent for cups of coffee from the restaurant; one falls into the eastern way of doing things.

He told me what he wanted, and it was as I had supposed. This first flight to Australia was in the nature of a test of a new mode of operating their vast concern. They were thinking in terms of a much freer exchange of staff and equipment between their properties in the Persian Gulf, in Central Burma, in Southern Sumatra, and in North Australia. They had in mind a regular service once a fortnight linking up these places if this first flight proved to be a success, and this trial service would continue for at least six months. It might be, after that, that it would need to be stepped up to once a week, or else they might want to run a smaller and more comfortable aircraft for passengers only on alternate weeks with the freight machine.

We started then and did a little figuring. To run the Carrier or the Tramp from Bahrein to East Alligator River via the other places was going to cost them £4,500 for the return trip, so that the fortnightly service was going to cost them about £120,000 a year. It was a fleabite to them apparently, but it was the hell of a lot of money to me.

I told him that I could handle it for him, and I convinced him with facts and figures that I could. I think he wanted to be convinced, and indeed he said as much. "I'm very glad to hear that you're happy about the fortnightly service," he said presently. "I should be sorry, personally, if we had to put the business elsewhere. For one thing, your quotations have always been lower than anybody else's, and yet you seem to make your business pay."

"It's the hundred-per-cent Asiatic labour that I use," I said.

He nodded. "It's partly that, and partly your own ability. We like the use you make of Asiatics. We think you're on the right lines, politically. I think you'll have fewer difficulties in running a service for us through Pakistan, India, Burma and South-East Asia than a wholly European concern might have."

"I think I will."

"And you're quite happy that this thing won't overstrain your resources?"

"It's about the limit I can do upon my present capital, Mr Johnson," I said frankly. "I shall put the new Tramp on the service and use it for nothing else. When you decide to start, I shall get another spare engine and put it in Australia with a couple of engineers; I'll have to have some staff out at the other end. The utilisation of that Tramp will be at the rate of 2,100 hours a year. Well, that's reasonable. We can do that. We may have to send the Carrier occasionally when the Tramp is in for C of A or for an engine change, but that should be all right."

"Your Carrier's pretty well occupied, isn't it?"

"That's so," I replied. "As I say, a contract of this sort would pretty well fill me up. I can handle it all right, but if any more work comes in I'll have to get another aircraft – somehow or other."

He smiled quietly. "We shan't be difficult about the schedule. We can adjust the date of the flights by a day or so to help you, if you give us plenty of notice. Only our own people are involved. It's not as if it was a public service."

"That may be a great help," I replied. "We might want that for an engine change."

"Will you have any difficulty in expanding further, if more work comes in?"

"Not technically," I replied. "I can get the aircraft and I can get the staff. Every Asiatic ground engineer in the East seems to want to come and work here – I don't know why. The only difficulty will be finance."

"You've got a good business," he said. "I shouldn't have thought you'd have much trouble with finance."

"There's been the hell of a lot of trouble over the last lot," I said candidly.

"Sheikh Abd el Kadir?"

"That's right. It seems my name stinks round these parts."

He nodded. "I know they aren't pleased at the Residency."

"Do your people object?"

"I don't think so," he said slowly. "I don't think we object at all. We have to pay the sheikhs these vast sums in royalties for the oil that lies under their deserts, really huge sums of money that they've done nothing to earn. If some of that money finds its way back into your business, I don't think we object at all. It means that part – a small part – of the money we pay out comes back to do a useful job for us. I think we rather like it."

He went away quite satisfied, and I went on with my work. I stayed at Bahrein for about ten days before we took off for Australia, and in that time I didn't fly at all. There was too much to do upon the ground. The growth of staff continually made new organisations necessary in the business; what had been adequate for a staff of two was quite inadequate for a staff of thirty. The stores were a headache now. I had one or two long talks with Connie about that; we were having rather a curious trouble. There was practically no pilfering from the hangar, most unusual for the East; I could only put that down, uneasily, to the supposition that the staff regarded our hangar as a holy place. Tools and materials, however, were continually getting lost; one day there would suddenly be no quarter drills in store, and next day six or seven would be found in various drawers or other parts of the hangar. It was the same with gasket material and taps and dies and things like that.

I worked out a new stores system and put it into force with the help of Connie and his sister. Nadezna was a great help. She was quiet and efficient, and she was always there; moreover, she took an interest in the business and, living with her brother as she did, she could learn the ropes without having continually to bother me with questions. Like most girls in an office, she had an aptitude and a liking for routine work, and she filled a very necessary place in our business. It was always a burden to me to check invoices, release-notes, and all the many documents that every aeroplane must have for every part put into it, but it was no irritation to her to trace out the pedigree of a spare length of flexible petrol pipe and enter it under the proper reference numbers in the aircraft logbook. She seemed rather to like that sort of job.

I commented on that once, and she said, "I like seeing everything all entered up and right, and the job properly done. It makes me feel good."

"You're very like your brother," I remarked. "That's what he tells people in the hangar."

"I know it." She paused, and then she said, "Quite a few people round these parts seem to be taking an interest in what Connie says in the hangar."

"Didn't you know about that – when you came here?"

She shook her head. "He always was a bit that way at home, but nobody ever listened to him. I don't mean that he got up and preached. He never did that, although there's plenty of people in California who do. No, he just had ideas. But nobody paid any attention to them, back at home."

"We wouldn't pay any attention to them in England," I remarked. "But they seem to fit in out here."

She sat in silence for a minute. Then she said, "Have you seen the way they treat him in the souk?"

I shook my head. "How do they?"

"I don't know. It's like he was a prophet or something. Some of them get up and do a sort of a salaam when he walks by."

I hadn't heard that one. "There's no harm in that."

"I know. But one or two of them have started doing it to me. Do they do that when you go walking down the souk?"

"Only beggars. Do they come and beg off you?"

She shook her head, "These are well dressed old men, merchants, you know, sitting in their shops. Not poor people."

I laughed, because it seemed best to take it as a joke. "I look too English. Nobody salaams to me unless they want something."

"I wish they didn't do it to me," she said uneasily. "It makes you wonder what it is that's going on."

I didn't pursue the subject; it seemed better to let things sort themselves out in their own way. In a sense, I was relieved. The girl and her brother were a mixture of the East and the West, and when first I had heard that she was living in the souk I had been a bit troubled. If respectable old men got up and bowed when she passed it probably meant that she was perfectly safe down there; it seemed to indicate that she was already known and respected. So far as it went that was all to the good, and resolutely I put the matter out of my mind.

We took off for Australia in the Tramp a few days after that, Gujar Singh and I, with a load of four passengers and about three tons of technical equipment. We left at dawn and put down in the early afternoon at Karachi to refuel; after an hour we got going again and spent the night at Ahmedabad. We refuelled at Calcutta next day and slept at Rangoon, and on the third day we got to Diento after stops at Singapore for fuel and Palembang for Customs. On the fourth day we stopped for fuel at Sourabaya and went on down the island chain of Indonesia, and then over the Timor Sea to Australia. We put down on the big aerodrome at Darwin just after dark, and ran our heads straight into a pack of trouble.

Australia is a white man's country, and nobody could have presented Gujar Singh as a white man. I found in the first ten minutes that everyone knew that my aircraft were normally flown and maintained by Asiatics, and that a strike of the air line staffs, Control officers, and ground engineers throughout Australia was threatened if my aeroplane was handled by the Customs or allowed to fly into Australia at all.

Preoccupied as I had been with all my own affairs, I hadn't foreseen that one. The row broke in the darkness on the tarmac, and it went on for hours. The Customs refused to clear the goods in the aircraft or, at first, to pass the passengers through immigration. Somebody said at one stage that I could have fuel and fly away back to Indonesia with the load and passengers and all. After an hour and a half of argument they allowed the four passengers to go into the town to the hotel, but the machine was placed under a military guard till the morning. At about ten o'clock they said that I could go down to the hotel, but when I asked about Gujar they said flatly that no hotel in Darwin would accept him. I was so angry by that time I said they could take their hotel and treat it unconventionally, and went off to sleep with Gujar in the cabin of the Tramp, having sent a radio message to the Arabia–Sumatran Company at East Alligator River to tell them my predicament.

I found Gujar Singh waiting patiently by the Tramp; he had very wisely kept in the background while all this was going on. "Look, Gujar," I said. "I'm very sorry about this. They've got this colour trouble on their minds here, and we've got to make the best of it." I told him what had happened, and then I said, "We'll sleep in the machine tonight, and see what happens in the morning. It looks as though the idea of running through to the East Alligator River will have to be revised a bit."

He smiled gently. "Don't be upset about it," he said. "This is nothing new to us."

"I *am* upset," I answered hotly. "By God I am. I've never heard such bloody nonsense in all my life."

"My people do things as silly, or sillier than this," he said. It was just after the British had left India, and Pakistan and India were at each other's throats and mass deportations of pitiful refugees were taking place from both countries. "All countries are stupid in these things," he said. "It does not matter."

"It's economic," I said. "They know that we can undercut their rates because we employ Asiatics. I don't believe we've got a hope of operating in this country."

"There are plenty of other countries," he said philosophically.

"You've said it." I was still very angry. "They can keep this one."

There was no trouble about sleeping in the machine, of course. Darwin is hot all the year round, and we had no need of coverings. In the rear fuselage we had the engine covers and the cockpit covers which I had brought with me in case we had to leave the aircraft parked in monsoon rain, and these great masses of canvas were quite new and clean. We were both well accustomed to this sort of thing, and we made beds of this stuff in the cabin behind the load, and made ourselves comfortable for the night.

I lay awake for some time, worrying about my business. This regular fortnightly charter for the Arabia–Sumatran was a very big thing to me; a steady contract running at the rate of £120,000 a year was not one that I could afford to let slip through my fingers. At the same time, I had heard enough about Australian reactions to the flight that evening to realise that it would be quite impossible to operate my aircraft in White Australia. My Asiatic pilots and staff were a valuable asset to me all the way from Bahrein to Timor; they smoothed the way politically for the free passage of my aircraft and they made it possible for me to quote low prices for my freights. The last leg of the journey, however, was impossible for me to operate at all.

Half waking and half sleeping, for I was tired with the strain of four days' hard flying, I wondered if I could operate to the nearest extremity of Indonesia, and make arrangements with an Australian air line for the last leg of the route. Suppose I flew as far as Koepang in Timor, and transhipped the loads there to an Australian machine with an Australian crew, which would fly to Koepang from Darwin, pick up the load, and take it to East Alligator River? To operate like this would put the costs up, but the cost of the service to the oil company would still be far less than if the flight all the way from Bahrein were carried out by a "white" company. And in this way they would keep the political advantage of running an Asiatic service all the way through Asia.

I drifted into sleep, thinking about this one.

They allowed Gujar and me to go out of the aerodrome next morning to a small café just outside the gate, but they sent a soldier to stand guard over us while we were eating our breakfast. I asked him to join us at the bacon and eggs and after some hesitation he agreed; he was a good, clean lad, and said a little awkwardly that you had some pretty funny things to do when you were in the Army.

When we got back to the Control office there was a signal there for me from the East Alligator River to say that they were sending over a representative, and at about ten o'clock a Grumman amphibian landed, carrying a Mr Fletcher as a passenger.

Mr Fletcher knew all about us and our way of operating aircraft; indeed he had been at Bahrein when first I went there with the Fox-Moth, and I remembered him when I saw him as a passenger that I had carried once or twice in those early days. Knowing Australia as he now did, he was not in the least surprised that we had run our heads into a brick wall. His first concern was to secure the release of his passengers and freight, but he listened to my proposals to end my service at Timor and make arrangements in the future for the goods and passengers to be brought into Australia on an Australian aircraft. After half an hour's talk he left in a taxi to go into Darwin for a conference with the Administrator of the Northern Territory, Mr Walker.

He didn't invite me to go with him, so I stayed up at the aerodrome and had a long talk with the pilot of the Grumman, a Dutchman called Beebs who spoke very good English. Beebs knew Australia well, and had flown the

Grumman repeatedly between East Alligator River and Diento in Sumatra. He thought that the proposal to stop my service in Indonesia was sound, and he suggested that Maclean Airways at Alice Springs would probably be the best people with whom to negotiate for bringing the loads on into Australia; he said they had a Dakota which they used for freight. With the encouragement of regular work for this Dakota operating from Darwin, he thought Eddie Maclean would so adjust his services as to use this aircraft more in the northern part of the country, and so make it available to me.

As regards the terminal point for my service, he suggested Dilly, Koepang, or Bali, as these three places all had Customs organisation and good fuel supplies. He pointed out that Customs would be necessary. He showed the geography to me on the maps. The island of Timor is half Dutch Indonesian territory and half Portuguese. Dilly is in the Portuguese bit and the authorities there were pleasant and easy-going, and delighted to see Australians or anyone else who came to visit the colony. Koepang, in Dutch territory at the other end of Timor, was a military airstrip where civil aircraft were tolerated as a necessary nuisance. Of the two places he preferred Dilly. The third alternative was Bali further back along the chain of islands, to the west. Bali, he said, was a friendly place with very good Dutch officials and very suitable as my terminal, but it was a good way further back and would bring up the last leg of the route to be operated by white Australian aircraft to no less than eleven hundred miles, with a corresponding increase in the costs.

Mr Fletcher came back from Darwin presently with his four technicians, my passengers to Australia. He had settled the business, got his technicians through the immigration, and secured permission to unload the cargo from my aircraft; he planned to take the technicians back to East Alligator with him in the Grumman and to send over a truck for the three tons of cargo. Unloading the cargo was a headache, because the labourers at the aerodrome belonged to the wharfies' union and refused to touch it. With pilots, technicians, and Mr Fletcher there were eight of us, however, and we got it out of the aircraft in an hour of sweat in that hot, humid place, and carried it all to a store.

I had a talk with Beebs and Fletcher then about the future operations of the service, and we went down to Darwin in a car and had beer and lunch with Jimmie Corsar, the local agent for Maclean Airways. We told him what we proposed and found, as I had expected, that he was keen on getting the business, and saw no difficulties. Beebs and Fletcher left to go back to the aerodrome to fly to the East Alligator River in the Grumman with their technicians, and I went with Jimmie Corsar to his office and wrote a long letter to Eddie Maclean in Alice Springs. Then I drove back to the aerodrome.

It was four o'clock when I got there, and Gujar had had the Tramp refuelled and was all ready to go. I think he was tired of Darwin, and I don't blame him. However, I had decided to go back by way of Dilly, and the strip at Dilly was right up against hills and with no night-landing equipment except paraffin flares; I didn't fancy that so much in a strange place, and anyway, we hadn't got permission to go there. I went to the Control office and made a signal asking for permission to land, and arranged to leave at dawn next day. Gujar and I had high tea in the café by the gates and walked round the aerodrome a bit, and then we went to bed in the cabin of the Tramp as we had done before.

We took off for Dilly about half-past six next morning. We crossed the Timor Sea to the north end of Timor, skirted the mountains and flew westwards down the north coast till we came to Dilly, a pretty little tropical town on a white coral beach with mountains behind, much damaged by the Japanese. The strip was right up against the town and fairly short, but we got down without difficulty as we had no load, and taxied to park outside the hangars.

We stayed in Dilly with the Australian consul for a day. The Governor and all the Portuguese officials were kind and co-operative, but they had a regular storm in a teacup vendetta on hand with the Dutch in Indonesia, and relations were very strained. It seemed that the colony had one ship, the bottom of which was dying of old age, so they had sent it for repair to the Dutch naval dockyard at Sourabaya. The Dutch had estimated a high price for the job, and had demanded that the whole estimated cost of the repair was to be paid in United States dollars before they would begin. If there was any change, they would give it back in dubious Indonesian guilders. The ship was in no condition to go anywhere else, and in Dilly the Governor was furious. He maintained communication with Portugal by flying his airmail to Koepang and sending it to Portugal by the Dutch airline; his angry comments about the ship stung the Dutch to retaliate by refusing to handle his airmail. Accordingly he was now flying his mail to Darwin and sending it by BOAC, and in this far corner of the world there was almost a complete diplomatic rupture between the Portuguese and the Dutch. Probably their governments in Europe knew nothing about it.

I liked Dilly, although the strip wasn't very good for the operation of a large, heavily-laden aircraft; in the heat of the day the take-off might be dicey. The chance of political trouble, however, was more than I could face. My aircraft would have to enter and clear Customs whenever they passed from Indonesia to Timor or vice versa, and if those two were at each other's throats my aeroplanes might feature as pawns in a quarrel that was no concern of mine. Regretfully I washed out Dilly, and took off for Koepang in Dutch Indonesian territory at the other end of Timor.

Koepang had a good airstrip, but it was ruled entirely by the military and garrisoned by troops. At that time the Dutch were conducting a full-scale war against the Indonesians in

Java and Sumatra, punctuated by somewhat dilatory truces and negotiations. I broached my business to the military commander of the aerodrome, a Colonel Rockel, but when I told him that my pilots would be Asiatics and I wanted to station Asiatic ground engineers with a spare engine and stores on the airstrip, he turned sullen and obstructive. He said that the airstrip was only nominally a civil one because it was used by the internal services of KLM, and that only the smallest aircraft with limited range ever used it nowadays for flying to Australia; in consequence there would be continual difficulties over Customs. He said that he could not agree to have my Asiatics in the Dutch military zone that he commanded without reference to his superiors in Batavia, who would probably seek guidance from the Hague.

This didn't look so good. It was just possible that we might force our way in there, but there would never be co-operation and there would always be the risk that we might be turned out of Koepang at any time for military reasons. The Dutch in Indonesia at that time were troubled and a little bitter with the world; pursuing a policy that they sincerely believed to be right, they were badgered by well meant advice from UNO and infuriated by criticism from India. The civil administrators seemed to stand this strain better than the soldiers; after an hour's discussion with Colonel Rockel I could see little future for my service in Koepang, and we took off at dawn next day for Bali.

Bali was totally different. The strip is a good one on a narrow isthmus of land between two very beautiful bays; it was long enough for anything we wanted, with no high ground near it so that you could approach it in bad weather by flying along the coast at a hundred feet until you got there. To my delight I saw a very large hangar by the strip with a roof in good condition; I studied this as we went round on the circuit and pointed it out to Gujar Singh, who elevated one thumb. We found on landing that this hangar had been put there by the Japanese Navy during the war; it was big enough to take a Carrier or a Tramp, but it was seldom used, and normally was only occupied by the Governor's Auster.

We landed and taxied to the airport building and stopped the engines. A young Dutchman in clean whites came out to meet us, a cheerful young man called Voorn. He said he was the airport manager and KLM representative. He was very pleased to see us, because at that time his service only came to Bali twice a week and so good a chap found spare time heavy on his hands. He said there were no military on the aerodrome, and very few soldiers in Bali at all. He didn't want to see our passports, and had only a casual interest in our papers; when we asked about Customs he said that the Customs officer lived in Den Pasar, the chief town of the island ten miles to the north, and he would invite him to the hotel for a drink that night.

This looked good, and we went into the airport building and had a fresh lime squash and broached our business to Mr Voorn. He saw no difficulties at all. Bali, he said, was an island run by the Dutch administration purely for the benefit of the Asiatics living there; it was a happy and a prosperous place that imported little and exported less. The balance of payments was made up by what the Dutch in Indonesia spent when they came to this delightful place on leave. He thought that there would be no objection at all to the presence of a few Asiatic engineers upon the aerodrome; in fact, he said, we should probably be offered a contract to maintain the Governor's Auster. He was interested in our colour troubles, but assured us that we should find nothing of that sort in Bali, perhaps because the girls were so attractive and the people so friendly.

He drove us into the hotel in Den Pasar. I had heard vague stories of Bali from time to time in my travels about the East; I had not known it was so beautiful. The island itself was beautiful, a place of palm trees and rice-fields, and white coral beaches, and a great volcanic mountain in the middle. The people were peaceable and friendly, and very artistic so that every beam of every house was carved and ornamented, and stone carvings were everywhere. I found later that they had a deep religious sense and spent a good part of their lives, in that good place where food was easy to come by, in prayers and temple festivals, but their religion was a form of degenerate Hinduism unworthy of their sincerity. The women, I found, were normally beautiful and attractive, and they frequently went naked to the waist, though they were very careful not to show their legs. The most attractive of them went about in this way in the home, but when they went out shopping they would usually have a shawl of some sort to put round themselves if they saw a stranger or someone they didn't like. I thought Bali was a grand place; so did Gujar Singh.

We met one or two of the Dutch officials of the administration during the afternoon, serious, competent people whose one concern was for the welfare of the people of the island. They went into our proposals with some care but they raised no obstacles. I think they welcomed the idea of an Australian aeroplane coming to the island now and then, because at that time consumer goods were very short in Indonesia, and small things such as Thermos flasks and electric torches which mean so much in the East were almost unobtainable. We were taken to call upon the Governor that evening and received his approval of the proposals; next morning we had a detailed talk with a Dutchman called Bergen who seemed to be the second in command, and fixed with him the rentals for the hangar and the landing fees.

I should have liked to stay in Bali and rest there for a time, but the demurrage on a Tramp is a heavy charge, and I had to go on. I told Bergen that I would come out with the first series flight and stay ten days and go back on the next machine, in order to see the engineers settled in and the show running smoothly. We went down to the aerodrome about midday and had a last look round the hangar. Then we took off again and flew through to Batavia, and spent the night there, and flew on next morning to Diento to pick up a small return load for Bahrein.

We got back to Bahrein three days later, and I went into a huddle with Gujar Singh and Connie that evening. "They just won't have us in Australia," I told Connie. "Too bad, but that's the way it is." And then I told him about Bali and about Maclean Airways.

"Who do you think of sending out there?" he asked presently.

"What about Chai Tai Foong?" I asked. He was the Chinese ground engineer who had been with Connie and Dwight Schafter at Damrey Phong; he had been with us for two years or more, and he had come on a lot. I always reckoned him in my own mind as second in command upon the ground staff.

He nodded. "He'd be all right. He's got an Arab wife here; I don't know about that."

It was a point that I had missed when talking to the Dutch administrators at Bali, whether foreign Asiatic women would be acceptable. "I shouldn't think there'd be much difficulty," I said slowly. "I'll write and ask if there'd be any objection. Find out first, though, if he'll go and if he wants to take her."

I suggested that we should send a young Egyptian called Abdul with Chai Tai Foong, but Connie said they would quarrel; he preferred a Siamese that we had with us, whose name was Phinit. That was a better choice as it turned out; the Siamese are a gentle and artistic people and Phinit was mentally much closer to the Balinese than Abdul would have been. He was unmarried, so that complication didn't arise. I left it to Connie to put the matter to these two and then to bring them in to see me in the office.

It was dark by the time all that was finished, and I couldn't get hold of Mr Johnson at the Arabia–Sumatran office. I had to see him soon to find out how he reacted to the whole idea of transfer to an Australian machine at Bali; it might well be that he would wash out the whole thing and give the contract to a British company with a white staff; the cost did not mean a great deal to them. I worried over this a lot that night.

As luck would have it, a cable came in that night from Maclean in Alice Springs. I was in bed in the radio operators' chummery where I still had my room; the operator on duty saw it was important and sent it over to me by a boy. In it Maclean gave me his quotation for the return trip of a Dakota once a fortnight between Bali and East Alligator River. It was exactly what I wanted; I got up and went over to the office on the aerodrome, and stayed there for two hours revising my quotations to the Arabia–Sumatran, cutting everything as close down as I dared. When I'd finished I still had a figure that was about fifteen per cent lower than anything my white competitors were likely to quote for the whole journey from Bahrein to the East Alligator, and I went to bed moderately happy about the job.

I was over at the office bright and early next morning, and when Nadezna came in I had the new quotation ready for her to type out. She ran through it in half an hour and I rang up Mr Johnson, and by nine o'clock I was in his office showing him the new figures and telling him all about it. He had already had a cable from Fletcher at East Alligator River telling him about the difficulties, and he wasn't at all happy about changing airlines at Bali; he was afraid, quite reasonably, that one or other of the aircraft wouldn't be there on time and so his men and loads would get hung up at Bali.

"There's worse places to be stranded at than Bali," I remarked.

He glanced at me. "I've never been there. I've heard that it's a very lovely island."

"It is," I said. "It breaks my heart to think you won't see much of it – not travelling this way." I turned more serious. "You're absolutely right," I said. "There is a danger of a hold-up there. What I propose doing, if you go on with this, is to go to Australia and either form a new white company to do this last leg, or take a financial interest in Maclean's show – if I can. I'll have to get control of that last leg."

He grunted. "It's just possible that we might operate it ourselves from the East Alligator River ..."

He wouldn't say yes or no to the new scheme at that meeting; he said that he wanted to talk it over with his colleagues and he'd telephone me later in the day. I went back to the aerodrome worried and anxious, wondering if my £120,000 contract had gone down the drain. I roamed about restless and irritable in and out of the office and the hangar, unable to settle to anything or attend to anything. I had a miserable day. So did everybody else in the party.

At about four o'clock in the afternoon Johnson came on the phone. He said they had decided to try the service in the way that I suggested, in co-operation with Maclean Airways. He said that I must have escape clauses to the contract enabling us to get rid of Maclean if he was late at Bali, and he wanted to see me about that. He wanted to talk to me again about the possibility that they should operate a Dakota themselves for the last "white" leg of the journey. He suggested I should come and see them next morning, and he said they wanted to start the service on a six months basis with a flight leaving upon Thursday week, in nine days' time.

I put down the telephone, and I was so relieved I could have wept. It was all right, after all.

Nadezna had been standing by my desk. She had come in while I was talking, and was waiting to say something to me.

"Major Hereward is here, waiting to see you," she said. "Shall I bring him in?"

Even the Liaison Officer couldn't worry me at the moment. "Show him in," I said. "Look – slip over to the hangar then and find your brother and Gujar. Tell them it's all okay – Johnson has accepted the Bali scheme and Maclean Airways. I'll be over there as soon as I've found out what this chap wants."

She smiled at me, radiant; perhaps it was my own relief that made her look like that. "I'm just terribly glad it's all come out all right," she said.

"My God," I remarked with feeling. "So am I."

She brought in Major Hereward, and I got up to greet him. "Good afternoon," I said. "I'm sorry to have kept you waiting, but I had someone on the phone." I offered him a cigarette, but he refused it.

"I'm afraid that what I've come to tell you may be rather unwelcome, Mr Cutter," he said. "It's about your man, Shak Lin. We feel up at the Residency that the influence that he is building up here is quite undesirable, and could even be dangerous."

"I see," I said. The sun seemed suddenly to have gone in.

"It's very unwise to play about with religious matters in this country," he said seriously. "I've been here twenty-five years, and I know. A new sect makes a schism, and in this country schisms may break out into an open riot, any time. I'm afraid we cannot tolerate a British subject who gains influence in this country by starting a new sect."

"There doesn't seem to be much harm in it," I said dully.

"Well, that's for us to judge, Mr Cutter. Shak Lin is a British subject, and you're a British subject, and in this I'm afraid you'll have to do what we decide."

I was silent.

"You'll have to get rid of him, Cutter," he said, not unkindly. "I'm very sorry about it, and so is the Resident. But Shak Lin's got to go."

CHAPTER SEVEN

God be thy guide from camp to camp; God be thy shade from well to well;
God grant beneath the desert stars thou hear the Prophet's camel bell.

JAMES ELROY FLECKER

MAJOR HEREWARD WAS adamant that Connie had to leave the Persian Gulf. He said that I could see the Resident if I liked, but it was obvious that they had made their minds up. He made it pretty clear, too, that if they had any trouble with me they'd kick me out too. They didn't seem to have a lot of use for any of us, and yet, I think we'd done a useful job while we were there. Perhaps it would have been better if I'd gone into the officers' mess, as I could have done long before. I should have got invited to the Residency parties then, and got alongside them more. Perhaps I had stuck too closely to the job.

Using his own words, I told him that what he proposed raised rather large issues. "Maybe I shall wind the business up," I said. "The chief engineer is a key man in a thing like this. In any case, I'm not going to decide anything tonight. I may go to London and talk it over with your people there. Mr Shaklin has done nothing but talk a very harmless and sincere form of religion."

"Not Christian," he said.

"No," I replied. "Not Christian. Does that make a difference?"

He shrugged his shoulders. "I can't enter into that. Where British subjects are concerned, one expects Christianity. However, Mr Cutter, there it is. I don't want to upset your business unduly, but I want Shak Lin out of this district within a fortnight. We can't have him here any longer than that." He got up to go.

I got up with him. "I understand what you want. I'll think it over, and let you know what I'm going to do."

He went out and got into his car and drove away. I went back to my chair and flopped down into it, tired and depressed. Nadezna came back from the hangar presently, and found me sitting so, staring idly at the pad in front of me, wondering with a dulled brain what I was going to do. She said, "They're all very pleased. Gujar was asking if you're going on the next Bali trip yourself, or if you want Arjan Singh to go with him, or what."

I could not take in what she was saying. "What's that?" I asked.

She looked at me curiously, and repeated the question. "Arjan – no – I don't know," I said. "I'll have to think about it."

"Is anything the matter?" she asked.

I shook my head; I wanted time to think about things before spilling them to anyone. "I'll be going off in a minute. If you've got the letters I'll sign them now."

I think it was on that day that my business stopped being fun. Up till then, it had been a game to me. I had made money out of it, it is true, but this had been a paper profit that I had seen nothing of. I was still the same Tom Cutter living with the radio operators as I had been when first I came to Bahrein in the Fox-Moth. I had no more goods, no better clothes or food than in those days. Figures on white typescript sheets might say that I was worth thirty thousand pounds or so, and it was just like any other fiction to me, as unreal as a page in a novel. No Rolls-Royce had yet come my way; I drove a 1940 Dodge station wagon that I had bought in the first year. The only difference in my life was that I had more work even than in those early days, and larger aeroplanes to play with.

And it had been play. It was a game to all of us in those first years, a game that we all played together as a team. We had all been of the same mind, I think; the fun that we had had in working the thing up together had been the real essence of it. Now, it seemed, the team was to be broken up, and we should go on one man short. Fun is a delicate flower that doesn't stand up very well to changes of that sort. You can't play about with fun. You can kill fun very easily, as easily as you can kill a wife.

I didn't sleep much that night. Towards morning I gave up the idea of going to London to argue with the Foreign Office. They would only take the advice of their officials on the spot; I had no prestige, no influence or reputation that would weigh against the vagaries of these foolish people. I was just Tom Cutter, ex-ground engineer, who made too much money to please civil servants. If I had been Sir Thomas Cutter, Bart., deep in debt and divorced three times, I might have commanded some attention in official circles, but as just plain Tom Cutter I hadn't got a hope.

Connie would have to go to Bali and set up the party there, and Chai Tai Foong must take command of the ground staff at Bahrein in his place. Connie and Phinit to Bali. I reached that conclusion towards dawn and dozed a little then, thinking unhappily of what I had to say to Connie, and how Gujar Singh would react, and all the rest of the party.

I don't like stalling when there's anything unpleasant to be done. I walked over to the hangar soon after the men came in at half-past seven, and called Connie out on to the tarmac. "Look, old boy," I said as soon as I got him out of earshot of the others. "We're in for trouble, I'm afraid."

He faced me, smiling gently. He had a wonderful smile that sort of comforted you. His sister had it a bit, too. "I know," he said. "They want to get rid of me. That's it, I suppose?"

"You've heard about it, then?"

He nodded. "The Imam came and told me a couple of days ago. That's what Major Hereward came up about last night?"

"How did the Imam get to know about it?"

He shrugged his shoulders, still smiling. "The bush telegraph works very well, here in Bahrein. Far better than the Residency know."

"Those bloody fools," I said bitterly. "I've been trying to think of some way out of this. And I can't think of one."

"Don't let it trouble you," he said. "I know it's going to be a set-back to the business, but it's no injury to me. It's time that I went on, in any case. I've been here long enough."

"It's good of you to take it that way," I said. "I don't believe you, but it's nice of you to say it. I don't believe you meant to make a change."

"No," he said thoughtfully. "I wouldn't have left you, just as you wouldn't leave us. But I've done all I can in this place, and I should go on."

We strolled into the shade of the hangar, for the sun was getting hot already. "I've been wondering if you'd care to start up Bali for me," I said. "Let Chai Tai Foong go on here in your place, and you go down to Bali with Phinit. There's not a lot of work there, I'm afraid, but it's all I've got to offer."

He smiled again, that wonderful, comforting smile. "I'll go there," he said. "I'd like to go somewhere for a bit now where there's time to think things out. Bali is what I should have asked for, if you had suggested any change before this happened. It's no injury to me to go there." He paused, and then he said, "There's only one person damaged by this nonsense."

I glanced at him. "Who's that?"

"You."

"I'm not damaged," I said. "Nothing's happened to me."

"Nothing that you can't ride over," he said, "because you were born a valiant and courageous man, and you can take hard blows. But you were going to sell this business, weren't you?"

"I did think of it," I said. "I gave up the idea."

He nodded. "And with it you gave up England, and wealth, and an easy life in a beautiful place, and love, and the children that you long for. You gave up all these things, and came back to the Persian Gulf. Why did you do that?"

I stared at him. "How did you know all this?"

He smiled gently. "You're thinking I've got second sight," he said. "I haven't. Your mother told Gujar Singh about these things, and he told me."

I stared out along the tarmac of the runway, already shimmering in oily waves of heat. "It didn't seem to be a very good idea to sell the business, after all," I said. "One does what one thinks is for the best."

"You thought it for the best to give up all the delights of the world, and come back to this hot, barren place of difficulties and insults," he observed. "Why did you do that, you hard-headed man? Did you do it for a penance?"

"I don't know," I said. "If I did, I've got plenty to do penance for."

"So have all men," he replied. "But all men don't do it."

"I don't know that I'm doing it either," I said. "As regards selling the business, I very nearly did sell it. I only rejected the idea on final inspection."

"Half a thou too small," he said. "The difference between Right and Wrong. Half a thou bigger, and it'ld be Right. As it is, it's Wrong, and you can't cheat about it." He smiled

229

again. "Too bad when God gives you the mind of an Inspector, isn't it?"

I laughed. "You'd better get into the hangar if you're going to talk that sort of stuff."

He smiled. "I shan't talk my beliefs here very much longer. When do you want me to go?"

"I'm laying on the first flight down to Bali on Thursday week, provided Maclean Airways can play at such short notice," I told him. "Will you and Phinit come with me on that? I shall take Arjan as pilot so that he can learn the route."

He nodded. "I'll tell Phinit."

I stood staring out across the wide expanses of the airfield to the sea, revolving all the problems in my mind. "There's your sister," I said. "I suppose she'll go with you."

He glanced at me. "You'd like to keep her here, wouldn't you?"

"That's all right," I said. "I can get along without her."

"No," he said. "I think you'll need her. I think she'd better stay here."

I hadn't got the heart to combat that one. If Nadezna went with Connie, as was only fair and reasonable, my office and my works would be disorganised at the same time. "It's all very well for you to talk like that," I said. "Nadezna's got a mind of her own. She won't want to stay here alone, with you in Bali, about five thousand miles away."

"I'll have a talk with her," he said. "You didn't run out on us. I don't see why she should run out on you."

"Don't force her to stay here if she doesn't want to," I said. "I don't want anybody in the party who's unwilling."

He smiled. "I think she'll want to stay. I don't think you'll find that she's unwilling."

We stood in silence for a time, for there was nothing else to say. I broke it at last. "I think I'd like to get the Carrier's engine change done before you go," I said. "Give Chai Tai

Foong a break when he starts off. I don't want to land a big job like that on him in the first month."

He nodded. "I was thinking that, myself. You'll send the pair that's in her now to Almaza?" We talked about the details of the engine overhaul for a few minutes, hard, simple facts that were so easy to discuss. Then I turned to go back to the office.

He strolled a few steps with me. "The Residency want me to go because they're afraid I may make trouble, I suppose?"

"That's what they said," I replied. "The cock-eyed bloody fools."

"I should never make any trouble," he remarked. "But they will."

I stood for a moment in thought. "Will there be trouble in the souk because you've been kicked out?"

"Not while I'm here," he said definitely. "But after I have gone, there may be trouble. Some of them will miss me."

I shrugged my shoulders. "That's just one of those things."

"If there should be any trouble," he said. "see that some fool of an officer doesn't go and close the aerodrome with an armed guard. They may want to come up here to say their prayers."

I laughed shortly. "I'll do what I can. But whether I'll get Major Hereward to see it from that angle, I don't know."

I went back to the office and drafted a long cable to Eddie Maclean about the Dakota that he was to send to Bali in the following week to meet us there. I was too worried to settle down to office work, and so I went out to the tarmac where Hosein was just about to take off in an Airtruck for El Haura with six lorry wheels fitted with new tyres and two truck radiators, and put him out of it and flew the machine myself. It's good to have something physical to do, when you're a bit worried.

I spent the middle of the day with the repair gang at El Haura, and flew back in the evening with an air compressor set that had got sand where no sand ought to be. I landed shortly before dark and handed the machine over to Connie, and went into the office. Nadezna was still there, waiting for me. She had one or two minor matters for me, notices to ground engineers and information circulars.

I glanced them over. "Okay," I said to her. "You can get off now. No need to wait."

She hesitated. "I wanted to see you, Mr Cutter. I've been talking to my brother."

"Sit down, then." I dropped into my chair myself. "He's told you about everything?"

"I think so. He's told me that he's got to go to Bali."

"That's right," I said. "I'm sorry about that, but it's the only thing to do. You'd like to go with him, I expect, wouldn't you?"

She shook her head. "I'll stay here while you've got a job for me."

"I thought the only reason you came out here was to be with him."

"I know it. And now he's got to move on, when I've only been here a month. But all the same, I think I'd rather stay here, for a time, at any rate. If you'll have me."

I smiled at her. "I'll have you all right. But are you sure you wouldn't rather be with your brother?"

She shook her head. "I've got a job to do here, and I'm getting interested in it. In Bali I'd have nothing to do at all. It's not as if I shall be out of touch with Connie, either. There'll be machines going and coming to Bali all the time from now on, won't there?"

"Oh – yes," I said. "Once a fortnight certainly, and probably more often."

"If he got ill or anything, could I go to him on one of the trips?"

"Of course. You can get on one of the machines and go and see him any time you like. The weight won't make any odds."

She smiled. "In that case, I'll stay here."

A point that had been worrying me all through the day while I was flying came back to my mind. "When your brother goes, where are you going to live?"

"I'll go on where I am," she said.

"Will that be all right?" I asked uneasily. I suppose after all that time I still had something of an Englishman's dislike and fear of the native quarter of an Eastern town.

"Surely," she said gently. "I live in a house owned by a very respectable old man, Mutluq bin Aamir; he's a silk merchant. He's a great devotee of Connie, and he knew my father. And Gujar Singh lives only just across the way."

"You'll be all right there, living alone, after your brother's gone?"

"Of course," she said, smiling a little. "I should never come to any harm down there."

If she was happy about going on there alone I didn't see that I could raise any objection; moreover, I didn't know of anywhere else where she could live any better. I asked her, "How are you for Arabic? Can you get along without your brother?"

She nodded. "I'm learning it. I can ask for all the ordinary things now, and anyway, lots of the people know a little English. Really, I shall be quite all right. You don't have to worry about me."

I couldn't press it any more. "Well, of course, I'll be very glad if you can stay," I said. I sat in silence for a minute. "It's going to be a big loss when your brother goes," I said quietly. "Things have gone very smoothly under him."

"And under you," she said.

"I mean, in the hangar. I've had nothing much to do with the ground engineers since he came."

"I know," she said. "But under you, he has been able to teach people in his own way. When Connie started talking his religion over the fifty-hour schedules and the daily inspections, not everybody would have allowed it to go on. You must have been very puzzled sometimes."

"Yes," I said. "I was."

"Because you saw virtue in his way of teaching engineers to do their work you let him go on in his own way, although it was not an English or an American way. If the results are good, a share in it is yours." She paused. "His way has spread a long, long way from here, and may spread further. Engineers worship in the hangar in his way in Rangoon and Bangkok, in Karachi and in Abadan. She paused again, and then repeated, "And it may go further."

There was a long silence. "What is this thing, Nadezna?" I asked at last. "Is it a new religion?"

"What is a religion?"

I was silent. I couldn't answer that one.

"As I see it," she said thoughtfully, "it's a way of life that brings men to worship through their work, who wouldn't worship in the old-fashioned way. If that's what a religion is, I suppose this is one. But does it matter what we call it?"

I shook my head. "The only thing is to accept it, and just see what happens. After all, there isn't any harm in it."

"No harm at all," she said. "Only a lot of good."

There was a tension in Bahrein in those last days before we left for Bali. I wrote a note to Major Hereward telling him what I proposed to do, and I got a short and not unfriendly reply in acknowledgment. I did not see him again before we left, and nor did Connie. On the Friday Connie asked for a Proctor to go over to the Sheikh of Khulal at Baraka, and Gujar flew him over; nothing seemed to happen as a result of that. Years later Gujar Singh told me that the visit had averted a major clash between the Sheikh and the Resident, and Johnson of the Arabia–Sumatran once hinted at the same thing. But at the time I knew nothing of all that.

There were more worshippers than ever at the sunset prayers outside the hangar in those last few days. Each evening more bus loads of men arrived from the souk and the surrounding district; on the last evening before we took off for Bali there must have been nearly five hundred people there, including the Imam, who led the *Rakats*. I know I counted eleven buses parked by the roadside, and some of them had made more than one journey. Many of these people were what in Bahrein would pass as intellectuals, grave, white-bearded old men in flowing Arab clothes. But with them there were men who had to do with things mechanical; every taxi-driver and every truck-driver in the district must have been there, and men from the waterworks and from the refineries, and from the electrical power station. We had a failure of the power supply that night.

There was no demonstration, and no sign of any emotion. They came and lined up for their prayers outside the hangar with the Imam leading in the motions of the *Rakats*. They went through it all as I had seen them do so many times before, only now there were far more of them. None of them seemed to pay any attention to Connie and the other non-Moslems kneeling apart, and after it was over they went back to their buses and got into them; the engines started up and the old vehicles moved off. There were no speeches, no farewells, no protests or debate. Watching this from a distance, I was vaguely uneasy. It seemed unnatural that if they loved him well enough to come out of the town to pray with him, they should go so quietly. It didn't seem right to me, but then, I reflected, I knew nothing really about the East.

We loaded up the Tramp before dawn next day. There were eleven great metal rods that I was told were drills, each about six inches in diameter and nine feet long, swathed in sacking; these weighed together about four tons. There were five passengers from the Arabia–Sumatran, one of whom was getting off in Central Burma and two at Diento; the other two were going through to the East Alligator River with the drills. Then there was Arjan Singh as pilot and myself as copilot, and Connie and Phinit travelling with us to Bali. All told, we had a pretty full load, even for a Tramp.

We took off for Karachi with the first light, and I left everything to Arjan Singh, only flying the machine myself while he was at the navigator's table. The route eastwards was becoming a well-worn track to me by that time, but my pilots had flown it less frequently, and I was anxious for them to get in the maximum experience. We went up to about ten thousand feet in dusty air conditions, so that it was difficult to see the ground or sea except immediately below, and navigated by radio; we got fixes from Bahrein and Sharjah till we were well past Bandar Abbas, and soon after that we picked up the broadcasting station at Karachi and began to home on that, getting a few cross bearings from Jiwani as we passed.

We began to lose height when we were half an hour out from Karachi. The dust haze was quite thick and Arjan had to be on the job of piloting the whole time. To help him I relieved him of the radio work, and picked up the microphone and called the airport to announce our arrival in their zone. "Karachi Tower, this is George Able Nan How Victor, from Bahrein. ETA one one five zero, Zebra. Over."

A high-pitched, Pakistani voice speaking clipped English acknowledged the call and cleared us into the zone. I laid the microphone down and told Arjan; I kept the headphones on and the set going, on a listening watch. And a couple of minutes later they came through again.

"George Able Nan How Victor, this is Karachi Tower," said the Control officer. His English was not very easy to understand. "Is ... on board your aircraft? Over."

I could not get the missing words, and asked him to repeat. This time he spoke more clearly and distinctly. "Is Mr Shak Lin on board your aircraft?"

"Karachi Tower," I said, "Roger. Shak Lin is on board."

"How Victor, Roger. Thank you. Out."

One cannot ask questions about non-essential matters on the radio, and it was difficult to understand the Control officer on any but the standard routine calls. I sat wondering, uneasy, for a few minutes; then I passed the microphone to Arjan and got out of my seat, and went down the ladder to the cabin and to Connie, seated behind the load. "Karachi Tower have just asked if you were on board," I said. "Are they expecting you?"

He shook his head. "Not that I know of."

"Well," I observed, "they are."

"Somebody must have got on the blower from Bahrein," he said. He meant the radio telephone that connects the aerodromes all down the eastern route; the operators are talking to each other all the time.

I nodded. "Thought you'd like to know."

"Thanks."

I went back to the cockpit and slipped into my seat again. Arjan knew the Karachi district very well, and found the airship hangar without difficulty in the thick haze, and we got cleared for landing as we passed down wind, and put down on the one long runway, and taxied to the Control Tower. As we swung round into wind and stopped the engines, I saw brown men in overalls running towards us down the tarmac from the hangars. I pointed them out to Arjan Singh.

He nodded. "I think they know that Shak Lin is with us."

I slipped down into the cabin and went first to the door. When I opened it, the first man I saw was Salim, the Pakistani ground engineer who had been with us at Bahrein, and who had left to take a job with Sind Airways here in Karachi. I said, "Hullo, Salim. How goes it?"

"I am very well, Mr Cutter, thank you," he replied. "Mr Cutter, is Shak Lin with you?"

"He's here," I said. "Do you want to see him?"

"Oh, yes. Many, many people here want to see him."

I got out of the machine. "Don't keep him too long, Salim," I said. "We've got to go on as soon as we've refuelled. I'm going through to Ahmedabad today."

"May we have one hour?" he said. There was a considerable crowd behind him now, brown men in oil-stained overalls, and more were coming up. "It is important to us, Mr Cutter. Just one hour."

It would take us most of that time to get refuelled and get the necessary clearances from the Control. I glanced at my watch. "All right." My watch was all wrong of course, and I glanced at the airport clock. And then there was a low murmur from the crowd, and several of the men touched their foreheads. I turned, and Connie was standing behind me in the door. I said, "Connie, I want to take off in about an hour. Let's say three o'clock, local time by that clock. Salim here wants you."

He nodded. "Okay. I shall be ready."

He got out of the aircraft and went away towards the hangars with Salim and the crowd, and from the airport building officials in blue uniforms, Customs officers perhaps, or bus-drivers, came out and went with them, making a small stream of people down the tarmac in the brilliant sun.

The Shell refuelling truck arrived and Arjan Singh gave them the instructions, and we left Phinit in charge and went up to the Control office with the documents and logbooks. I knew the Controller slightly from previous visits; he was a lean, brown Pakistani who had been in the Royal Indian Air Force in the war. His name was Khalil. He smiled when he saw me and I offered him a cigarette, and we smoked together while Arjan got on with the job with one of his assistants.

He asked, "You are taking off again at once?"

"In an hour. My chief engineer is with me, Mr Shak Lin, and they want to see him in the hangar. Was I speaking to you about him on the R/T?"

"Not to me personally," he said, "but I passed the message. The men down there, especially those working for Sind Airways, wanted to know very much if he was coming."

"They know about him here, do they?"

He smiled. "Oh yes, they know about him. We call his method here the New Maintenance. It seems to be a system which maintains an aeroplane according to ethical principles, so far as I can understand it. Is that right?"

"I'm blowed if I know," I said. "My men have all been very devout since Shak Lin came to work for me, and the maintenance has been first-class. I've let it go at that."

"That is what the managing director of Sind Airways tells me, that the men have become devout and the work has greatly improved." He hesitated. "Some of my staff go down sometimes to the hangar for the sunset prayers," and though he would not admit it to an infidel like me, I knew that he was telling me that he was in the habit of going himself. "I think it is a very good thing."

"I think it is," I said. I left Arjan Singh to get the met report and clearances for Ahmedabad, and went down to the restaurant for a quick meal. There was a chap there called Harrison who had been a pilot in Almaza during the war; he was working for a small charter company operating from Bombay now; I knew him slightly, and went over to talk to him.

"My word, Cutter," he said, "your GEs have started something, haven't they?"

"I don't interfere with what they do," I said. "If Asiatics like to say their prayers, it's not for us to try and stop it."

"All going round the bend, if you ask me," he said. "You can't get a thing done up here until they've said a prayer or two, and now it's starting in Bombay. I came in yesterday in a Commuter, and she was missing a bit on the front bank, so I took her into Sind Airways for a plug change. It was like being in a bloody church."

"Did they do the plug change all right?"

"Oh, they did that. They found one or two cowling cracks, too, that our lazy muggers down in Bombay hadn't noticed. They're quite a good crowd in Sind Airways, if it wasn't for all this religious nonsense. I think they've come on a lot lately."

Connie did not keep me waiting. He came back down the tarmac punctually at the end of the hour with a crowd of forty or fifty engineers tagging along behind him as he walked with Salim. There was no ceremony and no trouble as he got into the machine; he paused in the door and looked back at them with that wonderful smile he had, and then he was lost to their view in the cabin. The rest of us got in and shut the door, and Arjan and I got up into the cockpit, and started up the engines, and taxied out for the take-off to Ahmedabad.

We stopped there for the night, and took off next day just before dawn, landing for fuel at Calcutta about midday. Nothing much happened there, and we took off again for Rangoon after an hour, and flew down the coast of Arakan past Akyab and Ramree in the evening. Passing Sandoway I went down into the cabin to talk to Connie.

I squatted down beside him on the load. "I'm night-stopping at Mingadon," I said. "We shall find U Myin there, probably."

He nodded. "He's with BNA."

"He'll want to see you." I paused. "Do you know anything about an old man called U Set Tahn?"

"The English monk?"

"That's right," I said. "U Myin took me to see him once. If he's alive still, he'll be very anxious to meet you. I was wondering how this would be. We're night-stopping tonight at Mingadon and going up to Yenanyaung tomorrow with this chap who's getting off there, and picking up two more bodies for Diento. I'm reckoning to be back at Mingadon tomorrow night and on to Diento next day, fuelling at Penang. Would you like to have a day off in Rangoon? There's no sense in you coming with us to Yenanyaung unless you want to."

He said, "I'd like that, if you're sure you won't need me. I'd like to meet U Set Tahn."

"I shan't need you," I said. "There's quite a bit going on here in your line; U Myin's introduced a lot of your ideas, from what I can make out. Have a talk with the chief engineer, Moung Bah Too, if you can manage it. He's a very good type."

I went back to the cockpit to my job. We cut in over the Arakan Yoma at a point just south of Sandoway and made for Rangoon across the Irrawaddy delta. The sun set before we came in sight of the city, and we put down at Mingadon airfield in the dusk and taxied to a parking place. We spent the night at the rest house upon the aerodrome.

I left Connie in the rest house when I got my party out at four in the morning for a cup of coffee in the restaurant and a dawn take-off for Yenanyaung. It's only an hour's flight or so and we landed in time for breakfast. I could have got back to Mingadon by noon and gone on to Bangkok that day, but I didn't want to hurry Connie in his conference with U Set Tahn, and I had promised him the day. I stalled a bit at Yenanyaung and was glad when one of the passengers asked if he had time to go to the head office there. So we stayed there on the airstrip all the morning, and had lunch from what we carried with us in the aircraft, and took off for Rangoon at about one o'clock and landed back at Mingadon in the middle of the afternoon.

As we taxied in I could see there was a considerable crowd on the tarmac round the entrance to the Burmese National Airways hangar; there seemed to be a rope barrier keeping a clear space upon the tarmac in front of the building. We parked the aircraft and I sent my passengers to the rest house, and set to work with Arjan Singh and Phinit to get the Tramp refuelled and ready for the morning.

I sent Phinit to make contact with the fuel manager and get the petrol bowser up to the machine. He came back presently without it. "No driver," he said. "Drivers and fuel men all over at the hangar, listen to Shak Lin. Manager says, in one hour, will that do?"

It would have to. "Shak Lin's over there now, is he?"

He nodded. "Many pongyis there too, very holy men." He hesitated. "May I go?"

There was little for him to do till the bowser came. "All right. Find the bowser driver, and bring him back here in an hour's time."

He went running off to join the crowd. I finished cleaning up the aircraft with Arjan and then, twenty minutes later, I strolled down myself to see what was going on at the BNA hangar. There was an old Anson parked outside it. Connie was standing up upon the wing of this and talking to the crowd. There were several pongyis, monks in the yellow robe, standing by the wing, and in one of them I recognised the old man I had visited in his ashram, U Set Tahn, at one time Colonel Maurice Spencer of the RASC.

I stood on the outskirts of the crowd, but they were so massed I could not hear what he was saying. He was speaking in English; I could hear that much, and in the crowd of Karens and Burmese and Chinese and Indians there was a good deal of whispered translation going on, which made a low hubbub drowning all but a few sentences of what he was saying. He was impressive, standing up there on the Anson wing, speaking quietly, with that wonderful smile he had.

I had not seen him quite like that before. Looking up at him silhouetted against the sky, it struck me suddenly how very thin he had become. He had always been a lean man, but now, and from that point of view, he looked almost emaciated. It was a good thing, perhaps, that he had left the Persian Gulf for the milder and more generous climate of the isle of Bali. Two years of the desert seemed to have taken a good deal out of him. I wondered vaguely if it had not taken a good deal out of me.

I couldn't hear, and so I turned away and walked around outside the crowd. On the other side of the Anson I met Moung Bah Too, the chief engineer of the airline. He recognised me, and came towards me with a smile.

"I'm sorry about this," I said quietly, indicating Connie on the Anson wing. "It seems to have stopped work a bit."

He shook his head. "I allowed it. We heard that Shak Lin was to come through here four days ago, and I arranged a holiday. We are treating it as a duty day." He meant, as if it was a Sunday.

He paused. "It is a great honour," he said quietly. "He is a very wonderful man."

"I've only just come up," I replied. "What has he been talking about?"

He said, "He took as his thesis the Mingala-thut, our sermon on the Beatitudes," he said. "He took the words to the Buddha in the list of the blessed things, that a man ought to hear and see much in order to acquire knowledge, and of study all science that leads not to sin. He has been saying that in studying the stresses and the forces in the

243

NEVIL SHUTE

structure of an aircraft, the thermodynamics of an engine or
the flow of current in the oscillating circuits of a radio
transmitter, we are but following the injunctions of
Gautama, who said expressly that we were to learn these
things. The world is full of suffering and pain caused by our
wrong desires and hatreds and illusions, and only knowledge
can remove these causes of our suffering ..." He paused.

He listened for a moment. "Please forgive me," he said.
"It may be years before he comes this way again." And he
left me and pressed through the crowd towards the Anson.

I stood on the outskirts of the crowd and listened, and for
a few sentences I could hear him plainly. "You know that
aeroplanes do not crash of themselves," he was saying. "You
are intelligent men. You do not think there is a jealous God
who stretches out a peevish hand to take an aeroplane and
throw it to the ground. Aeroplanes come to grief because of
wrong cravings and wrong hatreds and illusions in men's
hearts. One of you may say, 'I have not got the key to the
filler of the oil tank. I cannot find it. I looked yesterday and
there was plenty of oil. It is probably all right today.' So
accidents are born, and pain and suffering and grief come to
mankind because of the sloth of men ..." His voice was lost
in the murmurs of the crowd.

It was the same message that he had preached so often in
the hangar at Bahrein, that the maintenance of aeroplanes
demanded men of a pure and holy life, men who would turn
from the temptations of the flesh to serve their calling first.
Here the message was transmuted into terms of Buddhism,
but it was the same set of ideas, that good work and good
living were one and indivisible.

I turned away, and strolled back to the Tramp, deep in
thought. It seemed to me that Connie had done something
quite remarkable. He had gained support for his ideas both
from the Imams of the Persian Gulf and from the pongyis of
Rangoon; he had succeeded in impressing both Moslems

and Buddhists with the same message. True, it was all coloured by the fact that he was talking to the men who maintained aircraft, whose profession made a bond of internationalism which might transcend the narrower boundaries of their religion. But all the same, it seemed to me to be a remarkable achievement. I wondered if he would make his mark upon the degenerate Hinduism of Bali.

After a time the meeting broke up, and presently Phinit came with the bowser and we refuelled the Tramp. When that was over I went back with Phinit and Arjan Singh to the rest house. There was a small crowd of Burmese around the veranda and the door of Connie's room was closed; squatting outside it was U Myin, the Burmese lad that we had found at Damrey Phong.

I greeted him. "Evening, U Myin," I said. "Is Shak Lin inside?"

He got to his feet. "The Teacher is very tired, and he must rest."

"May I go and speak to him?"

He hesitated, and then stood aside and opened the door for me. Connie was lying stretched upon the charpoy in a short pair of pants; it was very hot in the room with the door shut, and he was sweating in streams, so that dark patches showed upon the sheet on which he lay. I noticed again how thin he had become.

He raised his head as I came in, and then raised his body on one elbow. "Evening," he said. "I was just having a lie down."

I grinned. "Takes it out of you, I suppose – all that talking."

"A bit."

"Let me send over for a whisky – a chota."

He shook his head. "I never touch it. You know that."

I nodded. "Have you eaten anything today?"

He shook his head. "I'll wait till the crowd's gone, and then I'll slip over to the restaurant."

"That crowd's a fixture," I said. "I'll send one of the boys over for a tray. They've always got a curry there. Curry and rice?"

He thanked me, and got up, and went across the room and had a long drink of water from the chatty. I went out and spoke to U Myin and Phinit, and U Myin went to the restaurant leaving Phinit to guard the door and keep the crowd away. He came back presently carrying a tray covered with a white cloth, a meal of curry and rice and fruit. I went into Connie's room and saw him settled down and eating it.

"Take-off at dawn tomorrow morning," I said. "Refuel at Penang and enter the Dutch Indies at Palembang, and then to Diento for the night. That okay with you?"

He nodded. "I've got nothing more to do here."

"What about all those chaps outside? There's one or two monks with them."

"I'll go out presently and say good-night to them. Tell U Myin to tell them that, would you?"

I nodded. "I'll tell him."

He looked up at me, smiling. "I sometimes think that you're a very patient man."

I grinned. "I'm a chap who's been operating aircraft for three years without a sniff of engine trouble," I said. "If the price is to send for a meal of curry and rice over from the restaurant, well, that's okay by me."

We got to Diento at dusk next day without incident, and spent the night with those hospitable people in their tropical country club by the riverside. Next day we flew on. We passed Batavia and went on down the length of Java to Sourabaya and landed there to refuel; then we got going again and flew to Bali. We landed on the airstrip there about the middle of the afternoon. There was no other aircraft there, but just as we were preparing to leave the strip to drive into the city, Den Pasar, a Dakota appeared from the east, circled once, and came in to land. It taxied to park by our Tramp and stopped its engines.

I had not met Eddie Maclean before, though we had cabled and corresponded. He drove with me in to the hotel, and when we had had a shower and changed our clothes we met in the wide, airy forecourt for a drink. At his end everything was working out all right, and he was anxious to retain the contract and prevent the Arabia–Sumatran people from operating the service themselves; I said that that was his affair. He was anxious to examine my Tramp and very interested to know how much it cost, and he had heard a garbled tale of Connie Shaklin that I had to put right for him. I liked him well enough, and we sat for a long time together in the blue of the night in the cool forecourt of the Bali Hotel, drinking Bols and talking about aircraft and their maintenance. From time to time Balinese young men and girls passed by in the road, talking and laughing softly together in quiet, musical voices. Both men and women wore much the same clothes, a sarong with a blouse or shirt above, for they were in their best clothes now and walking out together. They seemed to me to be a very beautiful people.

We all went out to the aerodrome early next morning and transferred the load from the Tramp to the Dakota, a troublesome business because each of the great drills weighed seven or eight hundred pounds. It took us two hours with a gang of men to get the eleven drills out of the Tramp and into the Dakota, and then we set to work to refuel. Finally Maclean took off in the Dakota and vanished over the island of Lombok in the direction of Australia, and I was left upon the airstrip with Connie and Phinit and Arjan Singh.

I stayed two days at Bali with them, which was all the time that I could spare. With the changes that had taken place at Bahrein I had to get back there as soon as possible; I could not spend a week or ten days holidaying in Bali as I had intended. I went and called upon the Dutch administrator, Bergen, that I had met when I was there before, and took Connie Shaklin with me and introduced him. With Bergen and Voorn, the airport manager, we went back to the strip and inspected the store and workshop building that I wanted to rent, built into the side of the hangar. The buildings were in fair condition and the rents were not too bad, and having no option in the matter I arranged to rent them there and then.

The next day was spent in arranging with Voorn and Connie the alterations that were needed. We had brought with us in the Tramp one spare engine and a fair assortment of tools and spares, enough to carry out minor maintenance work and repairs. We found a carpenter to come and work under Connie to put up all the necessary racks and shelves, and got that going. Then we had to fix up some accommodation for Connie and Phinit.

At that, I must say, I was a bit out of my depth. They were both Asiatics, and though in that place of no prejudice it would have been quite possible for them to live in European style in Den Pasar, they both declared that they preferred to live with the people in some village closer to the strip. They had a point there, because Den Pasar was ten miles from the airstrip, and I had no car to leave them, nor would it have been at all easy to buy one or get petrol for it in that place. If they wanted to live with the Balinese in Asiatic style, that suited the work best, and suited me.

The major difficulty was, of course, the fact that they had no common language; if the Balinese spoke anything at all but their own tongue it would be Dutch. However, Connie made light of this point when I raised it; he said that it would be an inconvenience for the first week if he could not converse with the people, but after that the language would present no obstacle. So we went and talked to Voorn and Bergen, and went out that afternoon with a young man called Andel from the administration office driving us in a jeep, to look for somewhere for Connie and Phinit to live.

He took us to a place called Pekendang, a village about a mile to the south of the airstrip, in the other direction to the city.

This village was a lovely place. It was built in a grove of coconut palms a little away from a white coral beach; in fact, a proportion of the men were fishermen. Behind it, rice-fields stretched in terraces up the hill. The village itself seemed to consist of three or four walled enclosures grouped around a temple enclosure, and the high walls which surrounded these enclosures were pierced only by narrow entrances or gateways with carved limestone ornamentation.

I asked Andel if the people put these walls up for defence. He grinned. "Defence against bad spirits," he said. "These walls, they put up to keep out the ghosts at night."

He stopped the jeep outside one of these gateways. "A man is here I think will help," he said. We all got out and followed him through the wall.

Inside, the wall enclosed a space about a hundred yards square. The ground was of hard beaten earth, and dotted about in the area were a number of single-storey dwellings, wooden structures with palm thatch roofs and walls. Each seemed to consist of one or two rooms; the floors were raised about three feet above the earth. As walls were absent on one side of each house, if not on two sides, the effect was that of a number of deep verandas which disclosed sleeping charpoys in the dim background.

"This is a house temple," said Andel. "Each house for one member of the family with his wife and children." Arranged around a central square were six or eight shrines, small alcoves on masonry pedestals raised five or six feet from the ground. There did not seem to be an image in any of them, but a few artificial flowers of palm fronds were laid in a few of the shrines, as offerings.

The whole area was well shaded with palm trees. Men and women were sitting about, the men mostly working at fishing nets or carving woodwork, the women weaving or cooking on open fires behind the houses or nursing their children. In the confines of this family enclosure both men and women went naked to the waist in a sarong. They were well developed, happy people, golden brown in colour, going tranquilly about their daily life in the warm sun. It struck me that they had achieved a better life than I had, who dashed hurriedly from country to country in an aircraft, pursuing God knew what.

They paid little attention to us, except to smile as we went by. Andel stopped at rather a larger house, apparently the home of the head of the family. An old, grey-headed man got up from squatting on the steps as he approached, and smiled at him.

They talked together in Balinese for a time. Then Andel turned to us and said, "This is I Wajan Rauh." Rauh was the name, and Wajan meant first son of his father, an indication of his standing in the community. "Wajan says that the village can accommodate your friends if they have no objection to living as the people do. He says they can have a room to themselves."

I said, "May we see where they would have to sleep?"

The old man led us to another house. I said to Connie, "What about it? Is it a bit primitive? You can live in Den Pasar if you'd rather."

He said, "I would rather live here, with these people."

"What about you, Phinit?"

The Siamese boy said, "It is similar to how they live in my mother's village, near Hua Hin. I should be happy to live here."

The house that Wajan showed us was a single room with one charpoy in it, apparently kept for putting up a casual traveller. He could produce another bed. As regards food, he had a daughter who would cook for the two strangers, and he sent a child running for his daughter. She came in a few minutes, a striking-looking, smiling woman of about forty perhaps, but very well preserved. She was wearing only a sarong, but as she had come to meet the strangers she had thrown a towel over her shoulders with the ends hanging down her back so that her firm, fine breasts were partially hidden. She talked to her father and to Andel for a minute or two, smiling, and then nodded.

The Dutchman said "This is Mem Simpang. Simpang is her son; Balinese women take the name of their first child, unless there is another to make a confusion. You call her Mem Simpang."

Connie repeated that, and the woman nodded, laughing with him. He indicated himself, still laughing, and said, "Shak Lin." She repeated it, and then turned to Andel and asked something. He replied in the negative.

"She asked if you have a caste," he said. "She thinks you must be an aristocrat."

Connie shook his head. "Tell her we're just ordinary people."

"I will do that." A little conversation ensued, while a small crowd of people gathered round. A girl of seventeen or eighteen with a very sweet face, with a piece of cloth thrown over one shoulder and breast as a sign of good manners, came and stood by Mem Simpang. Presently Andel turned to us again.

"She will provide food and cook for you," he said. "They are asking for three guilders a day each, for food and lodging. I have told them that it is much too much, and they should be ashamed to treat strangers so, but they say you are highborn people and must have the best."

Three guilders a day is about six English shillings. Connie laughed and said, "Ask her if she'll take two if I help to look after the children."

Andel translated, and for some reason that sent the fine, middle-aged woman off into fits of laughter, and the people round laughed with her. Andel coloured a little. "She has only two children," he said. "The eldest, a boy, is away fishing." He indicated the pleasant-looking girl. "This is the younger, Ni Madé Jasmi. You call her Madé; that means, second child. She will probably do most of your work."

He paused, and then he added, "I am afraid you will find that these people have a very broad sense of humour, Mr Shak Lin."

Connie said, "Most country people have, in all parts of the world. Tell her that we will pay three guilders and Madé shall look after us."

We went back through the houses to the wall entrance, having made arrangements for Connie and Phinit to get their gear and move in next day. Passing the open space with the shrines, Connie said, "They are Hindus, aren't they?"

Andel said, "Of a sort. I do not think that Indians would recognise much of their religion in what these people do. It is a very complicated religion, Mr Shaklin; there are over forty thousand temples in Bali, and each has a festival two or three times a year. The people here spend most of their spare time in going to festivals or making up offerings to take to the next one. They are very devout. And yet, I do not think they really know what their religion is about. Certainly, I don't."

Connie said quietly, "It will be interesting to learn about it."

Andel said, "You will learn plenty about it as soon as you can talk to them, because their whole life centres round the temple festivals. They are a very religious-minded people."

As we drove off in the jeep I wondered uneasily what would come of putting Connie down to live in such a place as that.

Next morning Arjan Singh and I took off in the Tramp for Diento on our way back to Bahrein. We left Connie and Phinit to get on with it and set up the small maintenance base I had planned. I left a credit at the bank for him, and told him not to economise too much on cables; it would pay us to know what his requirements were before the next trip left Bahrein to come to him.

We got to Diento that day after a stop at Batavia for formalities and fuel. We loaded up with about a ton and a half of machinery and three passengers for Yenanyaung and made Rangoon next evening after one stop at Penang. At Yenanyaung next day we picked up five passengers and two tons of load for Bahrein and got back to Mingadon by dinner time, refuelled, and made Calcutta for the night. Next day took us to Karachi, where we night-stopped before going on to Bahrein.

We stopped outside the airport building at Karachi and Arjan went up to the Control office to do his stuff there; I went and fixed up accommodation for my passengers in the airport hotel. Then I had to move the Tramp because it was in the way of other aircraft, and I got in and started it up, and taxied it down the tarmac past the hangars to its parking place for the night.

It was evening by then, and after sunset. I was very tired; we had flown and worked continuously for four days since leaving Bali, and even in so well-equipped an aircraft that can be a strain. I stopped the engines and locked the controls. There were things I should have done that night, but it was nearly dark and all the jobs could wait till we were fuelling at dawn. I got down from the cockpit into the big, empty fuselage and walked down to the door, and got down on to the tarmac, locking the door after me.

There was a man waiting for me by the tailplane. He came towards me, and I saw that it was Salim, the lad who had worked for us at one time and was now with Sind Airways. He came forward and said, "Good evening, Mr Cutter."

"Evening, Salim," I said. "How goes it?"

"I am very well, Mr Cutter," he said. "Mr Shak Lin, he has not come back with you?"

"No, he's staying down in Bali for a time," I said. "He's looking after things for us there."

He was silent. Then he said, "Mr Cutter, you heard about the trouble in Bahrein?"

I turned to him quickly. "I haven't heard of anything. Has something happened there?"

"They say there has been fighting in the souk," he said. "Much trouble, very much trouble. It is because the Teacher has been sent away."

Nadezna lived in the souk, but Gujar Singh lived near; surely, he would have been looking after her? "What happened in the souk, Salim?"

"An English officer was stoned," he said. "They say he was very badly hurt. He would have been killed, but the Sister was there."

"Who was this English officer?"

"It was the Liaison Officer, from the Residency."

"Major Hereward?"

"I do not know the name. It was the Liaison Officer. The people of Bahrein say it was because of him that the Teacher was sent away, and so they stoned him. And then the RAF stopped men from going to the hangar by a guard, and when the people came the guard fired, but they fired into the air and the people went on and said their *Rakats* at the hangar as usual. One of the bullets fired into the air fell down and killed a goat. Then the guard was taken away, and now the people go and say their *Rakats* every night. Many people go, every night."

God, this was awful. It was just what Connie had warned me might happen. I had done nothing to prevent it, but there was probably nothing that I could have done; the Residency would not have listened to anything I said.

"How is the Liaison Officer?" I asked. "Will he recover? When did this happen?"

"It happened the day after you came through here with the Teacher," he said. "Eight days ago."

"How is the Liaison Officer?"

"He is in the hospital. It is all right, because the Sister was there and she saved him."

I was puzzled. "Which sister was that?" I was thinking of someone from the hospital.

"The Sister of the Teacher," he said. "The one who works for you as secretary."

"Nadezna? Was it she who saved the Liaison Officer?"

"Yes," he said. "The Sister."

"Do you know what happened, Salim?"

"The Englishman was driving in his car alone in the Muharraq road towards the Causeway," he said. "Someone threw a stone and broke the windscreen. And the man stopped and got out of his car, and more stones were thrown, and one hit him on the arm and broke it, and one hit him on the head and then he fell down beside the car, and more stones were thrown to hit him as he lay upon the ground, by many people. But God, the Compassionate, the Merciful, took pity on him. The Sister, who was in the street, came running, and she saw the crowd and the men throwing stones. And the Sister came to the crowd and they made way for her, and she went forward through the stones that men were throwing and stood over the Englishman who was lying on the ground. She said, 'This is a bad thing, and the Teacher will be angry when he comes to hear of it.' Then the men stopped throwing, and she called to two of them to take up the Englishman and lay him gently in the back seat of his car, and that was done, and the Sister got into the car and drove it to the hospital, and the crowd made way for her to pass with the car. And when they came to the hospital men came with a stretcher and they put the Englishman upon it and took him inside, and he will recover from the stoning. And when that was done, the Sister was ill and she was sick in the road by the car, because she is a woman and had been afraid. And one came and said, 'Sister of the Teacher, shall we take you also to the hospital?' But she said, 'I will go back now to the souk, to my own place. Go you to the Residency and tell the guard to come and drive this car away, and see that no harm shall come to it.' And that was done."

I walked back with him to the main airport building, but he knew nothing more than that. It had all happened a week ago. A machine of Orient Airways had been through Bahrein upon a pilgrim flight to Jiddah and the crew had heard all this and brought the news back to Karachi, but since then there had been no authentic news of what was going on. "I think everything is quiet now," said Salim. "If there was still trouble we should have heard, because the radio operators talk to each other all the time."

Outside the main building we met Arjan Singh walking towards us in the tarmac lights. He said, "There has been fighting in Bahrein," but it turned out that he knew no more than we did, and had the same story. We talked about it for a time, but there was nothing we could do except get going for the Persian Gulf as soon as possible in the morning; so we dined and went to bed with an order to be called at four o'clock.

We landed at Bahrein about midday next day. Gujar Singh and Hosein were both out on jobs, Gujar flying the Carrier and Hosein one of the Airtrucks. Chai Tai Foong was in the hangar, however, and he came out and met us as we stopped the engines on the tarmac. I got down quickly from the door ahead of the passengers, leaving the machine to Arjan, and walked over to the Chinese engineer, and said,

"Morning, Tai Foong. How are things here now? They tell me that you've had a bit of trouble while I've been away."

He smiled. "All is quiet now. It was only one day. The people were angry with the Major Hereward and they hurt him with stones, but now they listen to Mem Nadezna and there is no more trouble."

"Was there trouble here, about the people coming in to pray?"

He nodded. "One day only. After that Mem Nadezna went to the CO and said the people meant no harm in coming here to pray. And Flight Lieutenant Allen, he spoke on the radio to Air Vice-Marshal Collins at Habbaniya near Baghdad and said – his own words, Mr Cutter, I am sorry – he said the local Jesus had been crucified and he was in a mess and wanted some advice because there was nothing in the book to tell him what to do. And next day the Air Vice-Marshal flew down from Habbaniya in his Devon, and after he had talked to Flight Lieutenant Allen they both came here to the hangar and talked to Gujar Singh, and then they talked for a long time to Mem Nadezna. And after that the guard was taken off the road and there was no more firing, and the people now come here to pray each evening. It is quite all right now, Mr Cutter. No more trouble at all."

I went into the hangar with him and he showed me what had been going on in my absence, but I had only half my mind upon his maintenance jobs. I told him to get on with the routine checks on the Tramp since she would be leaving again for Bali in a few days' time, and I went over to the office. It was the lunch hour and the babu clerk was there eating something that he brought with him every day done up in a cloth; he told me that Nadezna was over in the restaurant having lunch, as she usually did. I went there to find her.

She was eating curry and rice at a table by herself, and at first she did not see me. I crossed the room thinking how small she was, how delicate, with her slim figure, her black hair, and her kind, thoughtful features. It was incredible that this slight girl had pressed through a yelling crowd of furious Arabs stoning a man to death, to walk through the flying stones and stand over him, and tick them off. It was more credible that she had been sick afterwards from nervous exhaustion. I walked towards her not quite knowing what to say, because she had become very dear to me, and I was shocked at the risks that she had taken.

She heard my step and looked up, and got up to meet me. "Mr Cutter! I didn't know you were back. Have you come back in the Tramp?"

"Yes," I said. "We landed about a quarter of an hour ago."

"I had no idea. I'm so sorry – I'd have come out to meet you. Have you had lunch?"

I shook my head. "I'll join you, if I may." I pulled out a chair and sat down opposite her. "They tell me that you've had a bit of trouble here."

"Nothing to speak of," she replied. "It was just one afternoon, down in the souk. The people were a little upset. But that's all over now."

"How's Major Hereward?"

"He's still in hospital. He's going to be flown home on leave in a few days' time. His relief, Captain Morrison, was flown up here from Aden yesterday."

"Is this one any better?"

"You mean, as a liaison officer?"

I nodded.

"They say in the souk that he was quite popular at Aden. I don't think Hereward was very bright."

"I don't suppose we'll see him here again," I said. "They'll probably send him to another district, after this." I smiled at her. "He ought to be very grateful to you, but I don't suppose he is."

She said, "Oh, but he is. He sent a message asking if I'd go and see him in hospital, and all he wanted was to say thank you." She hesitated. "It was a bit pathetic. He didn't know what he'd done wrong to make the people so angry."

"Didn't he realise that sending your brother away was likely to make trouble?"

"I don't think he did. I think he thought he was preventing trouble when he sent Connie away."

You cannot argue with stupidity; you just have to accept it patiently as one of those things. I said, "You didn't get hit by any of the stones?"

She shook her head. "They stopped throwing as soon as they saw me."

"Thank God for that," I said quietly.

She looked at me curiously for a moment, and then coloured a little. "There wasn't any danger," she said. "They wouldn't do anything to me. I knew that from the first."

"Like hell you did," I said. "That's why you were sick as soon as it was all over."

She stared at me. "However did you hear of that? Did Chai Tai Foong tell you?"

I shook my head. "Salim told me, last night at Karachi. He's a Pakistani lad who used to work for us here. He's with Sind Airways now."

"He told you I'd been sick outside the hospital?"

"He mentioned it in telling me the story."

She looked me in the face with her thoughtful eyes. "They know about that in Karachi. Do they know that I was sick in Rangoon, in Bangkok, in Bangalore and in Bombay?"

I was silent.

"Does every little thing we do here in Bahrein go halfway round the world?"

I met her eyes. "If you want a straight answer to that one, Nadezna," I replied, " – I think it does."

She smiled. "A goldfish in a glass bowl has more privacy than we have, if I can't even be sick without the whole of Asia knowing."

"Much more," I agreed. "But that's what comes of having Connie for a brother."

"How did you leave Connie?" she enquired. "What sort of place is Bali, anyway?"

I told her what had happened on our flight out as we sat over lunch in the airport restaurant, and about that far-off village he was living in, Pekendang. "It's very quiet, very lovely there," I said. "It's not like this at all. It's tropical, of course, but it's a gentler place than this, with plenty of rainfall, plenty of shady trees and greenery. And cleaner, gentler, happier people than live here. He hasn't got a lot of work to do. I think he should be able to rest there, and put on weight a bit. It seemed to me that he was getting very thin."

She nodded. "I know; he's terribly thin. I think he's been in Bahrein long enough."

I sat thinking for a time, wondering if I could ask her what was in my mind. At last I said, "I wonder if you'd tell me something. Was Connie ever married?"

She shook her head, smiling. "Never came within a hundred miles of it."

"Was he ever in love with a girl?"

"I don't think so. Not that I know of, anyway. He always thought too much about religion. What's all this about, Mr Cutter?"

"I don't want to be nosey," I said. "It's just that he's stuck down there in a very lovely place with very lovely women to look after him. I was wondering how he'd make out."

She smiled. "Like a hermit or a monk or something. I wish he was different, more like other men. If he'd go around with girls and fall in love I'd be much happier about him."

"I know," I said. "Everyone ought to do that."

She coloured a little, and then she said, "I'll have to be getting back on to the job, Mr Cutter. Can I ask Arjan for the journey logbook of the Tramp?"

"That's all right."

"I'll get the airframe and the engine logbooks written up, then, right away. Oh, Mr Cutter, Tarik wants to see you as soon as you can fit him in."

"What does he want?"

"He wants to go down to Bali to work under Connie. Tai Foong came and told me all about it."

"What does he want to go there for? This is his home town."

She sighed a little. "He's writing up the Gospel according to St Tarik in a lot of five-cent exercise books. He's afraid there'll be a gap."

I suppose I was dead tired. I just sat back and laughed as if that was something very funny. I knew it really wasn't funny at all, and yet for a few moments I couldn't stop laughing. I saw her face change, and she came across and laid her hand upon my shoulder. I think that was the first time she had ever touched me.

"Stop it, Tom," she said gently.

I think that was the first time she had called me Tom, though I had called her Nadezna for some time. I never had been quite sure if Shak Lin was her surname, or what.

I took a pull upon myself. "Sorry," I said. "Tarik can't go down there. He's got Phinit with him. That bit will have to be the Gospel according to St Phinit."

She nodded. "Don't bother about that any more. I'll see Tai Foong and Tarik. Go to the chummery and rest an hour or two. There's nothing very urgent in the office."

"I can't do that," I said. "I must go up this afternoon to the Arabia–Sumatran and tell Johnson how the trip went off."

I went and got the Dodge out of the hangar and drove into town to the Arabia–Sumatran office. I told Johnson

261

how the trip had gone and fixed with him the details of the next one, to start in four days' time. We spent half an hour talking of the business, which was going smoothly from his point of view. Then, as I got up to go, I said, "I hear that there was some trouble the day after I went."

He nodded. "It was very foolish of Hereward to advise the Resident to expel your man Shak Lin. Very foolish indeed. As it is, he's lucky to be alive today. He wouldn't have been but for that girl Nadezna."

"I know," I said. "I heard about it."

He thought for a moment. "We owe a lot to her," he said. "I'd give her a medal if I had one to give."

"Things seem to be quiet enough now," I remarked. "I suppose the people in the souk have accepted the position?"

"The souk? Oh – they don't matter. It's the Sheikh of Khulal and his oil that I was worried about. I'm a bit worried still, I don't mind telling you."

"The Sheikh of Khulal?"

"I see you don't know the half of it," he said. "The Sheikh of Khulal was behind that business in the souk. Not a doubt of it. He was in Bahrein that day. I think we might have had a first-class riot if your girl Nadezna hadn't gone to see Wazir Hussein."

I was startled. "When did she do that?"

"The same evening. She put on one of those black milfa veils to hide her face and went to see the Wazir at Sheikh Muhammad's palace, where they were staying."

He paused. "It would be very awkward for our interests if an open breach were to develop between the Sheikh of Khulal and the Resident," he said thoughtfully. "I wish you to bear that in mind, Cutter. We want peace in this country. In a way, I think perhaps you and Nadezna can do more to bring peace back into this district now than the Resident can. Bear it in mind, and just do what you can. Especially if anything crops up that has to do with Khulal."

I left him and went back to the aerodrome. As I crossed the causeway I saw an Airtruck on the circuit, coming in to land, and when I drove up to the hangar Gujar Singh was just taxiing in. I met him on the tarmac, and walked with him to the office.

He told me about the various flight jobs that had been going on in my absence. About the disturbances, he knew little that I did not know already. "I think things are becoming quiet now," he said. "I think that when Air Vice-Marshal Collins took the guard off the road and let the people come back here to pray it made a great deal of difference."

"I should think that would begin to tail off now," I said. "Now that he's gone away, they won't be quite so keen to come out all this way just to say their prayers."

"I do not know," he said. "I have not counted them, but it seems to me that more of them come here to pray each evening. I think there are more coming now than when Shak Lin was here." He paused and then he said, "I think a movement such as this is strengthened if you try to repress it."

I told him that I wanted him to take the Tramp on the next trip to Bali with Hosein as copilot, and discussed the route with him a little. There was not much to talk about, because he had flown it already once with me; he had plenty of time in the next four days to study his maps and radio information to prepare for the flight. I left him presently, and went back into the office and started on the correspondence.

That was the bad part of my job, the office work. I had been flying and working hard for five days in the tropics, all across the world, and as a solace and a rest I came back to a desk piled high with papers to be dealt with. I dictated to Nadezna for three quarters of an hour and gave her more than she could cope with that day; then I sent her out to get on with the typing and sat on at my desk turning over the remainder of the stuff with a mind dulled with fatigue.

Presently outside my office Arabs from the town began to pass along the road; it was getting towards sunset and the time of evening prayer. I could not concentrate enough for useful work; I got up and went out of the office and watched what was going on from a distance. A string of motor buses and taxis were parked on the road, and men were streaming from them to the empty space reserved for prayer just by the hangar. There were a great many of them. I did not try to count them, for I was too tired, but as I stood there watching it seemed to me that there were many more than I had seen before. There was an Imam with them, and presently he stood up in the semicircle of white stones that faced to Mecca and began to lead them in the evening *Rakats*.

I stood and watched them for a time, most desolately alone. I could not go and join them because I was a European and a Christian, and because I had never done so. I just stood at the corner of the restaurant watching as they laid their troubles before God and cleansed their souls with the ritual; I was tired and depressed, and I would have given anything to be there with them, joining in their prayers. And presently I couldn't bear it any longer, and I went back to the office and sat there with my head resting on my arms upon the desk. If I had been able to I would have wept, but I had not wept since I was a child.

And presently Nadezna came in with the letters. I raised my head, and I said heavily, "The post must have gone. I'll sign them in the morning." She came to my side and put the letters down upon the desk. And then she put her hand to my head and caressed my hair, and said, "You're very, very tired. You must go home and rest."

She was comfort and security and stability to me, a touch of everything that was lacking from my life. I pulled her hand down and kissed it, and she said softly, "Poor Tom." We stayed like that for a long time, perhaps ten minutes.

It was no good starting off upon another Beryl. Presently I got up and smiled at her, and said, "Thanks, Nadezna. That was good of you." And then I went out to the old Dodge station wagon, and drove in a daze down to the chummery, and went and lay down on the charpoy. I didn't sleep much that night: perhaps I was too tired.

CHAPTER EIGHT

And God shall make thy body pure, and give thee
knowledge to endure
This ghost-life's piercing phantom pain, and bring thee out to
Life again.

JAMES ELROY FLECKER

FROM THAT TIME on there was a period when everything
went well. It was autumn, for one thing, and with the onset
of the winter weather nerves became less strained, tempers
less ragged. As the nights got colder so that first a sheet was
necessary over you for sleep, and then a blanket, everybody
slept better and was able to relax. The summer is a bad time
in the Persian Gulf, even if you can stand it. Every one of
our party was accustomed to great heat or we wouldn't have
been there, but even so – the summer's a bad time.

In Bahrein, the new Liaison Officer, Captain Morrison,
turned out to be a great success. He was quite a young chap,
not more than about thirty but, my God, he was good. He had
come into the Army when he was about twenty for the war,
and had found his way into some branch of the Intelligence
in Egypt and the Sudan. He had stayed in after the war was
over and had been seconded for civil duties; he had travelled
very widely in Arabia with the Bedouins. He spoke Arabic
fluently, and half a dozen dialects of it. He was unmarried.

He came up to the aerodrome soon after he arrived and
came into my office. He had a shy, diffident manner, very

unlike Hereward; there was no professional charm about him at all. It was difficult to believe that he was in the Army; he seemed just like an ordinary person.

He said, "I suppose you know what I've come for."

I must say, he got me a bit confused. As a matter of fact, I *did* know. Gujar Singh had told me that morning that he was coming to see me to ask me to have dinner with him in his quarters at the Residency. Gujar had heard that in the souk, of course. The gossip was that this young man had told the Resident that he wanted to tackle things in Bahrein from a different angle. He had told him that I, Tom Cutter, was one of the most influential people in the district, and that it was absolutely necessary to get my co-operation and advice in tackling the religious difficulties that seemed to have arisen. All this had got down to the souk in about five minutes, and ten minutes after that one or two grave, white-bearded old men had visited the house of the silk merchant, Mutluq bin Aamir, to tell the rumour to the Sister of the Teacher and ask her what she thought about it. Gujar Singh told me that Nadezna had told them gravely that it was a good thing and that the Teacher would certainly approve of any such co-operation from the Liaison Officer; so everybody in the souk was happy. As for me, didn't know what to say to my shorthand typist, so I said nothing.

I temporised with Morrison. I said, "How on earth should I know what you've come for?"

"I just thought you might have heard something," he said awkwardly. "I wanted to ask you to have dinner with me tonight."

It was a friendly approach, meant in a friendly way. I was a bit embarrassed in my turn, because essentially I was a fitter come up from the bench, and I'd never had time for any social life or anything like that. "I'd like to do that," I said. "But there's just one thing. I'm afraid I haven't got a dinner jacket."

He said that didn't matter because there'd only be him and me, and so I dined with him that night. We sat on his veranda for a long time after dinner drinking his whisky, and because he was simple and really anxious to learn what had been going on, I told him everything I knew.

We must have sat like that talking for over an hour after dinner, looking out into the still blue night, with the moon making a bright track across the sea. I told him everything right from the first day I met Connie in Cobham's Circus; I even put in a word or two about my marriage. I told him about Dwight Schafter, and I told him about U Set Tahn.

In the end he said quietly, "What do you really think about Shak Lin, Mr Cutter? What sort of a person do you really think he is?"

I stared out over the dim sea. "I think he's a very good chap," I said at last.

"I know. But there are a large number of people here who think he is divine."

"He's not," I said. "He's just a very good ground engineer with a bee in his bonnet." I paused, and then I said, "If I thought he was divine, I couldn't very well dictate my letters to his sister."

"No ..." he said thoughtfully.

I could not put it into words, but what I meant was that Nadezna was a human being, a girl like any other girl. She was somebody that one could get to care for very much and to depend upon. It was unthinkable that her brother should have qualities above humanity; it was a gross fallacy that had to be put right, at all costs.

"I can assure you, there's nothing like that," I said positively. That was the first time I denied him.

He got up and went and got some papers from the room behind us, and when he came back he poured me out another whisky, and got a fresh bottle of cold soda water from the refrigerator. Then he sat down beside me again.

"Did you know about the RAF plans for expansion here?" he asked.

I shook my head. "Not a thing."

"It's in a very early stage," he said. "I think they're planning to put a squadron on the aerodrome at last. Of course, the trouble is that you are occupying the only hangar, and that's right on top of the RAF camp."

"I see," I said. "Do they want to kick me out?"

"Not from the aerodrome," he said. "They realise that your business mustn't be disturbed. The proposal is that they should build a new civil aviation hangar for you, at the south end of the north-south runway." He unfolded a plan of the aerodrome and showed me where they meant to put it. "Here. At the same time, they want to extend the present hangar by building over the vacant land to the south of it, here. The present hangar won't be large enough for them, apparently."

I stared at the plan in consternation. "Hell," I said. "They can't possibly do that. They can't build over that bit to the south. That's where the people come to say their prayers."

"It's all RAF land, of course."

"It's holy ground," I retorted. "Honestly, you've got to put a stop to this. If they prevent the people coming there to pray you'll have all hell break loose."

"That's because it's the bit of land that Shak Lin used for praying on?"

"That's right," I said. "It's very holy ground."

He smiled gently. "And yet, you don't think Shak Lin is divine?"

"Of course I don't," I said. "But other people do." That was the second time.

He sat studying the plan. "I think as you do," he said at last. "I don't think we can let them put their hangar there – not just at present, anyway. It's going to make a lot of difficulties I suppose, but I think they'll have to put their hangar somewhere else. Let you stay in the present hangar, and choose another site for their new buildings."

We talked over the details for a time. It was certainly an odd position, that a holy place had come into being in the middle of an RAF camp. I told him that I thought that Air Vice-Marshal Collins might be reasonable about it; he seemed to have acted with understanding at the time of the previous trouble.

Presently he laid the papers down. "I don't feel that the present situation is a static one," he said. "Do you?"

"I'm not sure that I know what you mean," I said.

"Well, what I mean is this. Either this cult of Shak Lin will die out in a few months, or else it will increase and be a bigger thing than ever. I don't believe that two or three hundred people will be coming up to the aerodrome to make their *Rakats* every evening, in two years from now. There may be more or there may be less, but not two or three hundred."

"I think I'd agree with that," I said slowly. "I think there'll be a change."

"If we could guess which way the change would be," he remarked, "we'd know what to tell the RAF about their hangar. If the people have forgotten all about Shak Lin in two years' time and nobody goes to the aerodrome to pray, then the RAF can take that bit of land and build on it."

I shook my head. "I don't think it'll go like that. There's been no sign of any diminution so far. This thing is growing now at a great pace. Shak Lin has never been anywhere near Bombay, and yet his cult is strong amongst the engineers there now. So far as I can see, it's growing every day, all through the East. I haven't seen a sign of any falling off yet, not in any place. You'll have to work on the assumption that this thing won't die out here. I think myself that it will grow."

He said quietly. "You're saying, in effect, that we must work on the assumption that Shak Lin's divine."

"God damn it," I said angrily. "I tell you he's not. I know him, and he's just a damn good engineer who's going round the bend a bit. That's all there is to him." That was the third time.

"A damn good engineer who's going round the bend a bit," he said thoughtfully. "It wouldn't have been a bad description of the Prophet Mahomet, only he was a damn good merchant."

I got to my feet. "Time I went home," I said. "I'm sorry if I spoke strongly, but I know Shak Lin very well. And I know his sister, too. They're very ordinary people. She works in my office, you know." I could not possibly admit that there was anything different about Nadezna. I was growing to depend on her too much.

"I expect you're right," he said. "We've passed the age of miracles, except the ones that come from nuclear fission." He came down with me to the courtyard to my old Dodge station wagon. "It was very good of you to come this evening," he said. "It's a great help to have a talk to somebody who really knows what's making this place tick."

It was nice of him to say that. I said something or other of the same sort in reply and drove back to the chummery, feeling that at last the Administration would be guided on the proper lines by this young chap.

Gujar Singh took the Tramp down to Bali on the first of the regular trips with a load of passengers and freight for Yenanyaung, Diento, and East Alligator River. He was back in nine days in accordance with the schedule, bringing with him four passengers and about half a ton of fresh fruit for the oil company's employees, mangoes and pawpaws and pineapples, things that we didn't very often see in the Persian Gulf. He brought me in a basket of this fruit to my office, and told me about the trip and showed me the journey logbook; it had been a good, uneventful journey except that he had had a bit of trouble with the monsoon at

271

the intertropical front over north Malaya. He hadn't been able to get high enough to over-fly the cloud banks and it looked so bad ahead that he had been unwilling to go through them, so he had gone under and had flown for five hundred miles in heavy rain along the beaches, only fifty feet up. Coming back it had been easier.

I asked him how things were going at the Bali end. He said that Connie and Phinit were getting quite a good little workshop going in the hangar; they had taken on two Balinese lads temporarily for whitewashing and painting and they were getting the place shipshape. The Governor wanted them to maintain his Auster, as we had supposed. Gujar had a list of tools and materials that they wanted to be sent down on the next trip.

"How's the accommodation working out?" I asked. 'Did you go to the village where they live, Pekendang?

"Oh yes," he said. "We went there to sleep and spend the evening with them, Hosein and I." He hesitated, and then said, "I was not sure if we would have been accepted in the Bali Hotel, or if that is only for Europeans."

"I'm sure that would have been all right," I said. "There were Asiatics there when I was there. I ought to have told you. I'm sorry."

He smiled. "We liked it in Pekendang. It is much cheaper, too. We did not pay at all, but in the Bali Hotel it would have cost ten or fifteen guilders. It is better for us to stay in Pekendang with Shak Lin and Phinit."

"How are they getting on there, Gujar? Are they hitting it off with the villagers all right? It's pretty primitive accommodation."

He said, "They are very happy there, Mr Cutter. I think Bali is a happy country, where people can live well and still have time to work upon their arts and serve their temples. I think that they are very happy there indeed."

"I'm glad to hear it," I replied. "I was just a bit worried that they might not have fitted in. That woman Mem Simpang, is she looking after them all right?"

He said, "I think so. I only saw her once. Her daughter brings the food and keeps the room clean and mends Shak Lin's clothes."

"That's the good-looking girl? Ni Madé Jasmi?"

"They call her Madé," he said. "I did not hear the other name."

"She does for them?"

He hesitated. "There is another girl who seems to take care of Phinit. They call her Ktut Suriatni. The two girls do the work between them, but Madé works mostly for Shak Lin."

I said, "Is Phinit behaving himself, Gujar?"

He laughed in his great black beard. "With Ktut Suriatni? I do not think so. The village would probably be very insulted if he did."

"Not going to make any trouble?"

He shook his head. "He is a good lad, from a country that is not so far away, and he knows the rules by which this game is played. He will do whatever is the right thing in the eyes of the village. There will be no trouble, Mr Cutter."

"I'm glad to hear it," I said. "What about Madé?"

He looked more grave. "Ah, Madé," he said. "She thinks nothing of Phinit, and in any case he could not have two women at one time. I do not think the village would approve of that. But Madé only serves the Teacher."

"And is she getting any joy out of that?"

He shook his head. "No joy."

I did not think she would, but it was an interesting situation. "Will the village take that as an insult, then?"

He smiled. "I do not think that they are very touchy. But in any case, Shak Lin is different to Phinit, and the village know it. Phinit is one of them, but Shak Lin is different."

"How do Connie and Phinit spend their time, Gujar?"

273

He said, "They are at the airstrip working most of every day. But in the evenings they sit in the village and talk with the people. They can talk to them now fairly well."

"What do they talk about?"

He grinned broadly. "What would Phinit talk about to Ktut Suriatni, Mr Cutter? Your guess is as good as mine. But Shak Lin talks to the old men a great deal. A Buddhist priest came to the village the night I was there. He had walked from Besakih, a great temple in the middle of the island, to see the Teacher. He stayed after we had gone."

"I thought they were Hindus?"

He laughed. "I think you English call every religion that you do not understand, Hinduism. But there are Buddhists in the island, just a few."

"Shak Lin is finding out about the religion, I suppose?"

He nodded. "I think so."

"And that's bad luck on Madé?"

He nodded gravely. "He could have happiness for the asking, and give it, too. But the Teacher is different to other men."

There was no arguing about that one. "I'll go down there myself one of these trips, Gujar," I said. "Stop over for a fortnight till the next one. It's time I took a bit of leave."

He said, "I think that would be a very good thing. It is a lovely island, and you should rest sometimes, Mr Cutter. I think that would be very good indeed."

We left it at that, but the idea stayed in my mind. Late that night before going to sleep, as I luxuriated in bed in a cold room with two blankets over me, I got what seemed to me a pretty good notion. The more I thought of it the more I liked it, and I drifted into sleep with a smile on my face. It was still there when I woke up.

I could hardly wait till I had finished dictating to Nadezna next morning. "Look," I said when the last letter was done. "I've been talking to Gujar about your brother and how they're getting on down there."

She nodded. "I've asked Gujar about Connie, too."

"Oh." I grinned at her. "Did he tell you about Madé Jasmi?"

She smiled. "That's the Bali girl who's looking after him?"

"That's the one. She's a very beautiful girl."

"So Gujar says."

"What I thought was this," I said. "I want a bit of a holiday. I was thinking we might get everything cleaned up here in the office and go down there, and stop over for one trip. Not this coming trip, but the one after. That gives us a clear fortnight in the office here to get everything buttoned up so that Dunu can look after things while we're away. Go down on one trip and come back on the next one. That would mean we'd have about a fortnight there. We should be away from here about three weeks."

I hesitated, and then I said, "You'd like to see your brother, wouldn't you?"

She sat silent with her eyes cast down, tracing a little pattern faintly with her pencil on the cover of her pad. I was disappointed that she had not welcomed the chance of a visit to Bali, but a man gets used to disappointments as his life goes on. I said gently, "Wouldn't you like to come?"

She said, "May I think it over, and tell you this evening?" She hesitated. "I don't think we ought both to be away at the same time."

"Think it over," I said. "Gujar and Dunu can cope with anything that's likely to crop up. I'd leave Gujar here in charge."

I went on with the day's work in the office, but it was a weary day. I had counted on her coming with me for this holiday, and I didn't see what there was against it. It couldn't possibly be that she wanted a chaperon or anything like that, and I knew she was becoming fond of me. I wanted to be with her, to get to know her better, to find out what she liked and didn't like outside the office. She must have known I'd never do her any harm. I spent the day uncertain, worried and impatient.

In the evening, as she was putting the cover on her typewriter, I said, "Thought any more about this Bali business?"

She turned and faced me. She was wearing a white drill frock, very simple. "I've been thinking about it all day, Tom," she said. "I don't think I'd better come."

I suppose I'd known that was coming, though I didn't know why. My face must have shown my disappointment, because she looked up at me and said, "I'm just terribly sorry. It's not that I don't want a holiday with you. It's Bali."

I sat down on the edge of the desk. "What's it all about?" I asked, as kindly as I could. "What's wrong with Bali?"

She said, "I don't want to go there, not just now."

"Don't you want to see Connie? I thought you'd like the chance."

She shook her head. "I don't want to see him for a bit."

I reached out and took one of her hands in mine. "Tell me why," I said. "I'm only trying to help."

"I know you are," she said. She smiled a little. "You're doing that in your own way all the time. That's why this party runs so well."

"I'd like to know why you don't want to go and see Connie," I observed.

"I know you do," she said thoughtfully. "Otherwise you'll think that it's because I don't want to go away with you, and it's not that at all."

"Thank God for that, anyway," I said.

She raised her eyes and looked at me. "I want to leave him alone for a bit," she said. "I don't mind you going. It might be quite a good thing if you did. But I don't want to go myself, not now. I think he's better without me."

"Why is that, Nadezna?"

She withdrew her hand, and walked over and stood by the open window. The people were beginning to go past to the place by the hangar for the evening prayer. She was silent for a bit, and then she said, "Did you meet this girl, Madé Jasmi?"

I was amazed that she should raise that thing again. Surely, she wasn't jealous? I said, "Yes, I just met her. She was with her mother when we were settling how much they were to pay. I didn't speak to her, of course. I couldn't."

"Is she nice, Tom?"

"She's got rather a nice face," I told her. "To look at her, you'd say she would be kind and even-tempered, and probably faithful."

She nodded slowly. "That's what Gujar said. Did Gujar tell you much about her, Tom?"

"He said that she looked after Connie mostly. There's another one who's looking after Phinit."

"Did he tell you that she was in love with Connie?"

"Yes," I said. "He told me that."

She stood looking out at the muddled buildings between us and the hangar, with glimpses of the tarmac and the sea beyond. "If that's true," she said, "it's the first time it's ever happened."

"The first time anyone has ever been in love with him?"

"I think so. You don't know of anyone, do you?"

I shook my head. "I never saw him take an interest in a girl, or any girl in him."

"Nor did I," she said. "But now, if Gujar Singh is right, there is a girl, and she's in love with him."

I thought about this for a moment. "Well, you can put it like that," I said at last. "I don't know much about the Balinese, and I don't think Gujar Singh does, either. She's a very lovely girl, Nadezna, but it's a very primitive village. She may want to go to bed with him. Probably she does.

277

But whether you can put it any higher than that, I wouldn't know."

She said, "I only wish she would."

I grinned. "Think it'll do him good?"

She said gravely, "I know it would."

She came and stood by me again. "I want you to try and understand about Connie, Tom," she said. "There's such a lot of nonsense being talked about him that one can't deny, because it means so much to so many people. So many people think that he … that he's a prophet, or something. They do, honestly, down in the souk. They think that he's a sort of prophet."

I took her hand again, and examined it. "I know," I said. "Some people quite high up are starting to say that."

"You don't believe that, do you, Tom?" She looked at me appealingly.

I smiled at her. "I don't. I think he's just a damn good chap who's got a bee in his bonnet. Perhaps he's been out in the East too long."

She nodded. "I think he has. He always was interested in religions, ever since he was a little chap. And then, when we lived in America, we were Asiatics, you see – different to the rest. Mother was Russian-born and we always reckoned we were European, but we weren't really – not Connie and I. And of course, it made a difference. I don't think Connie ever had a girl friend in his life, not one. And his religion made up."

"I see," I said. This was a new light on the man I knew.

She said quietly, "Tom, I believe this is his chance, and it may be the last one that he'll have. I don't care who she is so long as she'll be kind to him, and make him happy like an ordinary man, and give him children. If she's an Asiatic, well, he's Asiatic too, and so am I. I want her to have him. He's never had a girl in love with him before, and that's what's made him into what he is. I want her to make him love her, and make him an ordinary man."

I stood studying her fingertips, holding her hand in mine. "You think that's what he's missed?"

"I know it is," she said. "He's always been incomplete, because he's never had that. He's slid deeper and deeper into his religion, just to compensate."

I stood thinking, perhaps, more about Nadezna whose hand I was caressing than about Connie. I was wondering if the same Asiatic nature of her birth had denied her boy friends, too. It might well be so. But she had had her mother to look after, and perhaps she had found compensation in that way.

"You're a good bit younger than Connie, aren't you?" I asked.

She nodded. "Eight years," she said. "There were two others between us – both boys. There was a typhoid epidemic in our street down by the harbour in Penang, and my father and Ivan and Victor all died. After that, Mother took Connie and me to London, because my father died fairly well off, and Mother didn't want us to grow up as Chinese. My father had helped Sir Alan Cobham on one of his flights through Penang, and Mother wrote to him in London, and Sir Alan took Connie on as an apprentice. That's how he got started in this business."

I came back to the point that we had started from. "Why don't you want to go to Bali, then?" I asked.

She said, "I might frighten her, and spoil it."

"I see."

She said, "Gujar and you say she's just a village girl, living in a very primitive place. But Gujar says that she's in love with him, and Phinit, living there with him, is living with another of the girls there, one of Madé Jasmi's friends. If ever Connie had a chance of knowing what love means it's now.

And if he can have that, I think he might snap out of all this prophet stuff, and come back to us as a normal man."

"Why do you think you'd frighten her?" I asked. "You're on her side."

Nadezna said, "If she's a village girl like that, she'd never believe it. Different clothes, different speech, different colour … If I turned up there as his sister she'd be terrified of me, and angry, too, because she'd think that I resented her and wanted to take him from her. I'd never get her to believe that I want her to have him."

"No," I said thoughtfully. "I don't suppose you would."

"I think I'll have to keep away," she said. "However much one wants to help her I think this is a time when another woman just can't help at all."

"Would you rather I kept clear of them, myself?" I asked. She shook her head. "I think it might be helpful if you went, if you can spare the time. Connie thinks so much of you, Tom. He may want to talk to somebody before he takes her." She smiled. "He's such a bunch of ideals," she said. "He's quite capable of keeping a girl hanging round while he consults a friend to ask him if he's doing the right thing."

I laughed. "You want me to push him into it."

"I do," she said, but she wasn't laughing at all. "I think that it's the only thing to save him now."

There was real pain and anxiety in her when she said that, and for a moment I thought that she was going to start crying. I put an arm clumsily around her shoulders. "It's not as bad as that," I said. 'After all, nothing's going to happen if he doesn't get this girl."

"Only one thing," she said sadly.

"What's that?"

"I think he'll turn into a prophet."

I was silent.

"I don't know how a man becomes a prophet," she said quietly. "But thousands of people, spread all through the

East – they think he's one already. I suppose that if a person gives up earthly things and preaches a new, simple way of life to people who are hungry for his teaching – I suppose that's what a prophet is, isn't it? Or is there something more to it than that?"

I pressed her shoulders gently. "Look," I said. "I don't know what a prophet is, or what makes one. I only know that it's a very long time since there's been a prophet in the world. Far as I know, Mahomet was the last, and he lived about fourteen hundred years ago. That's a good long time ago. I don't know what a prophet is, but I do know this: that it's pretty long odds against our having one here in our little party, now. In all these ages, people must have been thought to be prophets who weren't really, just ordinary chaps who'd been out in the East too long. That's all that Connie is, Nadezna – honestly. And if we treat him that way, it's the best thing we can do." I paused. "I'd like to see him have a job in a cold climate for a time. In England or America."

She smiled, and pressed my hand, and said, "Dear Tom. But he wouldn't go."

"No …" I thought about it for a minute. "Well then, I'd like to see him get this girl. I think you're quite right there. I think that it would do him good, perhaps."

She looked up, smiling. "If he became the father of twins it'ld knock him off his perch, wouldn't it?"

I burst out laughing, and she freed herself from my arm and laughed with me. "Well, anyway," she said, "you go alone this time and find out what he's up to, and give him a push the right way." She was calm and matter-of-fact about it now, all apprehensions of the unknown put away. "I'll stay here and look after things with Dunu." She paused. "But don't think it's because I won't come with you for a trip, Tom. I'd like to do that – but not to Bali. Not just now."

"All right," I said. "I'll go and see what I can make of it."

Arjan and Hosein took the Tramp down for the next journey to Bali, and I went on quietly at Bahrein, making my preparations to go down on the following trip and spend a fortnight there. I flew one of the Airtrucks once or twice upon a local journey, and I spent some time in the hangar with Chai Tai Foong and the ground engineers. Most of the time I spent in the office, because it was there that I liked to be now. There was always something to talk about with Nadezna, something to make a joke about with her.

I never took her out anywhere, for the very good reason that there was nowhere to take her to in Bahrein. There was no restaurant where we could have a meal together, or anything like that. If one drove out in the car you got out into the dry, parched desert in a couple of miles, without a tree or any vegetation whatsoever. I did think once or twice of taking her bathing, but that's not much catch in the Persian Gulf; you can't go in more than knee deep because of the sharks, and there's no shade at all, which makes it rather trying. I'd never felt the need of anywhere to go except the office up till then, and now it was in the office that we met and got to know each other. It was very pleasant there in those few days.

Hosein and Arjan came back in the Tramp according to their schedule, and I warned Gujar Singh and a new pilot that we had, called Kadhim, that they would be the first and second pilots for the next trip down to Bali, the one I should be going on. Hosein and Arjan Singh had spent the night in Pekendang with Connie and Phinit, but they were neither so observant or so much in my confidence as Gujar Singh, and I didn't like to question them too closely about the women. I learned nothing from them. Nadezna asked Gujar to find out anything he could from them, but they had little information for him. They were both devout followers of Connie, Hosein in particular, and it had probably never entered their heads that the Teacher could take any interest in a woman.

Two days before I was due to leave for Bali, I was in the hangar with Tai Foong when Nadezna came to me. "Wazir Hussein's just arrived and wants to see you, Mr Cutter," she said. She always called me Mr Cutter in front of other people. "He's in the office, waiting."

I left the hangar and went over to the office, wondering what he wanted. I was up to date with my payments on the loan to buy the Tramp, and with the work that the machine was doing I could step the payments up, if need be. I thought about that quickly as I walked over to the office, past the maroon car with the Arab chauffeur.

I went and greeted him, "How very nice of you to come," I said. "Let me order coffee." I nodded to Nadezna in the doorway and she nodded back that she would send for it, and closed the door softly behind her, so that I was alone with Hussein.

We began to talk about the weather and the crops as usual, and very soon he asked me how the Tramp had been behaving, so I knew it wasn't that that he had come to talk about. I told him all about it and the work that it was doing, wondering all the time what he had come for if it wasn't that, and he listened politely and said all the right and courteous things at the right time. Then Dunu brought a tray with the small cups of Turkish coffee, and put it on the desk between us, and went out and closed the door behind him.

Presently the Wazir said, "And where is Shak Lin now, Mr Cutter?"

"He's at Bali in Indonesia," I said, "looking after the far end of our service there." I told him what Shak Lin was doing and how he was living. I found he did not really know where Bali was, and he wasn't too sure about Indonesia either, so I took him to the big map of Asia that I had pinned up upon the wall and showed him where Bali was and how the aircraft flew there every fortnight to meet the Dakota coming up from Darwin. He was an able man with an alert mind, and he grasped the various points very quickly.

We went back to our chairs. "And will El Amin be coming back here to Bahrein in the near future?" he asked.

"I don't think so," I said carefully. "As you must know, there was a small amount of friction here about him, and the Liaison Officer suggested to me that he should be sent away." He inclined his head, and his face darkened; with his black beard and aquiline features framed in the white cloth of his head-dress he looked quite an ugly customer for a moment. "Things are much more pleasant now," I said. "I think perhaps if I were to ask for his return the Government might allow it." I paused. "On my side, I don't need him back here. He's doing good work for us where he is, and the Chinese boy, Chai Tai Foong, who has succeeded him, is doing well." I added, "Doing well in the straight performance of the work, I mean. No one could replace Shak Lin as a teacher of ground engineers, or as a man."

He nodded gravely. "That is very true. He is not likely to return here, then?"

"I don't think he is." I hesitated. "I doubt if he would want to, himself. When he left here, he felt that his time here was over, that it was time that he moved on, in any case. He went without resentment, for that reason."

He nodded again, and we sat together for some time in silence. At last he said, "My master, the Sheikh Abd el Kadir, is becoming an old man. He will not live for very many months more. He is not ill, but he is tired now and ready to put down his burdens. He wants very much to meet El Amin once again, to pray with him and take his blessing before he lies down to die."

"I see," I said. The old man, after all, had lent me sixty thousand pounds at a time when I needed it badly. I still owed him most of it. "That's very easy to arrange," I said.

"Shak Lin can come back here on one machine and go down again on the next trip. He'd have about four days here, if he did that. I should have to ask the Resident, of course. But this new Liaison Officer, Captain Morrison, would help us there. And as for Shak Lin, I know he'd be glad to come."

He said evenly, "My master would not ask the Resident for any favour in this matter, nor would he allow you to do so."

There was another long silence while he left that to sink in. I had known, of course, that there was some bitterness; I had not realised that it was quite so strong as this. Time would heal it, of course, because the old Sheikh would be dead before so very long, but it seemed to me to be a sad thing that official clumsiness should have produced such lasting ill feeling. If anyone could ease the matter for the Resident and Captain Morrison, perhaps now, queerly, it was me.

"What can we do about it?" I enquired at last. "How can I help your master, who has helped me so much?"

He said, "My master would like to travel to El Amin. I do not think that he would ask so great a man to come back here, halfway across the world, to visit him. My master wishes to arrange that you should fly him to El Amin in your large aeroplane, with some members of his household, so that he may see Shak Lin again and talk to him before he dies."

I thought quickly. The Sheikh would have to go in his own aeroplane, the Tramp; no doubt that was his idea. Because of the relationship between the Arabia–Sumatran and the Sheikh by which they paid for his oil, Johnson would probably forgo one of his fortnightly trips for this purpose, if I put it to him. We could free the Tramp for the job. But the Tramp was a bare box inside, unfurnished, unheated, and unsoundproofed; a poor vehicle for an invalid old man to live in for four days to Bali, and four days back, all through the tropical extremes of heat and cold.

I said, "Of course I will do that, Wazir. If that's what he wants to do, he shall do it. I can arrange for him to fly to Bali in the Tramp, the large aeroplane which he lent me the money to buy, or I can arrange for him to charter a more comfortable aeroplane, that an old man can travel in without so much fatigue." And I went on to tell him of my doubts about the suitability of the Tramp.

We walked over to the hangar together for me to show him the Tramp. We got up into it and stood in the great empty cabin, floored with duralumin, with bare stringers and formers supporting the outer skin of the walls, innocent of any upholstery. I showed him the toilet that my mother had admired so much, back in distant Eastleigh; that was about all the passenger accommodation that there was. "As an alternative," I said, "I can arrange for him to charter a York from BOAC. That would have a crew of five or six, probably with two stewards in uniform, with proper arrangements for serving meals. It would be warmer for him, and much less noisy. I can't say quite what it would cost; probably between five and six thousand pounds for the return journey."

He said, "The money is not important ..." He looked around the inside of the Tramp. "Could we put a carpet on the floor, and a couch for my master to lie on?"

I said, "Of course we can, Wazir. If he would like to use this aeroplane we can do anything like that, only limited by the amount that we can carry, which is five tons."

He said, "I think my master would prefer to go in one of your aeroplanes. He would not want to go upon his pilgrimage in luxury and carried by a crew of unbelievers." He glanced around him at the bleak functional utility of the metal cabin. "This is more suitable." He turned back to me. "My master would prefer to be carried by devout men."

"Of course." I thought for a minute. "If he wishes," I said, "I can arrange for the whole crew to be Moslems. I can arrange for Hosein and Kadhim to go as first and second pilots; they're both Iraqis. Then I should send two of my Bahrein men who are accustomed to travelling by air to act as servants – Tarik and Khail, I think. But frankly, I should like my chief pilot to go with your master upon such a journey – Gujar Singh. He's a Sikh. If your master has no strong objection, I should like to send Gujar as chief pilot and Hosein as second pilot."

"It does not matter that the crew should all be Moslems," he replied, "El Amin himself is not a Moslem. My master knows Gujar Singh, and everybody trusts him."

As we walked back to the office I told him that the Arabia–Sumatran had first call upon the Tramp under their contract, and that I would see Johnson at once and see if I could get him to release the aircraft for one trip. I told him that I was going down to Bali on the next flight myself, and we arranged that the Sheikh's journey should be the trip after that, so that I should be at Bali to meet the aircraft when it arrived, and could make arrangements for the accommodation of the party. Then I would travel back with them to Bahrein on the return journey.

He was staying with Sheikh Muhammad, with his master, the Sheikh of Khulal, at the palace just outside the town. I told him I would see Johnson at once and call on him at the palace later in the day. Then he bowed to me and said, "May God protect you," and got into the back of his maroon Hudson, and was driven away.

I went and saw Johnson and got him to agree to stand down for one trip; as I had thought, he was very ready to oblige the Sheikh of Khulal in this way. I went to the palace and drank coffee with the party and confirmed the arrangements with the Wazir, and told him how much it would cost him, and got away from there after only an hour and forty minutes – good going in those parts. Then I went back to the aerodrome. Gujar Singh was there, and I had a talk to him about it in the office. We rearranged the pilots' schedules to send Arjan on the next trip with Kadhim since Gujar was to pilot the old Sheikh, because I didn't want my chief pilot to be away from the home base too much.

As he got up to go, Gujar said, "This is the next phase, then."

"What's that?" I asked.

He said, "This is the first pilgrimage to visit Shak Lin."

Nadezna was in the room, taking some papers from the basket on my desk. I felt her check and stiffen. "This is exceptional," I said uncertainly. "This won't happen again."

He smiled. "We can't do anything to stop it, if it does."

He went out, and Nadezna was still standing there, motionless by my desk. "It *is* exceptional," I said gently. "It doesn't mean anything ..."

She said dully, "Only that an old man who is dying thinks it worth while to go six or seven thousand miles to get Connie's blessing."

I tried to cheer her up. "Perhaps Madé Jasmi's done her stuff by this time." And then I said, "You're sure you wouldn't like to come down with me?"

She sighed a little. "No," she said, "I couldn't help. You go alone, Tom, and do what you can."

I left with the Tramp two days later, and travelled like a passenger, resting in a long chair in the cabin with the load. The pilots were getting the hang of the journey by that time, and were making longer stages. We were circling the airstrip of Den Pasar on Bali by midday of the fourth day, half a day ahead of time. The Dakota from Darwin wasn't due until the evening; I made a note to put its times forward by a day.

Connie and Phinit were on the aerodrome to meet us, and began to work at once to check the aircraft and the engines, and to refuel. We had two Australian scientists and a Dutchman with us to go on as passengers to East Alligator

River, and for courtesy I had to stay with them and not go off alone to Pekendang. Moreover, it wouldn't have benefited me to do so, because Connie and Phinit would be working very late upon the Tramp, perhaps all through the night, to get it ready for the trip back to Bahrein. Probably they wouldn't get back to Pekendang themselves that night.

I sent my passengers into the Bali Hotel in the KLM car, and set to work with the pilots and the engineers to get the aircraft serviced and the load ready to tranship to the Dakota when it came. It turned up just before dusk and taxied in, and as we were all there and working we changed loads that night. It was most of it light stuff that could be carried over from one aircraft to the other, all except one motor generator set that the Dakota had brought for us to take back to Diento; this weighed over a ton and we had to rig the sheer-legs for it. It was nine o'clock by the time we could leave for the Bali Hotel, and Connie and Phinit were still working on the engines of the Tramp when we went.

They were there when we got out to the airstrip next morning at about half-past seven. Connie said that they had finished about one o'clock and had slept for a few hours on charpoys in the hangar; they had the engines running and the machines all ready to go when we got there, so they had probably been working again at dawn. The crews and passengers got into their respective aircraft and made ready with the usual deliberation; then the machines taxied out and down the strip together. The Dakota took off first and headed straight out from the strip towards the east. The Tramp followed and climbed straight ahead till it was at about five hundred feet, slowly raising flaps; then it turned in a wide circle and flew past north of us, climbing, and set a course to the north-west for Sourabaya and vanished up the coast.

Connie, Phinit, and I were left upon the ground, tired, they with a night's work and I with four days flying. Connie said, "Where are you going to stay? Will you stay in Den Pasar or come with us?"

"I'd like to come and stay in Pekendang, if that can be arranged," I said. "Would they mind having a European in the village?"

"Not a bit," he said. "I thought you might want to come there, for a day or two anyway. I've fixed up a room for you to yourself, and a bed, and a mosquito net. But it's all a bit primitive, you know."

I nodded. "If I get fed up with it I'll go back to the Bali Hotel. But I don't suppose I shall."

"They've got very interesting techniques of woodcarving," he said. "There's quite a bit to see."

I had brought my bag with me to the aerodrome, and he sent one of the Balinese labourers to get it; we locked the workshop and closed the hangar doors, and started off walking across the airstrip towards the village. We went slowly because the sun was getting up and the heat increasing, but when we got off the aerodrome the track led through scrub and palm trees, and it was shady and cool and pleasant. After about half an hour we came to the walled family enclosures that made up the village, and turned into the one that I remembered, and into the internal square with the shrines round it.

Connie and Phinit, I found, now lived separately. Connie was alone in the one-roomed atap house that I remembered, but Phinit had moved out and had gone to live with one of the families of the village, the family of the girl Ktut Suriatni who looked after him. He was, in fact, living happily and openly in wedded bliss. Connie was living alone. He had got another single-roomed house for me a few yards away and he took me there; a little place with a thatch roof and atap walls, the floor raised about three feet off the ground. There was no door, and not much privacy except what would be provided by the darkness when night fell.

"People will come in and have a look at all your things," he said. "They won't take anything."

A girl came up as he was showing me the little house, Madé Jasmi, that I remembered from my previous visit. She had her long black hair gathered behind her head and hanging down her back; she wore a little cotton jacket which represented her best clothes in deference to me because I was a stranger, open down the front for coolness. I smiled at her in recognition and she smiled at me, and then she asked a question of Connie.

"She wants to know if we want food," he said. "I'd like to rest this afternoon, if you don't mind. I was up most of the night. Shall we eat something now?"

I said that that would suit me. "What do you eat here?"

"Rice," he said. "Always rice. Usually with something curried on top – dried fish or meat. They eat a good many vegetables, and a certain amount of fruit. I leave it all to Madé here, and she feeds me very well." He spoke to her and she smiled shyly, and went away.

She brought us food to Connie's house presently; he had a table and two rickety chairs. She brought two wooden bowls filled with rice, and two spoons, and a number of broad leaves upon a tray each with a small portion of curry or dried fish upon it. "I'm teaching her western ways," he said. "The people here eat everything off leaves so there's no washing up. I told her that I had to have a bowl and a spoon, and you'd want one, too." He had two glasses, and Madé brought water in an earthenware jug with a curious long spout. "If you're a Balinese you can drink out of that by pouring it into your mouth. Very hygienic. I can't do it without choking, though."

"It looks as if you make quite an unreasonable amount of work for her," I said.

"I don't think she minds that," he said. "She wants to learn how people do things in the West."

The girl settled down upon the edge of the small balcony or floor before the hut, and watched us while we ate. The food was good, well cooked and appetising. As we ate, Connie asked me how Tai Foong was settling down into the job at Bahrein, and I told him about that, and about the new Liaison Officer, and how the work had been going generally. He was interested in the proposal of the RAF to build on to the hangar. "It would be better if they didn't build just there," he said. "It's not very important, though. It's only sentiment, because I took our people there to pray after work, and then the others from the souk got into the habit. But that could very easily be changed. If the RAF really need that bit of land, let me come back there for a week, and I'll see that they start praying somewhere else."

"It's not necessary," I said. "There's all the land in the world there. The RAF can put their hangar on the north side of the long strip. They've got to have a civil aviation hangar, anyway."

"If it's going to make any trouble," he said, "we can easily put it right."

He spoke to the girl, and she smiled, and got up and went away. "I asked her to get fruit," he said. "They've got some quite good things like grapefruit here."

"You've learned the language very quickly," I remarked.

"I never have much difficulty with that," he replied. "I was brought up to speak Canton in Penang when I was a boy, and I speak Malay, of course. These languages are all very much the same."

The girl came back with a wooden bowl full of fruit and put it on the table, and went back and sat on the edge of the floor again. "Phinit eats in his own place, I suppose," I said.

He nodded. "He's gone to live with the other girl's family just over there." He smiled. "Quite a married man."

"That's all right, is it?" I asked.

He said, "I think so. Madé here tells me that it's a very good idea." The girl, hearing her name spoken, looked up and smiled. "But I'm afraid she's got an axe to grind."

I didn't follow that one up, and presently I got up and went to my own hut, and dropped off my two garments, and blew up the air pillow that I carry on these journeys, and lay down on the charpoy. From where I lay I could see out into the brilliant sunlight across to Connie's hut; he also had gone to bed, and the girl had carried away the remnants of our meal. I lay dozing before sleep while the sweat slowly ceased to run, and presently she came back with a flat basket of palm leaves, and sat down on the corner of his hut in her usual position, and began doing something with her hands. Later I found that she was making lamaks, woven panels of dark green and yellow palm leaves in a chequer design, and stylised artificial flowers of the same craft, for offerings at the shrines of the house temple. I fell asleep and slept for about an hour in the heat of the day. When I woke up she was still sitting there making her offerings, waiting, perhaps, to be ready to fetch Connie anything he wanted when he woke.

I got up presently and put on my khaki drill trousers and bush shirt, and a pair of sandals, and went to the entrance of my little house. Madé saw me and got up, and moved softly into the room behind where Connie was asleep. I crossed over to where she had been sitting to look at her basket and examine what she had been doing; she had been using a crude knife of hoop-iron to split the fronds of the green leaves, and her basket was half full of her offerings. She came out of the room, and she was carrying her earthenware pitcher of water and a glass, and she poured out the cool water for me. It was no good trying to talk to her, so I smiled at her and took it from her, and drank, and she smiled gravely in return, and put the pitcher back in the shade and the draught.

She offered me the bowl of fruit, but I refused that and strolled slowly through the village. There was a girl weaving at a loom, and a young man roasting a pig upon a spit over a wood fire, and a very old man carving an elaborate wooden sculpture of a girl dancer, a very advanced and refined piece of artistry, or so it seemed to me. I stood and watched all these for a time, and then I went out into the road and down towards the sea. Two or three children followed me at a safe distance, quiet and a little timid, watching everything I did.

There were fishing-boats on the beach, and a few children bathing. The boats were beamy, well-built vessels with one big lateen sail; there was a lighter type also, a sort of dug-out canoe stabilised with an outrigger formed of a large bamboo log. I sat in the shade of the trees at the head of the beach for a time watching the boats come in and go out; women were washing and gutting the fish nearby and salting them, and spreading them out to dry in the hot sun. Both men and women on this job were less crude in their manner than fishermen and herring girls in other countries; it seemed to me that they must make their living more easily, permitting greater attention to the arts and graces of their lives.

I left the beach presently, and went back into the village in the late afternoon. There was a temple there, an enclosure of brick walls with facings of a soft white limestone, most elaborately carved with fruits and gods and gargoyles. Inside there were a number of platforms with thatched roofs, and a number of shrines, but the shrines were all empty and unattended, and the whole place was swept and clean and empty. I learned later that there was a festival there three or four times a year, when the whole countryside came to make offerings and pray, but at other times it stood empty and unused, the daily worship taking place at the shrines in each house.

I came out of the temple and looked around. There was another one a short distance away, and here I was brought up with a round turn at a statue before the door. It was a stone figure, more than life-size, of a hideous old woman, perhaps a witch. She had huge, pendulous breasts, and the face of an animal; her body appeared to be covered in hair. In the talons of her hands she held a baby, and she was about to eat it.

The children were still following me. I stopped and stared at this monstrosity, and they gathered around me. One little girl went and patted the stone figure and said, "Rangda." Whatever the thing was, it didn't seem to worry them a bit.

I left the enigma, and found my way back to my own place. Connie was up and sitting at the entrance to his house in a deckchair; Madé Jasmi was still sitting at the corner of his house weaving her offerings. He said something to her and got up to meet me, and she came back in a minute with another deckchair and I sat down beside him.

I told him where I had been and what I had seen, and I asked him about the hideous statue outside the temple. He laughed. "Oh, that's Rangda," he said. "That's the Death temple, where they do cremations. Rangda symbolises death, and evil – all the bad things of this world. To make it perfectly clear, she's usually shown eating a baby."

"Well," I said. "That doesn't seem to leave much doubt." He smiled. "No. The opposite to Rangda is the force of Good, or Life. He's the Barong. The Barong's an animal that's a cross between a lion and a bull, very fierce. At one season of the year mummers go round every village and act a sort of play. They have a pantomime Barong with two men in it, and this has to fight a pantomime Rangda. It goes on for hours. I'm not sure who wins, but everybody gets very excited about it, specially the children."

"Is all this Hinduism?" I asked uncertainly.

He shook his head. "It's something much older – animism, I think you'd call it. It's not got much to do with the daily worship, although, of course, it all gets a bit mixed up. What Madé here is making – " she looked up at the mention of her name, and smiled – "is offerings for the shrines here in the house. Those are for the Hindu gods in the shrines. The one in the big shrine in the corner is the kingpin – that's Surya, the sun god. Then there's Brahma, and Vishnu, and Shiva, and Ganesh, and half a dozen others. Madé doesn't know them all. The only ones she knows are Surya and Shiva. She picked Shiva when she was a little girl, because the shrine was the fourth from the left and she liked that one best. Perhaps she was four years old. She's always said her prayers to Shiva ever since. She asked the pemangkoe once – he's the local priest – she asked him who lived in that one and he told her Shiva, so she says her prayers and makes her offerings to Shiva."

I asked, "Is there an image in the shrine? I didn't see one."

He smiled. "No image. Shiva likes to come down and live in a bit of quartz. She got the pemangkoe to show it to me the other day. He keeps it in a sort of cupboard with a lot of other bits of things – a piece of coral, a bit of lava, a bit of carved ivory, one for each god. Shiva's spiritual home is this bit of quartz. On holy days the priest takes them out and puts each in its own shrine, and then the god comes down and takes possession of it. The soul of the god, that is. She works for days before that holy day to make offerings that will please the god. Not only palm lamaks like these – she'll kill a duck and roast it and dress it up nicely as a cold roast duck, with little sweet rice cakes all round. She mustn't smell it, if she can avoid it, because that takes the essence of it, that's reserved for the god." He paused. "When the great day comes she takes her offering and lays it down before the shrine, roast duck and all, and kneels down to say her prayers. The priest comes along and sprinkles it and her with holy water while she prays. And the soul of the god comes down out of the shrine while she is praying, and he takes the soul of the roast duck, and the soul of the rice cakes, and the soul of the lamaks. She stays there praying for an hour or more than that, and she feels good after it, so she knows that the god is pleased with her. Shiva doesn't want what's left of the roast duck and the rice cakes; he's taken their soul, and so only the husks, so to speak, are left. She can have those, and so she picks them up when she's done praying and takes them away to eat, and has a feast with her friends. I got a bit of Shiva's offering for supper the day before yesterday."

I couldn't make out if he was making a joke of it all, or not. I said uncertainly, "That sounds like a very debased sort of religion."

"Is it?" he said thoughtfully. "I'm not so sure. It keeps her praying."

I didn't quite know what to say to that one. "What does she pray for?"

"All the usual things," he said. "She prays for her mother, for her good health and long life. She prays for her father, that he may rest quietly and that his ghost shan't come and trouble them. She prays for a good rice crop and for good fishing, and she prays for her brother and for her cousins who are children, that they may grow up clean and good. And because she's a girl, she prays for a man that she can love and respect, and she prays for children by him, and that she may stay faithful to him, and he to her, until they die. She probably spends an hour upon her knees in prayer each day, and double that on holy days, apart from the amount of time she spends in making up the offerings. I don't know that you can say that it's a bad sort of religion."

"I don't know that you can say it's a good one," I replied. "It seems to me that these people are naturally devout, and that's all about it."

"Maybe so," he said thoughtfully. "Somebody once said it doesn't matter much what you believe in, so long as you believe in something. These people here believe that their religion helps them to lead better lives. If we think that the impulse is from their own nature, not from the religion – does it matter? Does it matter much if they believe in Jesus, or Shiva, or Mahomet, or Gautama, so long as the results are good?"

"Blowed if I know," I said. "Perhaps it doesn't. I don't know."

"Nor I," he said. "I only know that the results here are good, and I like to see it."

I glanced at him. "You like this place all right?"

He nodded. "Yes," he said. "I like it here."

"I was afraid there might not be enough work for you," I said. "Enough interests in training and directing other people, which is what you're good at."

He smiled. "Can't you believe that I'm a normal man, and that I like to draw my pay for doing nothing, and be lazy?"

"No," I said. "It would be all too easy if you were like that."

"Why do you think I'm not?"

"You'd be living with Madé Jasmi, if you were as you say," I remarked. "Phinit hasn't wasted much time."

He sat silent for a little. Behind his hut the sun was going down; the small buildings were casting long shadows, and the air was golden with the light of sunset. "I was very tired when I came here," he said at last. "It was time for me to get out of things and sit quiet for a time, and think where I was going. These weeks have been very good for me, I think."

"And where are you going, Connie?" I asked him. "Do you want to go back into the active life again, or to stay here?"

"What do you think I ought to do?" he asked. "You know me well enough by now to say."

Perhaps it was as Nadezna had said: he wanted someone to advise him. I said, "Well, this job is pretty stable, far as one can see. I'll probably be getting a small passenger machine before long, a Dove perhaps, and then we'll run that down here turn and turn about with the Tramp. That means there'll be an aircraft down here every week within a few months, and you'll have a bit more work then."

I was talking to gain time, and he knew it. "I think you ought to settle down here," I said quietly. "Take what's given you, and be happy with it. Marry Madé Jasmi and raise a family, like any ordinary man."

He smiled. "And you," he said. "Are you an ordinary man?"

I wasn't ready for that one. "You mean, I'm a fine one to talk?"

"I know that you have been married," he said, "and that it ended in a tragedy. But is that any reason why you should not marry again? Will you ever be really happy till you do?"

"All very well to swing it over on to me like this," I said. "It's you that I was talking about. You and Madé Jasmi."

He smiled. "And I was talking about you."

"That's not fair," I said. "Stick to the subject."

"She would marry you if you asked her," he observed. "I knew that, of course, when I lived in Bahrein, and Gujar Singh, he tells me that she is in love with you."

Gujar, it seemed, was something of a two-way street. "I wouldn't ask any girl to marry me and raise a family in the Persian Gulf," I said. "The summers are too bad. If I did that, I should want to give up everything and go and find another job in a cold climate, in England or America perhaps. I don't know that I'm ready to do that yet. I've started something, and I've got to see it through."

"So the work comes before the chance of marriage and children, and a quiet home," he said.

"If you put it that way," I said, " – yes, I think it does."

"And so it does with me."

There was a pause. "We are two men of the same temperament," he said. "Madé would marry me tonight if I should say the word." I don't think she knew what he was saying, but she heard her name and knew that we were talking about her, and she looked up, smiling. "If we did that, I should stay here, of course, probably for ever. Living is cheap and easy here, and while there are aeroplanes, and an airstrip upon Bali, there will be casual work for an engineer, to let him earn the few guilders that mean wealth among these people. I would not take her from this place, into the world outside. Here she is known and loved and happy, but in the outside world she would be treated as a savage. Marriage with one of these people means a life spent in this place, and there are few better places in the whole wide world to spend one's life." He paused. "Only the work prevents."

We sat silent for a little, and then he went on, "This power of the job, so much greater than we ourselves! When you came to Bahrein with one Fox-Moth to do a little charter work, you never thought that you were setting up a power that would rule your life, impede your marriage, dictate where and how you were to live. When a good man employs others he becomes a slave to the job, for the job is the guarantee for the security of many men. So when a man speaks candidly in the hangar of the things, the ethics of the work, that he believes in, he may bring others to believe in those things too, and to depend upon his words. Then he, too, is a slave to his own job, because if he relaxes his endeavours to teach men proper ways of work and life, he may destroy the faith he has created in them, and so throw them back into an abyss of doubt and fear and degradation, lost indeed." He paused. "I think that we are very much alike, you and me. Both, in our own way, in the same boat."

"Both going round the bend a bit, if you ask me," I said, a little bitterly.

"Yes," he said thoughtfully. "Perhaps the road has a curve in it. Perhaps it is necessary to go round the bend a little before you can see clearly to the end."

"Nadezna would be very happy if you were to marry Madé," I said. It was my last argument. "She wants to see you married, very much indeed."

He smiled gently. "She's been a good sister, Tom. Not many women would have left California to come to the Persian Gulf, to live as an Arab woman in the souk, merely to look after me. Will you give her a message from me?"

"Of course I will," I said. "What is it?"

"Tell her that I should be very happy if she were to marry you."

"I can't tell her that."

"I think you can."

I hedged. "I might in my own time, but not just yet."

"Tell her in your own time," he said. "But be sure that you tell her."

It was nearly dark. The girl got up from beside our feet and said something to Connie; he exchanged a word or two with her, and she went away "Supper," he said. "We have it soon after dark here. I usually go to bed after that, and get up before dawn. It's the best routine in a place like this, I think."

I said something or other agreeing with him, and then I said, "Nadezna was going to come down with me on this trip, for the holiday. But then she thought she'd better keep away, till things were settled between you and Madé."

"Things are settled now," he said. "But not the way she wanted them to be."

"Madé knows that, does she?"

He nodded. "If it looks like being difficult for her, I shall go away. Live in Den Pasar perhaps, and buy a bicycle, and come to work on that." He paused. "But very soon, I think that there may be a change."

"What sort of change?" I asked.

301

He said vaguely, "A change. I don't know what sort of change, but I think perhaps a change is coming, and quite soon."

"I see," I said.

He glanced at me. "Have you got any other message for me, that you have not told me yet?"

"Not exactly a message," I said slowly. "But there is something you'll have to know. I had a visit a few days ago from Wazir Hussein. The Sheikh of Khulal is a very old man now, perhaps dying."

He nodded. "I know that he is near his time."

"He's very anxious to see you before he goes," I said, and then I hesitated. It seemed such a stupid thing to say to my chief engineer. "He – well, he wants to get your blessing. He's chartered the Tramp, and he'll be coming here to visit you on the next trip. He'll be here in about ten days from now."

"He's liable to die upon the journey, isn't he?"

"I don't know. If he is, it's a risk that they're prepared to take. We're rigging up a bed for him in the fuselage."

"Is the Imam coming with him – the Imam from Baraka?'

"I don't know," I said. "I know there's quite a party coming to look after him, seven or eight of them, at least."

"I would have gone to him," he said. "Why strain an old man to come all this way?"

"I offered that, Connie, but they wouldn't have it," I told him. "They seemed to think that he should come to you."

He nodded. "You see the workings of the job," he said. "Once you start something, you must see it through. I am as much enmeshed in my net as you are in yours. Only by an act of treachery to those who believe in us can either of us escape."

CHAPTER NINE

And God shall make thy soul a Glass where eighteen thousand aeons pass,
And thou shalt see the gleaming Worlds as men see dew upon the grass.

JAMES ELROY FLECKER

I LOOK BACK on the ten days that we spent in Bali before the Arab party came as one of the happiest periods of my life. For the first time in many years it was impossible for me to control events in any way. That of itself might not have freed me from the worries and the strain of my responsibilities, but being with Connie did. We had no more serious conversation. There was little to do in the workshop except painting and distempering, which was being done by a couple of Balinese boys from the village, who were doing it very well. Each morning soon after dawn we would stroll over to the hangar and see them started working under Phinit, and as the sun got warm we would go off and go down to the beach and bathe. It would have been just perfect if Nadezna could have been with us.

We didn't go far from Pekendang. There are forty thousand temples in Bali, I believe, but I only saw the one. I never was much of a sightseer; Connie had wandered fairly widely inland and had been up to the central volcanic mountain, Kintamani, but transport wasn't easy, and he seemed to think that when one had seen and absorbed Pekendang the rest was largely repetition. We went once or twice to a place the other side of the strip called Sanoer, where a Belgian artist was married to a very fine Balinese woman. I think that was the most wonderful house I have ever been in, the walls covered with paintings of the Balinese and their way of life, and full of Balinese young men and women so that it was difficult to say in memory which of the scenes remembered from that house were real ones and which were paint.

We saw a good deal of the headman of the village, Wajan Rauh. He used to come and sit and talk to us sometimes, about the crops and the fishing, and about the Dutch and the full-scale war that they were waging against the Indonesians in Java and Sumatra. I could not understand these conversations, and I used to sit back, smoking, watching the old man and his friends, watching Connie as he talked to them.

One did not need any interpreter to see how greatly they valued his advice. All through my life I had seen him gain this influence over people; it had been the same story even in Cobham's Circus, as a boy, I think, and certainly it had been so in Damrey Phong, in Rangoon, in Bahrein. I do not think he ever worked for it, or sought this influence. When simple people came and told him things that troubled them, which they did very often, he gave them straightly what advice he could, and his manner of doing it encouraged them, so that they came back with more important and more intimate matters for his ruling. I think that's all there was to it.

He told me that they thought little of the war in Java. They did not greatly care who ruled them, whether the radjas who had ruled before the Dutch came, and who still ruled them in name, or whether the Dutch. The Balinese had no national ambitions. All they wanted to do was to get on with their farming and their temple festivals and let the world go by them; they had no desire whatever to become involved in great events. If the Dutch or the Indonesians or anyone else wanted to come and rule them, they were welcome to do so, thought the Balinese; they were shrewd enough to know that in the case of one small, self-supporting island it could not make any great change in their daily lives.

Because they thought so very highly of Connie, and because I was his guest, the village went out of their way to show me all their arts. They put on a dance one evening, a most complicated and picturesque affair of stylised dancing by little girls eleven or twelve years old, dressed heavily in gold-embroidered skirts and jackets sewn with tiny mirrors, and enormous golden head-dresses. This dance was called Legong; it was danced to the music of an orchestra of bamboo xylophones and small brass gongs. It went on for over three hours, and seemed to be an affair for the whole village; when one xylophone player tired another took his place, and the little dancers danced in relays too, though the two chief ones danced the whole evening with only short pauses for rest. The village sat around in a rough square that formed the stage, and children played about among the dancers, who avoided them skilfully, and dogs walked through; from time to time a mother would get up and go out on the floor to adjust the clothing of a little dancer that was slipping, and the dance went on. At about ten o'clock at night it stopped quite suddenly and for no particular reason, and the people all streamed away to bed, gossiping and chatting, well content.

Cockfighting was a sport of the men, and they held a main in my honour. I had never seen it before, although it still goes on in England, quietly and illegally. It is a cruel sport, of course, because the fight is to the death and usually bloody. It was not the sadist angle that appealed to the

Balinese, though, but the opportunity for betting. They are tremendous gamblers, and bet furiously on their cockfights, though I think that this is general in South-East Asia. Phinit told me that in his mother's village in Siam they breed small fish, three or four inches long, that will fight fiercely to the death when put together, and the people bet on those.

They put on a play for me one night, entirely incomprehensible to me and, I think, to Connie also. It was quite colourful, and it was amusing to sit in a deck-chair and watch. Madé Jasmi, I think, didn't understand much of it either, because it dealt with very high-born people, kings and princes, who for the sake of verisimilitude spoke a regal dialect called Kawi which nobody of common clay can understand. Madé Jasmi evidently thought I needed sustaining through this entertainment because she kept bringing me glasses of toeak, palm-juice beer. In the end the performance came suddenly to an unexpected finish, as the dance had done, and people and actors melted quickly away.

I cannot describe the grace, and the charm of that small village. It was like nothing I had ever seen before; I shall find nothing like it in this world again.

I suppose there always must be something, or there would be nothing to distinguish places such as that from those that we have been taught to look forward to in the world to come. In this case, it was the physical condition of Connie Shak Lin that began to worry me. As I have said, he had grown very thin. I doubt if he weighed more than about eight stone at that time, and yet he was a big man, five foot ten or eleven in height. When we went bathing together I could see every bone in his body, so it seemed, and I began to get a little worried about him.

He ate fairly well, though nothing like as much as I did. He didn't smoke or drink; he never had. He was well in himself, at least, when I was there, but he had little energy and spent a good part of each day within his hut, lying upon the charpoy, dozing or asleep. He had a great store of nervous energy that he could call upon, however. It had not distressed him unduly to work most of the night upon the aircraft when it had been there, and he could sit for hours in the evening talking and discussing with the old men. There seemed to be nothing really wrong with him, and certainly nothing that required a doctor. But – well, I was a bit uneasy over him. As I have mentioned, he was very thin.

After a few days of this idyllic life we began to make preparations for the Arab party. It was a bit tricky, because I had to get the permission of the Dutch Governor for the party to come to the island at all, and though I didn't expect any difficulty it did mean that I had to disclose the fact that they were coming on a pilgrimage five thousand miles or so to see my chief engineer, which was unusual, to say the least.

The Governor spoke no English, and in any case he was too high a dignitary for me to approach direct. I went and called on Mr Bergen, his second in command, who had served with the American Army in the war and spoke English as well as I did.

He was interested to hear that this Arab Sheikh and his retinue were coming to visit Bali. He had already had a telegram about them from his headquarters in Batavia, which was quite incomprehensible to him, and he was glad to find somebody who could inform him on the matter. Only the crews of aircraft, people such as myself and my pilots and ground engineers, can move easily about the world these days, and Sheikh Abd el Kadir and Wazir Hussein and all the rest of them had to have passports and visas for their journey. Before I left Captain Morrison had been getting busy with all this, and the Foreign Office in London had requested permission for their visit from the Dutch Ambassador in London as a matter of diplomatic urgency. Morrison must have been very positive with the Resident back in distant Bahrein, because cables had been flying backwards and forwards halfway round the world in English and in Dutch, so that a notification of permission for this visit had come to the Governor of Bali from his immediate superior without any information what the visit was about. Probably the people in Batavia didn't know themselves.

I suppose I was a coward, but I really didn't feel equal to explaining to this Dutchman that the Sheikh of Khulal was coming to get Connie's blessing. I felt that it was better to go softly on the religious side. I stressed the vast wealth of the sheikhs, and their power to indulge their slightest whim. I said that this Sheikh and Connie had become great friends during his time at Bahrein, and now that the old man felt his end approaching he wanted very much to see Connie again and say goodbye to him. I said confidentially that to Europeans like us a journey of this sort might appear unreasonable, but that he, of course, was accustomed to Asiatic ways of thought, which were not always quite upon our lines. I said that the desire of the old man to see his friend for the last time had become an obsession with him, and his position in the Persian Gulf was such that the British Government were anxious to oblige him. Hence the permission which had been requested for this visit on the highest level, and which had been granted by the Dutch in Holland.

This went down all right, and Mr Bergen went out of his way to help me to arrange accommodation for the party. There were few people staying on the island at the time, and the Bali Hotel, built for a considerable tourist trade before the war, was not more than half full. As is common in the Indonesian islands, this hotel was built in bungalow style and spread widely as a number of little suites built around courtyards, somewhat in the manner of a very good American motel. I got a row of six of these rooms for the party, each with two beds and a bathroom and a sitting veranda, and I arranged for two cars for their use.

The Tramp came in to schedule, in the late afternoon. Connie and Phinit and I were there to meet it, of course. We stood in the shade of the hangar and watched it touch down on the strip and run to a standstill; it turned and taxied towards us and I saw the familiar, bearded face of Gujar Singh in the chief pilot's seat on the port side. He taxied to the hangar and swung it round accurately into position for pulling in; then he stopped the engines, and we went forward to the door.

Tarik opened up from the inside and put down the steps, and Wazir Hussein came down first, grave and dignified in long white skirts, as ever. He told us that the old Sheikh had stood the journey well; he was tired, but not unreasonably so. There were nine of them in the party all told, including the Imam from Baraka and the Sheikh's personal physician, a French-speaking Arab who came, I think, originally from Tunis. I told him the arrangements I had made, and I showed him the two cars which were at their disposal; then I handed over to Connie, who went up into the machine to greet the old man, and I retired myself into the background.

Gujar Singh came out of the machine in a few minutes, and came over to where I was standing by the bowser, ready to refuel the Tramp. I asked him how the trip had gone. He said it had been normal; the old Sheikh had been interested in the details of the flight, and had followed their journey on the maps with a good deal of intelligence. At every night stop the most elaborate arrangements had been made for them; at Karachi and at Calcutta and at Singapore a fleet of cars had been waiting on the tarmac to meet the aircraft, and suites of rooms had been reserved at the best hotels.

"The difficulty was to prevent taking on more passengers," he said, smiling. "It is not possible to keep a journey that concerns Shak Lin a secret. At every stop ten or fifteen engineers came to me, or to Hosein, or to the Wazir, asking if they might join us, to come here to listen to the

Teacher. The Wazir consulted me, and I advised him to refuse them all. I think that was the best. Otherwise, there would have been too great a crowd, that would have tired the Sheikh too much."

"It was like that, was it?" I asked thoughtfully.

"Everywhere people knew about this journey," he said. "It is the radio operators, of course, talking with each other. Everywhere people wanted to come too. I could have filled the aircraft three times over."

While we were talking the Arabs were getting out of the aircraft, organised by Connie; there was a bustle of flowing white skirts and black beards, and then the old Sheikh himself appeared, helped down the steep duralumin steps of the Tramp by a couple of his retinue. I went up and said something to welcome him, and he recognised me, and smiled, and Wazir Hussein translated for him. Thanks be to Allah, he said, they had had a safe and an easy journey in the hands of Gujar Singh; he was not tired, and he was grateful to me for the arrangements I had made for his comfort. I replied that anything I had done for him was nothing in comparison with what he had done for me, and he smiled again when that was translated; then he turned away and spoke to the Imam, and said something about sunset prayer.

That didn't concern me, of course, as a European and an unbeliever, and so I excused myself and went up into the cabin of the Tramp with Gujar to inspect the aircraft and the journey log. Hosein was there tidying up and putting maps and instruments away into their stowages, and I told him that prayer was about to take place and he could go down to it if he wished. Gujar didn't want to go; he often used to go to Connie's prayer meetings outside the hangar at Bahrein, but not, I think, when there was an Imam conducting the *Rakats*; perhaps that made the prayers too officially Moslem, so that a good Sikh could not participate.

I stood at the chart table in the Tramp behind the pilots' seats watching the Arabs through the little navigator's window. Connie had marked out a small, square area of ground beside the hangar with white stones, and he had had the grass cut here by two Balinese boys so that it made a small, level sward. The square was carefully oriented towards Mecca, and in the north-west side there was the usual semicircular indent. Tarik and the other servants brought three carpets from the Tramp and spread them on the ground inside this square; the Imam took his place in the indent, and they began their devotions. Connie knelt beside the old Sheikh in prayer, motionless, all the time; he did not follow the others in the ritual of Moslem devotions, the standing, the kneeling, the prostrations. He remained kneeling all the time.

The old Sheikh had one of his retinue each side of him, who helped him to his feet each time from the kneeling position. He was evidently getting very feeble.

Phinit was there, praying with them. Like Connie, he remained kneeling all the time, but his position was just outside the square. He was a Buddhist. I think it must have been something quite exceptional that Connie should have prayed inside their prayer ground amongst the Moslems, and yet not go through the ritual of their devotions.

The prayers lasted for about a quarter of an hour or twenty minutes. Then they were over, and I went down and drove with the party into Den Pasar to see them comfortably installed in the hotel. Connie stayed with Phinit at the airstrip to refuel the Tramp; it is better in the tropics to keep fuel tanks always full to prevent condensation troubles. They were not going to work late, however, as the aircraft would be there for a full day, and could be serviced normally in working hours.

I stayed that night in the hotel myself to be on hand to assist the Arabs if they got into any difficulty; I had a room on the far side of the courtyard from them, in order to be near and yet not be obtrusive. They had brought a Moslem cook with them to ensure that no unclean meat was prepared for their food; I took this chap along and introduced him to the kitchen staff, and I arranged for one of the cars with a driver to be permanently on call parked near their rooms. There was nothing else they wanted, so I went and changed and had a bath myself, and had a Bols, and dinner.

They had Phinit up there that evening, but not Connie; from my suite across the courtyard I could see him squatting on the ground talking to the old Sheikh and his Wazir. I found later that Connie had spent the evening quietly in Pekendang; apparently he was in a position to dictate to these Arab princes who had come six thousand miles to see him, when he would see them and when he would rest. In default of Connie they had got hold of Phinit, and I had little doubt that they were hearing from Phinit heavily embroidered stories of the asceticism of the Teacher. Madé Jasmi would come into this, I thought, but there was nothing I could do about it. Once, talking with the desperate humour of fatigue to Nadezna, I had spoken of the Gospel according to St Phinit. Perhaps, I thought, as I looked out across the courtyard, the first chapters of that Gospel were already taking shape.

When I got up next morning soon after dawn, the Arabs were already gone. They met Connie down at the hangar on the airstrip for the sunrise prayer at about six o'clock. They must have stayed there for two hours or so, because when I was ready to go down to the airstrip at about half-past eight, they arrived back in the two cars. I waited till the Sheikh was settled back into his room and then went over to see Wazir Hussein, to find out what his plans were. He told me that they were to meet the Teacher again in the cool of the evening, and that they would like to start back for Bahrein next morning, after the sunrise prayer.

I got a car and went down to the airstrip to see what was happening to the Tramp. I found Connie and Phinit working to give her the routine check over, with Gujar and Hosein helping them; they had got the cowlings open and they were checking the filters, changing the sparking plugs and examining contact breakers; there was a defective directional gyro to be changed. Nothing indicated that there was anything unusual about my party at all; it was just a large aeroplane being serviced by a good crowd of Asiatics.

I found that Connie already knew about the plan to start back for Bahrein next day, and he was working through the heat of the day to get the servicing of the aircraft finished by mid-afternoon. There was nothing much that I could do to help them. I told Connie that I would move back to my hut in Pekendang for that last night, for I was going back to Bahrein with the Sheikh's party. I wanted to spend the last night of my holiday in Pekendang rather than in the civilised luxury of Den Pasar.

My car was waiting for me at the small airport bungalow. I walked from the hangar to it across the sun-drenched tarmac. As I got near the bungalow another car drove up, one of the two allocated to the Arabs. It had only two people in, the Sheikh's personal physician and the Wazir Hussein.

I went up to their car as it came to a standstill, and spoke to the Wazir. I told him that I was just going back to the hotel to check out, and said that if he wished I would settle the bill for their party and invoice him for it in Bahrein; I told him that I was going to spend the night myself in Pekendang, and that I would join them for the return flight at the airstrip in the morning. We talked about these matters for a few moments, and then he said: "I am glad that we have met you here, Mr Cutter. There is another matter which I came here to discuss with you, if I could find you." He turned to introduce his companion. "This is Dr Khaled."

I bowed and said something or other. The doctor was dressed in a grey European suit and a Panama hat. He had a short black beard trimmed to a neat point; he might have been forty-five or fifty years old. Conversation with him was difficult because he could only speak French and Arabic; I know hardly any French and my Arabic, at that time, although adequate for the hangar and the direction of casual labour, wasn't good enough for a prolonged conversation on any subject but aircraft.

The Wazir said, "Dr Khaled is worried about the health of El Amin, Mr Cutter. He would like to ask you a few questions, and perhaps talk also to the Teacher."

"Of course," I said. "I'm not too happy myself." I took them through into the small veranda with a few chairs and tables that served for an airport restaurant; it was a shady place where we could talk quietly, looking out over the strip. I ordered coffee, but that was difficult, so we drank fresh lime squashes. "I'll tell you anything I can," I said.

The Wazir had to translate for us; I think Dr Khaled understood a little English though he could not speak it. He wanted to know at once what Connie weighed, but I could not tell him that. He asked if his emaciation was a recent matter. I told him that Connie had certainly been heavier when he had joined me nearly three years before, but that I had not noticed any very sudden change. He asked if he had been ill, and I said that he had never had any time off. He asked if he was eating well, and here I was able to give him some definite information about Connie's habits of life, having lived with him for ten days. He was interested in his lassitude when there was no work to be done, and asked several questions about that. He asked about women.

After a quarter of an hour of this the Wazir asked if I thought Connie would permit the doctor to make an examination of him. I said I thought that was a very good idea, and that Connie should certainly take this opportunity to be checked over. I indicated as politely as I could that though Connie might be a prophet to them, he was an employee to me, and that if I said he'd got to have a medical examination he'd bloody well have one.

We walked back to the hangar, and I got Connie down off the machine and introduced him to Dr Khaled. Connie spoke fluent Arabic, of course, and he knew Dr Khaled well from his visits to the Sheikh's palace at Baraka. He made no objection to a medical examination, and they went off together to the workshop, Dr Khaled carrying a black case in his hand. I took Wazir Hussein back to the restaurant and sat with him there till the doctor joined us.

He came after about three quarters of an hour; Connie had gone back to work upon the Tramp. The Wazir questioned him at once, and translated his replies to me. The examination had revealed nothing particularly wrong, beyond the obvious fact that Connie was exceedingly thin and had only small reserves of physical energy. In general, he was careful with his health, apart from the fact that throughout his life he had been in the habit of eating what the native peoples of the countries that he lived in ate, and drinking what they drank. He had had malaria, of course, but it had not troubled him recently, perhaps because I always issued ample supplies of Paludrine to any of my party who were travelling away from Bahrein. That's an economy measure, of course, because if an aircraft gets delayed because the crew are ill you can lose hundreds and hundreds of pounds, easy as wink. I always made the money side of illness clear to everybody, and my pilots and my engineers appreciated that, and took far more care over my money than they would ever have done over their own health. Connie had taken Paludrine regularly while he had been in Bali, and his malaria had not recurred.

The doctor said that he had taken samples of sputum, blood, and urine, and he had these in test tubes in his case. There were no facilities in Bali for an analysis of these samples. He had good connections with hospitals in Karachi and in Cairo where such things could be investigated, and since the aircraft would be passing through Karachi in three days' time he proposed to put his test tubes in a thermos jar full of ice, and stop off in Karachi while the analysis was carried out, and come on to Bahrein by air line as soon as he had the report. He wanted to know if the Wazir would agree to this, or if he would prefer him just to leave the samples and travel to Bahrein with the old Sheikh, in which case the report from the Karachi hospital would come on by post.

The Wazir was emphatic that he must complete the journey to Bahrein with the Sheikh, and see him safely installed back in his palace at Baraka. After that, and if the Sheikh was in good health, he could return to Karachi if necessary for a consultation about Connie's samples. He asked me if I could provide an aircraft to take the doctor back to Karachi, if that should be necessary.

I said, of course I could do that if there was no convenient machine upon a scheduled service. I went on to suggest that perhaps it might be a good thing to make some contact with the Dutch doctor in Den Pasar now, since if any treatment should prove to be necessary it would hardly be practical for it to be directed from Bahrein.

The Wazir said blandly that if any treatment should be necessary, he did not think that his master would agree that it should be put into the hands of the local doctor in Bali. Until the samples had been examined it was impossible to say what was required, but if the matter should be serious in any way, his master would consider the health of El Amin to be as important as his own, and much more so. If that should be the case, he was sure that his master would say that a specialist should be engaged in Europe and should fly to Bali to be in attendance upon El Amin for as long as was required. He did not think that his master would like a local doctor to attend El Amin.

We left the matter so. I had already had a good deal of experience of how these fierce, proud Arabs who led simple and ascetic lives themselves could handle the unlimited money that was at their command in any cause that touched on their religion. People who would lend a man like me sixty thousand pounds merely to keep the business that employed El Amin free from usury would not hesitate to pay a man from Harley Street ten thousand pounds to drop everything and fly to Bali and stay there a month. To suggest that they would do otherwise would be offensive to them, as suggesting that they put their riches before their religious beliefs.

I did not see Connie until late that night, or not to talk to. I went back to Den Pasar and did my business with the hotel, and packed my bag, and took a car back to Pekendang. I got there about midday and Madé Jasmi came to me as soon as I arrived and asked by signs if I wanted to eat. I ate what she brought me, and then, as Connie had not turned up, I managed to make her understand that she was to take a bowl of rice and curry to the hangar, and she went off carrying the bowl wrapped in a cloth, and a basket of fruit.

Connie came back about the middle of the afternoon and went straight to his charpoy; he did not appear till half an hour before sunset, when he went over to the strip again, to meet the Arabs for their prayers. I sat in a deck-chair and waited for him to come back, and presently Gujar Singh appeared strolling through the village, and I called him, and he came and talked to me.

An hour after sunset Connie came back to the village, walking slowly, and flopped down in a deck-chair outside his house. I got up and went over to him; Gujar slipped away. I sat down on the wooden step that led up to Connie's house, the place where Madé usually sat. "Tired?" I asked.

He said, "A bit. It takes it out of you, talking to these people. You've got to be right, so exactly right, the whole of the time."

I nodded. "We'll all be gone tomorrow," I said. "Then you can rest for a week if you want to."

He was silent for a time, and then he said, "Did that doctor tell you anything?"

I shook my head. "So far as I know, he didn't find anything the matter with you. He's going to have those samples analysed."

He said, "He found something all right."

I glanced up at him quickly. "What did he find?"

"I don't know. Nothing that you can put your finger on, perhaps. But he's good, that chap – and cagey, too. He'd never say a word to anyone till he was certain. He thinks there's something wrong with me, and he's got an idea in his head of what it is. I couldn't make him tell me, though."

I was disturbed. "He didn't give us that impression."

"Perhaps he found he could fox you more easily than me."

"What sort of thing does he think is wrong with you?"

"I don't know. With a man like that no one will know until he's certain of his facts."

I didn't pursue the subject because I didn't want to turn his mind to sickness; instead I asked about the Tramp and got his report; she was all ready to go first thing next morning. He said he thought the sunrise prayer would take half an hour or so; then we could put the old Sheikh straight into the aircraft and get started up.

Madé came with food, but he ate very little. I said presently, "Nadezna was coming down with me this time, Connie. But then she decided not to. You wouldn't mind her coming down here if she wants a holiday?"

"I'd like to have her here," he said. "It'ld be good for her to get away from the Gulf for a bit." And then he said, "You will give her my message?"

"In my own time, and when I think she wants to hear it," I said. "Yes, I'll give it her."

Nothing more happened that evening. He was evidently very tired indeed, and that I put down to the fatigue of his religious ministrations to the Sheikh. He only pecked at his food, and ate half an orange, and very soon he went into his hut and lay down on the bed.

We were all up before dawn, as usual, but early as I was, Connie was earlier; he had already gone down to the strip when I came out. Madé Jasmi brought me coffee and fruit as a breakfast, and I packed my small bag, and waved the farewell that I could not say to the villagers, and walked down to the airstrip. The sun was just coming up when I got there, and the Arabs and Connie were at their devotions in the marked out square beside the hangar, with the Imam leading in the *Rakats*. The Tramp had been drawn out of the hangar and parked in front of it, and as I walked across the strip I could see Gujar already in the cockpit, busying himself with the preliminaries of flight.

Prayers lasted for about half an hour, as Connie had said they would, and then we were ready to go. While Hosein made out the flight plan and went through the formalities in the Control office, Gujar and I helped the old Sheikh up the duralumin ladder into the cabin of the Tramp, and saw his retinue install him comfortably on the divan bed. Then Gujar and Connie went up into the cockpit and started up the engines; in that climate motors don't take very long to warm up, and in five minutes they were running through the cockpit drill. The run-up over, they stopped both motors again and waited for Hosein to come, and while we were waiting, Connie came down and sat cross-legged on the floor, talking quietly to the Sheikh sitting on his divan.

Then Hosein came and got into the aircraft, and went past up to the cockpit, his hands full of documents and logbooks. Connie got up and glanced at me, and I nodded and said, "Ready to go now." He turned to the Sheikh and said quietly in Arabic, "May God strengthen you," and the old man said, " 'Alaikum as salam," which means, "On you be peace". Then Connie got down on to the strip and put up the ladder to us from the ground. and I closed the door and Tarik stowed the ladder. I went forward and got up into the cockpit and sat at the navigator's table, and Gujar in the pilot's seat with Hosein at his side started the motors, and we taxied down the sunbaked turf to the end of the runway, and took off.

That journey was just one of many journeys that I made along that route, and I cannot now remember much about it. I think we stopped at Penang and at Allahabad, but for the life of me I can't remember, and it doesn't matter, anyway. I know we got to Karachi about midday after a dawn start, and as we hoped to get the old Sheikh back to Bahrein that night for him to sleep in comfort in the Sheikh Muhammad's palace, Wazir Hussein put Dr Khaled in a car with his samples, and told him to drive quickly to the city hospital, and leave his samples to be analysed, and come back immediately so that we could take off. Karachi civil airport is about fifteen miles out of the city, and it was an hour and a half before he came back and we were able to get under way again.

We were all of us in a hurry to get on, because none of us were particularly happy about the condition of the Sheikh. It was obvious that the long journey to Bali, and the excitement there, and the strange accommodation, and the long journey back, had tired him very much. There is an insidious sort of fatigue in travelling in an unsoundproofed aeroplane. After the first few minutes you don't notice the noise at all, and you think nothing of it, but at the end of the day you may find yourself too tired to eat, too tired to sleep without a drug. The pilots knew all about this, of course, and none of us ever flew in my machines without our ears being stuffed with cotton wool, which makes all the difference. Gujar had tried to get the old man to use cotton wool on the flight out, and I tried on the way back to make him use it, but although he did make some effort to co-operate he never kept it in for very long – partly, I think, because his ears were full of hairs and the wool worried him.

Because of this, he was very, very tired on the last leg of the journey home. He sat, or lay propped up with cushions on his divan, and he no longer wanted to look at the maps, or hear where we were, or any of the details of the flight. He did not talk to anyone, and he refused all food, though now and again he took a few sips of water. I know before we reached Karachi Dr Khaled had suggested to him that we should stop there for the night, or possibly for more nights than one, but he had got a bottle from the old Sheikh, who was only anxious now to get back to the places and the people that he knew. He wanted to be back in his palace at Baraka, even if it killed him.

We made a night landing at Bahrein at about half-past eight, local time. I had been talking to them on the radio for the last hour and telling them to ring through to Sheikh Muhammad's Wazir to tell him that the Sheikh of Khulal would be arriving at the aerodrome at eight-thirty, very tired by his long journey, and to ask for cars to be on the tarmac for the party without fail to meet us when we landed. One of my pals from the chummery, a bloke called Alec Scott, was in the Control room, and I didn't scruple to call him every ten minutes in the last hundred and fifty miles to make sure that he had passed on all my messages.

So, when we taxied to a standstill before our hangar in the floodlit darkness and stopped the engines, the maroon Hudson was alongside the machine before we could get the steps down. We were able to get the old man down on to the ground and into the car within five minutes; he could hardly stand alone, and drove away with one of his servants sitting on each side of him on the broad rear seat to hold him erect in case he should fall sideways on a corner. He was as bad as that.

There were other cars there for the rest of the party and their luggage, and in ten minutes or so they, too, were gone. I stood with Gujar Singh and watched the last car disappear into the darkness. We were all tired, too. "Well, thank the Lord we've got him home safely," I said heavily. "I wouldn't have liked it if he'd died on the way home."

"I was afraid of that," said Gujar. "It would have made great trouble if he had died in India, a Hindu country. I do not think he could have been buried there ... If that had happened, I would have suggested that we just flew on as quickly as we could, and brought him home."

"We couldn't have done that," I said. "Not for two days, in heat like this."

"We could have flown high, above the freezing level."

"We'd never have got him through the Customs at Karachi," I said. "But anyway, he didn't die on us, so that's all right." But I was only partially correct because, in fact, the old man never left his palace again. He died a few months later. He'd known that he was near the end, of course, before he started on his journey to see Connie.

It was a disappointment to me that Nadezna was not there to meet us; I didn't look forward to the prospect of telling her that I had failed to make Connie consider marrying Madé Jasmi, but I had looked forward to meeting her, all the same. I went into the office and found my desk completely empty and bare, not a paper on it except one little note, which read,

DEAR MR CUTTER,
I know you'll be tired when you get in, so I've taken the IN basket away and locked it up. There's nothing urgent in it. I hope you'll take the hint and go to bed.

Best wishes,

NADEZNA.

I grinned, and took the hint, and went to bed.

I was in the office bright and early next morning, but Nadezna was there before me, and my desk was stacked with correspondence, invoices, receipts, release notes, official pamphlets, and all the other paper clutter that a business can accumulate in a fortnight. Before beginning upon this, I told her about Connie and the girl. "I didn't cut any ice at all," I said. "I don't think he's got any intention of marrying."

"No," she replied. "I don't think he has. It was a chance, though. Tell me, is she nice?"

"She's a very nice girl," I told her. "She's just a village girl, of course – she can't read or write. He'd have to make his life there if he married her, but there are worse places to live than that. They live simply and eat well. Her mother must be forty-five at least, and she's a beautiful woman still. A man who was prepared to settle down and live there quietly could have a very happy life."

"I thought it was like that," she said. "But that's not Connie's way." She paused, and then she said, "Oh well, that's over, then. How was he in himself?"

"You mean, his health?"

She nodded.

I thought for a minute before replying. I did not want to alarm her unduly. "He's very, very thin," I said at last. "He seems to get tired easily, too. I think he's quite all right, though. Dr Khaled examined him." I told her about what was going on at Karachi.

She wanted to know a lot of things then, how he was eating, how he was sleeping – all the usual enquiries. I had one or two to make of her. "Has he ever had anything like this before?" I asked. "Any sort of illness?"

She shook her head. "Not that I know of. He's always been thin, and he's always lived a great deal on his nerves. I mean, I've seen him get very tired sometimes, when he's been talking a lot. But I don't ever remember him being in the doctor's hands at all."

"It's probably nothing," I said. "He may need something with his diet down there – cod liver oil and malt, or something like that."

I settled down then to pick up the threads of my business, and I worked with Nadezna on the papers for the whole of that day. Johnson came on the telephone in the middle of the morning wanting to know the earliest date for the Tramp to leave again for Bali and for the Maclean Dakota to meet it there; having given up a trip to the Sheikh of Khulal, the Arabia–Sumatran Company had an accumulation of scientific equipment and staff wanting to go through to the East Alligator River oil field as soon as possible. I checked the work on the machine with Chai Tai Foong, and came back to the office and rang through to Johnson and told him the machine could take off at dawn the day after tomorrow. I got a cable off to Maclean Airways, and then I sent for Arjan Singh and warned him for the trip, with Kadhim as second pilot.

I got up before dawn that morning to see the Tramp loaded, and to have a final word to the two pilots before they went. I always think it helps if the boss shows up on an early morning show like that, especially if it's the start of a long flight. There was really no need for me to be there, of course; Arjan had done the trip several times before, and though Kadhim was new he'd got over a thousand hours in

324

with the Iraqi Air Force and Iraqi Airways on the Baghdad–Mosul route.

I said to Arjan, "Tell Shak Lin we got the old Sheikh back all right. He's still in bed, though – I think he's pretty sick. Shak Lin's sure to want to know how he is."

He nodded gravely, "I will tell him everything."

In the first light of dawn the Tramp taxied down to the far end of the runway, and took off over the sea, and swept round in a great left-hand turn to get on course, and vanished into the sunrise. I went back to the chummery and had breakfast and shaved, and went to the office. I had a Proctor booked to take a couple of surveyors out to a place called Marib in the desert later in the day, and I intended to take them myself since I should be fairly clear of office work.

At about half-past eight, half an hour before the surveyors were due, the maroon Hudson passed my office window with Dr Khaled and Wazir Hussein in it, and swung round to park. I was dictating to Nadezna at the time. "Christ," I said. "Look, pack up this. Nip out and see if you can find Gujar Singh, and tell him I'd like him to take this Proctor to Marib, because I'm tied up here after all. And look – tell Dunu to go over to the restaurant and order us three cups of coffee – Turkish."

I got up to meet my visitors as they came in. "This is a great honour," I said. Probably they had come to talk about Connie, but one had to let them start it in their own time. "I hope the Sheikh of Khulal was not too tired by the journey?"

They said something or other, and we made the usual polite conversation till the coffee came. When Dunu had gone out the Wazir came to the point.

"We have received the report about El Amin from Karachi," he said. "It is not good."

"Oh," I replied. "What does it say?"

He spoke to Khaled, who produced a white printed form, filled in with a few words of typescript. The Wazir handed it to me; it was in English. There were spaces for sputum and for urine, and opposite each of these was typed the one word, "Negative". There was a space for blood, and here was typed,

Red cells, 2 ½ million.
White cells, 275,000, with immature cells present.

There was a further space at the bottom for remarks, and here it said,

Chronic Myelogenous Leukaemia, indicated by the blood count figures above. From the number of primitive white cells present the disease would seem to be entering an acute phase.

That, with a signature, was all there was.

I looked up at Hussein. "Well, this doesn't mean a thing to me," I said. "What is Myelogenous Leukaemia? I've never heard of it."

"Dr Khaled tells us that it is a disease of the blood," he said. "It is a very bad disease."

"How bad?" I asked. "What's the treatment?"

He turned and spoke to the doctor in Arabic. It was evidently the continuation of a discussion that had, perhaps, been gone over many times. The doctor spoke emphatically with some gesticulation, but he spoke Arabic with a strange accent to me and he spoke quickly, so that I could not get very much of what he said.

The Wazir turned back to me. "It is a long and complicated treatment," he said. "It needs X-rays to cure it, and very modern things that are not found in many cities of Asia. It would be better that Shak Lin should go to Europe, Dr Khaled says. He can arrange treatment in Paris."

"I see," I said. I sat in thought for a few minutes. There was no question of expense in my mind, or of the work. Connie's job at Bali was a sinecure that could be done by any good reliable engineer. If this thing was serious he must come straight back to Bahrein and go on to Paris or to London for his treatment; I could get him back to England from Bahrein in a couple of days.

I raised my head and spoke to the Wazir. "He shall certainly go to Europe for his treatment if he's really got this thing," I said. "If we get him back to Karachi for a start, could we have him properly investigated at the hospital there in the light of this report, to get a second opinion?"

Dr Khaled said that could be done.

"The next thing," I said to Wazir Hussein, "is just this. Will he come?"

"He will come if you say that he must come," the Wazir said. "I think that you are right. He would not change his way of life or travel to Europe for his health, for himself alone. But if you say he must do that for reasons of your business, I think he may agree."

I bit my lip. I wasn't a bit sure, myself. Connie was so much a part of the East that it was difficult to visualise him as a patient in a hospital ward in London or in Paris, in countries where he had no friends at all, where nobody had any reverence for him. "I think the first thing to do is to get him back to Karachi for a proper examination," I said at last.

Dr Khaled spoke quickly to the Wazir. As I had thought, he could understand English all right, though he was reluctant to try to speak it. The Wazir turned to me. "My master wishes to spare no expense," he said. "If he is to come to Karachi for examination, it would be better that a specialist should come from Paris or from London to examine him at Karachi, in the hospital. My master insists that he should have the best advice." He paused, and then he said, "This has been a great trouble to my master; this news of El Amin."

I said, "It is a great trouble to me, too." I sat in thought for a moment. "It's bad luck that the Tramp left this morning for Bali," I said. "It will be back here in nine days, and going down again" – I glanced at the calendar – "on the fourteenth. To get him back here on this trip means I must try and explain the situation to him in a telegram, and persuade him to come back to hospital at Karachi. That's not going to be very easy."

Wazir Hussein asked, "If he came by the next trip, when would he reach Karachi?"

"On the twenty-second or the twenty-third," I said. "It means he wouldn't reach Karachi for about three weeks from now."

We discussed this for a time. If he could be induced by skilfully-worded telegrams to come back to Karachi with the present trip he could be there in about seven days' time. It was doubtful if the Arabs, with all the power of their wealth, could get a specialist from Europe there so soon as that. They would have to write to their agents in London and the letter would take three days; the man then had to be found and induced to leave his work in London or Paris to fly to Karachi. No specialist of any repute would leave his other patients in mid-air and unattended, whatever the fee paid. It seemed to us that such a man would need at least a week to settle his affairs before coming out to Karachi, and then the flight would take at least two days. It would be a fortnight at the earliest before he could be there.

Dr Khaled, pressed by the Wazir, said that he did not think that El Amin's physical state would alter very greatly in a fortnight. The disease was probably getting worse, and if unattended death might well occur in a year or eighteen months. Since the specialist could hardly reach Karachi for at least a fortnight, if Connie came on the next trip the greatest time that would be lost would be one week.

We decided that that would be the best course, that he should come back upon the following trip. Wazir Hussein said, "Will you write him a letter?"

"Yes," I said slowly. "I'll write to him by airmail." I thought quickly. "It can go by Orient Airways tomorrow to Karachi, and I'll get the pilot to see that it gets on to the KLM for Batavia there." I knew that any letter for Shak Lin would get whatever special treatment was required. "Wazir," I said. "Would your master, the Sheikh of Khulal, write a letter to El Amin, too? We shall have difficulty in persuading him to leave his work and come to Karachi to hospital. I know a letter from your master would have weight with him."

He nodded gravely. "It shall be done. I shall bring it here tomorrow after sunrise, so that it can go with yours."

Dr Khaled said something, and the Wazir turned to me after a brief exchange. "It would be well that we should be certain that El Amin will come to Karachi," he said. "Perhaps it would be better that the specialist should go direct to Bali."

But Bali had no technical facilities such as Karachi hospital had. We talked about that for a time. "I tell you what I'll do," I said. "I'll take the next trip down to Bali myself, as pilot. If his sister wants to come, I'll take her, too. Then we'll bring him back with us to Karachi and meet the specialist there."

That settled that, and they went away, and I walked over to the hangar, not because I had anything to do there but because I wanted to get out of the office for a few minutes to think over how I was to tell this to Nadezna. I went back presently and called her in from the other office, and when she came, I said, "Bit of bad news, Nadezna. They did a blood count at Karachi. It seems that Connie's got a thing they call Leukaemia." And then I told her all about it.

She took it amazingly well. Asiatics do take these things well, of course; they never show their grief by any extravagant display of emotion. All she said was, "That's fatal, isn't it? He's going to die?"

I was from the West, and perhaps we kid ourselves more than they do. "Oh, it's not as bad as that," I said. "He'll have to go into hospital for some sort of treatment, possibly in Europe. He'll be all right."

She shook her head. "I think this is the end of it," she said. "I've heard about this thing."

"What have you heard?" I asked.

"There's no cure for it at all," she said quietly. "They may take you into hospital and mess you about, but once you've got it, you die just the same."

"I can't believe that's true," I said.

"I think it is."

I turned the subject and told her about the letter I was going to write. She agreed that Connie ought to come up to Karachi and be properly examined, and she said that she would write as well. And then I said, "Look, Nadezna, I think I'll go down to Bali myself again on the next trip, probably with Hosein as second pilot. I think it may take a bit of arguing to get him to come. Will you come with me this time?" I hesitated. "It's not the holiday I wanted it to be, but I think it'd help if you came. And then we can take him straight back to the hospital at Karachi."

She said quietly, "You can't go away again so soon, Tom. You've only just come back."

"There's nothing for me to do here," I said. "The business runs all right without me."

"Does it?" she asked. "I don't believe it does." And then she said, "I sometimes wonder who this business is supposed to benefit, you or Connie."

"I make money out of it," I said.

She smiled. "No, you don't. I've never seen you spend a penny, except on other people. You could live in a big house with plenty of servants and run a Bentley. But you don't.

You go on living in the chummery and the sergeants' mess, and you drive a station wagon. You don't make money at all, Tom. You make aeroplanes, that's what you do. Every penny that you make goes back into the business."

"What if it does?" I asked. "I like aeroplanes. I wouldn't want a Bentley, anyway."

"I suppose you'll tell me next that you're going down to Bali again because you like flying in the Tramp."

I laughed. "Many a true word." And then I said, "Will you come with me for the joyride?"

She said, "Dear Tom. You've never quite got used to having me around, have you?"

"No," I said. "I don't suppose I ever shall. It's a fresh wonder every day I come into the office, to find you here."

She smiled, and smiling she was very lovely. "All right, Tom. I'll come to Bali with you, and we'll do what we can for Connie."

After that, our life at Bahrein went on smoothly for a few days. I saw Wazir Hussein again and heard of the energetic steps that he was taking to get a specialist out to Karachi. These efforts finally resulted in them getting a Frenchman called M Serilaud, who seemed to be the authority on leukaemia in Europe; Dr Khaled said that he had worked in New York and in London and spoke English fluently, which was a help. The earliest that we could get him to Karachi was the twenty-seventh, which gave us a good margin of time to get Connie there to meet him.

I rang up Captain Morrison, and he came to see me one evening, and I told him everything that was going on. He was friendly and helpful, and said that if I wanted to bring Connie back to Bahrein there would be no difficulty from their end at all. He indicated that he, personally, would welcome his return as a gesture that would help to heal the breach that had arisen with the Sheikh of Khulal.

Inevitably, the news got round in the souk that Shak Lin was ill, and was coming to Karachi for examination. I don't know how these things get out in Asiatic places; I didn't tell anyone, and I don't suppose the Arabs in the Sheikh's retinue did much talking, though they may have done. In any case, it was all known in the town within a day, and Nadezna told me that wherever she went, in the streets, in the market, in her house, there were continuous enquiries. After a day of this she had to give up going out into the streets, and I sent the station wagon down to pick her up each morning and drive her home in the evening.

On the ninth of the month the Tramp arrived back from Bali, dead on schedule. It came in and landed about three o'clock in the afternoon. I walked out on to the tarmac to meet it when it came in. The five passengers got out and were met by a young man from the oil company, and then Arjan came out and walked across to me. He said that they had had a good trip, with no special incidents; there had been bad weather over Sumatra which had delayed them half a day on the outward journey, but on the homeward trip they had got through the inter-tropical front without much trouble. And then he said, "I have letters for you, from the Governor and from Shak Lin. I will fetch them and bring them to the office."

"Okay," I said, and I went back to the office myself, because it was hot out on the tarmac. Arjan Singh appeared in the office in a few minutes and laid them on my desk, and then he went through into the other room, perhaps to speak to Nadezna or Dunu. I opened the first letter.

It was from the Dutch Governor in Bali. It ran:

DEAR SIR,
It is with regret that I write to say that the continued residence of your engineer Shak Lin in Bali is no longer

acceptable to the Royal Netherlands Government of Indonesia.

I must demand that this man is removed from Bali very soon, and should be replaced by another engineer with neutral religious associations.

B HAUSMANN,
Governor.

I bit my lip, and read it through again. Then I opened the one from Connie. He said that by that time I should have received a letter from the Governor ordering him out of Bali. He was sorry that this had happened, and that it was not due to any action on his part, but due to circumstances out of his control that Arjan Singh could tell me about. He thought that it would be better now that he should leave my service, and he suggested that I should send down another engineer to work with Phinit by the next machine. He himself would leave on the same aircraft, and he proposed to make his way to Bangkok.

At the time he wrote that letter, of course, he hadn't received our airmail letters to him about leukaemia.

I got up heavily and went into the other office. Arjan Singh was there talking to Nadezna; she had an open letter in her hand. From her face I guessed that she had had the same news. I did not want to talk about it in front of Dunu; I told Arjan and Nadezna to come into my office, and when the door was shut and they were sitting down, I asked: "What's all this about, Arjan? This trouble down at Bali?"

He said, "Two Dakota-loads of pilgrims."

"What?"

He said, "Three days after you left Bali, a Dakota came to Bali from Bangkok. It was chartered from the Thai-Cambodia airline by a party of about thirty ground engineers from Don Muang. Most of them were engineers, but some I think were from the Siamese Air Force. They came to visit Shak Lin and to pray with him. They went away after one day. Then another Dakota came, with Indians from Allahabad and Calcutta. The Dutch administrators were angry, and they say that you should not have sent a man with a religious following to Bali. They do not encourage missionaries in Bali; they prefer that the people should continue in their own religion. The Governor gave me that letter to give you." He paused. "That is all I know."

I was silent for a time. Then I said, "Did you hear of any other machines going to Bali with pilgrims?"

He replied, "I heard talk at Karachi airport that a Dakota was leaving very soon, with pilgrims. I told them that it was forbidden, but they said that Shak Lin was ill. I think they mean to go."

"They mustn't go," I said. "When did you hear this?"

"Last night – and this morning."

In favourable conditions, usually late at night, we could get Karachi from Bahrein on the radio telephone. In a case such as this, Alec Scott would probably let me speak to Karachi myself. I might be able to stop that machine from leaving.

"Who pays for all this?" I asked. "It must cost somebody a packet."

Arjan said, "I asked that, also. The machine from Bangkok was provided by the Thai-Cambodia for a nominal charge only – one hundred rupees, somebody said. The engineers at Bangkok had agreed that each would work ten hours on the machine without pay in the next month, so that the servicing and life of the aircraft should not suffer. The pilots flew without pay, of course, being pilgrims themselves. The engineers serviced the machine upon the flight without pay. All the expenses to be met were petrol and oil, and insurance, and landing fees. They say that each man had to pay two hundred and fifty rupees. Some of them had not got the money, and their companies advanced wages to them so that they could join the flight, and they would work the time off later, so much in each week, to repay the loan."

Two hundred and fifty rupees is about twenty pounds. It was a big sum for an Asiatic engineer, but it was by no means prohibitory, and if the air line companies were prepared to help their men to go off on a trip like this by allowing them to work the advanced pay off over several months, it might be that many such journeys would take place. I already had abundant evidence that Shak Lin's teachings had spread widely through the East and had resulted in a marked upgrading in the quality of aircraft maintenance. If the employees of an air line wanted to go off on such a pilgrimage, a worthwhile manager would encourage the project and make it easy for them to go, knowing that such a religious experience would encourage the men and lower his maintenance costs. If my own people had come up with such a proposition I should probably have taken that line myself. There was no telling now where this thing would end.

"What started this, Arjan?" I asked at last. "What put the idea into their heads? We've never had anything like this happen before."

He said, "It was the Sheikh of Khulal's pilgrimage."

"I see ... They saw that trip go through, and thought they'd do the same?"

"Also," he said, "the word got around by radio that Shak Lin is dying." By my side Nadezna stirred, and then was quiet again. "I do not know if that report is true or not," Arjan went on, "But it is all over the East now, that Shak Lin is a dying man. And so, on all the aerodromes, engineers who work according to his teaching but have never seen him – such men desire more than any earthly thing that they should see Shak Lin before he dies, and hear his voice, and hear his blessing on their work. This is a thing that many men want more than anything else in the world."

"So we're likely to get a good many more Dakotas going to Bali," I said thoughtfully.

"I do not think that they will be able to go now," he said. "I think the Dutch will stop them. It is too far for a Dakota to fly from Singapore to Bali without landing for fuel, and when they land, at Palembang or at Batavia or Sourabaya, I think the Dutch will stop them. I do not think that such machines will get clearance from Singapore now, any more, to fly to Indonesia."

That seemed likely enough, though whether the authorities at Singapore would have the power or the will to raise a hornet's nest by standing between Dakota-loads of resolute pilgrims and their religious goal seemed to me to be doubtful. Arjan Singh was obviously tired with his eight days' flying, and I let him go soon after that, telling him that I was going to take the next trip down myself with Hosein as copilot. He was pleased to hear that I was going down myself again. "I think that is very good," he said. "I think it will be good that you should be with the Teacher at this time, for a few days."

"How is he taking it all, Arjan?" I asked. "Is he very much upset?"

He said a little pityingly, "Was he upset when he left here, Mr Cutter? He is not like ordinary men. Nothing that is written for him can cause him to grieve. Only the errors of mankind do that." He paused, and then he said more practically, "There is a woman there who serves him, Madé Jasmi. She sees that he lacks nothing, does not grow too tired. I think she will attain a great advancement in the life to come."

He went away to eat and rest, and I was left alone in the office with Nadezna.

She said, "Poor old Connie – to be kicked out of a second place, for his religion! And when we've just written to him about leaving, and telling him about the blood count. It's too bad, Tom."

"I know," I said. "He doesn't have much luck." And then I said, "He's going through a bad patch now, of course, but he'll get through all right. I suppose it was a mistake sending him to Bali, though it didn't seem like it at the time. After he's got rid of this leukaemia thing we'll see if we can find a place for him where they'll like his religion. Somewhere in Burma or Siam would suit him best, I think. A Buddhist country."

She smiled faintly. "But, Tom, he's not in your employment any more. He's resigned."

I said quickly, "He can't do that to me, after being with me all this time. I'm going to send him a cable now to say I won't accept his resignation."

"You won't accept the fact that he's dying, either, will you?" she asked.

"No," I said, "I won't. I won't accept that any more than I'll accept his resignation. He's going to get well."

She came over to where I was sitting, and bent down and kissed me. I stood up and held her in my arms for a minute. "It's going to be all right," I said. "There are times when things are a bit of a battle, and this is one of them. But it's going to be all right."

We broke away presently, and I sat down and wrote a cable to Connie. I said,

Won't accept your resignation now or ever. Coming down myself next trip with Nadezna to take you to Karachi; specialist arrives Karachi 27th. After treatment have new job for you in Siam.

CUTTER.

Nadezna stared at this. "What is this new job in Siam?" she asked.

337

"I haven't thought it out yet," I said frankly. "I'll have it cut and dried before I see him. We've got to give him something to look forward to, and hang on to."

"But you don't operate in Siam at all, Tom."

"I didn't operate in Indonesia six months ago," I said.

I took her down to the souk myself in the old Dodge that night; it was not possible to get the car up to her house, so I stopped it at the end of the narrow alley and walked with her to the flight of steps that led up to her room. Then I went back and got into the station wagon again, and on an impulse I drove out to the Residency compound at Jufair and went to call on Captain Morrison.

The Liaison Officer was out, but he was somewhere not very far away; his boy offered to go and tell him that I was waiting to see him and his bearer brought me a whisky and the paper. Morrison came in about five minutes and apologised for keeping me waiting in his shy, diffident way.

"I've come about Shak Lin," I said. "He's been chucked out of Bali." And I told him all I knew.

He took it very seriously. "The bloody fools," he said bitterly. "They've done just the same as we did here."

"I don't see that we can blame them for that," I said.

"No. I suppose that, down in Bali, they're right out of things; they couldn't know how fast this Shak Lin cult is spreading. It's up in Baghdad now." He glanced at me. "I suppose you know about that."

I nodded. "It's in Teheran, too. And it's all through India, from Lahore to Trincomalee."

He said, "It's gone right through the East – so far, only with one limited class of people, on the aerodromes. You can't say that it's a very strong cult, yet. It hasn't touched the peasants, or the politicians, or the intellectuals. But it's strong enough already to rouse vast resentment if we Europeans take to kicking Shak Lin out of every place he tries to settle in."

I agreed with him. "It's just not got to happen again," I said. "For one thing, he's a sick man now. After he's got rid of this thing, I think a Buddhist country would be best for him. I'm thinking of Siam. He's always been very well thought of in Bangkok. He'd be all right there."

"He'd be all right here," said Morrison. "The Foreign Office are quite aware that a mistake was made. You don't think he could come back here again?"

"I doubt if he'd want to," I said. "I think he feels that he's done all he can in this part of the world. You see, he's much more of a religious teacher now than a chief engineer. And as the cult grows, he goes further that way every day. I'd like to see him back in the hangar on the airstrip here, running the maintenance of my aeroplanes. But you can't put back the clock."

"No," he said, "you can't do that. When you make a mistake, sometimes, it's made for good." He stood in silence for a moment, staring out into the night. "Do what you can to get him back here for a little while, Cutter," he said. "Even if it's only for a visit, for a week. We made a blunder over this, and there's no doubt that it's affected British prestige in the Persian Gulf. People may call the Sheikh of Khulal an old fuddy-duddy, but he's an important man in these parts. If you could get Shak Lin back here if only for a visit so that we could make amends, I think it might be very helpful. Just bear that in mind."

"I'll do that certainly," I said. "I'll get him back here for a little if I can. But everything depends upon his health; this treatment at Karachi or in Paris must come first."

I went back to the aerodrome for dinner in the restaurant. Alec Scott was in the Control Tower; I went up and talked to him about Karachi. Radio telephone connections were not very good at the moment, and he said they would get better as the night went on; I went back at about midnight and Karachi was coming through as clear as a local call.

I asked to speak to the Controller, and I had luck there, because it was Khalil, the chap that I had spoken to once before, who was himself a follower of Shak Lin. I asked him to deter any aircraft that might be taking off for Bali with pilgrims and make it clear to them that they would almost certainly be stopped upon the way. I told him that I should be going down in two days' time myself and bringing Shak Lin back to hospital in Karachi. There was no point in any pilgrims going anywhere, since Shak Lin would himself be in Karachi in a fortnight and they could see him there.

He thanked me for the message, and said he would explain what I had said to the engineers. I only just got through to him in time, because the Dakota was already chartered and was to take off at dawn.

We left two days later in the Tramp. I made Hosein chief pilot and went as second pilot myself, and I put Nadezna on the manifest as navigator, and she travelled in the navigator's seat most of the way. We had eleven passengers for various destinations on the route, all oil men of course, and about two and a half tons of miscellaneous machinery and stores, so we had a pretty good load up.

We passed through Karachi in the early afternoon. Wazir Hussein had arranged for his agent to meet us on the aerodrome and this chap turned up. The hospital bed was all arranged and everything laid on. I took his name and address, and promised to send him a cable to tell him our exact time of arrival back with Shak Lin, so that he could meet us with a car upon the tarmac. I made these arrangements with some difficulty, because Hosein was up in the Control office with the paperwork, and Nadezna and I were beset with continuous enquiries from the engineers about Shak Lin. Finally a Pakistani customs officer in uniform came to our assistance and got a couple of the aerodrome police to keep the people off us, and to explain to newcomers what we had already told them many times.

We took off presently for Ahmedabad and spent the night there. Next day we flew on to Calcutta and Rangoon, and then in the evening light up to Yenanyaung, landing just at dusk. We set down some of our passengers there and took on others, spent the night in the oil company's rest house, and went on next day down the Kra Isthmus.

I had cleared the machine that morning from Rangoon for Kallang airport at Singapore, because when making a long journey I always like to get a good long stage done in the early part of the day, and a short one in the afternoon; it's less tiring doing it that way than the other way about. We were passing the Siam–Malaya border about noon and beginning to think about lunch; I was flying the machine with Nadezna by me in the copilot's seat, and Hosein was down organising the lunch baskets, when Nadezna said, "Are we going to land at Penang?"

I didn't think for a moment. I said, "No – Singapore." And then I said, "Why, of course – you were brought up in Penang. It doesn't matter – I can go in there and fuel just as well. Would you like to? I can get upon the blower."

She said, "Oh no. I'd just like to see it."

"We'll go past," I said. "Go past between Penang and Butterworth. You can see the harbour and the town that way. I'll drop off height and come down to a thousand feet or so." I throttled back a bit and retrimmed the machine. "How long did you live there?"

"Only till I was five," she said.

"Remember anything about it?"

She smiled. "Oh yes. I used to go to a convent school; I remember the nuns very well. They were so kind. There was a rocking-horse there, and a swing."

"I tell you what we'll do," I said. "We'll night-stop there on the way back, with Connie. I often do that. Then you can get a rickshaw and go down and see the school."

She said, "Oh Tom, that would be fun!"

341

I brought the machine down on a long descent, and Hosein came up from the cabin to see what was going on and I told him, "Nadezna was born here!" and he grinned, and went down again to reassure the passengers. We passed Georgetown on Penang Island quite close, and Nadezna looked up flushed and excited and said, "Oh Tom, I believe I can see the street we lived in!" And I said, "Bunkum. You were only five years old." And she said, "I'm sure I did."

"We'll come back this way and spend a night," I promised her.

It was a grand day that, spent flying the Tramp in fine weather down the coast of Malaya with Nadezna by my side. I made her fly it while I ate my lunch, touching the wheel now and then to bring the machine back level when I thought the passengers would be dying of heart failure. Hosein kept bobbing up to see what was going on, and once he asked me why I didn't use the automatic pilot. I said, "I am," and indicated Nadezna. I think he went down and told the passengers that I was in love, and they'd all probably be killed. We had a fine time up in the cockpit, that afternoon.

We put down at Kallang for an hour to refuel and then went on over the Linga Archipelago and Banka Strait down to Diento. It was a lovely evening; the sea blue and green around the coral atolls, the coastlines with their massive forests dim on the horizon. Nadezna and I were in the pilots' seats as before, and now a new problem was right upon me, not altogether unpleasant. Connie had ordered me to give his sister a message, and I hadn't given it to her. I should be meeting him the next day, and he might ask me about it; he was quite capable of asking her. It seemed to me that I'd better see about delivering it, and Diento was as good a place as any.

They had Customs at Diento since our flights had become regular, so we didn't have to waste time by putting down at Palembang. We landed just at sunset and were met, as usual, by cars from the oil company. It was dark by the time we had refuelled the Tramp and got her shut up for the night. The others had gone on, and Nadezna, Hosein, and I drove the five miles through the scented tropic night in an open car, to the refinery club. There was a great full moon, just coming up.

She said, "Oh Tom – this is a marvellous place! It's everything the tropics ought to be, and aren't."

It was, that night. The Dutchmen had arranged bedrooms for us in the club, as usual, but because we came there so frequently now they had given up the effort of entertaining us, and the routine now was that they just turned us loose to swim in their swimming pool, eat their food and drink their liquor, and dance to their dance band with the shorthand typists of the refinery. We did all that, that night. Hosein had a girl friend there and he went off with her, and Nadezna and I swam and changed and dined and danced in that lovely place beside the tropical river. I couldn't have staged a better evening for her if I'd taken her to the south of France.

We had flown all day, down from Yenanyaung, over ten hours in the air. We were both tired, and by eleven o'clock we both felt like packing up and going up to bed. We lingered a little on the terrace by the river, bright in the moonlight; sampans moved about on it with little lanterns, going upstream with the tide.

She said, "It's been a marvellous evening, Tom. Thank you so much."

I squeezed her arm a little. "Why say that? You know I've enjoyed every minute, being with you."

She raised her face and smiled, and I kissed it. She said, "Oh Tom. Think of all the Dutchmen!"

"They've probably got a rule against that," I said. "We'll get chucked out of the club."

But nobody seemed to have noticed us, so we moved into a bit of black shadow and did it again.

"I had a message for you from Connie, that I've never given you," I said presently. "Would you like to hear it now?"

"I don't want to hear anything about Connie just now," she said. "Not tonight."

I raised her face to mine and stroked her cheek. "I think you'd better have it," I said quietly. "We shall be seeing him tomorrow, and it's kind of relevant. He came back at me when I told him that it would make you very happy if he married Madé. He seemed to think that was a bit of lip. He said that it would make him very happy if you married me."

I paused, and then I said, "He said I was to tell you."

She stood quiet in my arms. "He isn't very practical," she said. "You're English, Tom, and I'm an Asiatic. You wouldn't want a quarter Chinese baby."

"If it was yours I'd want about a dozen of them," I replied.

"That's a fine way to propose to a girl," she said. "I ought to push you in the river."

"You can do that, if you'll marry me," I said. "Will you?"

She stood silent for a time, and then she said, "Not just like that."

"Like what, then?" I caressed her shoulder.

She said, "We're such very different people, Tom. I know you like the East, and for an Englishman you get on wonderfully well with Asiatics. That's probably why you want to marry me, because you think of us as people like yourself, not different. But we *are* different, all the same. You're English, and I'm Asiatic."

"Does that matter?"

She said, "It might not, but it might ruin everything. I wouldn't want to marry without children, Tom. And I wouldn't want to marry and try and raise a family in the Persian Gulf – there'd be no joy in that. You're English, and

344

some day you'll want to go back and live in England. All your roots are there, not in a place like this." The sampans moved on the dark water at our feet; over our heads the flying foxes wheeled under the full moon. "Suppose we went to live in England. I look Chinese now, and I may look more so when I'm older. Suppose someone said something about us, in the subway or a restaurant or something. I couldn't bear that, Tom. I'd have to get out of England if that happened, and where would we be then?"

I was silent.

"There's the children, too," she said. "I couldn't bear it if the others called your children Chinks, at school."

"Look," I said. "All these are serious things, Nadezna. I think you're worrying too much about them, making too much of them, but still, I know they're there. I wouldn't want to live anywhere where my wife would be insulted in the street, or my kids have a bad time in school just because they were yours. But there's lots of places where those things don't happen; we could live in one of those."

"There aren't so many white countries where those things don't happen," she said. "I know."

She turned in my arms, and put her face up to me. "I do want to marry you, Tom," she said. "If we got half a chance, I could make you very happy. But I'm not going to marry you till I can see things a bit clearer than they are just now. Some day, if you ask me again, I'll probably say, yes."

"You wouldn't like to say it now?"

"Not now. All I'm going to say now is, goodnight."

She got kissed goodnight, and it took about ten minutes, and then we broke it up and went to bed. I really hadn't expected anything much different, I suppose, and perhaps as you get older you get philosophical about these things, and don't go off the deep end as you do when you are young. You get to count your blessings, and my blessing

345

that night was that Nadezna loved me, and that there was a very good chance she'd marry me one day.

We went on in the Tramp in the morning, stopped at Sourabaya for fuel, and put down at Den Pasar airstrip in the middle of the afternoon. Connie was there to meet us with Phinit; I got out of the machine with Nadezna and left the work to Phinit and Hosein for the moment, and walked with Connie and his sister into the shade of the hangar.

"One damn thing after another," I said. "First leukaemia and then pilgrims."

He smiled. "I told you that that Arab doctor had found something wrong."

"I know you did," I said. "The crafty little mugger. He never said a thing to me till he got his samples reported on from Karachi."

Nadezna said, "We're going to take you back to hospital in Karachi." She told him about the specialist from Paris and the arrangements that had been made. "It's going to be much better if you have it all done there."

He smiled. "If I've got to get out of Bali I might as well go there. The only thing is this, and it's quite definite. I'm not going to Europe."

Nadezna said, "It may be that the best treatment is there, Connie. There's something about X-ray therapy."

He said, "They can keep it. I belong in these countries, not in France or England."

There didn't seem to be much point in arguing about it there and then. "In any case," I said, "the first thing is Karachi. Will you be all ready to start tomorrow morning?"

He nodded. "I'm all ready now."

"Okay," I said. "Now look, about these ruddy pilgrims. I'll have to go into town and see the Governor and smooth things over with him, Connie. I heard about two Dakotas coming here. Has anything else happened?"

"Three," he said. "It was two when Arjan Singh was down here ten days ago. One came in from Bangalore after that. It had a lot of people from the Hindustan Aircraft Company."

"Any more coming?"

"Not that I know of," he said. "But then I didn't know those were coming, either."

"I don't suppose that there'll be any more," I said. "They won't clear pilgrim aircraft at Kallang, because the Dutch don't like it."

I left them to get on with the refuelling and transfer of the load, after warning Connie not to do any physical work himself, and I drove into Den Pasar to see the Dutch authorities. I went first to see Bergen. He was quite polite, though somewhat distant. He said that the policy in Indonesia was to interfere as little as possible with the indigenous religion of the peoples in Dutch territory, and that they had naturally assumed that this policy was known to me and that they would have my co-operation. They had nothing against Shak Lin except that he appeared to represent a new creed of some sort, and that aeroplane loads of people from all over the East had started coming to see him. It was quite impossible for that to be allowed. They understood that this man had been expelled from British territory in the Persian Gulf for similar activities, and they considered it a little underhand of me to have introduced him into Bali without disclosing his record. In any case, I must remove him now, and I must understand that no activities of a religious nature by my staff would be tolerated in the future.

There was nothing to be gained by quarrelling with them. I said I was exceedingly sorry this had happened. It seemed to me that this was hardly a religious matter; Shak Lin had done no missionary work among the natives, and had not, in fact, infected any Balinese men or women with his ideas. All that had happened was that visitors had come to see him from considerable distances, and had left again without troubling anybody or making any contact with the Balinese. I told him that Shak Lin in any case was a sick man and would have to be removed to hospital immediately, outside Dutch territory; I proposed to promote Phinit to be chief in his place and send down a young Chinese called Pak Sza San to work with him. I said that I hoped there would be no further trouble.

We went in to see the Governor then and Bergen explained all this to him in Dutch, and he delivered a rocket in Dutch which Bergen translated to me, and then we all smiled and shook hands, and it was over. I said goodbye to Bergen and went out to my taxi to drive back to the airstrip. The young Dutchman, Andel, was waiting for me by the car; he was the man who had first taken us to Pekendang, in the jeep.

He said, "Is it true that Shak Lin has to go?" I suppose he was too junior in the Administration to have been told.

I said, "Yes. He's a sick man, anyway. I shall be sending down a young Chinese to work with Phinit."

He said quietly, "I am very, very sorry, Mr Cutter. It may not be my place to say so, but I think it is a great mistake."

I wrinkled my forehead. "Why do you say that?"

"I think he is a very great man," he said simply. "Perhaps the greatest that has ever visited Bali." And then he said, "I am interested in all that has to do with aeroplanes. I served in the war with the RAF in Bomber Command; I was the rear gunner in a Halifax. I have been to Pekendang several evenings, to be with Shak Lin and to listen to him talking. He is the greatest man that I have ever known."

It was nearly dark when I got back to the airstrip. The Dakota had come in and both lots of passengers had gone up to the Bali Hotel. Refuelling was just finished but the loads had not been changed; we would do that in the morning. I knocked everybody off for the night, because I

348

knew that if anybody worked late on the aircraft Connie would insist on working too, and I wasn't going to have that. We shut up the machines when the bowser had driven away, and then I asked Connie if there was room for us at Pekendang.

"I think so," he replied. "There's only three – you and Hosein and Nadezna?"

"That's right," I said.

"Hosein usually goes with Phinit. There's the hut you had before – that's ready for you. Are you sleeping with Nadezna yet?"

She was in hearing, but I didn't dare to look at her. "No, I'm not," I said. "We haven't got as far as that."

"Pity," he said. "Well, she can come in with me. We've shared a room often enough before."

We all walked over to the village carrying our small overnight bags. It was dark and shadowy when we got there, a friendly darkness with brown people moving about in it and welcoming us, in the light of a few coconut oil wicks and a hurricane lamp or two. Connie took Nadezna to his room and sent Madé Jasmi to organise an extra bed. I dropped my haversack down in the hut that I had occupied before and went to find Phinit to talk over the new organisation with him.

I sat with him on the steps of his house in the dim light, telling him what I wanted him to do; he knew Pak Sza San, and said he would fit in all right in Bali. I had chosen Pak Sza San because he came from Singapore, and so his home was geographically close to Indonesia, and he might be expected to know the customs and the ways of the Balinese by hearsay, anyway, better than, say, an Iraqi engineer from Basra. We sat there talking for about a quarter of an hour, and then a girl, bare to the waist, came up and spoke to him. I peered at her in the dim light, and it was Madé Jasmi.

Phinit said in English, "She wants to ask you something, Mr Cutter."

"Of course," I said. "Ask her what I can do for her."

There was an exchange in Balinese. "She says, is it true that Shak Lin has to go away to a hospital in a far country?"

"Tell her, I'm afraid that's true enough."

They spoke again. "She says, may she go with him to the hospital to cook his food and wash his clothes."

I sat in silence for a minute. That's usual in rural hospitals in the East, of course. A man's wife always goes with him to hospital and sleeps on the floor beside him. They think it is a very cruel custom of the West to separate husband and wife when one is ill. They think that in the great distress of a bad illness husband and wife need each other most.

"Tell her," I said gently, "that she can't do that. She's not his wife."

They spoke. "She says that Shak Lin has no wife, and he will never have one. She says that he will be unhappy if he is alone, and that she knows what he likes to eat, and when, and she knows all his clothes and how he likes them washed. She says he cannot look after himself when he is tired and ill."

I replied, "Tell her that he is going to a fine large hospital, larger than the Bali Hotel, a hospital such as Europeans go to when they are ill. Tell her that every person there has two or three servants that the hospital provides, and these are taught to do everything in the way the doctor says. Tell her that it is better that those servants should look after him, because he will get well more quickly, because they know everything about this illness."

She said something a little scornfully.

"She says, if they know everything about this illness, then they know that he is going to die."

I didn't know what to say to that one. Presently she said something again, and all the scorn was gone out of her voice.

"She says, Shak Lin will not stay in hospital for very long, because he is only going there to please you and his sister. She says that presently he will become too weak to travel, and he will go then to a quiet place beside an airstrip, and live there until he dies. She says, when he goes to that quiet place, may she get into your aeroplane to go to him, to be with him, to cook his food and wash his clothes."

She had a simple faith, apparently, that my aircraft would always fly direct from Bali to Shak Lin, wherever he might be.

"Yes," I said. "Tell her she may do that."

CHAPTER TEN

His speech is a burning fire;
   With his lips he travaileth;
In his heart is a blind desire,
   In his eyes foreknowledge of death.
He weaves, and is clothed with derision;
   Sows, and he shall not reap;
His life is a watch or a vision
   Between a sleep and a sleep.

A C SWINBURNE

FOR A NUMBER of reasons, I worked to a slower schedule than normal on the homeward flight. Work upon the aircraft was not finished, for one thing, so that a dawn start was out of the question, and for another I had promised Nadezna that she and Connie should revisit the scenes of their childhood in Penang, so that I planned to get there early in the afternoon and stop there for the night. Accordingly, we took off from Bali about ten o'clock in the morning, and made a short day of it to Diento, arriving there about three o'clock in the afternoon and stopping over for the night; next morning we went on at dawn and stopped for the night at Penang at about midday, to the surprise and delight of our passengers, who had no objection to an afternoon in Penang at their company's expense.

I had sent a cable from Diento to reserve accommodation for my passengers and crew, and since the passengers were all European I had reserved it at the best hotel in the town, the European and Oriental. Penang is a bit of a holiday place that planters come to when their isolation becomes unbearable, and everything in this hotel was of the best. It suited my passengers down to the ground, but it didn't suit Connie or Nadezna half so well, and I was out of tune with its luxury myself. They were going down to the Chinese quarter together. They suggested that I should join them down there later for a Chinese meal, and after some discussion about meeting we settled that I should meet them at six o'clock at the convent school that Nadezna had been to as a child, the Convent of the Sacred Heart.

I found it was a big place, with a school and an orphanage attached to it, down in the lower and less fashionable part of the town. Children played in the crowded streets all round it and the telephone wires overhead were tangled with their kites, and the streets were full of young women in flowered cotton pyjamas and old women in black pyjamas and young men in vests and shorts. The door was opened to me by an old sister in a coarse white cotton habit who showed me into a bare waiting-room, embarrassingly clean and scantily furnished.

Nadezna and Connie came very soon, and with them was the Mother Superior and a couple more sisters. Connie introduced the Mother to me, who was evidently Irish, and then they were saying goodbye to her. She wished Connie a good recovery from his illness. To Nadezna she said, "Remember that we deal in orphans here. If at any time you feel you have no home, come back and see us."

She said, "That's very kind of you, Mother."

When we were out in the street I asked her, "Did they remember you?"

She nodded. "They remembered us both. The one you saw, Mother Mary Immaculate, she used to teach me in the kindergarten. She looks just the same as she did then.

353

Connie sometimes used to come to take me home. She knew both our names, before I told her."

She paused. "They're so *stable*, those sisters," she said quietly. "Whatever else may change, whatever gets upset, you feel that they'll be going on there just the same, taking in orphans and bringing them up and putting them out into the world. Teaching the children ..."

I told my passengers when I got back to the hotel that night that I wasn't going to tire Shak Lin by flying very long stages. We took off at about nine o'clock next morning and stopped for the night at Calcutta. On the following evening we landed at Karachi. As usual, when we landed there a crowd of engineers was waiting on the tarmac to see Connie. I kept him in the aircraft and got out myself to find out what arrangements had been made. There was an ambulance from the hospital waiting for us; I got this backed up to the aircraft and got him into it and away while Hosein held the crowd off and answered questions.

Nadezna stayed in Karachi to be near her brother in the hospital, and I went on with the Tramp next morning to Bahrein.

The specialist from Paris, M. Serilaud, got to Karachi about the time that the Tramp went through again on its way down to Bali some days later. I had sent Arjan Singh this time, and I told him to night-stop at Karachi and go into town to see Nadezna, and then write me by airmail before flying on, to tell me what he thought about it all.

His letter came a couple of days later, and in the same mail there was one from Nadezna. And it wasn't very good news.

There is no known cure for leukaemia, only palliative treatments, and none of these are of great value. The disease is a sort of cancer of the blood-forming organs, and once you've got it medical science can't do a lot for you. Medical science, of course, is reluctant to admit this; the disease is a rare one, and human guinea pigs with it are not so plentiful, so that medical science has plenty of new suggestions for treatment when a case appears. There is not much evidence that anybody's life has been prolonged by such experiments, and no record of a cure.

Nadezna said as much to me in her letter. She said that Connie had agreed to a short course of X-ray therapy, not because he had any faith in it but because it would take a few days that he would have to spend in Karachi anyway. He wanted to come to Bahrein to see me, and he proposed to leave the hospital and travel to Bahrein on the Tramp with Arjan Singh on his return from Bali. Nadezna said that she had come to the conclusion that his time was limited, and as he had things on his mind that he wanted very badly to do, it would be best to let him do them.

Arjan Singh's letter was to the same effect. He made the point that a first-class ground engineer, accustomed to diagnosing the ailments of the most complicated aircraft engines and instruments from an examination of the symptoms, had little difficulty in mastering the functions of so crude and inefficient a mechanism as the human body. He said that the Teacher knew all about the prospect before him and he was not distressed. He wanted very much to come back to Bahrein for a short time, and Arjan proposed to bring him back on his return from Bali. In the meantime the Teacher was quite happy to rest in hospital, and let the doctors have their fun.

I saw Captain Morrison with these letters. He was pleased that Connie was willing to come back for a short time, and he sat down there and then and wrote a short personal letter to him to welcome him back to Bahrein; we got that off to him that night by air mail.

As I was going away, he said, "Let me know when you expect him to arrive, Cutter. I'd like to come out to the aerodrome and meet the machine."

I smiled, a little bitterly. "Shall I see if I can find a bit of red carpet?"

"We all make mistakes," he said quietly. "I'd like to come and meet him, if you'd let me know." I was sorry then that I'd said that, because, after all, the mistake had not been his.

The Tramp came in late one afternoon. I had got Gujar Singh to fix up Connie and Nadezna in the same rooms that they had occupied before in the house of Mutluq bin Aamir, the silk merchant; Nadezna had retained her room, I think, but someone had to be turned out of Connie's, which was done with great despatch. This of course put the news that he was coming back to Bahrein all around the souk, and when the Tramp landed there were close on a thousand people waiting by the hangar to see it touch down. Morrison knew about this, and he had laid on a few policemen to keep the crowd behind the rope barrier that I had set up, and when the Tramp taxied to a standstill Morrison went forward to meet Connie as he got out of the machine. Connie was bareheaded and dressed in khaki shirt and stained khaki drill slacks, and Morrison shook hands with him in front of the crowd. It was good of him to do that.

Connie wasn't very tired, though I think he was paler than when I had seen him a fortnight before. He wanted to join in the sunset *Rakats*, and as there was half an hour to go I took him round the hangar with Tai Foong and showed him what was going on in the shop. When it was time for prayer, he went out to the vacant ground with the Imam, and the crowd trooped on to it when we took away the rope, and the engineers formed a solid phalanx around Connie so that he would not be crowded. Then the Imam stood up in front of them and called on Allah, and I went over to the office with Nadezna, and gave her a cup of tea.

After the prayers were over, Connie came into the Office. I said, "I expect you'd better get down to the souk and rest." And I got out my keys and began putting the papers away and locking up my desk, because I was to drive him in the station wagon.

He sat down on a chair and said, "One thing, Tom, if you've got a minute. I came back here because I wanted to see you."

I stopped bustling around. "Of course," I said. "What's on your mind?"

"I want an aeroplane," he said. "I haven't got any money for it, but I was wondering if you could let me have a Proctor for a month or two."

I had two old Proctors. I had paid six hundred pounds for one and four hundred and fifty for the other; they were a fleabite in the total value of my aeroplanes, and both of them were pretty well written down in the accounts. "Of course," I said. "You can have a Proctor for as long as you like. What do you want to do with it?"

"I'm going to die of this thing," he said practically. "They seem to think I've got about a year, and I shan't be a lot of good after the first six months. Well, that's all right; most of us don't get so much notice. I've always said what I believed in, in the hangar, anywhere. And now I've started something. I don't know if what I've started will endure or not, but if it does endure, I think its quite a useful thing to have done. So many people now, in so many countries, on so many aerodromes, are talking about what I've said quite casually at some time, and repeating it, and writing it all down. And sometimes it's just hearsay – they're putting down things that I never said at all. Well, that's not right. If this thing's going to die out with me, it doesn't matter. But if it's going to endure, I'd like it to be right."

I smiled. "I see."

"If I had a Proctor," he said, "I could go round all these airfields and spend a day or two on each, just talking to the chaps. I want to do that. I want them to see me as a real man, not as a kind of God. I sweat like they do, eat like they do; I get tired and hungry and sleepy as they do. And ill, perhaps. When I tell them what I think about things, I want to tell them as a first-class GE, not as a bloody preacher. I want to go into each shop and hangar and tell them what I think of their routines and their inspection schedules, so that they'll remember me as someone who was good at their own job. Then if they like to pay attention to the things that I believe in, they'll be doing it on grounds of solid competence and fact, not just emotion."

"If you're going to go round all the airfields in the East where men are talking about you," I said, "it's going to take you all your time. There must be a hundred at least – more than that."

"I want to go on till I've got to stop," he said.

"Well, you can have the Proctor." I thought for a minute. "You'd better have Yoke Uncle – the engine's got about three hundred hours to go in that. That ought to see you through. If you want any more time, bring it in, and swap it for Nan Oboe. Who's going to fly it for you?"

He said, "Arjan Singh has offered to do that. He's coming in to see you in the morning. He wants you to give him leave without pay."

I nodded slowly. I knew that Arjan was a believer in Shak Lin, and he was unmarried; he could probably work without pay for a time. He was a good man for the job, too, because Sikhs are known and somewhat feared all over India. Arjan Singh in his best clothes was both an imposing and a ferocious figure; it would be a bold Bengali or Madrasi who would try conclusions with him. With Arjan Singh to run the practical affairs of life, Connie would be in good hands.

There would be no trouble about maintenance of the Proctor; at every aerodrome willing hands would seek to gain merit by servicing the Teacher's aircraft. "You'll have to have *some* money, Connie," I said at last. "I don't think you need bother about insurance – it's very little, and it can go on under the existing cover. Spares – we can fit you up with anything you'll need from the stores. But you'll have to pay for petrol and oil, or someone will."

"There's a chap called Noshirvan who lives in Bombay," he said. "A Parsee. He's a motor agent in a fairly big way. He came up to see me in Karachi. He wants to pay for the petrol and oil. I said I'd let him know if I could get the aircraft, and he'll take out a Shell carnet."

"We'd better get a cable off to him tonight," I said.

Next day I took Yoke Uncle off the list of operational aircraft and allocated her to Connie. He started in at once to do the fifty-hour maintenance schedules on her, working with Tarik. Arjan Singh came to see me and I fixed him up with unpaid leave for as long as he liked; I told him I'd be glad to see him back in the business whenever he was able to come. He said he did not know when that would be; as long as the Teacher wanted a pilot, he said, he would like to serve him in that way. He said that he had no home ties that would prevent him from devoting his life to religion. He told me then a thing that I had not heard before in all the three years he had been with me, that as a young man he had been married, and that his wife and son had died of fever while he was in the Royal Indian Air Force. Since then he had been unmarried. It takes an Asiatic a long time to get around to talking of his private life to a European.

Arjan and Connie got their Proctor going a couple of days later, and flew it over to Baraka to see the old Sheikh, who now seldom left his bed. They came back on the following day, stayed the night, and left for Abadan.

Nadezna and I stood in the shade of the hangar watching the thin line of the Proctor wing as it vanished into the haze to the north. Most of the other staff stood there with us, watching till it was out of sight.

"I'm glad you let Arjan go, Tom," she said as we turned back to the office. "I think he's about the best man to look after Connie. He's so very practical."

I nodded. "I told him to let me know at once by cable if he gets seriously ill."

She smiled. "I did that, too."

Nothing much happened after that for a couple of months. When Connie and Arjan had been gone for about a fortnight, they appeared again from the north and stayed one night; they had been to Abadan, Baghdad, Mosul, Teheran, Basra, and Kuweit, and now they were on their way eastwards to Pakistan and India. Connie was tired, but not more than one would have expected from such a strenuous journey. They went on to spend a night at Sharjah, and from there to Jiwani and Karachi.

About six weeks after they had gone through, Wazir Hussein came to my office in the maroon Hudson one afternoon. I got up to meet him and ordered coffee, and presently he came to the point.

"My master feels that he is near his end," he said. "Before he dies, he wishes to speak to the Majlis. He has sent me to invite you to be present, and the Sister, and Captain Morrison. He has matters of importance to tell you."

It was a very unusual summons, but everything about my relations with the Sheikh of Khulal was a bit unusual. "Of course," I said. "I should be very glad to come. When does your master wish to summon the Majlis?"

"If it is possible, tomorrow," he said. "I have seen Captain Morrison, and he is able to come tomorrow. He said that perhaps you would fly him over, with the Sister."

I fixed that up, and fixed the time that we would take off in the morning, and rang up Morrison to let him know. Hussein would come with us, and as there were to be four people I took one of the Airtrucks. The Wazir did not say what it was all about and I didn't care to question him.

Nadezna had no idea, but thought it had to do with Connie. As we were getting into the machine next morning I drew Morrison aside and asked if he knew anything.

"It's his will," he said. "He's calling the full Majlis. Can't be anything else."

We landed at Baraka an hour later, and drove to the palace in the Packard that came to the airstrip. Here we were shown into the same bare ante-room with the hard gilt chairs that I had been in before; this room was full of well-dressed Arabs, minor sheikhs and people of that sort, some of whom I knew from having met them in the desert or their villages in the course of various flights. There must have been about twenty of them. We waited with them in silence for a quarter of an hour, and then we were all led upstairs to the Sheikh's bedchamber.

This was a big, well-proportioned room, with little furniture in it except the one great bed. The old man lay propped up on this; he was much smaller and frailer than when I had seen him last. Dr Khaled was at his side. Huddled in a corner were several women, all heavily veiled in black burqas so that nothing was visible of them except their hands. We all grouped ourselves standing in a circle round the bed, and Wazir Hussein went forward and said in Arabic that everything was ready and that everyone was there.

The old man's voice was worse than ever, and I could only follow about half of what he said. Morrison gave it me in full that evening. First, he said his salaam to the Sister of the Teacher, who was the only woman in the place unveiled. He then gave his salaam to me, and to the various sheikhs assembled in the room, mentioning them all by name, and lastly to Morrison. He seemed tired then, and rested, and the doctor gave him something from a medicine glass to drink, pale pink in colour.

The old Sheikh revived after a few minutes and began to speak again. He said that his eldest son Fahad would inherit the Sheikhdom and would rule in his place after his death, and he would inherit all the incomes of the Sheikhdom including the oil royalties. All the old man's personal possessions, including his flocks and his herds and one half of all his moneys in the various banks, were to be divided between his wives and his children in accordance with the teaching of the Koran, and in this division was to be reckoned the sums owed by his debtors, but these debtors were not to be pressed to repay more quickly than had been agreed.

He rested again then for a minute or two, and then he went on. He said that it was fitting when a wealthy man died that he should provide for his family against all possible chance of want. Any money that there might be over should not be spent in idle luxuries, but should be given to further the work of God. He had given much thought to this matter, and had talked about it to the Imam many times. They were agreed that the stranger, Shak Lin el Amin, had done more than anyone in recent years to draw men back to God. In these modern times of machinery and inventions men who served such things, and more men served them every year, were tempted to abandon God, to their own utter destruction. El Amin, brought up to machinery himself and honoured in his calling, had shown them the folly of these ways, and had shown that only by turning back to God can men attain to Heaven. His teaching was a firm rock to which men could cling in a changing world, because it was the teaching of God. It did not seem to him important that El Amin shared his teaching with men of other creeds, with Buddhists and with Hindus and with Sikhs. His teaching was of God, and God knew best.

He therefore directed that the second half of all his moneys in the banks should be given to El Amin absolutely, since it would be used to bring men back to God through all the temptations of the new world of machinery. This was a legacy for a religious purpose in accordance with the fourth

Surah, and must not be disputed. He called everybody to witness that he was sane in mind and not subject to the influence of anybody in this bequest, which was made after due consideration for the furtherance of the works of God.

He was obviously very, very tired after all that. He rested again, and after a time he said, "God go with you," and we all trooped out.

There was nothing then to stay for, and no more to be learned. We flew back to Bahrein at once, and went down to Morrison's house for a talk about it, Nadezna and I. He said it was a perfectly valid will, and it was quite unlikely that anybody would attempt to upset it. If the Foreign Office should question it, he would have to testify that it was made strictly in accordance with Moslem law.

I asked him, "How much do you think is involved?"

"I simply haven't an idea," he said. "I'd only be guessing if I told you a figure. But it's a very large sum of money."

Nadezna said, "But Connie won't live to use it. It's given for his religious work. And he's a dying man."

Morrison bit his lip. "I know," he said. "That's just the hell of it. It's going to pass practically straight into other hands."

There was nothing to be done about it, and we went on with our work as usual. We heard of Connie from time to time as he ranged through the East, never staying longer than two days in any place. We heard once that he was in Patiala in the north of India, and three weeks later he was at Ratmalana airport at Colombo, and again, he was at Hyderabad, and again, at Chittagong. He went to Chiengmai and to Songkhla in Siam, and down to Singapore, where he spent several days.

It went on like that for about six weeks longer, and still the old Sheikh lingered on in his palace at Baraka. He must have been very tough. But then one day the inevitable happened, and Morrison rang me up to say that the old man had died during the night.

"What happens now?" I asked.

He said, "Well, the burial will be today and then there's three days of official mourning usually. I imagine we shall hear something from Wazir Hussein about the end of the week."

He didn't, but I did. The Hudson came to my office a few days later while I was dictating to Nadezna; we packed that up and I went out to meet them. The Wazir had a youngish man with him, richly dressed in Arab clothes and speaking perfect English; this was Fahad the eldest son, the new Sheikh, who had been educated at Shrewsbury and Balliol. He was then a man of about thirty, I should say.

I ordered coffee for them, but Fahad was of the new school and did not wait till we had sipped our coffee before starting on the business that had brought him to my office.

"I am sure you know what we are here for, Mr Cutter," he said. "My father, who died recently, left a bequest to Shak Lin, as of course you know. It is now a matter of implementing his wishes."

I nodded. "I was very sorry indeed to hear of your father's death," I said. "He was a great man, and a very good one." He bowed and I went on, "The sister of Shak Lin is in the next room. Do you wish her to come in?"

He said, "If you please."

I went and called Nadezna, and she left her typewriter, and the two Arab noblemen got up and bowed to her, unusual in the East. I told her briefly what had happened, and gave her a chair. Then Fahad said, "Where is El Amin now, Mr Cutter?"

"I don't know exactly," I replied. "He's travelling from aerodrome to aerodrome, staying no more than two days in each place. He has been in Malaya and in Siam, but when we last heard about ten days ago he was making his way back through Burma and East Pakistan to India again. I expect we could find out quite quickly where he is by the radio and Air Traffic Control."

Wazir Hussein asked, "Does he know that my late master gave a legacy into his care for the work of God?"

"I haven't told him." I turned to Nadezna. She shook her head, and said, "I thought it better not to."

"I think that probably he knows nothing about it," I said. I have told nobody. I don't suppose Captain Morrison talked about it either."

Fahad said, "It seems probable that he knows nothing about it, then." The coffee came at that point, and he waited till Dunu had put it on the table and gone out, and shut the door behind him. And then he said, "In that case, I should like to go to see him, with Wazir Hussein, to tell him that this thing is done because it was my father's wish, and mine also, that he should have this money to be used for God. Can you provide an aeroplane for us to travel to him in?"

"Of course," I said. "I can fix up that. How many will there be?"

He said, "If possible, I think the Sister should be present."

Nadezna said, "I should be glad to come, Sheikh."

I said, "Would you like me to come? That's just as you wish. I can send Gujar Singh to pilot the machine, or, if you wish, I'll pilot it myself. Just as you like."

Fahad said, "If you can spare the time, I should like you to come too, Mr Cutter. The sum involved is a large one, and it would be well that witnesses to the Majlis of my father should be present. And you are a completely independent witness, which perhaps was why my father asked for you."

I said, "I can come." And then I said, "How much money is involved in this legacy? I don't want to ask impertinent questions, but if it is a very large sum it may need some thought. Because, as you know, Shak Lin is a sick man."

Fahad said, "I know that, Mr Cutter. That has been in our minds, too, but my father's will must first be carried out before we think of anything else. As regards the sum, it seems to be about five hundred and twenty lakhs."

"Five hundred and twenty *lakhs*?" I repeated. A lakh of rupees is a hundred thousand rupees. I calculated quickly in my head – fifty-two million rupees. "You mean, about four million pounds?"

"Probably a little less," said Fahad. "Just under four million pounds, I think."

It may have been tactless before Moslems, but I said "Christ!" It's always a bit of a shock when the fairy tale comes true, and though I had heard for years that the old Sheikh had an income from the oil royalties that was a good deal more than half a million pounds a year, I had never believed it. I knew, of course, that he was wealthy, but sums such as that are bordering on fantasy, and one assumes instinctively that there is gross exaggeration somewhere. However, here it was, and it was true. The old man had just under eight million pounds in his various bank accounts, all in current accounts because of his hatred of usury. And by his will, one half of that sum was now due to Connie.

Fahad and Hussein were quite phlegmatic about parting with this vast sum, as well they might be, because the half that the family retained was free of any sort of tax or death duty. The income from the oil royalties was so vastly in excess of the requirements of their modest and ascetic way of life that the accumulated savings represented nothing but a burden and a responsibility. The old Sheikh had no idea of using money in the modern way; it was beyond his mental power to visualise the construction of roads, schools, hospitals, or sewage schemes as free gifts to his people; he would have thought that pampering them and leading them away from God into a life of sinful ease. Fahad, of course, had plenty of modern ideas, but he was new to the

Sheikhdom and had much prejudice to contend with. It would be many years before he could spend even the annual income from the royalties. I really think that they were happy and relieved that the old man had discovered a means of letting down the pressure in the Treasury for the service of God through El Amin.

We talked about this for a time, and then it became imperative to organise the journey to see Connie. There was a tendency for the party to grow on the Arab side; a cook was necessary to free the Sheikh from worries over eating unclean food, a servant or two were very desirable, and so on. I decided to take the Carrier as being bigger and more suitable than one of the little old Airtrucks, still doing yeoman service, and I warned Gujar Singh that I should want him to come with me on the flight, starting the day after tomorrow.

I took the Arabs up to the Control office then. Conditions were fairly good, and Alec Scott was in touch with Karachi by radio telephone. We got them to relay an enquiry to Air Traffic Control at Calcutta, and within a quarter of an hour we had our information. The Proctor had left Patna that morning for Benares; it was believed to be going on to Cawnpore, Agra, and Delhi.

We caught up with them at Agra five days later.

Agra, of course, is where the Taj Mahal is, the incredibly lovely and enormous tomb erected by a Moslem king to his beloved wife. To us Agra meant something different to that. It has a huge three-runway aerodrome with a long range of hangars and workshops; it is one of the principal bases of the Indian Air Force. There must have been thirty Dakotas parked there when we joined the circuit, and a mass of other aircraft.

Gujar was chief pilot for the flight and was flying the Carrier in for the landing; as we went round I scanned this mass of aircraft from the copilot's window to see if I could see the Proctor. And then I saw it. It was parked on the

367

tarmac between two Dakotas, and there was a great crowd of people round it; looking carefully I could see a figure standing on the wing beside the fuselage. I went quickly through into the cabin and pointed the machine out to Nadezna and the Arabs.

Then we landed, and taxied round the perimeter track to the Control Tower and stopped engines on the tarmac. I knew that Connie and Arjan Singh would have seen and recognised the Carrier as it came in, and they were expecting us because I had got a message to them at Cawnpore. It did not seem to be a very good thing to break in on their religious meeting, and so we cleared the necessary formalities regarding the aircraft, and telephoned for rooms at a hotel, and laid on two taxis, and then sat and waited until Connie and Arjan Singh turned up.

They came about half an hour later, driven by two officers of the Indian Air Force in a jeep, and followed on foot by a great crowd of enlisted men, all Indian, of course. I had not seen Connie for some months, nor had Nadezna, but we were both shocked at the change in him. With our intellects, of course, we had known that there must be a change, but I hadn't visualised it. He was thinner than ever, and obviously weak; when we saw him first, too, he was very tired because he had been speaking for over an hour. He was much paler than I remembered him, and he had lost a good deal of his hair, so that he looked ten years older. Sudden movements seemed to hurt him in his chest and abdomen.

He was very glad to see us all. I think he realised what the presence of the Arabs meant, because after a formal salutation in Arabic he said at once to Fahad, "Is your Father, the Sheikh of Khulal, well?"

The Arab said, "My Father is with God."

I broke in at that point, and insisted that we all went down to the hotel. The taxis were waiting, and I didn't like the look of Connie a bit; to start on a discussion of the legacy standing on the tarmac out in the heat of the sun, with all sorts of people listening, seemed very unwise. So we drove down to the Grand Hotel, and found it a big, spacious building in the grand style, now sliding into shabbiness and neglect since the departure of the British. In the vast place there were only two or three other guests, and we got a row of rooms in a ground floor arcade that opened on to a garden.

Connie and Arjan Singh shared a room as they were accustomed to do; it was only later that I came to know how much Arjan had done for Connie in those months, how good a nurse this robber baron with his great black beard had been. I got hold of Arjan Singh while Connie was having his bath and had a talk with him in my room. He said that Connie had never been actually ill in the sense that he had been unable to travel or to speak to his religious meetings, but he agreed that it was very near the time when he would have to give it up. He said that he slept very little, but rested a great deal; Arjan encouraged this, and kept him laying on the charpoy for as much as seventeen or eighteen hours in the day, only allowing him up to travel or to visit the aerodromes. He said that recently Connie had suffered a good deal from pains in his bones.

I asked if they were in money difficulties, if their travelling way of life could be made easier for Connie if they had more money. He said that money would make no difference. They were very seldom allowed to pay for anything; accommodation, taxis or gharries, and food were invariably provided for them free or paid for by the generosity of aircraft operators on the aerodromes. Landing fees were always remitted, wherever they went, except in Malaya, which was British territory; apparently the British civil servants didn't view religious travellers in quite the same way as Asiatics. He said that after nearly six months travelling they had spent no more than about four hundred rupees between them, and they had ample for their needs.

I asked him when it would be convenient for Connie to meet the Arabs, and he said that after dinner would be the best time; he said that Connie ate very little now, but that his evening meal was the best of the day, usually curry and rice and some fruit. After that he was alert and at his best, and Arjan suggested that the Arabs might come along at about eight o'clock or so to Connie's room, and we could all talk there. In that way it would be possible for him to recline on the bed if he felt like it.

I went and told Wazir Hussein this proposal, and then I went to tell Nadezna, but she was in with Connie. I dined alone in the hotel dining room that night because the Arabs ate privately in their own rooms, food prepared by their own cook. After dinner we all met in Connie's room.

There weren't enough chairs, so we sent the hotel boys to get some more, and presently we were all sitting in a row on hard, upright cane chairs in the bedroom, while Connie sat upon the bed, the mosquito net turned back over his head.

Wazir Hussein told the story to begin with. He said that his late master, the Sheikh Abd el Kadir, had been greatly troubled in his mind in his last years about the disposal of his money. After much thought he had decided that one half of his cash savings should be given to God, and they were then puzzled as to how this was to be done. Baraka was a small town that had a very good mosque already, and his master felt that if great sums of money were spent in the district the people of the country would become debauched. They decided that the money must be spent outside Baraka, and at one time they had played with the idea of spending two or three million pounds upon the erection of a vast new mosque in Bahrein. Then Shak Lin had appeared, the new Teacher whose ideas were refreshing and bringing up-to-date the old tenets of Islam without in any way destroying their original purity. His master had become convinced that this new teaching would spread through the Asiatic world and bring men back to God, and that if the spiritual power of El Amin were supported by the more material power of a great legacy to be devoted to religious purposes, then the new Teaching would be placed upon a firm foundation to the greater glory of God. Before the full Majlis, with some other witnesses, he had therefore left one half of his cash savings to El Amin absolutely, and this cash amounted to about five hundred and twenty lakhs of rupees.

Fahad, the new Sheikh, spoke then. He said that his father had made this decision after talking to him privately, and that he had agreed that this legacy was a fitting and a proper use for the money. He was entirely in agreement with his father's wishes, and he awaited a lead as to the disposal of the money.

I said a very few words then. I said that the late Sheikh had invited me to be present at the Majlis, which was a most unusual honour for an Englishman. Captain Morrison had been there, too. The old man was undoubtedly in full possession of all his faculties, and I had no doubt that this legacy was the result of prolonged and careful thought upon his part. Captain Morrison had told me afterwards that in his view the legacy was valid and completely legal, and that if any question were raised, he would advise the British Foreign Office so.

Connie said then, "I am very conscious of the honour that my old friend, the Sheikh Abd el Kadir, has paid me. Let me think for a few minutes."

He sat silent on the bed before us, his eyes on the floor. Then he got up and went to the door, and pushed aside the netted frame, and went out into the garden. There was a moon, and as we sat there in the bedroom we could see him through the netted door walking up and down upon the lawn in the moonlight. We sat there talking in low tones about unimportant things; I would have liked to smoke, but in that company of religious non-smokers that was hardly possible. There was a bowl of grapes upon the table, and we ate a few of these.

He must have been away for nearly an hour. At last he came in from the garden and sat down upon the bed again. He was calm and thoughtful when he spoke.

"My teaching has no need of temples," he said. "My temples are the fitters' shop, the tool room, and the hangar on the aerodrome. Nor do I need priests for what I teach, because each man who finds God in his daily work by working in a shop with other men, he is a priest for me."

He paused. "The Sheikh of Khulal was my friend," he said. "In the last years it has been one of the great pleasures of my life to visit him and talk to him about the ways of God with man, because he was kind and thoughtful, and compassionate to humble men, and wise beyond all belief. I knew that he intended this legacy; he told me when I visited him four months ago for the last time. I did not worry him in his last days by refusing his great kindness, even though I knew that it must be refused. If I did wrong in that, I ask your pardon."

Fahad cleared his throat. "It was not for temples or for priests alone that my father intended this money," he said. "I think he meant it for a pension fund in part, that men who turn to God in daily work and yet fall into ill-health or distress should be assisted by this money to regain their powers, or to die in peace. Also, he thought that men who followed your way of teaching should be helped to travel to far countries, where by their lives and work they would draw other men to God by their example."

Connie smiled a little. "Men who follow my teaching become good workmen," he said, "because good work and right thinking are as one. Such men need no money to help them travel, for if such a one should wish to leave his country and work, say, in Hong Kong to teach my ways, he will find there is a manager who will agree to pay his fare because he wants him in the shop. As for the old and the sick, you have provision for them in the Koran of the blessed Prophet. If this money is for them, it would be better that the Imam should dispose of it, not me."

There was silence in the bedroom. Presently he spoke again. "I have no possessions," he said. "Only the clothes I wear, my kit of fine tools and micrometers, and three or four hundred rupees. These things should go to my sister after I am dead. Because I have nothing of value, nothing of responsibility, nothing but the memory of my words will remain. That is the way I want it."

Gujar Singh spoke up. "Teacher," he said, "I know that what you say is true. Yet all the older creeds have found a use for money, and in some cases a good use. In Penang and many other places the Christians, the Roman Catholics and other Christian sects, maintain large buildings as schools and as homes for orphan children. Such deeds are good deeds, but the buildings have to be paid for. In that case the power of money has been used to do good things in the name of Jesus. May not the power of this money be used to do good things in your name, too?"

Connie said dryly, "I hope you're not comparing me with Jesus."

Gujar said defiantly, "I know that it is not the same. He was a woodworker."

Connie smiled. "Okay," he said. "Have it your own way. But Jesus didn't need five hundred lakhs to spread His word."

He was silent again, but presently he said, "This money is power. Great money is great power. But power has no place in what I teach; I do not teach men to be managers. I teach them to do good work and so serve God. Whether they sit at the manager's desk or whether they sweep the floor of the hangar is one to me. I shall die very soon. If I should receive this money, someone must administer it after me. And power corrupts."

"Many evils spring from power," he said. "Even from the power to do good. All power corrupts, and the intention to do good has little influence on the corruption. Either my words will last after me and be believed by men, or else they won't. Yet if one thing were required to kill them certainly, it is that my words should be spread after my death by the power of money. No teaching could survive a campaign of paid advertising."

There was a long silence. "I cannot take this money," he said at last. "Let there be schools and orphanages, and let my name be on the schools and orphanages if you wish, as one who loved Sheikh Abd el Kadir, but let these schools and orphanages be in Baraka. Let Baraka be a centre for learning and security in the Persian Gulf, so that no child, from Abadan to Muscat, shall need a home and not find one. And let there be a school for engineers, and an airstrip with hangars where men can learn my calling and my way of life, and find their way to God by doing first-class work. But let all these things be in Baraka and Khulal, to the honour of Sheikh Abd el Kadir and his friend."

He got up from the bed and said, "God go with you," in dismissal, and we all went out into the arcade, leaving Nadezna alone with him. The Arabs did not seem disconcerted at the refusal of the legacy; perhaps they had expected something of the sort. They did not discuss the matter then, but said good night with friendliness and courtesy, and went to their rooms. I think Fahad had some cause for satisfaction from the doings of the evening. Money meant nothing to him, as I have said; it would be years before he could spend even the income of the oil royalties. But an explicit direction from El Amin such as he had now received, to set up schools and orphanages for the whole of the Persian Gulf in Khulal was a help to him in dealing with the prejudice and reaction that was hindering the reforms he wished to make. A start was made on buildings for the orphanage and for the elementary school within three months of his return to Baraka.

I was left in the arcade with Gujar and Arjan; for a time we walked up and down upon the stone flags in the moonlight. "Everything has now been renounced," Gujar said at last. "No more temptations can be left. This was the final one, the temptation of Power to do Good."

Neither Arjan or I had anything to say to that, and we walked for a time in silence, the two Sikhs and I, each busy with our own thoughts.

At last I said, "What comes next, Arjan? He can't go on like this for very much longer. Do you know what he wants to do when the end gets near?"

He said, "I know that. He wants to go back to where it all began, to a place called Damrey Phong. I have never been there, but he says that you and Gujar know it. Is it in Cambodia?"

"That's right," I said. It's a very rural little village with one tarmac strip, about twelve hundred yards, I should think. It's about two hundred and fifty miles south-east from Bangkok, ten or twelve miles in from the coast, on a river. That's where he wants to go to, is it?"

"That is where he wants to go to live until he dies," he said. "He has told me that if he should become ill suddenly, wherever we may be, I am to put him in the Proctor and fly quickly to Damrey Phong."

"I see ..." I thought for a minute. "It's not on the map," I said. "I think the village may be shown, but there was no airstrip marked on my map. I can pencil it in for you in the morning. It's not difficult to find, though. When you're two hundred miles out from Bangkok, start looking for a peninsula like a hammer, with a little island off the south head of the hammer. Go on about fifteen miles and you'll find the mouth of the river. The strip is about ten or twelve miles up the river, on the west side, between the river and a ruddy great mountain about two thousand feet high. You want to watch it when you're on the circuit; it's a place rather like Penang."

"Is there a good house there?" he asked. "A house where I can care for him until he dies?"

I bit my lip. "I shouldn't think there is. There were two European houses by the strip, but that's three years ago. I shouldn't think they'd be much good by now, and the hangar had already fallen down. He definitely wants to go there, does he?"

Arjan Singh nodded. "That is where he wants to go to die."

We walked a few paces in silence. "I'll see if I can get something organised there, then," I said. "With five hundred and twenty lakhs going spare, there's no reason why he shouldn't die in comfort."

I put the matter to Fahad in the morning. "There's so little we can do for him, Sheikh," I said. "He will take nothing for himself. But if he goes to this place Damrey Phong for his last few months, he ought to have a house suitable for a sick man and a friend or two, and perhaps a doctor. And I think there should be a hangar for his aeroplane; in such a place he ought to have an aeroplane to keep in contact with Bangkok. Moreover, aeroplanes are his life's work. I can provide the aeroplane and a spare engine for it, and Arjan Singh wishes to stay with El Amin till he dies, so there will be a pilot. Will you provide the house and the hangar? I do not think that it can cost so much as one lakh."

He said, "I will do that gladly." We talked about it for a little time. "Surely," he said, "something should be done at once, because the matter is now urgent. Within a month he will be wanting to go there to die."

"I know," I said.

"Where is this place, Damrey Phong?" he said. "Is it possible for us to fly there now, and engage men to start the buildings?"

"We could do that," I said. "It would take us about two days to get there, by way of Calcutta and Bangkok."

"Let us ask El Amin if he will allow us to do that."

We went to see Connie, with the Wazir. Arjan and Nadezna were in his room, so we were all together. He was resting on the bed. "Look, Connie," I said, "we've been talking about what happens next." And then I told him what we proposed.

He was pleased at the idea. "I want to go back there," he said. "If you're going to do any building, keep it small and simple, so that simple people will come and see me. I'd like a bedroom with a veranda facing on the strip, and the hangar at right angles to the house, so that if I'm in bed on the veranda I can see into the hangar, and the aircraft landing and taking off on the strip, and everything that's going on."

"Okay," I said. "We'll have it like that. Now, Connie, there's another thing. Madé Jasmi, down in Bali – she wanted to come and cook for you and wash your clothes when you had to stop travelling. Would you like to have her there, or shall we give that a miss?"

"I'd like to have her," he said. "She'd be all right there. It's not so very different to her own place. If I hadn't been such a fool I should have married her."

"I'll see that she gets there," I said.

"Will you see that she gets back again to Bali after my death?" he asked. "She wouldn't be happy knocking around the world in towns or cities."

"No," I said. "I'll see that she gets back there right away."

There was one more thing. "Connie," I said, "we're going on to Damrey Phong from here, but none of us speak a word of Cambodian or Siamese. Can we make contact with anybody in Bangkok who can come with us to Damrey and act as an agent?"

"Tan Khoon Prasit," he said. "He's in Bangkok, and he's a friend of mine. He'll fix you up with everything you want. I'll give you a letter to him."

We all left Agra that afternoon. Connie and Arjan Singh went on to Delhi in the Proctor, and the Arabs and Nadezna and Gujar and I went to Calcutta in the Carrier. We stopped the night there and took off at dawn next day for Bangkok, and got there about midday after a six-hour flight.

I had sent a telegram to Tan Khoon Prasit, and he was on the aerodrome to meet us, a small, smiling Siamese who spoke good English. He was in the Treasury and he had something to do with the Government's airline, Siamese Airways. With the pull he had at Don Muang airport everything was made very easy for us, and we were driving down to the city with him within half an hour of landing.

He took us to his house, a villa on the outskirts of the town. He had Chinese tea for us, served ceremonially in little cups without handles, somewhat in the manner of Turkish coffee in the Persian Gulf, and then we settled down to tell him our story and what we wanted. It soon appeared that he himself was a follower of Shak Lin; he said that his teaching had influenced aircraft maintenance in Bangkok very much, both in the airline and in the Air Force. He had been a passenger on the Dakota that had gone from Bangkok to Bali to pay homage to the Teacher, and he remarked that he had noticed then how ill he looked.

He was practical and helpful over Damrey Phong. He said that the district was still held by the Viet Minh forces, but no fighting had taken place there ever, or was likely to do so. So far as he knew, the airstrip had not been used since Dwight Schafter had left it; he had never heard of anybody going there. He could supply an interpreter to go with us to Damrey if we liked and to negotiate any settlement that might be necessary with the local authorities before we started to build on the airstrip. He did not think there would be any difficulty at all. He suggested that he might make contact with the Buddhist hierarchy in Bangkok, who thought so highly of Shak Lin and of his teaching, and who might wish to send a priest with us to smooth out any points that might arise on the religious side.

We left next day with a young Siamese on board called Khun Phra Sanid and a Buddhist monk in a yellow robe whose name was Boonchuey, which means Helped by Merit. We came to Damrey Phong about an hour and a half later, and I circled it at about five hundred feet a couple of times. It all looked much the same; the two European houses were still there and apparently occupied, but the roof of one of them had been thatched with palm leaves, which didn't look so good.

The strip looked all right still, but I brought the Carrier down and flew ten feet up along the length of it while Gujar Singh and I studied the surface from our windows. It was crumbling somewhat at the edges and paddy melons were encroaching on it in parts and spreading over the hot tarmac, but we saw no holes. I took her up again and made a circuit and came in on a long, straight approach, and put her down.

She came to a standstill opposite the houses; I stopped engines and left her where she was; nobody else was likely to want the runway. We all got out, and the two Siamese began talking to the people who came out from the houses and from the town. They remembered the Carrier, and they remembered Gujar Singh and me from our visit to the place three years before. They said that no aeroplane had visited Damrey since then. They asked at once about Connie.

The two houses weren't too bad. One of them needed a new roof, and most of the glass windows had been broken, but although white ants had been at them a bit there was nothing that a few carpenters could not put right. Fahad told Khun Phra Sanid to buy them right away, and we flew back to Bangkok in the evening.

That night the Arabs chartered the Carrier from me for an indefinite period, with Gujar Singh to fly it. All the building materials and labour that were required could be obtained in Bangkok and flown to Damrey in the Carrier, with hospital equipment and linen, and everything necessary for a sick man. Nadezna stayed with them to organise that part of it. They got corrugated iron sheets, too, and steel angles for the framework of the hangar, and cement for the floor; all these things were to go to Damrey in the Carrier in repeated trips.

I could do nothing much to help all these arrangements and my business in Bahrein required me urgently. I left all this to go ahead and flew to Mergui in a Fairchild Argus of Siamese Airways, having cabled to Hosein to pick me up there on his way back from Bali in the Tramp. He arrived a day later, and two days after that I was back in Bahrein telling Captain Morrison about it, and tackling the huge pile of paper on my desk.

A fortnight after that Madé Jasmi got to Damrey Phong. I sent a letter down to Phinit at Pekendang and told him to explain to her that the time had now come when she could go to Shak Lin in the quiet place beside the airstrip that she knew about before any of us, to cook his food and wash his clothes. She put on her jacket as a concession to foreign ways and took a small rush basket with a few things in it, and got into the great aircraft with Hosein and his passengers, and went off as nonchalantly as the most seasoned traveller. Hosein put down at Mergui in Tenasserim as he had done for me, and Nadezna met her with the Argus there, and flew her to Damrey Phong by way of Bangkok.

Fahad was a good organiser, and he got the buildings up and ready in a very short time. He got the hospital equipment that he needed in Bangkok, because it was all simple stuff. Then Gujar Singh suggested that there ought to be electric light, which meant a motor generator set, and if they had electricity they might as well have a radio telephony equipment that would enable them to keep in contact with Bangkok. They appealed to me for these things, and I flew to Cairo in an Airtruck and got them there, and sent them down to Mergui on the next Tramp flight, and Gujar picked them up from there and took them to Damrey Phong. I sent a spare engine for the Proctor too, because it seemed to me that Connie's engine must be near its time, and with it I sent down a kit of spares and tools in case he wanted to do the overhaul of the old engine there himself. I had a hunch that possibly it was the kind of job that he might like to potter about with, on days when he was feeling well enough to work.

About six weeks after we had met him at Agra, his tour came to an end. He was talking from the wing of the Proctor to a crowd of engineers and pilots at Vizagapatam when he had some kind of a stroke and was unable to go on talking, and he might have fallen but for the fact that Arjan Singh was up there on the wing behind him, probably with that in mind. He was deaf on his left side after that, and the sight of his left eye was somewhat dimmed, and he decided to give up. Arjan Singh put him in the back seat of the Proctor where he could lie at ease, and flew him in two days to Damrey Phong by way of Calcutta, Akyab, Rangoon and Bangkok.

Nadezna told me that he was pathetically glad to see the Balinese girl, Madé Jasmi, waiting for him there. She said that he could hardly take his eyes off her on the first day, ill though he was.

He hadn't been there a week before the first Dakota-load of pilgrims came. They were Buddhists from Rangoon. Gujar had brought the Arab party back to Bahrein the day before, but Arjan Singh was there, and the Buddhist priest, Boonchuey. There were about forty pilgrims, and when the Dakota taxied to a standstill they got out and came and sat down in rows in front of the houses, patient and orderly, waiting for a sight of the Teacher. In spite of the protests of Nadezna and Madé and the Siamese nurse, Connie got up from his bed and went and sat on the veranda steps and talked to them for an hour, mostly about maintenance schedules on the Dakota aircraft. The Buddha was still in the same position at the edge of the airstrip, getting a bit weather-beaten now, and in the evening he went there with Boonchuey and knelt with the pilgrim engineers while the Buddhist monk held some kind of a service.

That was all right, perhaps, but there was no provision for feeding and housing forty pilgrims on the airstrip; they slept in the aircraft and in the hangar and all over the place, and ate the small village out of all its food supplies. That was no matter because Damrey Phong is in a rice growing district and the pilgrims paid for their meals. The villagers made money out of them, and looked for the next aircraft eagerly.

It came a few days later, this time from Calcutta, and with it came news of others on the way. Arjan Singh paid the villagers with money left with him by Wazir Hussein to build an atap dormitory hut, a simple affair that consisted of little but a board floor raised two feet above the ground, a thatched roof, and a lot of charpoys or string beds. The Hindus behaved well, but they were troubled by the Buddha, and they came to Arjan in a body before leaving and asked if there might be a Hindu shrine or temple there as well. He said that the Teacher would welcome it, and that Hindus might put up what they liked, provided that it was well back from the runway and generally in the line of the other buildings.

Arjan Singh wrote letters about all this to Wazir Hussein to account for the money he was spending, and Nadezna wrote to me every week. The Wazir turned up in my office one day rather concerned about what was going on, because it seemed that two or three Dakotas full of Moslems had been there, and there was no mosque at Damrey Phong.

There was a little Buddhist temple which the villagers were building up themselves out of the profits of the catering and urged on by Boonchuey, and a Bengali jute merchant had provided three lakhs of rupees for quite an imposing Hindu temple. The Wazir said that his young master was distressed to hear that there was no mosque on the strip and no Imam, and that he proposed to make good these deficiencies immediately. I said, of course, I thought that it would be a very good thing.

Connie had been there for over four months before I was able to free myself from my business in Bahrein for long enough to go down there again to see him – and Nadezna. I had replaced her in the office by an Iraqi shorthand typist, but he wasn't really any help to me; he could never act upon his own initiative to relieve me, as Nadezna had done every day. There came a time, however, when I realised that unless I went to Damrey soon I might not see Connie again, and so I called in Gujar Singh and told him to get on with it and cabled Arjan to meet me with the Proctor at Mergui, and went down on the Tramp with Hosein.

Arjan told me when I met him that a load of pilgrims came in almost every day, and sometimes two in one day; in fact, we got to Damrey Phong about the same time as a Dakota from Ceylon and had to make another circuit while it landed ahead of us and got off the runway. They had got into the swing of handling the pilgrims by that time. He told me that they had never had any sort of trouble, even when Moslems and Hindus had arrived together; this was probably because, being technicians, they were all fairly well-educated men, made more broadminded, too, by travel. To prevent any risk of clashes, however, he had had separate dormitory huts put up for each of the three main religions, and these stood each behind its own temple in an orderly array. With all these buildings, from the air Damrey Phong was starting to look quite a place.

I found Connie in bed on the veranda. He was looking very frail and white; it did not seem to me that he had very long to go. He no longer got up to speak to the pilgrims, nor did he pay much attention to them while I was there. The routine was that they went to prayer at their own temple, and there the resident priest explained to them that they must not expect much from the Teacher, who was now a dying man. Then they would come and sit down on the ground in front of the house where they could see Connie in his bed, and he went on talking to whoever happened to be with him, or dozing, paying little or no attention to them. In the evening they were called to prayer again, and ate, and slept, and took off again in their aircraft in the morning.

I sat with him on the veranda in the days that I was there for long periods, watched by all these pilgrims seated on the ground before the house; after a time one forgot about them, and took no notice. He was very pleased to see me, and grateful for everything that had been done to help him. Madé Jasmi sat all day on the veranda steps when she was not cooking or washing for him, making her palm leaf offerings in the Balinese way; the Hindu priest had made a special little shrine to Shiva for her in the temple, and she used to put them there, and pray. When pilgrims were about she wore her jacket, but at other times she usually left it off for coolness; when the Buddhist priest Boonchuey came to talk to Connie, which he did frequently, Madé was banished to the back quarters with the other women.

Connie liked to talk about the earliest days, when we had met in Cobham's Circus, when we had done the Gretna Green act together in the old Ford, when we had been bombed by the crazy-flying Moths and Avros with little paper bags of flour and rolls of toilet paper, and my skirt always got torn off. He could still laugh at the recollection of the fun that we had had together, even though it hurt him to laugh now.

"You've come a long way since those days, Tom," he said once. "You never thought that you'd end up by running an airline half across the world, and owning all the assets of the business."

I smiled. "You never thought that pilgrims would be coming from five thousand miles away to watch you talking to me, and to pray beside your house."

"No," he said thoughtfully. "No, I'd never have thought of that. It's funny the way things turn out."

Another time he said, "I didn't want to end up with this sort of reputation, Tom. All I ever wanted to be was an absolutely first-class ground engineer, the best in the world. And because the best teacher is the chap who's only one jump ahead of the pupil, I thought I could teach others to be first-class chaps. But the truth of it is, you can't do any job really well unless you're really good yourself. The perfect job demands a perfect man, and you can't separate the two. I didn't understand that when I started. It wasn't until I came out to the East and learned something about religious ideas here that I began to cotton on to what it was all about."

And another time he said, "They're making legends about me already, Tom. Try and tone that down. They're paying far too much attention to what that English pongyi, U Set Tahn, has been saying."

"You mean, about you being born in Tibet or somewhere?"

He nodded. "It's completely wrong. I was born in Penang, and I'm a British subject. I've got a birth certificate to prove it." He hesitated. "My father married my mother up at Barkul, true enough. But I was born in Penang. So that prophecy can't possibly apply to me."

I wasn't quite so sure about that, though I didn't argue the point. Some Asiatic countries have a different definition of when a man is born.

"Another thing," he said. "U Set Tahn and the Rangoon Buddhists say that the new Teacher's ministry will last for four years and twenty-three days. They're trying to pin that one on me, too."

"I know," I said.

"Well, when did I start teaching anybody anything?" he asked triumphantly. "I don't know myself. I simply haven't a clue."

"When did you first come to Damrey Phong," I asked.

"Four years ago last Thursday," he said. "I worked it out. But I never taught anybody anything while I was here. So that one's all wrong, too, because I was here three months, and I don't suppose I'm going to live that long. Try and put a stopper on this sort of thing, Tom, if you can. I want people to remember me as a good ground engineer with both feet on the ground. Not as a legendary mystic or anything like that."

"I'll do my best," I said. And as I sat there I wondered if he knew when he had been teaching or if, in those early days, his teaching had been largely unconscious. U Myin and Chai Tai Foong had both been with him at Damrey Phong, and they were among the most devout of Connie's followers.

That evening I walked out with Nadezna to the runway in the bright moon, and we walked up and down it for a time, thinking of Connie. And presently, at the far end where nobody could see us, I took both her hands, and I said,

"What about us? After this is all over, and it must be soon, I'm afraid – after that, will you marry me?"

She said, "I wanted to tell you about that, Tom." She hesitated. "I'm not going to marry anybody, ever."

I said quietly, "I don't think that's a very good idea."

She smiled. "I'm sure you don't. But it's what I'm going to do."

I held her a little closer. "Not because of your Chinese father?" I asked. "It's not reasonable to let that worry you. It doesn't worry me. You know it doesn't. We can work that out together. I don't want to go and live in England. All my work, and all my interests are out here, Nadezna. But it won't be any fun unless you're with me."

She freed herself a little, and I knew that I had failed.

"It's not that, Tom," she said. "I'm not worried about that now. I know that if I married you we'd get over the mixed marriage side of it all right. But we'd be letting such an awful lot of people down."

I was puzzled. "Who would we be letting down?" I asked.

She did not answer me directly. "I've learned a great deal since I've been here with Connie," she said. "You can't help being influenced by it, Tom – all these aeroplanes that come here every day, at such expense, full of people who believe in him. People who have spent all their savings just to make this journey, because Connie is a man that they can pin their faith to. All they want to do is just to hear him say a few words, or if that's not possible, then just to see him, or touch something that he has touched. It's – it's like the Bible, Tom. Like people that were wanting to see Jesus. They believe in him."

"They haven't been doing any worshipping, have they?" I asked. "Not like as if he was a God?"

She shook her head. "They haven't been like that. They know that he's a man, and that he's dying. Gods don't die. But they know, too, or they think they know, that he is such a man as they will never see again, and they go away feeling that just to look at him and touch what he has touched has done them good, and has made their lives complete, and justified spending all their savings to come all this way. They don't think that he's a God. But if you asked me if they thought that he was a man who had attained perfection as Gautama attained it – well, I think a lot of them do think of him like that. They do."

"You mean, as an example?" I suggested.

"I think that's it," she said. "They venerate him as an example of what any man can attain to if he can be as wise, and thoughtful, and self-sacrificing, and as good as Connie."

We stood together in the moonlight for a little, on the runway. Over against the strip the mountain loomed above us, scented in the warm night air. "He's my brother, Tom," she said simply. "One never thinks one's brother can be anything particular. I thought he was just nuts about religion, and it was all because he'd never had a girl in the United States, because he was an Asiatic who was out of place. It's not easy when you're brought up as an Englishman or an American, but you're really Asiatic, Tom. I know. I thought that Connie was just an ordinary brother, just like any girl might have. I thought that up till the time I came here. But now ... I'm not so sure."

I was silent. Perhaps I wasn't quite so sure, myself.

"These people that come here to see him," she said presently, "– they think he's a man, but a man touched by the hand of God, whichever form of God they happen to believe in. And because that's what they think, it does them good and gives them something to hang on to. Because, it means that God still cares about the world, and cares for them. That's why they come here, Tom. They come to see the evidence that God still cares, that He has shown that care in making of one man a perfect example, to show everyone the way to live their lives out in the modern world."

She turned to me. "It's bad luck on us," she said, "but I'm not going to spoil it for them. If I, Connie's sister, married and had children, and lived just a normal woman's life, going out shopping in the morning, going to the movies in the evening while you worked up a bigger business every year and we made money – it'ld detract from it. Maybe they'd get to feel that Connie couldn't have been something after all, if his sister wasn't anything. If they thought that, they'd lose the faith they have, and with that they'd lose everything that he has worked to give them. It's in my hands now, Tom, whether what he's started goes ahead or flops – at least, I think it is. And it's not going to flop."

I cleared my throat. "What are you going to do?"

"It's bad luck on you, Tom," she repeated. "You deserve a better deal than this. But if Connie could give up love to help along the things that he believes in, so can I. I don't have to give up children, though. I'm going to go back to Penang, Tom, where I came from. I'm going to go to Mother Mary Immaculate and ask if I can start in at the bottom, working in the orphanage. That's where I came from, and I reckon that'll be the best thing I can do."

I asked her, "May I come and see you there, sometimes?"

She said, "Please – please don't do that, Tom. And please, don't write."

I started on my journey to Bahrein next day, because I couldn't stay away too long. Connie lived for a month after that, gradually growing weaker. Then he went into a coma that lasted about thirty hours. He died just before dawn, and the cremation took place on the same day, according to the custom in the East.

CHAPTER ELEVEN

Only the road and the dawn, the run, the wind, and the
rain,
And the watch fire under stars, and sleep, and the road
again.

JOHN MASEFIELD

DAMREY PHONG HAS grown a bit since then, but the Proctor
still stands in the same tin hangar, with the engine that
Connie took out of it when he put in the new one standing
beside it on an overhaul trestle. He changed the engines
before he got too ill to work and got the old one stripped
down for overhaul with the sump off and the cylinder
heads, cylinders, valves, valve gear, and pistons laid out
neatly on a table in rows, all washed and clean and resting
on a blanket. He had to give up then and he never worked
again, and so the job remains just as he left it. The pilgrims
file past every day and look at the Proctor and these engine
parts laid out behind the wooden railing, and most of them
kneel down and say a prayer or two, according to their
creed.

It's not quite the same, of course. Sheikh Fahad went
there at a very early stage and had a sort of temple roof, a
temple with no walls except the roof posts, built over the
whole lot to protect it from the rains, so that the two little
European houses and the corrugated iron hangar with the

Proctor in it and the very lovely shrine that he set up to hold the casket of ashes are all under the same wide roof and safe for a considerable time. The house that Connie died in is kept just the same, with his bed and his few clothes laid out, all very simple. In the other house there is a small museum, and here his tools are displayed; he had quite a lot of fine precision tools and measuring instruments, micrometers, inside micrometers, feelers, thread gauges, callipers, vernier gauges – all that sort of thing. These are exposed to view, and may be touched and handled reverently by the pilgrims if they wish, and they are kept so carefully cleaned and greased that they are as bright and new as when he bought them.

In another room there are five pictures, and nothing else. Fahad, as a Moslem, will have nothing to do with pictures, of course, though I have been there with him and noticed that he spent a quarter of an hour in that room with them. Mr Ghosh, the Bengal jute merchant, commissioned Evan Stanley to come out from England to paint them, and a committee of the three priests on the airstrip decided that they should be of Connie Shak Lin himself, taken from photographs, and of the four people he loved best. So there is a very good picture of Connie in his stained khaki shorts and shirt, grave and intent, working on the engine of his Proctor, which stands in the background of the hangar behind him.

There is one of Arjan Singh, seated in the pilot's seat of the Proctor. They chose that because so many people had seen Arjan in that six months with Connie, and had seen how carefully he cared for him on that last journey.

There is one of Nadezna, a very good one. I can hardly bear to look at it.

There is one of Madé Jasmi, very sweet, but not quite natural because she has her jacket on.

And there is one of me, which oughtn't to be there at all.

Things are a bit different at Bahrein, too, on the aerodrome. There was a considerable demand from the people, backed by Sheikh Fahad, that a mosque should be built on the bit of vacant land beside the hangar that Connie had first used for prayers, and that the hangar should continue to be used for civil aviation so that the Moslem engineers should have the mosque available for prayer right by the hangar. This meant that the RAF would have to move away and leave that area undisturbed, although it is right on the edge of their camp. They have been exceptionally understanding and farsighted about all this, and have accepted the considerable inconvenience that must result to them. Their new hangars are going up at the south end of the north-south runway, nearly a mile away from their camp. The mosque is going up beside the civil aviation hangar.

A fair number of pilgrim aircraft come to Bahrein, perhaps one a week. Most of these are from Egypt or Iraq, places relatively near at hand, and most of these pilgrims are people who can't afford the long journey to Damrey Phong. Damrey is the main centre for pilgrimages, of course, since it was here that Connie's ministry began and finished, but it's a long way and an expensive journey for them, however much one tries to cut the rates. I have two new Tramps on order now specially fitted for pilgrims, and I hope to get the fares down to about sixty per cent of what one has to charge for a Dakota fare, but it's still an awful lot of money for an engineer to save. And yet they do it.

Some of them, perhaps one or two machines a month, go further still, right down to Bali, where Phinit shows them the hangar and the hut in Pekendang where Connie lived, and Madé Jasmi still sits quietly weaving her lamaks on the steps, oblivious of the brown people from far lands who have come to see the relics, of which she is one. I told her, through Phinit, when I took her back to Bali, that her service to Connie had been an episode of her youth, tender and lovely to look back upon. Now, I said, she ought to marry a young man of her people, and have children like a normal girl. I told her that, but so far there is no indication at all that she intends to follow my advice.

Nadezna is in Penang, living in the convent and working with the orphans. She came to some working arrangement with the Mother Superior and the Bishop that allows her to stay there; although she is far from being a Catholic or anything else, as yet, the Bishop seems to have agreed with her desire to be taken out of circulation. Gujar Singh and Arjan go to see her from time to time when a machine night-stops at Penang, and they tell me she is well and happy in her work. But I have not seen her myself since I left Damrey Phong before Connie died, and it may be that I shall never see her again.

I had several long conferences with Sheikh Fahad and Wazir Hussein in the months that followed Connie's death. I was lonely and troubled, and at first there didn't seem to be much point in going on with anything; I was very tired, and I didn't know what to do. I thought of selling out my business, to Airservice, perhaps, and going to live at Damrey Phong, for a time, anyway. It's quiet there, and one can think about things. But after a time I got settled down, and then it seemed to me that it would be a better thing to carry on the business and run it in the way that Connie liked, so that in a materialistic world my airline should be an example running through Asia to show that men can keep the aircraft safe by serving God in Connie's way, and yet keep on the black side of the ledger. I'd go so far as to say, from my experience, that only by serving God in this way can you keep out of the red.

So we go on as we did before. Sheikh Fahad is very anxious to do everything he can to help the pilgrims, and after one or two talks he asked me if I could find and operate some very economical machines equipped solely for the job. I borrowed from him, as I had borrowed from his father, the capital to order two new Tramps, short-range machines with rather longer fuselages equipped solely for the pilgrim traffic, and I hope to get these out to the Persian Gulf next month. I think at some time in the future I shall move my main base to Baraka.

These technical alterations have meant that the delivery time of the two Tramps has been extended to three months. I have taken that time in England as a holiday, leaving Gujar Singh in charge, because it was nearly three years since I had been home, and I was stale, and tired, and nervy. Before I left, Sheikh Fahad told me of his new project, the Six Books.

I think the Six Books are a very good idea. Already people are beginning to say that Connie was divine, and legends are already growing up about him. They are inventing quite fictitious miracles which he is supposed to have performed, although he never did anything of the sort.

Sheikh Fahad's idea is that the people who had most to do with Connie should write down what they know about him in a book, now, while the memory is still fresh and before these stupid legends have had time to grow. In that way proper evidence of what he was and what he did will be set down by people who knew him at first hand. Sheikh Fahad has engaged three scribes who between them speak English and Arabic and Burmese and Siamese and Balinese, to help those who aren't very handy at writing to get their evidence down on paper in a coherent form, and to edit all Six Books. When they are all done, the Sheikh is going to have them translated into several Asiatic languages, and possibly into English also, so that men who maintain aircraft and believe in Connie may know exactly what he said and did.

So first there is to be the Book of the Sister, which will tell us about Connie's early life and about his private life in Bahrein, and about his last months at Damrey Phong.

Next, there is the Book of Myin, which will tell about his first period at Damrey Phong under Dwight Schafter, when his ministry began.

The third book is the Book of Tarik, which is a very detailed record of his sayings in the hangar at Bahrein. There is good material for this, because Tarik was in the habit of writing down everything he could in penny exercise books, in Arabic, and there are about thirty of these books for the scribes to consult.

The fourth book is the Book of Phinit, which is an account of Connie's life in Bali, and of Madé Jasmi and her love for him.

The fifth book is the Book of Arjan, which deals with everything that happened on the six months' tour they made together in the Proctor, in which they visited so many aerodromes while Connie gradually grew weaker.

The sixth and last book is this one, the Book of Cutter. It's obviously right that anybody who can put down on paper any first-hand knowledge of Connie's life should do so, but Fahad asked me to go further than that, and put down everything about my own life that I thought would make the picture complete, and explain to future generations why I did the things I did which ultimately reacted upon Connie. So I have put down everything that I could think of that would make the story a complete one, and if Fahad's editors find any part of it unnecessary they can cut it out.

I have been glad to have this three months at home in England, in our little house in Southampton between the gasworks and the docks. Dad goes out to work each day, of course, and Mum is busy about the house and in the kitchen, and I have been able to write quietly all day in the back bedroom that we all slept in as boys. It's a good thing to get out of the East for a job like this, because you can look back and see what happened in perspective, and that helps.

Mum and Dad want me to stay in England now and find a job here. They don't think the East has done me any good, and that's rather sad, because I think it's done me all the good in the world. I know that I don't think about things now in quite the same way as I used to, and that in England people think me a bit queer. I know that in the aircraft industry there's a good deal of talk about my operations based upon the garbled tales that have got through to England. People are saying that I've been out in the East too long, and I've gone round the bend. Maybe I have, but then, I think that being round the bend is the best place to be. So I shall go back to Bahrein as soon as these two Tramps are ready for delivery.

And now, at the conclusion of this book, I still don't know what to think about Connie. To me he was always an ordinary person, a good friend from my youth, a very fine engineer, a very good man. He's still that to me – I think. But as I have sat here for the last three months in our back bedroom, writing down everything that I can remember about him, and meditating, I am beginning to wonder if I have been right. So many men, of so many races, are now turning to the memory of him, moulding their lives upon his example, praying that they may be made as he was. Could any human man exert such influence after his death? What makes a man divine?

I can't answer my own questions. I still think Connie was a human man, a very, very good one – but a man. I have been wrong in my judgments many times before; if now I am ignorant and blind, I'm sorry, but it's no new thing. If that should be the case, though, it means that I have had great privileges in my life, perhaps more so than any man alive today. Because it means that on the fields and farms of England, on the airstrips of the desert and the jungle, in the hangars of the Persian Gulf and on the tarmacs of the southern islands, I have walked and talked with God.

Nevil Shute

The Far Country

The Far Country relates the story of a young English woman's holiday in the Australian outback just after World War II. Travelling from a cold, rainy country she finds a land of plenty and falls in love with Australia's wild countryside. She meets an older doctor, a displaced person from Europe and their friendship begins to teach them about themselves and their adopted home.

In the Wet

Stevie, an ex-pilot, ex-ringer, drunk and drug addict lies dying in a remote hut in the Australian outback in the wet season. His passing is witnessed by an old Episcopal priest. As he lays dying, he dreams of his future incarnation as a pilot in the Queen's Flight. The priest shares his dream, and wonders if a corner of the veil has not been lifted for him.

Nevil Shute

Landfall

Jerry Chambers is a coastal patrol pilot in World War II; Mona Stevens is a barmaid at the Royal Clarence Hotel where Jerry drinks and dines with his friends. They meet and fall in love. All looks fine until Jerry is accused of making a terrible mistake in combat, and only Mona may be able to save his career.

On the Beach

Australia is one of the last places on earth where life still exists after nuclear war started in the Northern Hemisphere. A year on, an invisible cloak of radiation has spread almost completely around the world. Darwin is a ghost town, and radiation levels at Ayres Rock are increasing.

An American nuclear-powered submarine has found its way to Australia where its captain has placed the boat under the command of the Australian Navy. Commander Dwight Towers and his Australian liaison officer are sent to the coast of North America to discover whether a stray radio signal originating from near Seattle is a sign of life...

NEVIL SHUTE

PIED PIPER

Elderly John Howard goes off to the Jura in France on a fishing trip, except this is no ordinary time. Germany is at war with Europe. Friends at his hotel ask him to take their children back to England with him to safety as Germany is poised to invade France. Their harrowing journey begins by train and then proceeds on foot.

'Mr Shute not only writes vividly and excitingly of occupied France, but with a delightful understanding of children.' – *The Sunday Times*

A TOWN LIKE ALICE

Jean Paget survived World War II as a prisoner of the Japanese in Malaya. After the war she comes into an inheritance that enables her to return to Malaya to repay the villagers who helped her to survive. But her return visit changes her life again when she discovers that an Australian soldier she thought had died has survived. She goes to Australia in search of him and of Alice, the town he described to her.